ANGEL
IN THE
FOG

Also by TJ Turner

Lincoln's Bodyguard

Land of Wolves

ANGEL
IN THE
FOG

A NOVEL

TJ TURNER

OCEANVIEW ◐ PUBLISHING
SARASOTA, FLORIDA

ISBN 978-1-60809-375-5

Cover Design by Christian Fuenfhausen

Published in the United States of America by Oceanview Publishing

Sarasota, Florida

www.oceanviewpub.com

10 9 8 7 6 5 4 3 2

PRINTED IN THE UNITED STATES OF AMERICA

To my mighty girls, Cheyan and Sierra (Boo)—may you never know the challenges of Molly, but if they come, may you face them with the same grace, intelligence, courage, and ferocity as I know you can.

And to all the women warriors with whom I have had the pleasure to serve—there is a little bit of each of you in Molly.

ACKNOWLEDGEMENTS

So many people asked me to write Molly's story, that I will certainly miss a few who inspired me to put her struggle to paper. As always, writing may be a solitary art for the writer, but it takes a community of readers to hone that story. I am indebted to many who helped this novel come into the world.

First, I need to thank Nancy, my incredible wife. She continues to deliver fantastic editorial reviews—sometimes too honest, but she is always my first sounding board. Thanks also to my children: Cheyan, Jia, and Sierra who don't understand why I need them to get to bed so I can write. I must also thank my parents, Connie and Jim, for their feedback, and my mother-in-law, Gwyn Sundell. And, of course, the "Yellow Springs Wine Sipping Club with a Book Problem" read the manuscript and discussed it with me in between glasses of wine and fine cheese: Jen Clark, Karla Horvath, Liz Robertson, Kathleen Galarza, Eden Matteson, and Anne Noble. Then there is my cadre of kick-ass women whom I relied upon to ensure I captured Molly's perspective. They truly are my rogues' gallery of writers, spies, military professionals, and amazing women— Sharon Short, Sherry Stup, and Whitney Traylor. Thank you!

I am also forever indebted to Oceanview Publishing for taking another chance on my writing and letting me tell Molly's story. The team is fantastic. Thank you, Pat and Bob Gussin, Lee Randall, and Autumn Beckett for all the support.

And, of course, I owe an incredible debt to my amazing literary agent, Elizabeth Kracht (Kimberley Cameron & Associates). Her red pen is always sharp, yet what it removes only makes my writing better. Thank you, Liz!

Finally, the Antioch Writer's Workshop and the Bill Baker Award got me started on this writing career. I never would have gained the courage to call myself a writer without that supportive community of literary citizens.

ANGEL
IN THE
FOG

CHAPTER ONE

3 May 1860, New Orleans, Louisiana

BUSHES TORE AT Molly's dress as she flung herself into the darkness of drowning shadows. Her feet graced the dirt just long enough to make faint footprints, and her chest strained to keep pace with her legs, begging her to slow. She refused. The orange glow ahead violated the night and consumed her thoughts. The sun had set at her back, so what lay ahead was wholly unnatural.

"Miss Molly! Stop!"

Isabelle was chasing Molly to the end of her breath, yelling as best she could. Though Isabelle was a decade older than Molly, both girls had the advantage of youth. But Isabelle had never been as nimble, and she struggled through the tight spaces. The plea fell muffled on Molly's ears—as if a great distance separated them. Behind her, Isabelle's feet hit the ground with a pounding pulse. Isabelle wore shoes. Molly only used them if the formality of the situation dictated. This wasn't that time.

The light ahead built. The girls sprinted along the path until it spilled into the clearing of the great house. Smoke rose above the treetops, leaping from the orange tongues of flame until it congealed into the dark night. Though not all escaped. Some clung to the air until it teased their noses and burnt the back of their throats with each deep breath.

Molly was the first to break out of the woods. The scene across the clearing stopped her like a wall. Isabelle caught up. Her chest rose and fell. Both struggled to understand what they witnessed.

Across the clearing, the great house burned, its windows transformed to glowing eyes. The front door stood open as if the mouth of a monster. The staircase beyond the front foyer filled with ribbons of dancing flame. Fire grew from the roof, reaching into the night. The structure groaned and creaked. The noises it made matched its hideous appearance. Molly's hands gripped her head. Her fingers pulled through her hair in absolute anguish. The light of the flames danced across the dark skin of Isabelle's face.

They stood awestruck, confused. The fear that had driven Molly through the night distorted to shock and despair. So overwhelmed, it blotted her senses, blurring the men on horseback from her vision. They rounded up the plantation workers—Isabelle's people.

"Molly!" Isabelle wrapped an arm around the younger girl to drag her into the trail where the night would conceal them. "Who would do this?"

Molly's knees gave out. Isabelle clutched her as she sank to the ground. Once on her hands and knees, Isabelle pulled her tight.

The men on horseback had torches. They held them high, casting evil shadows. Other men with rifles, pistols, and whips forced the plantation workers into a ragged line. Molly knew each of these people—their faces, their stories, their children. More than half came with the land her father purchased. He added the others over the years. The crack of a whip reached above the roar of the fire. Molly startled when a man on horseback fired his pistol. The white smoke from the gun punched into the night like a plume of cottonwood seeds in a strong wind.

"Miss Molly. Who told them?" Isabelle's voice betrayed her agony.

Molly had no answer. She wiped her mouth and stared, rising until she knelt. Two of the men pushed a large colored man forward. It was Big John. They shoved him, prodding with a rifle in his back while the other man cracked a whip along the ground. Big John would never hurt anyone. He could scarcely swat the mosquitos that plagued during the summer months. But his size blinded most to his true nature. The man on the horseback, the one with the pistol, leveled the weapon and fired. Smoke leapt from the gun, like a white finger pointed at Big John. The large man stood for a moment. Then the man on horseback pointed the weapon skyward while he cocked the hammer again. As he leveled the pistol once more, Big John sank to his knees. Then he crashed like a giant timber upon the earth, his arms limp at his side, useless to break his fall.

"No! No, no, no . . ."

Molly crawled forward. Isabelle dragged her down, clamping a hand over the younger girl's mouth to silence her. For a moment the man on horseback turned in their direction. But another voice rose above the fire and the cracking whips. His Irish accent fell to Molly's ears.

Molly's father charged forward, breaking free from a group of women corralled near the front walk. His sleeves were rolled up, his usual jacket gone. The light of the fire flickered and blurred his features. As he stormed forward, one of the men struck him from behind with a rifle. The man fell to his knees near where Big John lay.

"Father." It came as a whisper. Isabelle still had her hand clamped over Molly's mouth.

The man on horseback swung down from the saddle. He landed in the dirt. Little eddies of dust kicked up from his feet. The fire behind them created a terrible wind, sucking the air as if caught in a chimney. The man walked calmly to where Molly's father knelt. In the flickering light Molly recognized the other man—Mason Cheeney. Her heart sunk. *This couldn't be happening.*

Cheeney stood over her father. They spoke, but from where Molly knelt, the words didn't reach her. She felt sick and pulled away from Isabelle.

Cheeney motioned to two of his men. They dragged Molly's father to his knees, holding his arms steady. Another man came from behind with a length of rope. One of the men bound her father's wrists as his protestations died. With the rope tightened, they tossed him backwards. He sat upon the dirt, his chest rising and falling with anger. Sweat rolled down his forehead, making it shimmer in the light of the fire.

Cheeney motioned again. This time one of his men dragged a woman from amongst the group—Molly's mother. Her father struggled to rise, but one of the men put a boot on his chest and kicked him down. Cheeney returned to his horse and tied a length of rope to the saddle horn. Then he dragged the other end of the rope out to where her father sat. He tied a crude noose.

"No," Molly muttered. "No!"

"Don't look," Isabelle pleaded. Molly couldn't help it.

Isabelle pulled her backwards. She dragged Molly to the edge of the woods, obscuring them both in what shadows they could find.

One of Cheeney's men yanked her father's head, holding him by the jaw and extending his neck skyward. Cheeney slipped the noose around his head and tightened it. In response, the bound man stiffened. He looked to the horse. Another of Cheeney's men held the reins, ensuring the beast would not spook and run off. It would only take a few steps by the large animal to snap his neck in the noose.

Cheeney walked toward Molly's mother, stopping once he stood in front of her. She spit in his face, defiant and angry. Slowly he wiped it away, and then slapped the woman across her face. When she fell, he grabbed her by one arm and pulled her upright. Molly's father struggled, then screamed. The man holding the horse forced the animal to take a half step forward. It dragged her father onto his back and stopped his fight. As the animal came to a rest, her father struggled to gain slack on the rope in order to sit.

Cheeney turned his attention back to Molly's mother. Once she stood on her own strength, Cheeney pulled her higher and onto her toes. Then with his free hand he tore at her dress, managing to rip one side. He dropped her to gain the use of his other hand and tore open what remained of her gown. She stood clutching her bare breasts as she held up the last remnants of her petticoat. One of Cheeney's men came from behind and grabbed her arms. Cheeney unhooked his suspenders, and then worked at his belt buckle. Molly's father screamed as her mother filled with shock. Then she pulled away to free one arm. Swinging it wide, she dug across Mr. Cheeney's face.

Immediately he dropped his pistol in the dirt, both hands clutching his face. When he turned back, one hand still covering his left eye, he struck the woman. She fell to the ground. His free hand worked his belt until he pulled it free of his pants. He began using the strap of leather to beat Molly's mother. Her screams drowned out the crack of his belt.

It was too much.

"Stop!" Molly screamed. She rose off her knees and broke out of the shadows in the tree line. Her vision narrowed. With uneven footing, she sprinted across the field.

Cheeney turned to see her.

"Molly! Dear God, no. Run. Run!" Her father yelled across the clearing.

Without hesitation, Cheeney nodded toward his man holding the horse. The man let go of the reins, and with a quick swat with a coiled whip, sent the beast up onto two legs. It landed stiffly, then bolted forward. Molly locked eyes with her father. He mouthed the word "Go." Then the horse yanked him into the darkness.

"Bring them to me!" Cheeney's voice carried above the fire. He stood framed by the burning house, as it moaned. The center of the roof began to collapse.

Isabelle caught Molly and pulled at her. The older girl was heavier and dragged Molly toward the open trail. Two riders from near the great house turned their horses in the direction of the trees. They spurred the beasts forward. Isabelle's voice became frantic.

"Molly! We have to go!"

"My mother." Molly pleaded. "Your sister."

"We can't . . ." Isabelle pulled at Molly, who stared at the carnage laid before them. Molly's mother looked in their direction.

"No," Molly said, barely above a whisper.

The woman nodded.

Isabelle grabbed hold, pulling with all her weight. Molly stumbled backwards, and both girls disappeared into the shadows.

CHAPTER TWO

5 FEBRUARY 1861, BALTIMORE, MARYLAND

THE BED CREAKED as Molly settled herself on the fresh linen. At least Mrs. Barbusca kept the place clean. She did it for the profits, not for the girls. But it was a small point of happiness for Molly—maybe her only one. Molly worked the top of the far bedpost, careful not to make a sound. *Just a little more.* She wiggled the top free and stared down the hollow center. Molly thrust the few coins she had received from the boy down the post. They clanked when they hit the others at the bottom.

The boy came every week, rapping at her window before the Barbuscas awakened. He would scale the building, clinging to the outside in a show of precision. Then he would brace himself as he reached through the bars. He came for the vial of bitter liquid next to her bed—laudanum. Together they would pour off her bottle into one he brought. Then they would fill hers with something that smelled as awful but contained none of the drug. He sold it on the street. Though she could make a good trifle more than he gave her, he had the one thing she didn't—freedom. She remained chained to the bed, the metal cuff cutting into her left leg. The boy also fancied her. She played to it. He brought her the few things she asked of him, things she kept hidden. The charcoal and white paste disguised the broken addiction to the morphine. Every day she rose and applied her own makeup concoction to make it seem she still had need of their bottle. Mr. Barbusca figured the chain was not enough to hold her. He was right.

The stairs outside her door creaked. She scrambled to replace the top of the bedpost. Normally at this hour the house had not yet stirred. But a brothel only napped—it never slept. And the Barbuscas were all too happy to appeal to the degenerate whims of Baltimore's underbelly.

She fumbled with the top of the bedpost, settling it in a haphazard manner. It didn't seat correct, but she had no time to fiddle with it. Instead, she flung herself over the bed, as if all along she had waited in the dark for the first visitor of the day.

As the hinges squealed, light streamed into the room. It blinded her. The man closed the door. Spots filled her vision where the sunlight had scorched her eyes. One of the unfortunate matters in pretending to be in need of the morphine was the lack of light. Someone still attached to it hated the sun, so Molly kept the curtains pulled tight. Between clients she would gaze outside in longing, planning her next escape.

The man settled into a padded chair that faced her bed. He wore a dark suit, with a matching vest, and carried a walking stick with a well-kept felt hat. He was more than a match for most who came through that door, at least in manner of dress. A trimmed beard adorned his face. Molly imagined it made him look older. Still, he had her by a decade—maybe two. His hair waved upon his head, affixed as if carved from marble.

Her thin nightgown felt immodest, and she shuffled the outer bed covering to hide the chain at her ankle. It felt heavy. Shame filled her, though her heart knew she had no call for such feelings. Her circumstances were beyond her control.

Silence grew between them. The man unbuttoned his vest and crossed his legs. His gaze was intimidating. When he had taken enough in, he broke the quiet.

"You hardly seem the dangerous creature Mr. Barbusca described. More a wretched girl than a fearsome entertainer."

Somehow the words fell hard upon Molly. She didn't quite know which among them made her most angry. The mention of Barbusca's name was a certain trigger. But this man had challenged her self-image. All her planning, her scheming to fool the Barbuscas about her addiction, her plotting to escape—those things had given her power. This man insulted all that with only a few words.

"What manner of man dresses in the latest fashion, grooms his beard and combs his hair to come to a whore house?" she fired back. "Are you afraid you might be rejected even here?"

Molly returned his gaze, meeting his blue eyes and locking hold of them. She made her expression fierce—no issue letting her hatred show. A smile formed on the man's face, then he broke into a low laugh. It deepened her anger.

"Does your wife know you're here?" she prodded.

His laughter stopped. He adjusted himself in the chair.

"That's more what I expected."

"Did my size fool you then?" Molly asked.

The man shook his head as he continued to take the measure of Molly.

"I learned long ago that size is not a predictor of someone's heart. With heart, anything is possible."

"Is that why you chose my room?" Molly asked.

Mr. Barbusca fancied himself a salesman. Evidently, he marketed Molly as a firebrand with an unpredictable manner.

The man had still not risen. Molly had never seen a man sit in the chair this long. Most didn't even bother to wait for the door to close before they started undressing. They came in already tugging at their jackets and ties.

"Mr. Barbusca offered you last—like an afterthought. He seemed rather concerned I might consider you. I figured if I am to pass time in this establishment, then I would find the lady most likely to keep me entertained with conversation."

"You want to talk?"

The man nodded. It made no sense. Men never wanted to talk—at least not the kind of men who came here.

"I came with a friend," the man explained. "He enjoys this place and spends much time with a woman down the hall. He felt I should join him. This is business, nothing more."

The explanation made no sense. His accent was familiar. It had a hollow ring, a mix of Southern gentlemen and something else. But it had been learned. He forced it—a disguise to hide behind. The thumb of his left hand stroked his ring finger while his hand lay upon the arm of the chair. But there were no rings upon any of his fingers.

"So, you are married," Molly said.

The man's thumb stopped rubbing the place where a ring should have been. A smile came across his face, but he fought it. She was right.

"Enough about me," the man said. "How does a girl like you come to a place like this? I am certain there is a tragic tale hidden behind your sharp tongue."

Molly shook her head, moving it only a small amount from side to side. Her eyes didn't leave the floor. Under the duvet her left foot twisted, checking if the iron clasp still held her ankle. The pain felt good, though she managed to move without making a sound. The great house, the fire coming from the windows, her father snatched away by the horse as the rope remained tight around his neck—*no. She wouldn't think on that.*

"Girls come here many different ways," Molly replied. She avoided the man's eyes.

"I imagine they do. But few are chained to their beds."

A tide of anger surged through her, then died off. Of course, Mr. Barbusca had told him of the chain. Most men didn't care. At most, they would see it for a moment, pity her, but continue to undress. Or they took it as part of the unpredictable mystique as they forced their fat bodies down upon her. No one ever asked why. Upscale or not, it revealed their true character.

The blanket covered her foot. She pulled at the linens until her feet felt the cold air of the room. The steel clamp had dug in deep on her leg. It had been weeks since Mr. Barbusca had closed it and turned the key. Even when she had leave to bathe, they walked her to the bath with the chain as a manner of leash.

"I heard you tried to escape."

"Twice. I almost made it."

"And you stole Mr. Barbusca's money?"

"I carried it. Do you see that fat bastard tied to a bed?"

The man's laugh was deep, covering the space between them. "It sounded like you would have made it, if you had known how to work the pistol."

She had taken off with Mr. Barbusca's pistol. The brothel keeper and his men had found her at the train station. She had only minutes to board the last line out of the city, bound for Washington. She didn't know that she needed to cock the hammer to make the revolver fire. Barbusca grabbed the gun from her hand and struck her about the head. She woke up chained to her bed.

"I only make mistakes once."

Molly willed her defiance to pierce through him as he sat smug upon the chair.

"I don't doubt it. Do you have another escape worked out?"

Molly didn't answer. She had been saving money, selling the laudanum. Beyond that, she had no plan. The bed next door began to creak. It swayed in a rhythmic manner as the end of the brass bedposts struck the wall with each beat. The door to Molly's room opened. Light once more flooded the space between her and this strange man. Molly's hands went to her eyes, holding back the onslaught of day. The smell alone revealed his identity—stale whiskey and smoked meat.

"Are you finding her as you desired?" Mr. Barbusca asked.

The man in the chair didn't turn.

"Out," he ordered. His eyes remained fixed on Molly.

"This is my establish—" Mr. Barbusca began, but the man cut him off.

"And I have paid handsomely for my time here. It is no concern of yours how I spend it. Get out, or we will have words upon my departure."

Mr. Barbusca hesitated and then closed the door. Molly's hand fell from her eyes as she replayed the man's words again in her head. They drew her attention. His accent. As he angered, he lost the Southern drawl. He formed his words with sharp edges, and a touch of the North seeped in. She had heard it with some of her father's associates.

"I apologize. Where were we?" the man asked.

Molly shook her head. Both of them looked to the wall at the head of her bed, which now rocked more violently with the couple in the next room. The bedposts hit hard a few times, then settled.

"I see your friend found what he was looking for," Molly said.

"Indeed. He will likely nap or have a cigarette, so we have time still."

Molly eyed this man and his peculiar manner. She was beginning to believe him—he had come for conversation alone. Her curiosity built, but she didn't know what to ask or how to pose the questions.

She had learned long ago to ask nothing—questions were how girls got beat. Curiosity was not looked upon favorably in a brothel.

"That man is not your friend," Molly said.

She surprised herself by saying it, and the meek volume to her voice betrayed her lack of confidence. Immediately she regretted letting her observation out into the space between them.

The man's expression washed away. His hand stopped fidgeting about his ring finger. His other hand stopped tapping the high arm of the chair. She held her breath. *Would he fly into a rage?*

"How's that?" There was urgency in his voice.

"That man, the one you came with—he's not your friend."

"What makes you say such a thing?"

She had piqued his curiosity. Puzzlement filled his brow as he furled it ever so slight.

"You're pretending to be his friend. But you're not."

He sat up in the chair, as if positioning himself to lunge forward upon her. From his face, he had no intention to move from the subject. Panic gripped her. She had crossed a line that would have been better left alone.

"You've never seen me before," he said.

Molly shook her head. "Of course not."

"I wasn't asking. But you've seen my friend?"

"I know him," Molly answered. "He's been here."

Her head motioned about the room, but she never took her eyes from the man who sat across from her. He pushed forward in his seat and leaned closer as he dropped the volume in his voice to just above a whisper.

"And what makes you think that we're not friends?"

Molly broke his glare. It was making her uncomfortable. She pulled her leg in, to give her some means of grabbing a length of the chain in case this man sprang upon her.

"How?" he demanded.

His patience grew thin. But there was another edge in his voice—fear. He was afraid the other man would find out.

"Your accent," she offered.

The man became puzzled. He eased back in the chair as his forehead furled deeper.

"You're not Southern. You're pretending to be, but I can hear it."

The man looked both amused and shocked.

"You can hear it?" His tone shifted to doubt. He didn't believe her.

"I can." Molly grew more confident. "You're from up North—maybe New York. But there's something else." She paused for a moment. "Britain. You're English."

Her father was from the Old Country—Ireland. When he drank too much, he would use an English accent and make fun of the barbarians from the big island—as he called them.

The man startled. He started to stand, but then looked behind him. The door remained secure. Molly hadn't heard any creaking from the floor outside since Mr. Barbusca had come and gone. The man leaned forward, as if he would grab her.

"Who told you this?" His face grew grim. Fear ruled his emotions.

"No one, I swear."

Molly moved away on the bed. His eyes darted to where she reached for her chain. He held his hands up.

"I'm not going to hurt you. But it's important that I understand how you came to know such things."

The man settled back in the chair but remained on edge.

"I told you," Molly said. "Your voice gives you away. I came from the south. It's subtle, but I can hear it. When you got angry with Mr. Barbusca, I heard it strong then."

The man nodded—he didn't quite believe her. From his stiff manner, she had alarmed him. He looked back over his shoulder. No one came.

"But it makes sense," Molly continued. "You're not his friend, but you want to know what Mr. Hillard plans."

"You know his name."

"I wish I didn't. His regular girl was gone once. He came here."

The man nodded. "I am sorry for that."

"Do you think he's serious then?" Molly asked.

"Serious about what?" The man's fear had abated, replaced by curiosity. Molly had him hooked once more.

"He wants Maryland to leave the Union. There's been much talk of it."

The man nodded. "And do you take him seriously?"

"I didn't," Molly said. "Not until today."

"Because of me?"

Molly nodded. "You're pretending to be a Southern gentleman, but you're not from here. You work for someone. Someone who wants to know Otis Hillard and his plans."

"Did he discuss those?" the man pressed. They could hear the room next door stirring. Their time was short.

Molly nodded.

"Tell me girl. What are they?" The man lowered his voice but didn't hide his urgency.

"He wants to kill the new president, Mr. Lincoln, when he arrives through Baltimore this month."

The man's face showed his shock. But also joy.

"How?" the man pressed. The floor outside the door squeaked. Someone battered upon the door. This wasn't Mr. Barbusca.

"Harry, all done?" a voice in the hall hollered through the thin door. It was Hillard.

"How?" The man pressed his point again, more desperate.

It gave Molly an angle. "Get me out of here and I will tell you everything."

"No. Tell me first, and I will see what I can do."

Molly crossed her arms over her chest, defiant. She shook her head. The door opened behind them. Light flooded the room, but Molly didn't flinch. Hillard stood in the doorframe.

"Do I need to rescue you from this one?" Hillard said. "She's a feral cat, she is."

Molly said nothing. She didn't even glance in Hillard's direction or shelter her eyes from the light. The man in front of her started to rise, reaching inside his jacket to remove his billfold.

"I already covered you," Hillard called out. "This time is on me. I hope you used my money well."

The man said nothing. He had yet to turn around and acknowledge Hillard. He stood, and then leaned in to Molly. As he kissed her on the cheek, he pushed bills into her hands.

"For your silence." The man pulled back until he could look into Molly's eyes. "And your next escape."

He turned and walked across the room to join Hillard. He buttoned his vest as he did so, making it seem he was getting dressed. The room fell dark as the door shut.

CHAPTER THREE

THE ENCOUNTER WITH the odd man consumed Molly's thoughts. Her mind raced. *What could she have done differently? Maybe held out more hope of Hillard's plans to force the man to take her with him?* She had grasped at sand and allowed it to slip through her fingers. Her melancholy was barely noticed by the men who filed in over the course of her afternoon. Or if they did notice, they ignored it as they did the chain about her ankle.

The next morning she awoke early as was her manner. She stood at the window and watched the street below, peering around the iron bars. Her chain fell loose upon the floor, lying like an old rat snake upon the wood floor. The bars worked with the chain to hold her latest escape at bay. She had worked the bottom of one bar loose, though she disguised her work so no one could detect it with only a cursory inspection. She should have been working on the top portion of the bar. Once she removed it, she could press her body through. But she had not the heart to keep working it loose. Instead, she let the bustle of Baltimore fill her room as she stared outside.

A carriage pulled up and stopped out front of the brothel. It wasn't ornate but appeared well looked after. The first patrons arrived earlier each week. Perhaps Barbusca advertised extended hours. He likely had, pushing his profits higher to make the return on his investments ever greater. There might even be a flurry of customers ahead of the presidential inauguration. Barbusca would be the second man she killed. She vowed it.

When the carriage door opened, a woman stepped out. Her dress was splendid—a deep scarlet with black trim. On the front she wore the black and white cockade of the secessionists. She held a box in one hand as a footman helped her to the ground. A wide-brimmed hat covered her face. Lace gloves transferred the box to and from as she found her footing on the rough cobblestones. The carriage remained as she walked into the Barbusca brothel.

Molly tried to follow her route inside, to see whom she met. But the overhang from the building obscured her view. Women didn't come here, at least not through the front door. The carriage remained parked out front. If not for the chain, she would have sneaked to the door and peered into the foyer below, where all the gentlemen waited.

With the carriage parked in the street, the rest of Baltimore competed for her attention. This was the only time sunlight graced her skin each day as she stood on the far side of the thick curtains. Soon men would arrive. The single merchants, the ones without wives and children, they liked mornings best. But the afternoons always picked up. Her stomach turned. This was the best, and the worst, part of her day.

The knock at her door startled her. She barely cleared the curtains when the door opened. Mrs. Barbusca stood in the doorframe. She held the box the woman had carried from the carriage. The older woman stared as Molly clutched the curtain behind her back.

"What are you doing there?"

Mrs. Barbusca was an unpleasant woman. Her voice most always held accusation or anger. Right now, it was the former.

"Just looking, ma'am."

"Planning on running again?"

"No, no . . . I like to see the day," Molly responded. "When it's not too bright," she added.

Mrs. Barbusca glanced toward the bottle of laudanum sitting upon the nightstand. It was empty, but the smell of the vile liquid remained.

"Well, it no longer matters. Get dressed in this."

Mrs. Barbusca tossed the box on the bed. Then she reached into a pocket hemmed to her dress and produced a key. She laid it on top of the package.

"I don't understand," Molly said.

"It seems you are leaving. You have a patron who bought all your debt." Then Mrs. Barbusca smiled as she added, "All your debt and then some. You will be someone else's problem. Though I told her to keep you chained so she will not lose you."

Mrs. Barbusca closed the door, letting the dark own all the little spaces once more. Molly stepped forward—tentatively at first. Then she turned and pushed her head through the curtain. The carriage was still there. She pulled open the curtains, until a large wedge of light fell upon the package. Rushing to the bed, she stood over the box. It was tied in twine, wrapped in brown paper. Molly pulled at the twine. Inside, a dress of the latest Baltimore fashion sat folded neatly. It was not the most expensive Molly had seen, but it was a match for anything worn in her current establishment.

Molly pulled it out and held it to the light. She pushed her face into the material and breathed deep. It was fresh store-bought, with fine stitching. The material was not fancy, but she hadn't seen a dress since her last escape. Mr. Barbusca had taken them—another means of discouraging her attempts to flee.

She searched the empty box. There was nothing—no note to offer any explanation. In the room next to her, the bed started its midmorning rocking. She tossed the dress upon the bed and searched for the key on the duvet. When her fingers found it, she fit it into the lock at her ankle and undid the clasp. She was free.

After rubbing her ankle, she rushed to pull the dress over her head. It was not strapped in the back, and she had no means to get it situated. It did not matter; she wanted free of this awful place. She pulled the top of the bedpost loose, and then upended the bed to get at the coins and money she had hidden away. Picking them up from the ground, she realized she had no bag in which to carry them. So, she gathered up the dress box, and placed the money into the large package. At the nightstand, she opened the top drawer.

In a twist of cruel satire, Mr. Barbusca insisted each girl had a Bible. Molly took hers and flipped to the back. She ripped the cover off. Hidden in the spine was a small medallion. She paused for a moment, tempted to leave the little bit of tarnished metal. The front contained some manner of symbol, and the back contained a man's initials. She put it into the box. There might come a time when she had need of it—*to find him*. Molly had pried it from her dead mother's hand, imagining the woman's dying wish had been this medallion.

Clutching her box, she rushed to the door. She had no shoes, but that didn't matter—yet one more thing that Mr. Barbusca had taken from her to maintain control. She would leave barefoot, if it meant the end of this place. As she closed the door, she thought better of it. Bounding back into the room, she stooped near her shackles and removed the key from the iron clasp. It dropped into the box with a metallic sound as it hit the coins. It served as another reminder—another awful thing to add to her collection and focus her anger. She would use it.

She made her way down the stairs without a sound. The third stair creaked in the middle. The fifth and sixth stairs had to be taken in one bound to avoid their tendency to groan under weight. She had mapped it out each time Mrs. Barbusca brought her down for her bath. Any detail might have been important, so she catalogued them to memory for the time she needed them most. Today it was just a game, a means to get down the stairs without thinking about what waited for her at the bottom.

The woman stood in the foyer as Molly bounded the last bit to land roughly upon the fake Persian carpet. She landed with such speed that she nearly tipped forward and ran into the woman. Instead, she caught herself and managed to stand upright in an awkward dance, her feet bare.

The woman in front of her did not appear amused. She looked down on Molly, more in her manner than in actual height. She was a few inches taller, and perhaps ten years older—like the man from the day before. She had removed her hat. It revealed dark hair pulled into a rigid and tight bun.

"You are the girl with the chain?" she asked.

Molly nodded, looking around her. Mr. Barbusca stood behind the counter of the bar at the far end of the foyer. He counted a stack of bills, feigning no interest in this strange woman.

"You have no shoes?"

"I don't need them," Molly said, trying to inject the right measure of urgency in her voice. All she had to do was sprint past this woman and into the street. But after almost a year under lock and key, her legs wouldn't hold. Not with the abuse her body had taken. It hurt to walk, let alone run.

"We will remedy that," the woman said. "But your hair. You did nothing to it this morning."

The woman reached out and picked up a lock of Molly's dark auburn hair. She lifted it and then let it fall, as if somehow examining her purchase. Molly had seen this before, when she accompanied her father to the slave markets. The men would examine all manner of things upon the chattel they thought to buy. It disgusted her then—it did so again.

"You are taking me from here?" Molly asked. She lowered her voice so that Mr. Barbusca might not hear her words.

"Don't you want to know where we would be going?"

"I don't care."

This woman had to be linked to the strange man from the day before. Nothing else made sense. Molly lowered her voice further.

"If you mean to discover what I know, you will take me now as I am."

Over her shoulder, Mr. Barbusca still busied himself counting the money. She fought her rising impatience. Daylight beckoned beyond the main door. It streamed through the frosted glass. *Could she make it?* Perhaps, but there was no way to know who this woman was, or what lay outside. She breathed deep and steadied herself.

"Very well," the woman said. She caught Molly's upper arm in a firm grip and guided her toward the door.

Mr. Barbusca called out, "Mrs. Barley, I am uncertain we agreed upon all the terms."

Molly turned the name over in her mind, committing it to memory. Mrs. Barley pushed Molly toward the door in a deliberate fashion. She did not bother to turn when she spoke to Mr. Barbusca.

"We agreed to all the terms. There is nothing left to negotiate." She kept her voice calm and confident.

"I was thinking—" Mr. Barbusca started to follow after the two women.

Mrs. Barley turned with such a start that she might have trained in the infantry. Rising a bit taller, she towered over the fat and balding man.

"There is nothing else to discuss."

Mr. Barbusca wiped his forehead with a stale handkerchief.

"When you are done with her, feel free to send her back. I can still tame the wild out of her."

Mrs. Barley had let go of Molly's arm. Molly stepped around her to where she almost faced Mr. Barbusca herself. Molly breathed in and spat upon the floor at his feet.

"You insolent—"

Molly did not hear Mr. Barbusca finish his insult. Mrs. Barley grabbed Molly by the arm and dragged her to the door. She pushed Molly through the foyer, and then into the street. Molly had to shield her eyes. But more importantly, she breathed deep. The air stunk of people, and horses pulling carts. It also held crisp and cold as she pulled it into her lungs, and her bare feet stung against the ice of the ground. It was wonderful. If not for Mrs. Barley's grip, she would have danced upon the frozen paving stones until her feet bled.

"In the carriage before you freeze."

Mrs. Barley guided Molly to the carriage that still waited in the street. The driver held the door open and Mrs. Barley urged Molly inside. Her grip eased. With no shawl, Molly was grateful. The seats were soft and upholstered in leather.

"At least take this."

As Mrs. Barley settled herself opposite Molly, she handed Molly her shawl. Molly accepted it and wrapped it around her shoulders. She sat upright to point her feet so only her large toes touched the ground. It would keep them warmer for a time.

"I didn't think about the shoes. I thought you would have some."

"They took them."

"After you last escaped?"

Molly nodded.

The carriage started with a jolt, the wheels jostling over the uneven paving stones.

"Do you want to know where we're going?" Mrs. Barley asked.

Molly shook her head. She didn't. Nothing could be worse than the brothel. For now, hope filled her. At least she would be happy during the time it took them to arrive.

"I find that hard to believe," Mrs. Barley said.

Molly stopped looking out the window and studied the older woman. She was quite lovely, though her manner came across as hardened. Molly suspected she had no husband—something about her spoke of a freedom enjoyed without a man. The women Molly had known without husbands were tough in a way that bespoke confidence. She longed for that manner of independence.

"Have you ever been someplace," Molly asked, "that was so horrible you would do anything to leave?"

Mrs. Barley nodded.

"Then you ask a stupid question," Molly said. "I don't care where I go."

"Well then, do you want to know who I am and why I came for you?"

"I know why you came for me."

"You do?"

"Of course," Molly said. "You are with the man from yesterday. If he is your husband, please know that we did nothing improper. He just wanted to talk."

Mrs. Barley laughed. It was the first time her rigid demeanor had cracked. Molly sensed her soften a little.

"I do not have a husband, nor do I want one."

Molly smiled—*she had been right*.

"I don't either."

"I can imagine. My name is Mrs. Barley, and I do work with the man who visited you yesterday. He said you were quick, and that your tongue was even sharper. He didn't tell me quite how wild you might be."

Molly sat upright and slid back on the bench seat—taking insult from the woman's words.

"I am not wild," Molly protested.

"Was it another girl who spat at her former employer?"

"But I was—"

"Shhh," Mrs. Barley cut her off. "Always conduct yourself as a proper lady. You will get further."

"Even when shoeless and leaving a brothel?"

"Especially when shoeless and leaving a brothel." Mrs. Barley paused, studying Molly, perhaps sensing the hurt feelings. "We will teach you."

"So, I will see him again?" Molly asked. She spoke about the man from the day before. Mrs. Barley understood.

"You fancy him?"

"No." The suggestion shocked her. "He was just . . ." She had to think of the words. "He was so odd. No one ever came to talk. I rather liked it."

Mrs. Barley nodded. "You will see him again. But first . . ." Her voice trailed off as she opened her handbag and pulled out a large black satin sash. "You may not care where we go, but we care that you might discover it. I will not bind your wrists nor your ankles, but I will ask you to place this over your eyes."

Molly accepted the sash. The material was soft and unwrinkled. It hadn't been used on anyone else. She met Mrs. Barley's eyes. The woman held no malice, and Molly would have use of her hands to grab at the blindfold if she had the need.

"Will you muffle my ears and plug my nose as well? One can see with more than their eyes."

"You *are* a clever girl, aren't you?" Mrs. Barley asked. "But your tongue will get you into trouble. A smarter move would have been to accept the blindfold without reminding me you would use your hearing to figure out where we went. You will learn. For now, place the blindfold on."

Molly took one last look at Mrs. Barley, and then nodded. Slowly she tied the black sash around her head, blocking out all the light. Her ears came alive—like those awful days lying in a dark room with the sounds of Baltimore below, as men sprawled on top of her body.

Mrs. Barley pounded on the side of the carriage to get the driver's attention.

"To Mr. Hutchinson's office. And take the long way."

CHAPTER FOUR

THE CARRIAGE WOUND through the city. Molly lost track of time, but she followed every turn. She didn't know the city well enough to have an exact bearing. But she had a broad idea where they were when the wheels finally stopped. During the ride, Mrs. Barley remained quiet. Molly appreciated the break in conversation. It gave her time to collect her thoughts. She would have to be guarded with these people—at least until she understood who they were.

When the carriage door opened, Molly reached for the blindfold.

"Not yet," Mrs. Barley said. Her hand pressed Molly's down to her lap. Another hand clasped upon Molly's upper arm from the direction of the open door. The firm grip guided her out of the carriage.

"Two steps, and you will be down."

Her stomach tightened at the sound of his voice. She reached for the blindfold to see him again, but then stopped. His accent was the same, though he seemed to try harder to disguise it. He eased her down until her feet met the shock of cold stone. She shifted between her feet, lifting onto her toes to get off the cold.

"She has no shoes," the man said.

"I know. It will have to do for now. Bring her inside."

The man guided her through a door where the air warmed her body and carpet lined the floor. His hand held her firm, but kind. They walked up two flights of stairs, and at the top he removed her blindfold. They waited outside a door in a short corridor. Daylight poured through a window at the far end of the hall. Molly blinked, getting used to the light.

"This is Mr. Davies," Mrs. Barley introduced the man from the brothel. "You will meet our employer, Mr. Hutchinson. He is not to be trifled with. Be direct and tell him the truth. He will treat you fair. But be mindful of your manner, especially your tongue."

Molly nodded. Concern filled the older woman's tone. She cared how this meeting went, likely to impress her boss. It didn't matter. Molly wouldn't go back to the Barbuscas' doorstep. She would flee before that happened. *Could she jump from the window? How high was it?*

As if he read her thoughts, Mr. Davies placed a hand on her shoulder. *No escape—not now.* He wore a different suit, though in fashion to the one he wore the previous day. He leaned close.

"We will not send you back, you have my word. Do not exaggerate what you know. Tell it to him plain so we understand. Then we will discuss what to do with you."

Molly fought to keep any reaction from her face. He meant his words as a kindness, but there was something in how he said it. Mrs. Barley rapped on the door. A voice called from within and she pushed into the room. Mr. Davies held the door open, but then closed it behind the women. He remained outside.

The office beyond the door was simple. A wood desk filled part of the space, with windows to let in the light and sounds of the city. Mr. Hutchinson sat behind the desk. He was older than Mr. Davies, perhaps by a few years—but his manner came across as more serious. Molly shrunk under his stare.

Mr. Hutchinson examined her from across the desk. Molly hadn't cared about her lack of shoes until now. And she had forgotten how she never tightened her dress all the way. She had meant to ask Mrs. Barley, but forgot once she placed the blindfold around her eyes. She felt out of place, cheap and tawdry. She hated how men could make her feel that way.

"Have a seat," he said. His voice was commanding. It left no question who was in charge.

Molly settled into the chair in front of his desk while Mrs. Barley stood to the side.

"My name is Mr. Hutchinson. Since you have me at a disadvantage, I will allow you to introduce yourself."

Should she tell him her real name? Did he know already? Likely he did.

"Molly Ferguson."

"And where do you hail from, Molly?"

"New Orleans, originally."

The man sat back in his chair and watched her more closely. His hair thinned on top, leaving him partially bald. His beard was full and bordering on the wild—he hadn't trimmed it into the latest fashion. His blue eyes pierced deep as he examined her, and he wore a gray coat with black lapels. A thin black bowtie held his shirt to his neck. His voice also held an accent Molly had heard before. It sounded a bit like her father's, but different—not of this land, north or south.

"And how do you find yourself in Baltimore?"

"I was brought here. Not on my own accord," Molly said. From his expression, Mr. Hutchinson wasn't satisfied. But she had no desire to relive the fire and watch her father ripped into the night at the end of a rope. "After my parents died."

"So, you are an orphan?"

Molly nodded. Her mother had once given her the name of an old family friend in Richmond. It belonged to a woman who might take her in if ever anything happened to her parents, but they had no kin. Her father's family, what remained of it, lay across the water in Ireland. And her mother had none left in the Virginia capitol.

"Sold to a brothel?" he asked.

"About a year ago."

"That is unfortunate," Mr. Hutchinson said. "I am sorry to hear of your circumstances."

Molly looked into her hands. "Thank you."

"Did Mrs. Barley or Mr. Davies explain why you are here?"

"I already know."

"Good," the man said. "That is what I want to talk about. *How* you know."

Molly didn't understand his exact meaning.

"It seems obvious. The man yesterday, he was interested in Mr. Hillard," Molly answered.

Mr. Hutchinson raised his hand, lifting it above the desk.

"We'll get there," he said. "What I want to know is how you know so much about Mr. Davies. The man you met yesterday."

Molly shook her head. "I know nothing of him. I only just met him when he came to my room."

"I disagree. From what he told me, it seems you know a great deal about him."

His accusation puzzled her. She searched her memory, trying to recall the strange conversation.

"I had never seen him before yesterday. He's English, that's all I know."

"Let's start there. How did you know that? Who told you?" Mr. Hutchinson asked.

"No one." Desperation seeped into her voice. "I didn't know his name until you said it."

"How did you know he was English?" Mr. Hutchinson's tone was stern.

"It's in his voice. When he became upset at Mr. Barbusca, his accent dropped. I could hear the English in it."

The man nodded. "That's a hell of a guess. What else did you hear?"

Mrs. Barley nodded, urging Molly to answer the man behind the desk.

"Maybe a New York accent. It wasn't Boston, though at times I get those mixed up."

"The accents?" Mr. Hutchinson asked.

"Yes."

"You've been to New York and Boston?"

Molly nodded.

"And you can hear the differences?" he asked, more forceful this time.

"Yes." She dropped her Southern inflection, the one she was born into, and mimicked her best New York accent. "I can change between them, too. My mother said I should act upon the stage, but my father would hear none of it. It wasn't respectable."

The man glanced at Mrs. Barley. He appeared taken aback.

"How do we know you're not acting now?"

"I don't understand."

Molly hoped some manner of explanation would present itself in Mrs. Barley's expression. There was none.

"How do we know you weren't hired by someone to play a part? To give me false information?"

The words stung. He didn't believe her, or he tested her.

"You think I'm here to lie to you? I've given you no information. You've asked for nothing." Molly's anger rose. "And you think I would be acting in a brothel, placed there in case you found me?"

Mr. Hutchinson shrugged, as if it wasn't an absurd suggestion. Images of the awful men who had come in and out of her room filled her thoughts, forcing themselves upon her until she had no hope. She had willed herself to live, if for nothing else than to escape and find the men who had dragged her to Baltimore. *And this man thought she was acting?*

"I have seen it before," the man said. "A poor story meant to confuse, or worse."

"Worse?" Molly asked.

"Meant to expose my operation."

"You think I wanted to be in a brothel?" Molly rose, but Mrs. Barley stepped toward her. "I don't know who you are, and I don't care a thing about you."

Molly reached down and pulled her left leg, landing it with a startling thud upon his desk. Pulling back the skirt of her dress, she let him see her ankle—the festering sores made by the iron clamp and shackles.

"Is this acting, too?"

Mrs. Barley reached for Molly, but Mr. Hutchinson raised his hand. He studied Molly. She never dropped her eyes. Instead, she lowered her voice, imagining it sounded menacing.

"I would have killed that fat bastard, too, if my father had taught me to shoot."

"She's speaking of Mr. Barbusca," Mrs. Barley explained of Molly's statement.

Mr. Hutchinson studied Molly's leg. When he looked up he couldn't hold her stare. He nodded, and brought his hands together by his mouth, resting his fingertips upon his lips.

"I apologize if I upset you," he began. "You must understand, in this line of work we must be absolutely certain of the things people tell us. From my perspective you are too good to be true. And now you tell me you are a poor orphan from New Orleans who has traveled to New York and Boston."

"I never said my family was poor. I said my parents died."

"A girl from means, with no family or friends who might take her in?" the man asked.

Molly pulled her foot from the desk. She gripped her hands together. She hadn't intended to talk about her parents. Even the thought of them brought forth tears. She tried to hold them back, but they came anyway. Her left eye broke first, the tear flowing down her hot cheek. It stopped before it could drip off, evaporated by the heat of her face—the anger fought the tears.

"My family owned a plantation outside New Orleans."

"How did they die?" the man asked.

"They were murdered."

"Why?"

She fought the sobs, but let the tears fall now, not bothering to wipe at them. Mrs. Barley placed a hand on Molly's shoulder.

"The plantation wasn't a plantation. My mother came from a line of abolitionists. She met my father after he had earned off his debt. He was indentured from Ireland. They named the place Salvation Acres. They bought slaves, but they owned none."

"He set them free?"

Molly nodded. "The minute they came to the plantation."

The man leaned forward, resting against the desk. His tone had softened.

"Didn't they leave?"

"They had their papers, but it was dangerous to travel. Almost everyone stayed. My father bought families, never separating children. It broke his heart to see ones he couldn't save. He brought me to the slave markets once, but then he never let me go back."

"Did he pay them?" The story had drawn Mrs. Barley's curiosity, too.

"Some. What he could after the bills were settled. We weren't poor, but we weren't rich. Most gave up their money for better cabins and a schoolhouse. My father bought more land, and then more slaves. A paid man, he used to say, was worth ten in bondage. He thought the idea could spread, but he had to be careful. He wanted to show it worked. He wanted to be more successful than any other plantation before he told anyone."

"But they found out?" the man across the desk asked.

Molly nodded. Her tears ended. She surprised herself. It felt good to talk about her parents, about the plantation. For so long she had only remembered those last moments. Now the other memories flooded back—the long lazy summer days, falling asleep in her father's lap, walks with her mother and Isabelle.

"Who told them?" the man asked.

Molly wrung her hands.

"I don't know."

"Secrets like that don't keep for long," the man said. "Everyone talks."

Molly echoed his words. "Everyone talks."

"And then they caught you?" Mrs. Barley asked.

"They caught me the next day. I hid in the forest until I thought they were gone. I came back to find my mother and Isabelle's sister. Isabelle was my nursemaid. She had a younger sister. I found my mother. They hadn't even buried her—just left her in the sun to rot. I never found Isabelle's sister."

Remembering the scene, her tears came back. Sobs worked their way to the surface. The sight of her mother's face was awful. She never had a chance to find her father. They came back too soon.

"They killed Isabelle in front of me."

"Who were they?"

"Mason Cheeney's men. He led a militia group and owned a shipyard. My father said he designed the best boats in all New Orleans."

The man nodded. "But they spared you?"

Molly's hands rose to her face and she sobbed. She fought for breath, sucking it in between each bout of sorrow that crashed upon her in waves. It only eased as Mrs. Barley knelt and pulled her close.

"The last thing I recall is Mr. Cheeney grabbing me by the jaw and forcing a bottle into my mouth. It was so bitter."

"Opium," Mrs. Barley said.

Molly wiped her eyes and face.

"I haven't touched it in months. I took less and less of it, until I had no need at all. They never knew."

Mrs. Barley smiled. "Clever girl."

"And that's when they sold you to the brothel?" Mr. Hutchinson asked.

"I don't know. Mr. Barbusca said I had a debt to earn. I figure he didn't think I would live that long, strung out on the bottle."

"And that's where you met Otis Hillard?"

"Yes," Molly replied "He fancies a girl at the house—that's what we called it. She was sick once, so he came to my room."

"And he offered you his plans?" Mr. Hutchinson asked.

"In a manner," Molly said. "Men cannot help but to brag. Even when they had me tied to the bed, they still looked to impress me—to show off. They are no better than peacocks. It was worse after I was chained. I think they felt guilty, so they tried to show me *I* was lucky for their company."

"What did Hillard tell you?"

Molly thought for a moment.

"He wears this medal around his neck. It has a palmetto tree upon it. I said I liked it, and he wouldn't stop talking. He told me he was the captain of some secret militia. They would help Maryland separate from the union, to fight the soldiers when they came. He was proud of it, so there was no trouble making him talk. And when he talked, he wasn't doing other things. He said they planned to kill the new president when he traveled through Baltimore this month."

"Mr. Lincoln?"

Molly nodded. "A mob will attack at the train station when the president-elect has to transfer trains. They will attend a rally to support Mr. Lincoln, and then seven or eight of them will pounce with knives."

The man behind the desk sat back. Molly wiped at her eyes, and Mrs. Barley gave her a fresh handkerchief.

"Do you believe me now?" Molly placed particular emphasis on the last word. She met his stare, never looking away.

"I do."

Molly used the handkerchief to clean up the remaining streaks down her cheeks.

"Do you know the other men?" he asked.

"Some of them. There's a saloon near the brothel; that's where they meet."

"Good. We'll get you cleaned up and some food. We will all talk further after that." The man rose from his desk, offering a hand across his desk. "You will help us?"

Molly didn't take it.

"On one condition," she said.

"And what would that be?"

"Teach me to work a pistol."

"Why?" he asked, his tone suspicious.

"There are men I am going to kill."

CHAPTER FIVE

THE MORNING LIGHT streamed through her window. It woke Molly gently, in a manner she hadn't experienced in over a year. She had left the curtains open to let the morning filter in with the rising sun. During the night she had woken once in a panic, uncertain of the room around her. When she pulled back the covers and found no chains bound to her ankle, relief sent her back into a deep sleep. A bath the evening before had even removed the smell of the brothel. There would be no callers. No makeup to put upon her face to fake addiction. No men smelling of smoke and whiskey who would smother her into the bed with their crushing weight. *No men.*

Molly sat upon the bed, her knees pulled to her chin. If it had been warmer, she would have opened the window to get at the sounds of the city. But she remained content with the light of day. Her thoughts wandered. Even with uncertainty, no worry gripped her.

Mrs. Barley entered with a soft rap upon Molly's door. She placed several packages on the bed. Then she sat upon a chair, off to Molly's side.

"Did you sleep well?"

The window held Molly's attention.

"I could never just sit in the sun," she said

"I know." Mrs. Barley's words were soft.

She let Molly have her peace. Finally, the younger girl broke the quiet.

"What business are you in?" Molly asked.

"Business?"

"Yesterday, when Mr. Hutchinson didn't believe me, he said something about your line of work. That people tell you false things. What business are you in?"

"It's not that he didn't believe you," Mrs. Barley said. "He had to be certain."

"I know. But what is it you do?"

Mrs. Barley sighed, letting the silence grow again. Molly turned to face her. The older woman struggled for an answer.

"We talk to people."

"And you find their secrets?" Molly asked.

"I guess you might say it like that. We find out what we're paid to discover, so that others can be informed."

"And who pays you now?"

The question caught Mrs. Barley by surprise. It spread across her face. She smiled, likely thinking how to answer.

"You ask strange questions."

"Is that bad?" Molly asked.

Mrs. Barley shook her head. "Maybe at the wrong time, but not now."

"So, then who pays you for the questions you asked yesterday?" Molly pressed again.

"That would be better answered by Mr.—" Mrs. Barley stopped. "Mr. Hutchinson." She had started to say another name.

Molly nodded, not pointing out the slip.

"And once you find these men I told you about, what will you do with them?"

"That depends," Mrs. Barley said. "We will let others know what we have found. And they will act as they see fit. We may help in that regard, or our work may be finished."

"And you are trying to save Mr. Lincoln?"

Mrs. Barley smiled. "I guess that much is evident—although it did not start in that direction. It appears our work crossed with a conspiracy we are only beginning to understand. What you know may be confirmation of this evil plot."

"And do you like him?" Molly asked.

"Mr. Hutchinson?"

"No, Mr. Lincoln." Molly turned to see Mrs. Barley's expression. There was so much more to learn from someone's face than from words alone.

"I guess I never thought on it," Mrs. Barley said. "Of course, I followed the election. I don't know who I favored."

"Whom would you have voted for if you could?"

"Does it matter? That is a decision for men."

"And yet you try to save a man you could not have elected," Molly said.

Mrs. Barley's smile filled her whole face this time. "You asked me what business we are in."

Molly nodded.

"I am a detective—maybe the first to ever wear a dress."

"I've never heard of a woman detective."

"And do you think it's a bad idea?" Mrs. Barley asked. It was her turn to probe Molly.

"No. It's wonderful."

Mrs. Barley nodded. "There are so few options for women like you and I. After my husband passed, I did not want to wait around for suitors. Nor did I feel the call to become either a nurse or teacher. Women are most useful in worming out secrets in many places.

Men become braggarts when they are around women who encourage them to boast. Though you know that already."

Molly nodded. "It seems Mr. Hutchinson agrees."

"Even he was skeptical. But he is a believer now."

"Have you worked with him long?" Molly asked.

"For many years." Mrs. Barley placed her hands upon her knees and stood. "Come. I brought you several new dresses, and a pair of shoes. I do hope they are the right size. I guessed based upon the dirty footprint you left on the carpet last night."

"What will become of me?" Molly asked.

"You will help us, and then we will see."

"You will teach me what I need to know?" Molly pressed.

"For the men you want to kill?" Mrs. Barley responded.

Molly didn't say anything. It seemed an absurd request. She was barely a woman, sitting upon a borrowed bed in a city far away from a home she no longer had.

"I assume you mean to find Mr. Cheeney."

Molly said nothing.

"You have to ask yourself," Mrs. Barley began, "do you seek vengeance or justice?"

"Is there a difference?"

"One fills you with hate. The other relieves you of it. But that's a path you will have to choose. I take particular pride in my judge of character. Molly, you have much to offer—much more than hate."

Molly glanced to her hands—the hands of a little girl.

"Come," Mrs. Barley urged Molly from the bed. "Let us get you dressed, and I will help fix your hair. No female detective can look in the manner you are in now and expect to worm secrets out of gullible men."

She wrapped an arm around Molly and guided her to a small vanity. Molly sat upon the bench while Mrs. Barley worked a hairbrush. She braided Molly's hair in a simple manner, so it fell in a neat style down Molly's back. Then she helped Molly into a dress, ensuring she tied the corset top. Wearing a dress two days in a row came as an odd sensation. As Mrs. Barley unpackaged the shoes, a knock sounded at the bedroom door.

"Come," Mrs. Barley called out.

"Is it proper?" The voice was Mr. Hutchinson.

"I wouldn't have said so if it was not. You may enter."

The door opened and Mr. Hutchinson stood in the doorway. He looked over the scene in front of him.

"I see you are still without shoes."

He looked at Molly's stocking feet.

"We are working to remedy that," Mrs. Barley responded as she loosened a single shoe from the box upon the bed.

Mr. Hutchinson nodded. He looked at the floor between the women as if he had interrupted something sacred.

"Is there some news you need to pass along?" Mrs. Barley asked.

"I telegraphed a colleague in New Orleans last night. This morning he responded."

"Something of note then?" Mrs. Barley asked.

Her tone was absentminded. She concentrated more on the placement of the first shoe upon Molly's foot. Molly cringed as Mrs. Barley tightened it. Weeks had passed since she'd worn shoes. Mr. Hutchinson met Molly's eyes for the first time since he entered the room.

"My colleague confirmed there was a plantation named *Salvation Acres* outside New Orleans. Patrick Ferguson held the deed, and he lost his holdings in a fire last summer. He lost his own life and his wife in the fire. There was a daughter, though no one knows what became of her."

"It was no simple fire." Molly clenched her teeth, forcing her words out as a hiss.

"It's alright," Mrs. Barley said.

"No, it's not! He doesn't believe I am who I say I am."

"I told you last night, in this business we need to be most careful," Mr. Hutchinson defended himself.

"In the detective business?" Molly asked.

Mr. Hutchinson shot a glance to Mrs. Barley. His expression made it clear he was not happy.

"I had to tell her something. She is clever enough she would have figured it out herself," Mrs. Barley defended her admission.

Mr. Hutchinson said nothing. He shook his head and looked to the floor between himself and the women. Molly stood from her bench, and then walked around the far side of the bed. A small nightstand held the box she had carried from the brothel the day before. Opening the box, she found the medallion and walked it over to Mr. Hutchinson.

"Maybe you will believe this?"

She held out the medallion for Mr. Hutchinson. He took it, examining the small metal object.

"I pried it from my mother's dead hand," Molly said, emphasizing each word as she fought the tears. A few escaped and streamed down her face.

Mr. Hutchinson flipped the medallion over in his hands, examining both sides. One held a Maltese-style cross and star, with the rays of light like the sun inscribed to the edges. On the backside, "MC" was carved deep into the metal.

"Knights of the Golden Circle," Mr. Hutchinson murmured to himself.

"You know it?" Molly asked.

He nodded. "A secret society, one formed in the Deep South—Louisiana."

He handed it back, looking right into Molly's eyes. She stood defiant in front of him, her fists clenched at her side. Slowly she took the medallion.

"I never said I didn't believe you. But we have much need to be careful. You understand what we have asked you, and if you are as clever as Mrs. Barley believes, then you know what we aim to do. This city would not be friendly toward us if our true manner were laid bare. Do you understand?"

Molly remained defiant for a moment, then softened. *He was right. They barely knew her.* It would be ridiculous to expect them to trust her without some means to verify her story. She nodded.

"Good. Please finish dressing, and then I would like to discuss more details of what you have learned." Turning to Mrs. Barley he continued. "And make certain she is ready. We will have need of her soon."

"Allan—"

He cut her off with a raised hand and a vicious glance. The older woman had slipped once more.

"Come outside with me," he said. As if to add emphasis, he added, "Now."

Mrs. Barley stood and passed the shoe she had been working on to Molly. Then she followed Mr. Hutchinson out the door and into the hall. They closed the door behind them. Molly waited only a moment, and then bounded as quiet as she might to the door, trying to hear what they said.

"She is not ready—not yet," Mrs. Barley said. Her voice was audible but muffled through the wood door.

"We don't have time for any other option. She knows who some of these men are. She can point them out to me tomorrow evening. Mr. Luckett is setting a meeting with the ringleaders. She will accompany me."

"We don't know how she will act. Or how she handles herself under the stress of the moment. That girl has been through so much. She is an excellent candidate, but she will need time. I have to teach her first."

"There *is* no time," Mr. Hutchinson responded. "The president-elect arrives in a fortnight. We need to know if this threat is real, and how far the conspiracy has gone. That is the only way we may prevent it. I feel certain this girl holds the key to it all."

"And what if she exposes you? What if she runs?"

"That's a risk we have to take. There is no time to do this right. The ends justify the means. She comes with me tomorrow."

There was silence for a moment. Molly was about to run toward the bed when the conversation began again.

"Kate, you have shown me the power of the female detective." Mr. Hutchinson spoke in a calm yet hushed manner.

Molly found she needed to get even closer to the door to overhear it all.

"You know that I am a true believer. I took a chance on you. Take a chance on this girl. I have a feeling she will help us unravel this whole nasty business. I see no other way. I can't take you to this saloon. You know this. Your cover identity is too upper class. No one would believe for a moment you could walk into that establishment. Help me get her ready and change her appearance such that no one from the brothel might take notice of her."

"Very well." Mrs. Barley sounded resigned to the outcome. "She's been through so much, I don't—"

Mr. Hutchinson cut her off. "I understand. We don't know how she will act."

"I was going to say, I don't want her hurt further. But that also worries me."

"Then make her ready. For if the new president dies in this city, this nation will tear itself apart. History will be our judge, and she will issue a harsh indictment shall we fail."

The floor outside the door creaked, as if Mr. Hutchinson had turned to leave. Molly bolted from the door, making it back to perch upon the bed before it opened. Mrs. Barley entered the room, closing the door. Her face remained set in a grim expression.

"How much did you hear?" she asked. She crossed the room and sat on the bench in front of the vanity.

Molly shook her head. "Nothing."

Mrs. Barley studied her a moment, then frowned. "I will teach you to be a better liar. Come here—let's get your shoes on. We have some work to do to change your appearance."

Molly nodded. Then, in a quiet voice, she dared to ask, "What is your real name?"

"It is Mrs. Barley, as I have told you."

"I doubt that very much," Molly said, speaking with more defiance. "I know his name is not Mr. Hutchinson. That's Allan Pinkerton, isn't it?"

There was no hiding the shock upon Mrs. Barley's face.

"How on earth did you figure that?"

Molly smiled—proud of herself.

"The accent again. His voice is similar to my father's, in a manner. He can't hide the Scottish in it. And you called him *Allan*. There's only one Scottish-born detective named Allan. Even in the South they publish his cases in the papers. Or in the dime novels my mother forbade. Isabelle and I liked them."

The revelation clearly disturbed Mrs. Barley.

"So, you understand exactly how precarious our position is? No one in Baltimore would be happy to know Allan Pinkerton was nosing around a conspiracy to kill the president."

Molly nodded but said nothing. Mrs. Barley studied her face, then turned back to loosening the shoe she picked up from the bed.

"What's your name?" Molly asked again.

The older woman stared at Molly for a moment, but then her face softened. There appeared to be no point in hiding it any longer.

"Kate Warne."

"I am who I say I am, Mrs. Warne. I swear it."

The woman studied Molly, and then met her eyes. Molly didn't waiver or look away.

"I believe you."

"And I can handle whatever you need tomorrow."

Mrs. Warne nodded, though she did not look as convinced on this point.

"Come, Molly."

She stood and guided Molly to the vanity. Molly sat upon the bench and looked into the mirror. She hardly recognized herself anymore. The carefree girl who ran through the trails in the woods and swamps had dissolved. Mrs. Warne pulled at Molly's hair, gathering it up in her hands.

"We will have to change this some. Perhaps black. Lucky for us, men do not have an eye for detail like women."

Molly turned from the mirror. She didn't want to see her image anymore.

"What is it?" Mrs. Warne asked. She sensed the change in mood in the younger girl.

"My father always used to say that we get what we deserve."

Mrs. Warne let Molly's hair fall. She placed both hands upon Molly's shoulders and looked into the mirror. Molly met her eyes in the reflection.

"No one deserves what happened to you."

CHAPTER SIX

MOLLY SPENT TWO days in debriefings from Mr. Pinkerton or in lessons from Mrs. Warne. Pinkerton desired any information about the conspiracy, even things she might think insignificant. In truth, her body ached from the abuse it had withstood. She would heal, but it hurt. She gave every possible detail to Mr. Pinkerton. He had asked many of the same questions again and again, looking for any inconsistency. She didn't argue. Instead, she answered the same way each time—the only way to build trust.

Hillard's coded system for writing letters turned out to be the most interesting to Pinkerton. She hadn't seen how it worked. But it raised Hillard's esteem in Pinkerton's mind. Someone with enough wherewithal to encrypt letters meant he had something to hide. Of course, Molly had only seen him use it once—the day Hillard spent in her room. After he had finished with her, he sat at the small desk and composed a letter. Stealing a glimpse over his shoulder, she made fun of his spellings. She meant it as an insult. He laughed and told her she was too simple to understand how he hid the intent behind the letters. Then he bragged about the Palmetto Guard and their grand plans, how she would soon know his name. It would be heralded throughout the land, he said. He offered all this without a shred of secrecy, because she insulted him. *Yet she was the simple one.*

Molly also told Pinkerton about the other men in the plot. Some came to the brothel, but most were just names. Among them was the ringleader—Cipriano Ferrandini—a hairdresser at Barnum's Hotel. Sometimes he accompanied Hillard to the brothel. On one occasion, Molly witnessed the men discussing something in a heated fashion. The girl Hillard fancied sat nearby and giggled.

After Mr. Pinkerton's sessions came Mrs. Warne. She had few questions. Mostly, they walked the streets to become familiar with the city that Molly had only seen from the window. They didn't trust her with the office location. Molly still didn't know exactly where that first meeting took place. Instead, they operated from a boardinghouse on Howard Street. It stood near the Camden Street rail station. There were multiple rail lines into the city, each with their own station. Trains to Washington left from the Camden Station, while those from Pennsylvania arrived at Calvert Station. That was the way Mr. Lincoln would come—through Calvert Station. Then he would transfer by buggy to Camden Station. He was vulnerable in Baltimore, precisely why Hillard's militia planned to attack as he transferred stations.

Mrs. Warne had dyed Molly's hair black as night and helped her apply limited makeup that added years to her age—perhaps a decade. It also didn't hurt that most who had seen her up close only saw her in a tattered nightgown and under dim light. The brothel was always in want of more light, even in the parlor. That way Mr. Barbusca could pass homely girls as the spritely water nymphs in the paintings that adorned the brothel walls. Dim light and alcohol distorted men's vision, especially those with wanton cravings.

Despite Molly's pleadings, Mrs. Warne refused to teach her how to use a pistol. She had established notions of how female detectives acted. They were to maintain their ladylike dignity. Under no conditions would they use the violent means found among their male counterparts. In Molly's opinion, this left her weak and vulnerable. But to Mrs. Warne, strength came from a quick intellect. This included the ability to deflect attention from oneself. She taught Molly how to change her appearance, even with simple tricks like a change of a hat or manner of walk. Mrs. Warne was adept at it, and in a crowd, Molly had a hard time finding her again when she meant to become lost. On their last session she gave Molly a small glass vial.

"What is this?" Molly examined the brown glass. A cork plugged a dark liquid inside.

"There will be times you may require more than your wits alone." She nodded toward the bottle. "This may buy you time, or equalize a situation where you cannot otherwise escape."

"Poison?" Molly didn't want to touch it.

Mrs. Warne laughed as she placed her arm through Molly's. The two women continued to walk down the street.

"Not poison. It is a strong sedative. You may have to be clever in its delivery. But the contents of that vial will put even the most robust man on his back for several hours. When he awakens, he will feel like he finished an entire bottle of rough country whiskey and reached for another."

Molly placed it secure in her handbag.

"It might be easier to shoot him."

Mrs. Warne pulled her closer as they walked. "You are an obstinate student. Men use such crude means. We can be subtle—more intelligent. Never let what you are crush who you are. Do you understand?"

Molly shook her head.

"You are a detective, or at least you will be. But who you are is a lady of the South with fine upbringing and refinement. Comport yourself in that manner. You will find you seldom, if ever, need to resort to crude methods. Our intellect is our weapon. Because they are physically stronger men think they control the world. But you or I can make them bend to our will, and all the while they never recognize it. That is true power, Molly. And when it fails, use the vial."

Molly was quiet for a moment. "I am not a refined lady from the South. I am a whore you rescued from a brothel. Nothing more."

Mrs. Warne stopped their walk and spun Molly toward her. With one gloved hand, she lifted Molly's face until the two women looked at one another.

"That is what they did to you. Don't let it define you. You fought them. You broke your addiction to the opium. You tried to escape two times, even banked money for your next attempt. They did not quench the fire. Don't give them power by letting that flame die. Instead, use it. Feel it. You are stronger for it, and they will regret it."

Molly replayed those words as she walked the Baltimore streets that night alone toward Barr's Saloon. As she hurried, she pushed the fear deep down, trying to do what Mrs. Warne suggested—draw strength from all she had been through. Mrs. Warne instructed her to arrive ahead of Mr. Pinkerton at the saloon. She would find a table and take the pulse of the establishment, presumably somewhere out of the way. Pinkerton wanted her along a wall, or in a corner—with everything in sight. She carried an umbrella. If the saloon appeared safe, she was to keep the umbrella upon the floor. If not, then she would place it upon her table. He would look for her when he first entered.

She hurried her pace. The cobblestones were rough in patches, and she had to make up time to arrive before Mr. Pinkerton. He came from a different direction. It would dispel any suspicion they were connected, in case anyone watched. The darkness had a scent about it, as it settled across the city—like after a light rain. As her feet hurried, she found some places slick with a thin sheet of ice. In the cold, her breath came out in a fog. It gathered droplets on her shawl.

This outing marked her first without supervision. She hoped it meant they trusted her. She had been to Barr's Saloon once already. Mr. Pinkerton sent her there the night prior. Mr. Davies—the man who met her in the Barbusca brothel—followed her all the way. She sat at a table in the back and watched. There were several other women that night. They were an upper-class version of the girls at the brothel. Likely, they worked for one of the criminal syndicates, or at least took their protection for a cut of the profit. A few women took extra notice of her. She might cut into their margins, but they allowed her to sit without protest. The bartenders paid her no mind, and the other men only glanced in her direction.

As she entered this night, the saloon felt much the same. A similar group of men stood around the bar—among them, Cipriano Ferrandini. The entire group wore the black and white cockades upon their lapel, or a gold badge. Both symbolized their inclination toward secession. The badge was the same as Otis Hillard's—the Palmetto Guard. Baltimore contained a seething hotbed of secession, and she had strolled her way into the lion's den. She listened as Ferrandini regaled the group with stories. The others appeared fixated on his every word.

She sat at the same table she used the night before. Once again, few noticed her. Holding the umbrella, she scanned the room. Nothing appeared different. Mr. Pinkerton would soon be here, and Mr. Davies would follow. That worried her. With Davies, Otis Hillard would be in tow. It would be the first test of her altered appearance. And it made all the talk of using her wits and not a pistol seem small and fragile—how she felt. She placed the umbrella at her feet.

It took a few minutes before Pinkerton arrived—as if he had watched and waited. He came with another man—someone he had befriended who would introduce him to the group. If he glanced her direction, she did not notice. As Pinkerton joined the other men, one of them caught her eye. He left his colleagues, making his way to her table.

"Madam, if no others are going to join you, then perhaps I may impress my company upon you for a time?"

Molly's heart beat fast. She had hoped to spend another evening in the shadows by herself. It would be easier to monitor Pinkerton without having to entertain at the same time, though she had little choice.

"Please." She swept her hand out, indicating the chair opposite the small round table.

As he sat, he moved the chair closer to Molly's side, so they were not quite sitting across from one another. He was a slight man, well dressed and composed. Black hair adorned his head, wavy yet combed. And a sweeping mustache covered his top lip, though it was also well tamed. On his lapel was a small black and white cockade.

"I have not had the pleasure," he said, holding out a hand to accept hers.

She placed her gloved hand in his.

"Miss Lawton. Hattie Lawton."

She used the cover name Mrs. Warne provided. It came with strict instructions—never to break from the role until safely back at the boardinghouse on Howard Street.

"Miss Lawton, it is a true pleasure. I am Mr. Booth—John Wilkes Booth. Have you heard of me?"

Molly nodded, surprised at the name. She did know it. He smiled, growing more confident. Taking her hand, he leaned forward and offered a light kiss. At the bar, Pinkerton used his newfound reputation as Mr. Hutchinson to make friends among the secessionists. He played the role of a strong supporter to the Southern movement.

"Are you by chance a theater connoisseur?" Booth asked.

"Regrettably, I am not. I find little time for it."

The words stung. He leaned back in his chair, disappointed. He had obviously used this introduction many times with a different result. His life upon the stage was well known, as were the rumors of the women he bedded along the way.

"That is unfortunate. There are few diversions as worthy as the theater."

"All the world is a stage, Mr. Booth. I find my entertainment elsewhere."

At this, his mood changed. Curiosity brought him back from the brink.

"Quite right, Miss Lawton—and all the men and women merely players. I see that you are not against fine literature. Perhaps you simply dislike its enactment for your entertainment?"

Molly shook her head. "It is so hard to find good renditions these days. I prefer to read and use my imagination. That way I am seldom disappointed."

Rather than the stinging insult that she meant, he seemed to take her words as flirtatious possibility.

"Then if you do not attend the theater, what, may I ask, takes up all your precious time? From my vantage I see only two types of women who would frequent a saloon such as this."

"And what would those be?" Molly prodded.

The group of men at the bar raised their glasses and toasted. Booth lost hold of Molly's question and watched them.

"Never shall Lincoln be president," Ferrandini exclaimed. His voice filtered to where Molly and Booth sat. "He must die—and die he shall! If necessary, we will die together."

Booth turned back to Molly, more serious after the words of his colleagues. There was little hiding their intent with such public proclamations.

"Either a lady of the night, or a federal spy." He said it in a manner half-joking. Her heart leapt in her chest.

"So, you give me only two choices. I am either a whore or a Unionist? Seems you have little regard for me then, and here I have just met you. Perhaps you leave out another possibility?"

Several new men walked into the saloon, pulling Booth's attention from Molly. Hillard and Davies were among them. Hillard caught Booth's eye and nodded. Davies made no sign of recognition. For a moment Hillard's stare lingered on Molly. It felt like time stopped. She held her breath. But his notice of her passed. He looked at her more with curiosity to see whom Booth worked his charm upon. Not as the girl in the tattered nightgown who had elicited the plans for his Palmetto Guard.

Booth returned his attention to Molly as Davies and Hillard joined the group of men at the bar.

"You were saying that I have misjudged your character?" he asked.

"I merely suggested you might have overlooked another possibility. Perhaps I am a spy, but not one for the Union."

At this Booth sat back in his chair. Examining Molly closer he seemed both taken aback, and amused.

"Now that would be something. But how would one prove it?"

The door to the saloon opened again. This time a pair of men entered. They did not talk or joke as most who had arrived. They seemed set upon some goal and eyed the entire place with critiquing eyes. They dressed in a similar manner. Though something felt distant in how they composed themselves.

"Friends of yours?" Booth offered. Again, he appeared half-serious—a trap, but a simple one to step around.

"Not of my acquaintance. I would wager they are not from Baltimore."

"I would as well. Perhaps we should ask them." He made to stand up, but Molly gripped his arm to pull him back to the table. She half-laughed at his suggestion.

"I would think that was not wise. Let them sit a spell and we shall watch them."

"Is that what your training in the service of our great Confederacy has taught you?" Booth asked.

Once more he provided a loaded question. Molly did not answer straightaway. The men at the bar had grown loud. They also noted the arrival of the strangers. The group shifted to a large table at the other end of the saloon, perhaps trying to keep their conversation from spilling toward the new men. Booth watched. Hillard caught his eye to make certain Booth saw where the group settled. Again, he gave no sign he recognized Molly.

"You were about to prove to me your Southern loyalties," Booth said.

Molly turned back to him. She had been watching Pinkerton's group.

"Yes."

With one hand she pulled at a chain around her neck. Mrs. Warne had given it to her. The medallion she rescued from her mother's hands hung around the chain. As did the key she took from the brothel. She let Booth see the medallion.

"Do you know this?" she asked.

"I've seen it before. But it is not a society for women."

"No, it is not," Molly said. "It was my father's. I took it from his effects when he passed."

It amazed her how easy it was to lie. In some manner it felt empowering. But it also made her sick to her stomach. Mixing her father's memory with that of Mason Cheeney felt a violation. Guilt overwhelmed her as she struggled to put the medallion back. She didn't want Booth inspecting the backside of it to find the initials inscribed. That would only lead to a tangle of lies.

"I offer my sincerest apologies for doubting you." He bowed his head.

As Molly contemplated what to say, the group of men stood and walked in their direction. They headed for the exit. Most made their way to the door, but Hillard stopped in front of them and leaned his hand on the table. In a hushed voice, he related their plans to Booth. Molly froze. She lowered her head and looked to her lap to give him no reason to examine her further.

"Those men are watching us." He looked back to the pair Molly and Booth had discussed earlier. "Cipriano doesn't trust them. They look like Unionists. We're off to the other place. Will you join us?"

Booth nodded. "I will be along." Turning to Molly, he made the introduction to Hillard. "This is Miss Lawton. A true supporter of the cause."

Hillard bowed his head and offered a hand. Molly swallowed hard. Fighting the tremble in her hand, she extended it for him. He grasped it and looked into her eyes—*nothing*.

"It is good to meet another of like mind, Miss Lawton."

He let go and turned back toward the men gathering at the door. At first relief filled Molly, then anger. This man had come to the brothel, disrobed her, taken advantage of her, and then insulted her. Yet he still could not recognize her. It solidified her hatred. Men like this were all the same—too stupid to be observant. So assured of their place and her inferiority. It burned. They used the women around them and thought nothing more of it. Mrs. Warne was right—it showed their weakness.

Booth stood.

"It appears I will be taking my leave of you. It was a true pleasure to meet you. I hope our paths cross once more." He leaned closer and lowered his voice. "Please assure your employers there is nothing but loyalty for the secessionist cause in Baltimore." Then he kissed her upon the cheek. "We will do what needs to be done."

With that he left to join the others, who filtered through the door. Surprisingly, both Mr. Pinkerton and the man he arrived with, Mr. Luckett, remained at their table. Pinkerton's frustration played across his face. He had not been invited to join the group for their next meeting. Although in a manner of good news, Mr. Davies left with his friend Hillard. So there remained hope. Pinkerton and Luckett spoke in hushed tones, all the while watching the two men who stayed in the saloon.

Molly sat uncomfortably for a few minutes, pondering if it would look awkward to leave. Pinkerton likely still watched her. His discerning eyes delivering a scathing critique. At the same time, she longed to deliver news of her conversation with Mr. Booth. This might be a revelation for Pinkerton's investigation.

While she struggled with the decision, one of the two strange men stood to leave. He looked around and made for the door. Pinkerton caught her attention. He looked to the man, then back to Molly. *Did he mean for her to follow?* Pinkerton and Luckett must have been left behind to watch these two men. And now the pair had split. Molly stood, picked up her umbrella, and followed outside.

Mrs. Warne had given her only the most rudimentary training in following someone. But it came well into play. Molly trailed for several blocks. She stayed far enough behind that she hoped he would not notice. Occasionally, he glanced over a shoulder but did not look far enough behind to see Molly. Whenever he turned a corner, she hurried her pace so she would not lose sight. Then she waited upon the corner to create the distance again.

As she walked, she struggled to silence her footfalls. They echoed off the cobblestones and rang out in the cold. At one point she slipped. The sound bounced through the night. She paused, terrified. Up ahead, the man turned another corner. Molly hurried.

When she rounded the corner, he was on the far side of the street. Near the entrance to an alleyway, he folded a piece of paper and placed it in a flower box hanging from the nearest building. Glancing both ways, he hurried off.

Molly waited until he was a half-block away, then she scurried across the cobblestones. Stopping in front of the flower box, she stood on her tiptoes. Only the corner of the paper stood out. She pulled at it and then unfolded the paper. *Blank. What did it mean?*

Down the street, he had vanished. There were only a few people out, and they were far in the distance. She panicked. *How did she lose him?* Slowly she walked down the street. *He must have used a door? Was there a boardinghouse nearby?* She didn't know the city well enough.

It mattered little. As she pondered what to do next, the man emerged from the next alley. He had used the paper as diversion. Grabbing hold of her arm, he dragged her across the frozen cobblestones and into the shadows of the alley. She screamed, but it did no good. He clamped a hand over her face and pressed her up against the brick. It felt like the brothel again. Her head ground into the wall. The more she struggled, the more he pressed against her. Tears flowed from her eyes.

"Who are you?"

He pressed harder. Perhaps he did not realize that by clamping his hand over her mouth she had no chance of answering. He looked back toward the street, then faced her again.

She had no time to answer. Over his shoulder a flash of movement caught her eye. The man turned. The shadow struck hard, hitting him about the head. He slumped forward, then slid down the length of Molly's body into the alley. She stiffened.

Mr. Booth emerged from the dark. He held out a hand. At first the terror still gripped her until recognition overcame the fear. She took his hand and he pulled her into the street.

"Hurry," he said. "Let's move from this place before he awakens, or his friend comes looking."

Booth guided her down the street, checking behind them every few steps.

"You followed me?" Molly asked. She blotted at her face with the handkerchief.

"Not exactly. We left Mr. Luckett and some new gentlemen at the saloon to look after those two men, to see if they followed. But Ferrandini does not much trust Luckett, and we know nothing of the new man. I volunteered to double back. That's when I saw him assault you—quite lucky if I may offer. This is dangerous work for women."

His words stung. She was angry that she had been taken by surprise. Angrier still at how helpless it made her feel. The tears felt like scars upon her cheeks, where they melted her makeup. She said nothing.

"Come, I will walk you to your residence."

"No, I am fine," Molly answered. She did not want to bring Booth to the Howard Street boardinghouse. That would be a huge mistake, luring the enemy to their base of operations. "I can walk myself."

"It was not a request." Booth's hand was firm upon her upper arm. She struggled to think.

Nodding, she acquiesced. His grip loosened as he felt her resistance fade. Focusing on breathing, she worked to clear her head.

"I must confess that I did lie to you earlier."

"Is that so?" His curiosity piqued. "So, you are a Northern agent?" He asked it in half-jest. He hid the intent behind his question.

"No. I was going to say that I believe I did see you upon the stage once."

"And, how was I?"

His tone softened, obviously pleased.

"Passable."

He was quiet for a moment. "Well, I pride myself in being good at many things. Acting is just one of them. Perhaps I would be better in your esteem with my other qualities. Yet, you have only the night as I leave for Albany in the morning. My *passable* skills must open a show there."

He said it with the right amount of deviousness in his voice. His reputation offstage was nearly as great as his acting upon it.

"And where is it you are staying?" Molly played the part, letting the same tone creep into her answer.

"I am on Davis Street."

The same street as the Barbuscas' brothel.

"Then your place is closer than mine." She had found her diversion. "Would you have a stiff drink there?"

"Indeed."

CHAPTER SEVEN

MOLLY LEFT BOOTH's boardinghouse on Davis Street before the sun lifted the night. By the time she reached Howard Street and her own boardinghouse, the horizon to the east was gray. She dragged herself up the stairs and entered her room. It lay bare.

Stunned, she stood and absorbed the scene. They had left nothing in the room. She walked down the hall to where Mrs. Warne stayed. The door stood open a crack. She pushed it open—*nothing*. They were gone. Her knees gave out and she stumbled into the room to sit upon the bed. Everything was gone. She had things to tell them, but they abandoned her. Anger and sadness spread through her. She had liked the time spent with Mrs. Warne. She felt . . . *safe*.

As she sat upon the bed, a melancholy took hold. The sun streamed through the window spreading in a wedge that swept across the floor. It lit the room and moved across the wall. A piece of paper sat upon Mrs. Warne's vanity—a note. Molly leapt up and grabbed the paper.

11AM—Calvert Street Station.

The flowing script was in Mrs. Warne's hand—her writing distinct. Molly flipped the note over. Nothing. *Was it left for her?* There was no way to tell, but the note was the only thing to go by. She gathered herself up and left the boardinghouse.

Despite her fatigue, she headed north to the station. With time to kill, she found breakfast and a warm place to wait in a bakery. There were a few other customers. They gathered after the churches let out from early morning services. She dozed. She only startled awake when a young boy selling newspapers burst through the door. He shouted at the top of his voice.

"Jefferson Davis has been elected President!"

The few other patrons looked to him. They began murmuring to themselves. Normally, there wouldn't be a Sunday paper, but the newsmen had made a special run for the occasion.

"Come here, boy, let me see that."

A man behind the counter took hold of the boy's outstretched paper, handing him a nickel in return. The man read for several moments. Molly breathed deep. She pushed the weariness from her head, to unclog the haze that hung in front of her vision. She had drunk two large glasses of whiskey the night before, while encouraging Mr. Booth to talk. He was much more reserved in his manner than Mr. Hillard. Perhaps he respected a woman's ability to listen more than his companion. But all the same, he let a few items slip that would interest Mr. Pinkerton.

"Well I'll be," the baker declared. "Mr. Jefferson Davis is the new President. It says it right here, duly elected by the Confederate delegates in Alabama. Now, if Maryland will get the vote together before that ape Lincoln makes his way through our good city. By God, we will strike him down if he tries."

The cheers of a few of the men standing close by startled Molly. Even one or two of the women joined the chorus. Molly gathered her belongings and hurried out of the bakery. For a Sunday, the city bustled. Several more newsboys hawked the latest edition of the papers. From all appearances, they ran low on supply. The demand for news flowing from the South appeared insatiable. Jefferson Davis' appointment meant a step closer to war. Even the thought of it energized the city.

Molly crossed the streets where they were least slick. Wagons passed her, delivering goods throughout the city. The breath of large horses hung in the air. Upper-class Baltimoreans, still in their Sunday best, drove through the traffic. Their buggies were more nimble. Molly had worn this dress for a whole day now and felt in bad need of both a warm bath and a change. A bed would have done her good as well.

When she arrived at the station, she stood outside. She had no idea where to find Mrs. Warne. The building towered above her, majestic and welcoming. Three arched entrances scribed the façade, with two towers reaching for the clouds on either end. She could run—take a train from here. But she had no one, and nowhere to go. *Who would take her in? What would she do?*

Maybe head south. She had no idea how much a pistol cost, but she could find one, and then find Mason Cheency. This time she would practice first, make certain how the thing worked. She gathered her skirts to cross the street.

The pace of the place felt daunting. No one slowed down for the Sabbath. Molly checked the time and the schedule. She still had a half hour until the time inscribed on the note, if it was meant for her. She found a bench to watch everyone coming and going. As she settled, the weight immediately fell upon her eyes.

A passenger sat on the bench next to her. It bolted her awake. A large clock stood in the middle of the station—11:25. Swearing, she stood to get a better view. No one looked familiar.

Panic seeped in. She walked through the station, checking faces, racing between the aisles. When she searched the whole station, she doubled back—nothing. The schedule hung behind the large ticket counter. A 12:15 train was scheduled for New York City.

She had no other clothes, no bags. She shook her head and walked to the entrance.

The streets were absent of anyone she recognized—no sign of Mrs. Warne, or Mr. Pinkerton. Loneliness set over her, as if she had pulled a blanket over her head. The weariness in her body clung to her legs and back until it threatened to drag her to the floor. The loneliness turned to despair and her eyes welled.

She resigned herself to take one more look at the boarding-house. Maybe she missed something. Maybe they left another sign for her. As she stepped down the stairs, a hand fell upon her shoulder. Mrs. Warne stood behind her. Relief coursed through her body, and then a twinge of anger. She might not have found them.

"I thought you had left me," Molly said, fighting back tears.

Mrs. Warne shook her head.

"But why?" Molly asked.

Mrs. Warne pulled her to the side, so they could talk discreetly as people passed.

"We didn't know what happened last night, and we couldn't take the chance. When you didn't return, we had to protect our interests."

"So, you left the boardinghouse?"

Mrs. Warne nodded. "Yes. But I left the note. I believed you would find us and would not have given us up."

"Of course not." The insinuation offended Molly. "Who would I have told?"

"Mr. Pinkerton expressed concern with your companion from the saloon."

"Mr. Booth."

"Yes," Mrs. Warne answered. "He is part of the conspiracy, is he not?" No one else was in earshot.

Molly nodded. "I believe so. He was not completely forthcoming, but he spoke more freely as he drank."

Mrs. Warne studied Molly's face. "Tell me what happened when you left the saloon."

"Mr. Pinkerton told me to follow a man—at least, I think that is what he intended. I didn't know exactly what to do, so I followed down the street."

"He told me," Mrs. Warne said. "That was his intention."

"I followed the man, like you taught me. Not too close. But it was hard. There were so few people out at that hour. Around a corner I hurried, and he was no longer upon the street. Then he grabbed me and pulled me into an alley."

"And then?" Mrs. Warne asked.

"Mr. Booth had doubled back. Ferrandini did not trust Mr. Pinkerton or Mr. Luckett. So, he backtracked to see if those strange men followed."

Mrs. Warne nodded. She stayed silent for a few moments, seemingly lost in thought.

"That makes sense," Mrs. Warne said. "Did you know that Mr. Pinkerton was close behind you?"

Molly shook her head. "Last night?"

"Yes. He waited a few minutes and then felt like he had fed you to the wolves, by forcing you to follow the first man. He was uncertain you were up to the task."

"I was fine."

The insinuation made her defensive. She didn't want to relive the helpless feeling as the strange man had pressed her up against the wall. She certainly didn't want to admit it.

Mrs. Warne raised her eyebrows. It forced Molly to look away.

"As I thought," Mrs. Warne said. "There is no shame in it. You have much to learn, and Mr. Pinkerton should not have sent you off

alone into the night like that. I have already chastised him for it."
Mrs. Warne continued, "But he saw you emerge with Mr. Booth
from the alley. That drew his concern. Mr. Pinkerton figured maybe
you were in league with him all along."

"No," Molly said. It came out in a rush. She was eager to beat
down any such accusation. "I only just met him last night. He sat at
my table. I had no desire to talk to him."

"Then where did you spend the night?" Mrs. Warne asked.

"He wanted to walk me back to the boardinghouse, but I couldn't
bring him there. So, I did the best I could."

Mrs. Warne nodded. The pieces fit. "So, you went with him."

"Yes."

"And did you . . ." Mrs. Warne paused, trying to find a way to put
it delicately.

Molly shook her head. "No."

She held firm, staring right at Mrs. Warne without breaking from
her eyes. Molly reached into her handbag and drew out the vial of
sedative Mrs. Warne had given her the day before. She uncorked it
and turned it upside down. Nothing came out. Mrs. Warne smiled,
then put her arm through Molly's as she angled her back toward the
station.

"It worked then?"

"Faster than I expected," Molly said. "He was revealing things,
and I managed to slip it into a second glass of whiskey. Before I
knew it, he was fast asleep."

"Good. I worried about you. I am relieved in how it turned out.
Mr. Pinkerton will be much relieved as well. We will send him a
telegram, especially after you tell me everything about Mr. Booth
on the train."

"Train? Where are we going?"

"New York."

"Why?" Molly asked.

Mrs. Warne held two bags. She handed Molly a ticket for the 12:15 train.

"Those men from last night were New York City detectives. We need to find out why they were here. It is too delicate a matter for telegrams—it requires a personal touch."

Molly nodded.

"And Mr. Davies discovered something else from Mr. Hillard last night," Mrs. Warne added. "We are to follow one of the conspirators to New York. He brings a message to a Confederate operative there. We need to discover who the man is in New York, and how deep this conspiracy goes. The messenger should be on our train."

"Who is it?" Molly asked.

"John Wilkes Booth."

CHAPTER EIGHT

11 FEBRUARY 1861 – NEW YORK CITY

GETTING TO NEW YORK turned into a sixteen-hour ordeal. Mrs. Warne secured a sleeper berth. No sooner had the older woman pulled the curtains shut than Molly's eyes followed the example. When she woke, the memory of stops along the line held little more than a fog. Occasionally, the high-pitch squeal roused her from her slumber. And the cars jostled, and the couplers made a racket whenever the brakeman pulled his lever. But she always fell back asleep as if the moment were a bad dream. Molly woke only when Mrs. Warne shook her shoulder and insisted she hurry from the train.

While Molly barely remembered the journey, Mrs. Warne appeared exhausted. As she hurried the younger girl off the train, she told Molly of her night. For the first portion of the trip, she searched the cars until she found Mr. Booth. Then she took up a seat behind him and kept vigil all day and then throughout the night. She had only caught a small amount of sleep to ensure he did not slip their grasp at any of the stops. He slept most of the trip, likely still feeling the effects of the sedative.

Now she hurried Molly, ensuring they did not lose sight of Booth. But Molly had trouble focusing. New York teemed with life—more than she had seen in a long time. The fog of sleep mixed with the bustle of humanity was overwhelming. Even the smell of the place was incredible—a mixture of people, horses, and the frigid air of winter.

Mrs. Warne pulled Molly close, weaving her through the crowd. She had an innate ability to sense where to go, and how to stay far enough behind that their quarry would be none the wiser. Ahead, Mr. Booth led a porter who dragged his extensive luggage upon a hand dolly. They stopped when they reached the edge of the rail depot. The porter helped Mr. Booth pile his luggage onto a waiting railcar pulled by a team of horses along an iron track. Molly pulled her wide-brimmed hat low to keep the wind from biting her face. The horsecar pulled away.

"We're losing him," Molly said.

"Shhh . . ." Mrs. Warne replied. She focused on the porter. When he walked by with his handcart, Mrs. Warne grabbed his arm.

"Excuse me, but where did that gentleman go?" Mrs. Warne asked.

"The man with the bags?" he asked.

Mrs. Warne nodded. She had opened her handbag and her hand emerged with a silver dollar.

"He was off to the Astor House. I believe he is some kind of actor. I didn't pay much attention."

"Quite right," Mrs. Warne said.

"I can get you on the next horsecar if you would like, ma'am."

Mrs. Warne pressed the coin into his hand. "That would be lovely. We only have the two bags."

She pointed to the ground. He picked up both bags, and turning the handcart around, he placed them upon it. They followed him through the crowd.

The Astor House was exquisite. Its impressive façade stood off Broadway, south of City Hall in Manhattan. Molly had worried about losing Booth as he disappeared into the car ahead of them.

But Mrs. Warne knew what she was doing. The first horsecar was still parked out front as the porters carried in Mr. Booth's luggage. Molly and Mrs. Warne stepped off their car. Mrs. Warne tipped the driver, and they waded through the front entrance of the hotel. A porter followed close behind with their bags.

The interior of the hotel surpassed Molly's imagination. After it opened, the Astor House fast became the most luxurious accommodation in the city. Indeed, it may have been one of the foremost luxury hotels in the world. At five stories, it boasted more than three hundred rooms. There were toilets and baths on each floor—a far cry from the brothel, or even the plantation. The central courtyard contained a glass rotunda, and under it a saloon. Marble columns marked the main hall, with blue-and-white mosaic floors.

The conversations of those loitering in the lobby bounced off the hard floor and pillars. The gentlemen dressed in suits, with full vests beneath their heavy coats. Most wore top hats. The occasional bowler hat also adorned the older gentlemen. The ladies who did venture out wore distinguished yet practical dresses and hats. They carried handbags and shawls to hold back the cold. The conversations around Molly rose and fell. In some manner, that comforted her. The congealed sound became a wall to hide behind.

Mrs. Warne led Molly to a small bench that bridged the span between two marble columns. The dark wood of the bench matched the beauty of the lobby.

"Sit here and make yourself unnoticed." She held her voice low. The porter stood behind them still carrying the bags. "I shall find us a room."

The porter dutifully followed Mrs. Warne to the main counter. Mr. Booth was farther down, dealing with another hotel employee. Mrs. Warne stood quite close to him. Molly turned her back. She hoped she might blend in with the surroundings should he look over his shoulder.

To steady her nerves, she focused on the room around her. The flow of people resembled a river, slow, yet unrelenting. The gentlemen walked with canes, letting the brass tips fall upon the hard floor in a jumbled staccato. Thick stone columns rose from the floor, as if they sprouted from the marble of the tiles.

When she finished, Mrs. Warne returned to where Molly sat. The porter with the bags had gone. Mrs. Warne pressed a key into Molly's hand.

"Take the back stairs, and head to our room. We are on the third floor. The room number is on the placard with the key."

"Where will you be?" Molly asked.

"I will wait here. Mr. Booth took the main stairs. He did not check his luggage, but rather had the porters take it for safekeeping."

"What does that mean?"

"He won't stay long. I suspect he is leaving for Albany and the theater production he told you about," Mrs. Warne answered. "He left the counter before I could follow, so we can only hope he comes back down. You go change, and then you will take my place while I freshen up. After that we will wait together."

Molly nodded and started off.

"And, Miss Lawton," the older woman called out. "Do hurry. It would be best for both of us to watch for our friends."

Molly nodded and headed for the stairs. Mrs. Warne had used her cover name—a reminder to once again resume her character.

Once upstairs, Molly unlocked the door and slipped inside. The porters had already carried the bags into the room, and Molly hurried into a new dress. The hotel staff even left warm water for their arrival—a luxury found only at the best hotels. She washed her face. Many a weary traveler welcomed such little touches of elegance from the hotel.

Once finished, Molly made her way to the lobby by retracing her steps. She found Mrs. Warne in a different place, concentrating upon the room around them. The older woman's face held exhaustion, but a focused drive shone in her eyes. When Mrs. Warne saw Molly, she motioned her over to where she sat.

"Take my place here. You can see the main door, as well as the stairs. Keep watch. I will be quick."

"What if they come while you are gone?" Molly asked.

"Then you follow. This is only half of our assignment. We need to know with whom Booth meets in New York. After that, we will deal with those New York detectives."

Mrs. Warne reached into her handbag, producing several bills and a few silver dollars.

"If you have to leave, keep your distance. Mr. Booth will no doubt recognize you. He has quite the reputation with the ladies. And I gather from the description of your last encounter, he would know you upon sight. It would be most hard to find an appropriate excuse for a chance meeting here."

Molly understood.

"And send a messenger for me," Mrs. Warne continued. "Any of these street children would happily earn a dollar for running a message. Pay them and promise another when they deliver the message. Agreed?"

"Yes," Molly said.

Mrs. Warne began to walk away. "I promise I will make haste and will not lie upon the bed. If I do, I am certain you would not find me until morning."

Despite her exhaustion, even the manner of Mrs. Warne's walk appeared elegant. Molly was still the rough girl who ran barefoot on the dirt. Or worse, the girl who walked barefoot out of a Baltimore brothel. She regarded her fortune in near disbelief. She had dreamed every night of escaping, but never of this.

Across the lobby, a man descended the main hotel stairs. Most of the men wore dark suits, especially this time of year—not this man.

He strode down the stairs in a light gray suit, wearing the black and white cockade upon his lapel. He wanted to be noticed. His large mustache made him easy to recognize, even if she had not seen the dark wavy hair—*Booth*. She struggled to find some explanation that might pass as truth for such an occurrence. She hoped Mrs. Warne would hurry, so she would not have to attempt another follow by herself. She forced herself to inhale, feeling the weight of the New York detective as he pressed her against the brick wall—*never again*.

Molly rose and moved behind a pillar, placing it between herself and Booth. She had little need to worry. He was deep in conversation with another man. This new stranger appeared older. He wore a dark suit. His hair gave the appearance he had fought a strong wind. White peppered the wild locks, and even invaded his beard, trimmed to barely cover his chin. His features were stockier than Booth's, with maybe a half-foot in height upon the younger man. He, too, wore the black and white cockade. They made no attempt to hide their political inclinations, not even in this Northern city.

Molly kept her distance, peering around the marble column. The men were so engaged in their own conversation they noticed little about them. They walked into the lobby. Then the river of humanity that filtered through the hotel swallowed them whole. Molly moved from the pillar to stalk her quarry.

Her heart beat faster as she pushed through the people, desperate to keep the men in sight. In this matter, Booth's suit gave her a particular advantage—easy to find as they made their way through the other guests. Molly followed at such a distance she would appear as another face in the crowd—nothing more.

The men made their way for the great dining hall. Molly stopped behind another marble column. The men spoke to the host—a diminutive creature dressed in a neat black suit with a white bowtie. He escorted both men into the great hall, and out of sight. Molly tried to see past the host station and into the dining room. Impossible. So, she pulled her hat down upon her head and walked up to the host station to look into the hall. Booth and the other man were at the far corner of the dining room, sitting alone at a table away from the other patrons. The hall was full, with a spattering of free tables spread throughout the room. However, the placement of the two men came across as odd, at least to Molly. Perhaps they asked for a table away from prying ears.

"May I help you, madam?"

The host reappeared after seating Booth and his friend—his tone condescending.

"I was looking for—"

The man cut her off.

"This is not a dining room for women. There is another smaller dining hall, but it has unfortunately closed for renovations. You will have to leave the hotel to find your meals."

Molly studied the man. He did not even rise to her full height. His hair fell neatly combed, yet looked plastered to his head. He held a haughty indifference, as if his position made him better than those around him. Behind him, several women dined at different tables.

"Forgive me," Molly began, "but there are women in the dining hall."

"They are escorted. We don't accept women by themselves. The Astor House is not *that* kind of establishment."

Something in his tone, condescension mixed with meanness, leapt at Molly. She glared at the little man, who rocked forward to puff out his chest. He took delight in his words, meaning them as insult.

"*That* kind of establishment?" Molly didn't understand his implication.

"We do not need women of your stature enticing our distinguished guests. I suggest you make off before I summon for someone to cart you to the door."

Her eyes fell to her dress. While not the height of fashion, it was far more than she ever wore to church when she lived upon the plantation. The tips of her shoes showed under her hem. She understood what he meant. She stood in a tattered night dress, barefoot and chained to a bed. *How did he see through her?*

At first, she walked from the dining room, then she ran. She pushed through the hotel guests, the river of humanity. She swam through it, her shoes making a din upon the hard marble floor. She didn't stop until she reached the place where Mrs. Warne left her. The older woman was waiting.

"What is it? What has happened?" Mrs. Warne asked. She stood and pulled Molly to her by her upper arms. "What happened, Molly?"

Molly shook her head. "It is nothing. Mr. Booth and an associate are in the dining hall."

Mrs. Warne studied Molly for a moment, offering her a handkerchief. Molly used it to wipe her face. She said nothing more about the tears, and Molly was glad she didn't press. Molly settled herself. She pushed the man's words from her mind.

"All right then, show me the way to the dining hall," Mrs. Warne said.

"No." Molly shook her head. "We can wait outside. They don't want women in the hall."

"I see," Mrs. Warne answered. She studied Molly, perhaps putting the pieces together. "Show me, anyway."

Reluctantly, Molly led her back the way she had just run. They waded through the scattered crowds, toward the dining hall. Once they could see into the hall, Molly stopped. She did not want to go near the little man again.

"Well, let us find a good table to observe our quarry," Mrs. Warne said. She stepped around Molly and toward the host stand. Molly grabbed her arm.

"They don't allow women in the dining hall. There is another dining room for us."

Mrs. Warne turned back to the dining hall. Several women were still dining with their male companions.

"Look, there are women."

"But they have an escort. That man . . ." Molly trailed off. The little man at the host station had caught sight of them. Mrs. Warne looked in his direction and then to Molly.

"Come with me," Mrs. Warne said. She marched directly for the man as he stared at them.

"Madam," he began, "I have already told you—"

His words were interrupted as Mrs. Warne's hand fell across his face. The blow sent the man reeling. He took a step to catch himself, and when he stood upright again she held his gaze.

"Do you have any idea who I am?" Mrs. Warne asked.

He shook his head, still clutching the side of his face. He glanced into the dining hall, as if help may come from that quarter. Mr. Booth and his companion were deep in conversation. No one noticed the commotion at the entrance.

"Get a table for myself and my niece, or I shall call upon Colonel Stetson."

Mrs. Warne held her voice low yet menacing. She stood near a foot taller than this man and used her height to good effect. It served to further intimidate him.

"Madam, it is not our custom here to—"

Mrs. Warne cut him off again. "Perhaps you did not hear me. Colonel Stetson is a dear family friend. He will be most disappointed to know that you called my niece a whore."

"That is not what I—"

"That is what you meant. A table, now!" Mrs. Warne stepped forward again. It caused the man to buckle under the pressure. He nodded.

"This way, madam."

He showed the women to a table in the more crowded portion of the dining hall. Mrs. Warne indicated that Molly should sit with her back facing Mr. Booth. They were some distance from the two men. It left no chance to overhear the conversation. But they could still follow the men when they left.

"This will suffice," Mrs. Warne said, sitting down.

"Yes, madam." He lingered a moment, certainly thinking of what to say. "I would hope that we could avoid any further misunderstandings."

"You hope that I will not report your behavior to the colonel. Apologize to my niece and we shall forget it happened."

He bowed toward Mrs. Warne, then turned to Molly. Anger filled his eyes, embarrassed at having his hand forced in the matter.

"I do hope you can—"

"Just leave," Mrs. Warne spoke up. She meant to interrupt him, adding a final insult. Mrs. Warne did not even look at him. She read the menu upon the table.

He paused, uncertain what to do.

"Better yet," Mrs. Warne said. "Bring us both coffee and toast. And the good marmalade, the one the colonel keeps in the kitchen for the most important guests."

The host nodded and started to the front of the dining hall.

"Who is Colonel Stetson?" Molly asked.

"He is an old acquaintance of Mr. Pinkerton, and the owner of the restaurant here. He knows us well and helps with anything we might need. We have occasion to come to New York often. They have a policy to keep the prostitutes out. When the hotel first opened, many came here and mingled as guests, trying to find gentlemen customers. The hotel is much on guard over their reputation."

"How did you know what he said to me?" Molly asked.

Mrs. Warne didn't answer. She looked to Molly, likely thinking of what to say. She reached across the table for one of Molly's hands. The waiter arrived. Mrs. Warne let go as he poured the coffee and left them with plates of freshly buttered toast. A jar of marmalade accompanied the plates. Mrs. Warne seemed pleased. When the waiter left, she reached for Molly again.

"I cannot imagine what you have gone through this past year, Molly. But there will come a time where you will have to make peace with your past. If not, it will forever haunt your future. You are ashamed of what happened in Baltimore—what they forced you to become. That is natural. However, you should embrace it. It is part of you. And you survived. Do you think that man would have lived through what you experienced?"

Unable to keep hold on Mrs. Warne's eyes, she looked to the table. Slowly she shook her head.

Mrs. Warne continued, "If you know who you are and are not ashamed, then words from little men can never hurt you. You will meet people in this world who will think they can control you, because they are larger or stronger. Most see physical strength as the only asset. But you have strength in a manner they will never understand. This is why I don't teach you to shoot or to carry a knife. Often those means fail, and that failure will be at your expense. Don't let words break you or make you feel small."

"But you struck that man," Molly answered.

"There are times nothing else works. This was one of those. He needed to be dealt with in a manner he understood. But you have to know when those times are and apply the right amount of force. You will understand, but you must make peace with yourself first."

"And what if I still want to kill the men who made me what I am?" Molly asked. Anger had replaced her shame. It felt good.

"Perhaps that is what you need to embrace yourself and accept it. But for men like that, there are fates worse than death. Ones that may be much more suitable for those you might seek revenge upon."

"Fates like what?" Molly asked.

If Mrs. Warne heard her question, she made no sign of it. She looked over Molly's shoulder.

"They are leaving."

Molly caught a brief glimpse. Mr. Booth and his companion stood, then shook hands.

"I will follow Mr. Booth." Mrs. Warne nodded in the direction of the men. "You follow the other one. That way there is less chance we are detected. Do your best to not lose him, and find out who he might be. We need to understand the depths of this conspiracy."

Molly nodded. "Where will I find you?"

"We will meet back at the room this evening. Wait for them to leave, and we will follow them out."

Mr. Booth left first, as his companion sat down again. Mrs. Warne watched Booth walk past, not recognizing or even seeing Molly with her back turned toward him. Mrs. Warne stood. She reached over and placed a hand upon Molly's.

"Remember, you are stronger than you know."

Then she walked out of the dining room and followed Mr. Booth.

Booth's companion stayed in the dining hall for some time after Booth left. Molly switched seats. It gave a better view. The host glanced at her like a hawk, especially after Mrs. Warne left. Molly paid him no mind. The other man drank a second cup of coffee and read a newspaper. When he finished, he folded the paper and stood.

Placing the paper under his arm, he picked up the coat resting over the back of his chair. As he strode out of the dining hall, Molly followed. When she walked past the host, he glared. She ignored him.

The man she followed walked through the lobby, stopping at the door to pull on his coat and place a bowler hat upon his head. He wrapped a scarf around his neck as he pushed out the front doors and into the cold. Molly stayed as close behind as she dared. She was determined not to let Mrs. Warne down.

She wished she had brought a coat or at least a shawl. The day had turned frigid, and she had not thought of needing to follow someone outdoors. But she remembered the words of the host at the dining hall. They burned in her mind. She would succeed in discovering the secrets of this man, despite the cold.

Once outside, the man turned north on Broadway and headed toward Town Hall. He made his way across the street. Molly darted between the carts and the horsecars, arriving on the other side. The man crossed into City Hall Park, seemingly unconcerned that anyone might be watching.

The park was small. It encompassed a block in front of City Hall—a magnificent building that exuded the power of New York. Molly slowed her pace as she made her way into the park. The man remained well ahead of her, headed for a group of three others awaiting his arrival. She forced her walk to a crawl so as not to overtake them before finding a way to turn from their meeting spot. But they had already stopped. The man she followed greeted one of the other men. Two others stood watch. They scanned, studying everyone who passed. As she walked by, one of the men stared, then turned his attention to someone behind her.

Molly made her way past them and found a place to turn off. She walked a few feet farther until the branches of the wintering bushes partly hid her. The group of men started in her direction—one of the bodyguards in front and the other trailing. Booth's companion strolled in the middle with the third man from this group. He was distinguished, wearing an impeccable overcoat and a well-kept top hat. He walked with a cane in one hand while his other remained tucked into a double-breasted inner coat. He was younger than Booth's friend, but the two spoke without formality.

Molly sat upon a small bench. As the cold seeped in, it slowed her senses. She longed for a warm shawl. Even her dress was no match for the cold from the bench. The tapping of the man's walking cane let her follow their progress. They headed toward City Hall. The cold sunk deeper. She shook as the wind pushed through the dead branches of the bushes. She gave the men a few moments, and then stood to follow around the corner.

She hurried her pace so she would not lose them, as Mrs. Warne had taught her. She pulled the hat down as the wind tried to lift it from her head, until it blocked her vision. Her eyes burned with the cold. She closed them for only a moment, losing her bearings in the process. She walked right into a man standing in the path blocking her way. He grabbed her arms to prevent her from falling.

"Let go," she demanded. His grip was tight and unrelenting. Something was amiss.

One of his hands let go of her arm, and it lifted her hat off her head. She recognized him—the bodyguard at the back of the group, the one who had studied her when she walked past.

"A little cold to be out like this, isn't it, miss?"

His voice was rough—a New York accent.

"I said let go!" she demanded.

"Where you off to in such a hurry? It seems you were following someone."

Molly drew her mouth into a tight line, defiant. She glared at the man.

"If you don't want to talk," he said, "then we'll figure it out another way. Take her!"

The man spoke to someone standing behind her. Another man, maybe two, grabbed hold. She struggled until one of the men bent her right arm behind her back and pinned it there. The other produced a bag and pulled it over her head.

"Take her to the superintendent. He'll know what to make of it."

CHAPTER NINE

FOR HOURS MOLLY sat in a dank cell, guarded by a rotted wood door. Guards brought her a putrid meal near dinner—molding bread with warm rice. Worms crawled out of the rice. The guards knew nothing and would tell her little beyond the fact that the New York City police had detained her. No matter how she banged her fists upon the door, no one came. It felt worse than the chain about her ankle. When the panic set in, she breathed deep and remembered Mrs. Warne's words. *She had survived before and would again.*

When the door finally opened a man in a suit stepped inside—the same man she ran into along the path. He smiled when he saw her. It wasn't the kindly smile of recognition. It was like the host at the hotel. He enjoyed her misery.

"Are you ready to talk?"

"Why am I here?" Molly snapped.

Her patience had exhausted, her rage soon to boil over. She fought it, trying to think her way through the situation, as Mrs. Warne would have done.

"What is your name?" he asked.

"You have no right to hold me. I've done nothing."

"Women don't walk around the city with so much money in their handbags. Or with medallions from secret societies."

They had searched her, taking her chain with the medallion and key. These men were aligned with the well-dressed man she saw in the park. And in turn, he met with Booth's companion. If they were truly New York police officers, then it seemed unlikely they were also Southern sympathizers.

"What's your name?"

Molly crossed her arms over her chest and stared at the man. He smiled. Then he stepped to her side, pulled the only wool blanket from her cot, and walked out the door. Before it shut he made certain to catch her attention.

"Maybe tomorrow you will feel different."

The door slammed behind him. It nearly blew out the only candle in the room, which would have plummeted her into darkness.

That night was miserable. The temperature dipped so low that Molly dared not sleep. She remained huddled on her cot, sitting with her arms wrapped around herself. She willed the sun to rise. There was no window in the cell, though from the feel of the far wall, it faced outdoors. The cut stone was colder than anywhere else in the cell. She feared she might freeze to death before the day came.

She drifted in and out as the night progressed, and only startled awake as the cell door opened once more. The candle had long ago died. She sheltered her eyes from the light. As she stood, she found the cold had worked deep into her muscles. Struggling, she managed to straighten her legs and rise. The man from the previous day entered. He didn't smile this time. He looked contrite, perhaps feeling guilty for making her suffer with no blanket.

"Is your name Lawton?" he asked. "Miss Hattie Lawton?"

How would he know that name? Mrs. Warne had called out to her in the lobby—a reminder to use her cover identity. No one else should know. But at the same time, it mattered little if this man knew her by her false name. If it got her out of the cold, that would be a welcome first step.

Molly nodded. "Yes."

The man shook his head, upset. He looked back through the door.

"Get me warm tea," he ordered to someone outside. Then he reached through the door and took the blanket from a guard. He stepped closer to Molly and wrapped the blanket around her shoulders. "It would have been easier if you told us from the beginning."

"Why?" Molly asked. "You had no right to kidnap me from the street. Why should I tell you anything?"

The answer upset him. He kept it to himself without taking it out on Molly. Another guard entered with a steaming cup. The man took it and held the cup to Molly. Her fingers could barely hold it they were so frozen. But she gripped the porcelain tight, letting the heat warm her hands. Slowly she brought it to her lips and drank. The warmth spread down her throat. She coughed at first, but took another sip. It felt amazing.

"I apologize for taking your blanket," the man said. "I meant only to get you to talk."

Molly didn't understand the turn in his attitude, but she didn't question it. She hoped to play into it, to figure out what her status might be and how to get hold of Mrs. Warne.

"Are you letting me go?"

The man said nothing at first. He nodded toward her cup. She took another sip, this time getting more of the hot liquid down. The warmth spread through her chest. Her fingers were slow, but they moved again.

"The superintendent would like to see you."

"Who is that? And what is this about?"

"I was told to fetch you," he said. "After you finish I will take you to his office."

Molly didn't want to pry further. It meant she would leave the cell, and then maybe reason her way free of the entire situation. And she was no closer to finding an identity to Booth's companion, or whom he met in the park. As the cold in her body subsided, anger took its place—the second time she had failed in her pursuit. *How would she find Mrs. Warne?* There was no way to locate her a second time if the older woman had left.

After she finished her tea, the man escorted her from the cell. He walked her down a dizzying array of halls, containing other cells. She clutched the blanket around her shoulders. He escorted her through an outside door and into a waiting carriage. No sooner had he closed the door than the driver lashed the horses and the carriage started with a jolt.

The ride lasted ten minutes. They brought her right to City Hall. The man led her from the carriage and up the long steps. He held her upper arm again, but not hard this time—more to direct her. His manner had softened. The danger of captivity had passed, that much was clear. *But how did he know her name?*

City Hall was more spectacular than even the Astor House. The white stone floors were immaculate, with marble columns extending to the ceiling. A double circular staircase led to the second floor. The man led her up the stairs and down a hall. They made a few more turns to arrive deeper in the building. With her mind slow from the cold, she was lost. They stopped in front of a wide mahogany door. The man knocked. Then he opened the door without waiting for a response.

The office inside was large, befitting a man who led the entire New York Police force. He sat in front of the window behind a large desk, wearing a dark suit. His eyes were intense, and with one hand he swept his dark hair back upon his head. A woman sat on the other side of the desk—*Mrs. Warne.* Molly filled with relief. She turned to see Molly, leaving her seat and rushing the few steps to her younger companion. Mrs. Warne grabbed hold of her, a hand brushing Molly's hair out of her face. The door closed behind her as the officer who had escorted her left the room.

"I have been most concerned about finding you," Mrs. Warne said.

"It would have been much sooner if she had told my officers her name."

The man behind the desk had also risen to his feet. His voice was tinnier than Molly expected. Mrs. Warne didn't respond. She smiled at Molly and let go of the younger girl. She lowered her voice.

"I'm glad you said nothing. That was the right play. But I am also glad we found you."

The man behind the desk motioned for Molly to sit in the other chair, next to Mrs. Warne.

"This is Superintendent Kennedy," Mrs. Warne explained. "The man Mr. Pinkerton sent us to see. And, sir, this is my associate Miss Lawton."

Mr. Kennedy nodded and then sat. Mrs. Warne followed suit and motioned for Molly to join her.

"Mrs. Warne told me of your purpose in New York," Mr. Kennedy began.

Mrs. Warne had used her real name. It left Molly puzzled why she had not given Molly's name as well. Perhaps she did not trust Mr. Kennedy. Molly longed to have even a moment alone, but that appeared unlikely. Her chain, complete with the medallion and her key, lay upon the desk in front of Mr. Kennedy. Her handbag and other effects were also there.

"I am still curious how you came to follow the mayor of our good city. That is why we detained you and provided such *luxurious* accommodations last night."

"She was not—" Mrs. Warne began, but Superintendent Kennedy held up his hand to cut her off.

"I will hear it from her."

"Miss Lawton is in my charge while in New York on Pinkerton duty," Mrs. Warne countered. "She acted upon my orders alone."

"Then there is little to fear, as she will relate much the same story that you already told me. Again, madam, I ask to hear it from your associate. I have already heard your side in the matter."

Mrs. Warne nodded in concession and looked to Molly.

Superintendent Kennedy turned back to Molly. "Why were you following Mayor Woods?"

"Mayor?" Molly asked.

She turned to Mrs. Warne for an explanation.

"You were following the mayor, were you not?" Mr. Kennedy asked.

"Was that the well-dressed man with the others—with the man who brought me here?" Molly asked.

Superintendent Kennedy nodded. Then he leaned forward on his desk and placed his hands together. They touched at the fingertips, likely how he sat during interrogations.

"I didn't know who he was until just now," Molly answered.

"Then why were you in the park, and with no jacket or shawl? It appeared you followed someone."

"I did," Molly said. "But I lost him in the crowd leaving the Astor House. I thought he crossed Broadway and headed into the park. But I must have been mistaken. Then I saw your officer. He stared at me most strangely as I walked by. It troubled me. I didn't know if I could return the same way, so I sat for a moment to let them walk past. I just wanted to return to the hotel."

"And whom were you following?"

Mrs. Warne nodded, encouraging Molly to go on. But there was more upon her face. This is where Molly's story had to match. There was only one name that made sense—the man who the New York detectives had already seen in Baltimore. Certainly they had told their superintendent whom they had uncovered within the conspiracy.

"Mr. Booth."

"The actor?"

Mr. Kennedy acted surprised, concealing a false ring in his voice. Molly nodded. He leaned back in his chair, seemingly in thought. Mrs. Warne smiled. Molly had guessed right.

"We heard he might be involved in some manner of plot," Mr. Kennedy said after a pause. "Do you have any idea what they may be planning?"

"No," Mrs. Warne answered. "That is precisely why Mr. Pinkerton asked us to New York, to speak with you direct. We didn't understand why New York detectives would be in Baltimore. But it seems we chase the same men."

"Indeed." Mr. Kennedy looked between the two of them. Then leaned forward again as if he would let them in on a secret he wanted no one else to hear. "I have been concerned that an attempt may be made upon Mr. Lincoln's life before he arrives in Washington. I assumed that New York or Baltimore were the most likely locations for such a daring move. I had hoped that it would be in Baltimore and not my city."

"I do hope you wish it will *not* happen at all, regardless of which city." Mrs. Warne sounded like a schoolteacher issuing a strong chastising.

Mr. Kennedy sighed. "Quite right. I hope it will not come to pass. I am, however, the superintendent of the New York Police. It would be a mark of dishonor to our glorious city if anyone even attempted such an act of treason here."

"And a black mark against you personally," Mrs. Warne added.

"Yes."

"So were your detectives able to uncover anything of such a conspiracy?" Mrs. Warne asked. She softened her tone, urging the man to talk.

He shook his head. "Not as of yet. We were in the infancy of our investigation. In fact, my detectives were newly in Baltimore when they heard of Barr's Saloon. They were advised that a rogues' gallery assembled there, and so they went to make their observations. I believe that is where you might have run into them, Miss Lawton."

He spoke of the man Molly followed—the one who had pressed her against the wall in the alley.

"Yes," Molly answered.

"Well, I am most relieved that there is another detective agency already upon this matter. And you, Mrs. Warne, have you uncovered anything further?"

"We have not. Our detectives are a few weeks in advance of your own. After we discovered your men operating in Baltimore, Mr. Pinkerton thought you might know more."

"Ah yes, Mr. Pinkerton. How did he become involved in this pursuit, if you don't mind my asking?"

"Not at all," Mrs. Warne said. "A railroad executive hired us to protect his rail lines. Of course, I cannot divulge more on the identity of our employer. But he feared his rails or bridges would be attacked to stop Mr. Lincoln from arriving in Washington."

"That makes good sense," Mr. Kennedy said. "I have not met Mr. Pinkerton myself. But he has an excellent reputation among the railroads—protecting their assets and the like."

"Well, the next time I am here in New York with Mr. Pinkerton, I shall make it a point to bring him to you for an introduction," Mrs. Warne said.

"I should much like that," Mr. Kennedy replied. "Where will you go now, Mrs. Warne?"

"Back to Baltimore. We shall check on the progress of the investigation with our other detectives in the field."

"Very well. And I assume if you find anything related to my city you would be so good as to send me a telegraph?"

Mrs. Warne bowed her head and then spoke. "I would be most happy to accept that task."

"I would be much in your debt," Mr. Kennedy said. "It appears our goals align quite well in this matter. I wish to protect the image of New York. You have a rail line to see safe. And we *all* wish Mr. Lincoln a speedy and uneventful journey to Washington. In the meantime, I will make preparations to receive Mr. Lincoln. I'll work under the assumption that an attempt on his life might happen in New York. He will be here in less than a week, and I will ensure we meet him with the full force of the New York Police as protection."

"That sounds splendid—more than he will likely receive in Baltimore."

Superintendent Kennedy turned to Molly.

"I would like to extend my apology on behalf of my officers for holding you in the manner we did. Perhaps we made poor assumptions."

"I hold no grudge," Molly said.

Superintendent Kennedy held up the chain from his desk. "I believe these are yours. But before you go, could you tell me who 'MC' is?"

"Another case we were working," Mrs. Warne answered. "It happened to come in handy for Miss Lawton in this matter."

Mr. Kennedy studied Mrs. Warne, then looked at Molly. She held her breath, trying to make her face as calm as she might. She forced a slight smile.

"Very well," he said. "Please take your effects. You will find my men outside, and they will be happy to take you anywhere you wish."

"Back to the Astor House is perfectly fine. We will rest this evening and then make our way to Baltimore in the morning," Mrs. Warne said.

"Well, I look forward to hearing from you, Mrs. Warne, if you find anything amiss."

He stood from his desk and clutched Mrs. Warne's hand, then Molly's. Molly gathered her handbag and chain from his desk.

"I will keep the blanket for the ride back, if you don't mind," Molly said. She hoped to end the conversation on a light note.

"Consider it a present from the New York City Police."

Molly smiled. She followed Mrs. Warne to the door. True to his word, Superintendent Kennedy had two men stationed outside. They escorted the women through City Hall and to a waiting carriage. Although the Astor House stood little farther than a block away, they drove Mrs. Warne and Molly to the hotel.

Once upstairs and safely in their hotel room, Mrs. Warne clutched Molly. It was an uncharacteristic moment for the older woman.

"I am relieved to find you. I spent the night quite worried and with no means to track you in this city."

"I was afraid you might have left," Molly answered.

"I figured I would start with the police. Since I had to meet with Superintendent Kennedy, I made that my first order of business. No sooner had I mentioned the circumstances than I knew by his face that they had found you."

"I didn't know that was the mayor," Molly said. She was exhausted and sat upon the end of one bed.

"Yes, that is a troubling development. You did splendid in Mr. Kennedy's office. I am most relieved that you chose to expose Mr. Booth and not our mysterious stranger. That was quick thinking. They already know of Booth."

"Do you not trust Mr. Kennedy?" Molly asked.

Mrs. Warne shook her head. "I am not certain about him. I am troubled by the connection with City Hall. Mayor Wood has strong feelings in regard to secession. He has called for New York to secede from the Union as well—to form their own city-state as it were. They worry about the cotton trade, and the shipping industry relies upon Europe. A civil war with the South would devastate New York."

"And the mayor is aligned with Superintendent Kennedy?"

"The mayor appoints the superintendent. That buys a lot of loyalty."

"Then how will we know if we can trust him?"

"I don't know that we will. I hope he is true to his word—concerned with the reputation of the city. Perhaps that will motivate him. I am afraid we will not know until Mr. Lincoln arrives in the city. If the police response is overwhelming, then Mr. Kennedy may be trusted."

"By that time it could be too late," Molly said.

"Indeed. That is why it would be nice to know the identity of the man you followed out of the hotel. I fear the opportunity is lost."

"So we go back to Baltimore?"

"No. Mr. Pinkerton wants us in Philadelphia. There have been developments, and he desires our help. Not everything is as it seems."

CHAPTER TEN

MOLLY SLEPT THAT night like she had upon the train—with no care in the world. She awoke to find Mrs. Warne packing.

"Already?" Molly asked.

She rolled over and pulled the blankets off. The room was cold, the floor worse.

"We should try for the morning train. It will take most of the day if our last journey is any measure."

Molly forced her legs to move, stiff as they were. She followed Mrs. Warne's example and packed her bag. Once done, she sat back down upon the bed, looking at the bag between her feet.

"If I had been better the other day," she said, "we might know the identity of that other man."

"Following someone is a hard art, and you did fine," Mrs. Warne replied. From her tone, she didn't note the disappointment in Molly's voice. Mrs. Warne busied herself going through her bag once more.

"But how are we to know if it will be safe for Mr. Lincoln once he gets to New York?" Molly asked. "We are no closer to understanding the conspiracy than before we started."

Mrs. Warne stopped what she was doing. She must have read Molly's frustration.

"This is never a business of certainty, Molly. That is the first thing you must learn. Our job is to uncover what we can, and then tell it plain. Others will paint the picture around what we know and what we do not know."

Molly found it hard to accept. No city might be safe for Mr. Lincoln, and the deeper they dug, the more enemies they learned he had.

"Why doesn't Mr. Lincoln go straight to Washington and forget the stops along the route? What if he took a new train and came a different time when no one expected him?"

Molly met Mrs. Warne's gaze. The older woman's eyes drifted off, looking out the window. She took a few moments, letting the low hiss of the gaslights fill the space between them.

"There is time yet to avert many things. With all we know, Baltimore is the most likely place for anyone to make an attempt against Mr. Lincoln. And for now, I see no more we can do in New York. We have no leads here."

Far below the window, the bustle of Broadway teemed with life. Working with Mrs. Warne, Molly believed she had a role to play in something larger—that she would be more than a random piece in the jumble of history. That feeling seemed far away.

"Come, Molly." Mrs. Warne's voice was soft and comforting. "We have much work yet before we see Mr. Lincoln through Baltimore."

Molly gave her melancholy another moment, then hoisted herself off the bed. She took her other dress from her bag and changed. At least she would not wear the same clothes she soiled on the cold slab that passed for a bed in the New York jail.

The two women finished in the room and headed down the main stairway. As they cleared the last landing of the stairs, a man walked past them. His stocky frame and unkempt hair with the white streaking gave him away. Molly grabbed Mrs. Warne's arm, nodding in the direction of the stranger.

Mrs. Warne understood. Together they followed a few paces behind. The river of humanity once more permeated the hotel lobby, but they stayed close. They followed him in the direction of the dining hall as he made his way through the hotel. His pace was faster than either woman could manage while holding their luggage. Then he stopped, engaged in a quick conversation with another man.

As they made their way past where he stood, Molly longed to slow her pace and overhear the conversation. Mrs. Warne gripped her arm and escorted her past.

"We'll stop ahead."

"He's going to the dining room," Molly answered.

"How would you know that?" Mrs. Warne asked.

"He has a paper under his arm, and no jacket. The other day he sat long after Mr. Booth left, reading the paper and taking his coffee. He'll go back there."

"Perhaps . . ." Mrs. Warne didn't finish.

Molly pressed ahead, pulling the older woman behind her. Stopping by a marble pillar, they watched the host stand. A different man stood guard over the dining room, not the same host from the other day. Looking into the crowd behind them, their target made his way in their direction. His conversation had ended.

"Take my bag," Molly said.

"What are you planning?" Mrs. Warne asked.

She made no attempt to take Molly's luggage. Molly gave up and placed the bag on the floor.

"Molly, what are you doing?"

"I'll find out who he is."

"How?"

Molly didn't answer. She searched for the man, still making his way toward them. She had to be fast.

"Please. Let me try."

Mrs. Warne studied her face. She must have seen the resolute look Molly placed there. She nodded, leaning down to take Molly's bag.

"I will wait where I left you to watch the lobby two days ago," Mrs. Warne said.

Molly didn't have time to respond. The man was close now. She had to beat him to the host stand. She stepped into the flow of people and cut through, arriving a few steps before the man.

The host looked at her as she approached. His face was similar to the man from the other day—a bit softer. Molly hoped he had the same stern policy for the dining room.

"I am sorry, madam, are you here with anyone?" the host asked. He held up one white-gloved hand to stop her approach.

Molly breathed deep, preparing for her act. Her heart beat furiously, and her head spun. There was no going back. Mrs. Warne watched. Working her best New Orleans accent, she tilted her head and played innocent.

"I am sorry, sir, I am uncertain I understand your meaning."

"We do not seat women by themselves," the man said. His voice adopted the bite of the host from the previous day.

"Why whatever for?" she asked.

The strange man stood behind her. A light breeze struck her back as he stopped. The brush of air held a smoky tinge.

"You must have an escort, or be dining with a hotel guest, madam."

"Well, I myself was a guest this past evening," Molly said. "I was hoping for a light breakfast before I have to catch my train."

"Madam, if you will step aside. I will seat this gentleman and then try to explain to you more discreetly."

Molly turned at the mention of the man behind her. For the first time she obtained a good look at him up close. Though in turn, he received the same view of her.

"Where would you be from, Miss . . ." he paused, indicating they were not acquainted.

Molly smiled, drawing upon all her acting skills for the occasion. "Miss Lawton—Hattie Lawton. I am from many places, sir. Originally from the great city of New Orleans, and have just managed to come from Baltimore."

"Madam," the host interrupted. "Please step aside and I will clear things up with you after I seat this gentleman."

"No need," the man said. "Can you not recognize a fine Southern woman when you see her? I will be most happy to escort her for breakfast and dine with her. That is if she does not have any reservations."

Molly managed a slight curtsy at the suggestion, though tried not to let her smile give her away.

"That would be most gracious, sir. I must admit I find this city and its customs most peculiar."

"Quite," the man answered. He looked at the host and tipped his head toward the dining hall.

"Very well, sir," the host replied. He led them into the room.

"My usual table will be quite fine," the man answered.

The host revealed a forced smile, then led them toward the table in the corner of the room. The man pulled out a chair for Molly to sit. As she took her seat she managed a glimpse of the entrance of the dining hall. Mrs. Warne still stood by the marble column, watching. Before the man sat he ordered breakfast for the two of them—eggs and toast.

Another man, deciding what she wanted.

"I must admit," the man started, "I am so glad I detected your accent. I seldom have the chance to entertain friends from my dear South. I hope you will forgive my manners. I have neglected an introduction."

Molly smiled, trying her best to watch his mannerisms for anything she might use. He forced his accent, no doubt on her account—making it more Southern. But it was nonetheless real, though careworn and rarely exercised. He was Southern in some manner but had lived elsewhere for some time.

"I am George Sanders."

"Well, that is a relief—and my pleasure, Mr. Sanders. I am most relieved to find a true friend to the cause." Molly nodded toward the cockade on his lapel. "I am most confused by the traditions in this city. I fail to see how denying a lady her breakfast before she travels is in anyone's best interest."

"New York is an interesting place," Mr. Sanders said. "It is neither here nor there."

Molly didn't understand his meaning. She must have made that fact plain upon her face.

"It is neither a true Northern city, nor yet aligned with our Southern brothers and sisters. It is in fact its own island in the sea of secession our nation now sails upon. Let us hope that it floats our way!"

"I see," Molly said. "I heard the mayor had a certain proclivity to support the South. Though I rather understand he has been rebuked by his associates."

Mr. Sanders nodded. "Mayor Wood is a good man, though I am not certain he would agree with our reasons for disunion. His are practical in nature. He would like to see more trade with Europe, and Southern cotton flow through his port."

He stressed the mayor's name, as if they were close personal friends; no doubt an effort to show how his relationships to the powerful—a peacock preening his feathers. Molly said nothing. Instead, she took a deep breath and hoped Mr. Sanders would continue to speak. Men liked to fill the silence.

"Well, look at my manners once again. I am boring you with politics. What brings you to New York City, Miss Lawton?"

The question caught her off-guard. Her mind raced, and her fingers twisted together as she wrung her hands under the table. She tried not to let it show upon her face.

"I came to see a friend. Though I believe he has already left the city."

"May I be of assistance? Is this friend another Southern gentleman?"

"Why yes, he is," Molly answered.

Her voice feigned surprise. Mr. Sanders' line of questioning gave her an idea. She would lure out his secrets. Mr. Sanders smiled and leaned back in his chair—proud that he had teased something from his companion. It was exactly how she wanted him.

"There cannot be too many men of good Southern upbringing in the city. At least not many with the character who would be meeting with a woman of your refinement."

"Mr. Sanders, you flatter me. Though I suppose the Southern gentleman would be a rare breed in this city. Quite identifiable for those of us with similar background."

"Indeed," Mr. Sanders answered. "Does your gentleman caller have a name?"

"Oh, my reason for being in this city is strictly about business, Mr. Sanders. I entertain no callers."

Molly pretended to take his comment as insult, adding a touch of scorn. She wanted him off-balance, thinking he may have trampled upon a social taboo. It placed him in her debt, at least in his mind.

"My apologies, of course. What business are you in, Miss Lawton?"

He was eager to change the subject, but she had opened another door, and he walked through it.

"I courier messages."

"Could that not be left to the telegraph?" Mr. Sanders asked.

He stopped his questioning as a waiter came and provided coffee to Mr. Sanders' cup. Molly declined the offer, waiting until he was out of earshot to continue.

"In most cases, yes. But there are those that must have as few eyes upon their content as possible. That is when I am commissioned."

"A most interesting career."

He drank from his cup, feigning disinterest.

"In that case," he said, "I wish you luck on finding your current assignment. If I can be of any help, please do not hesitate to call upon my services."

"Thank you, Mr. Sanders. I have only a small distance farther to travel, then I should be able to find him. Do you know how long the train takes to Albany?"

"Albany? Why that should be only a matter of a handful of hours."

The intrigue built upon his face as he puzzled the pieces together. No doubt Mr. Booth told him he intended to open a play in Albany. Mr. Sanders would be far more willing to talk about his friend if he made Molly out to be an acquaintance of the actor. He leaned forward and looked around the room. Then he lowered his voice.

"I do not mean to intrude upon your business, but could you be here to find John Wilkes Booth—the actor?"

Molly played it coy, passing a look of shock over her face. She glanced around the room as if she feared being lured into a trap. It worked. He read her fear.

"No, no, you are quite safe. I promise you that. I meant it when I said you are with a friend and true believer in the Southern cause."

Molly nodded, yet still made a point of looking around the room. She leaned closer, pretending his words revealed something further from her bag of secrets.

"How would you know the name of the man I seek?" Molly asked.

"It seemed quite natural, actually," Mr. Sanders said. He became more confident—more impressed with himself. "In fact, I met with him the other morning. We had breakfast in this very spot. He told me of his upcoming theatrical performances scheduled for Albany. And, look here . . ."

He paused as he opened his paper.

"I read just this morning that our good friend Mr. Booth had been injured in an accident upon the stage last night. The paper only has a limited account. Apparently, he injured himself upon a rapier during one scene. He completed the play while hurt. It must have been quite notable to make the city papers the following day."

Molly read the short article—a filler story between other news. Mr. Booth's performance had been well noted by the Albany press. He soldiered on despite a bleeding side. It required a doctor's attention immediately following the final curtain call.

"He does have the tendency for much physical acting, as they say," Molly said.

"Have you seen him perform?"

"Indeed, yes. I found him passable."

Mr. Sanders looked up. His brow furled and he tilted his head to one side. Molly caught his reaction out of the corner of her eye. She still skimmed the paper. Her heart pounded, and her hands clutched together once more.

"What was it you just said?" Mr. Sanders asked.

The older man appeared startled.

"I found him passable," Molly said. "I thought he overacted some portions of his role, as a means to impress."

A smile relieved Mr. Sanders' expression. It eased Molly some, but the way he stared made her uneasy.

"Have I said something wrong?" she asked.

"No, of course not. It's just that I know who you are."

He leaned further back in his chair and placed his napkin upon his lap. With a nod he motioned behind Molly. The waiter came bearing their breakfast. She remained quiet as the man placed several plates upon the table. They contained a simple breakfast—toast and eggs.

Molly took a deep breath and held it, searching Mr. Sanders for some sign of what he meant. His remarks disturbed her deeply. He thanked the waiter and took a piece of toast off his plate. Taking a bite, he focused the rest of his attention upon Molly.

She hated this feeling—small and out of control. He took a second bite, and then placed the toast upon his plate. Molly imitated him, still trying to mask her anxiety. The smell of butter filled her senses as she bit into the bread. The butterflies in her stomach barely allowed her to swallow.

"Mr. Booth was quite taken with you."

"He mentioned me?" Molly asked.

She hated the sound of her voice as it came out, a mixture of false innocence and worry. She feared Mr. Sanders would detect it. She would in his place.

"Indeed. Your words wounded him terribly."

Molly didn't understand. "Which words?"

"You did meet with him in Baltimore?" Mr. Sanders asked.

Molly paused a moment but could see no harm in admitting the fact.

"Yes."

"Well, he went on and on about how he received a most hurtful appraisal of his theatrical performances. It hurt all the worse as he indicated he was quite enamored with the woman who delivered the rebuke."

"I guess I fail to see—"

Mr. Sanders interrupted her.

"A moment ago you called him *passable*. It was that word which left him so injured. I can't imagine there are two women from Baltimore who have called Mr. Booth passable this past week."

Molly nodded. She had used that exact characterization of Booth's acting when she spoke with him in Baltimore. She had meant it as an insult. Apparently, he took it as such. More than she intended.

"But don't worry," Mr. Sanders said. "You are with friends, and I will not reveal your identity."

"I'm afraid I don't understand, Mr. Sanders." The words barely came out. *Identity? What could he mean?* Her mind raced over the layout of the room. *Could she run fast enough out of the dining room before he caught her?*

He placed his fork upon his plate and leaned forward to ensure no one else heard. Molly did the same, though she pushed her chair a little farther from the table to give her the space to bolt.

"Mr. Booth told me you were in the employ of our great Confederate government. He called you an agent of Southern delivery."

Molly made no effort to hide her shock. Without intending, she had forced her cover even deeper as a member of the Southern cause. And this man appeared to believe it.

"I, for one," Mr. Sanders began, "am grateful that we have young women of such obvious esteem and devotion to our nation. Your

bravery in working for our Confederate government is to be celebrated. I can understand what Mr. Booth sees in you."

He picked up his fork and took another bite of his egg. Molly
forced a smile. Inside she stood in a storm. Her knees were weak,
even though she sat. She studied Mr. Sanders' face. He appeared
sincere.

"Thank you, sir, I appreciate your discretion."

"The pleasure is mine, Miss Lawton. What a fortuitous meeting.
I may actually impress upon your service. You still intend to find
Mr. Booth?"

"Indeed, yes." She had no plan to head to Albany, but playing
along raised fewer questions.

"Then might I ask you to deliver a message for me?"

Molly's heart leapt. She had only hoped to learn the identity of
this man. Instead, she found herself wading deeper into his confidence. A new worry emerged. It would be easy to become lost in her
lies if she did not select her words with caution.

"Mr. Booth was to perform a task for me in Albany. But I am
uncertain if he can still perform his sacred duty if he is so injured."

Mr. Sanders pointed to the paper, indicating the article on
Booth's theatrical wound.

"Sacred duty?" Molly asked.

Mr. Sanders smiled, then leaned as far into the table as he dared.
Molly hesitated, but Mr. Sanders indicated she should lean in as well.

"He was to scout any weakness in the *rail-splitter's* security. We
wish to take advantage by the time that damned abolitionist reaches
Baltimore. Mr. Booth was also to recover a sum of money for us to
help in the exploit."

Rail-splitter referred to Mr. Lincoln—a common slur hurled at
the President upon the campaign trail. It made light of his begin-
nings working upon the railroads.

"After reading the paper this morning," Mr. Sanders continued, "I contemplated my own journey to Albany. But if you are already so dispatched, might you inquire what he has learned? I need to know if he is likely to get close to the special train bringing that ape to New York."

"Of course," Molly answered.

She surprised herself. Without thinking she grabbed at the opportunity. This man exposed the inner workings of the conspiracy, and his message might yet deliver more intelligence.

"Excellent. Should we do this in the usual manner?" Mr. Sanders asked.

Molly must have looked puzzled.

"I will write a benign note to Mr. Booth. With my signature he will understand that you are the bearer of my message. Then I need to know if Mr. Booth has ascertained the exact number of men guarding Mr. Lincoln aboard his train. And if possible, if those men are armed and the nature of those weapons. Also, if there are any scheduled changes to the itinerary. And the money. We need to know if he received the funds for our escape."

Molly nodded. "Of course."

He raised his hand to summon a waiter over. When the man arrived, Mr. Sanders requested paper and a pen. The waiter hurried off in search of the supplies.

"This is most helpful, Miss Lawton. I am in your debt. Of course, you will keep my involvement confidential?"

For the first time he seemed to realize how much he had revealed.

"Most certainly, Mr. Sanders. That is the nature of my business. I am a little confused, however." Molly created an opportunity to inquire further, though she hoped she did not dig too far. "There was talk of intercepting Mr. Lincoln's train in Baltimore, not New York. Has that changed?"

Mr. Sanders stroked his beard. Molly struggled to relax. She let her breath out slowly, hoping he would not see how fast her dress moved under her heartbeat. *Had she asked too much?*

"We have the mayor in our pocket here in New York, but not the police. Not like in Baltimore. Superintendent Kennedy plans a large presence to escort Mr. Lincoln out of New York. That is all well. It is better for Lincoln to fall in Baltimore," Mr. Sanders continued. "Maryland will vote to secede. Her honor will demand it, and force the governor's hand. When Maryland joins the Confederacy, it will cut off Washington from the North. Our war might end with a single shot, and the death of only one man. You understand what is at stake?"

Mr. Sanders studied her closely, as if he suddenly developed misgivings on his plan. Perhaps she had invoked his suspicions.

"I do," Molly said.

The plantation and the great house forced their way into her memory—Isabelle's ashen face and her mother's cold hands. Her eyes teared.

"I watched my father die for the South," Molly said. "I understand perfectly what is at stake."

She met his stare without hesitation. She didn't need to lie. Her father had died for his vision of what the South *could* become. Mr. Sanders reached out and placed a hand over hers. It made her uncomfortable, but she forced her hand to remain upon the table.

"We will all sacrifice for our dear South," he said. "You are a true friend, Miss Lawton. I will not forget this favor I ask of you."

The waiter returned with paper and an ink pen. Mr. Sanders scribed a note to his dear aunt. It said nothing, but it would further open the door with Booth. He stuck the note in the envelope, tucked the flap, and then handed it across the table. Molly took hold of it. Mr. Sanders did not let go. He met her eyes.

"*Sic semper tyrannis*. Do you know what it means?" he asked.

Taking the note, she maintained her lock upon his eyes.

"Thus always to tyrants," she replied.

CHAPTER ELEVEN

THE WIND BIT through Molly's shawl, forcing her to pull it tighter around her shoulders. It did no good. The cold hurt her nose as she breathed. Baltimore's weather had been bitter, and in New York she nearly froze inside the jail cell. But this felt heavier. The air sagged with moisture. It pulled toward the ground until it formed an icy fog that enveloped her. She pressed on. Her footfalls were muffled.

She left New York in a frantic manner, leaving Mrs. Warne to head to Philadelphia alone. Molly had succeeded beyond what they expected. A name to the mysterious man would have sufficed, so to expose his plans came as a stroke of luck. But it meant Molly must follow through. She had to deliver the message to Mr. Booth. Mrs. Warne gave Molly the address of a stockbroker's office in Chicago. It served as a cover for Pinkerton operations. She need only send a message, and they would relay it to Mrs. Warne.

Molly fought to steady her nerves as she closed in on the place Booth was said to congregate. Earlier she had gone to the New Gayety Theater on Green Street. Booth's name graced the playbill for that night's performance. But the manager confirmed that Booth had suffered a wound of his own making during the previous night's show. That development annoyed the man. His star actor had taken up in the local Stanwix bar and lobby despite the injury.

He felt that if Booth was well enough to drink, then he was well enough to perform. Instead, Booth joined in the frivolous invitations of theatergoers. He stayed out drinking to all hours, espousing his separatist politics.

Molly pulled open the heavy door of the Stanwix lobby. Darkness filled the space. Stepping across the threshold, it appeared she had passed from one night into the next. But she was happy to shake the cold. A few gas lamps burned along the walls. They glowed dim to enhance the ambiance. Rich green wallpaper covered the walls and ornate wood trim rose along the pillars to the ceiling. The place buzzed—alive with an upscale clientele. It even smelled like fresh flowers, though winter still gripped the city. What it lacked in light it made up for with the low churn of dozens of conversations. Molly moved away from the door as her eyes adjusted.

Mr. Booth had a small following about him. The men hung on his words, and the few women fanned themselves in a suggestive manner. Booth had found his element—a drink in one hand surrounded by his adoring public. Molly stepped into the room to better see who crowded the actor.

From the way he moved, his injury was significant—not enough to stop his drinking, but also not an act. Several times he spilled his drink as he motioned with his hand. His face winced. The dark liquid slopped over the rim. Each time he transferred the glass to his other hand and shook the wasted liquid from his fingers.

"Another drink!" he yelled out.

One of his fans went to the bar and fetched him a full tumbler. This was his calling—the center of attention. It would also be his downfall.

He lifted the fresh drink and took a sip, about to dive back into his story. But he saw Molly. A look of recognition fell about him. His expression turned to joy.

"Ladies and gentlemen, we are joined by greatness! Let me introduce—"

Molly shook her head, horrified at his lack of discretion. She let her anger show. His words fell silent, midsentence.

"My mistake," he said, once again talking to his friends. He went back to his story for a moment but watched Molly with quick glances. When he had finished, and the men roared with laughter, he nodded toward the back corner of the room.

Molly did nothing to acknowledge him. Instead, she moved in the direction he suggested. Several tables sat unoccupied. Behind her, he excused himself from his circle of fans. He made his way to where Molly waited.

"Why, Miss Lawt—"

Molly's hand fell hard across his face, cutting his words short with the slap—the same trick Mrs. Warne had used with the host of the Astor House. He stumbled and dropped his drink upon the floor—the crash of the glass was lost in the commotion of the bar. When he recovered, he stepped forward, enraged by her insult. She shoved him hard upon the right shoulder. The theater manager had said his injury was upon that side. He winced and slumped backward, landing in a chair. He caught himself as he fell upon the seat. Molly sat across from him.

"Whatever was that for!" he gasped. His breath had left him.

"Your indiscretion, for one. Keep your voice down."

Fear gripped her. But in truth, the anger was real. It upset her to deal with a drunk John Wilkes Booth again.

"You almost gave me away to an entire room of people whom I do not know. I will not have you toss my name around lightly."

Booth nursed his side. The anger faded from his face, and he now sulked. He pulled himself sideways on the chair, favoring his right side. He worried she might strike again.

"Very well, I apologize. I let my good humor get the better of me."

"Is that why you are speaking so freely of harming the President?"

Booth said nothing. Melancholy bore itself across his face, and he turned further in his chair. He had not expected this reaction.

"You should keep those opinions to yourself," Molly scolded.

"I do not need to be chastised by the likes of you," Booth began. "I have had a rough week of it. Though the critics found my performance more than *passable*. A pity you were not here for my opening."

"I heard all about it." She ignored his attempt to incite her with his phrasing. Mr. Sanders had been right—the slight bothered him.

"Is that why you are here then?" Booth pressed.

"It seems we have a common friend. He asked me to find you and deliver a message."

"We do?" Booth asked.

Molly fetched the sealed envelope from her handbag and handed it across the table. Mr. Sanders' writing scribbled across the surface of the envelope. He had addressed the letter to Booth. He read the contents, then his eyes skimmed the note again.

"I take it Mr. Sanders also read the newspapers?" Booth asked. "Is he worried that I will not fulfill my obligations?"

"Yes," Molly answered. "He was quite concerned that you had injured yourself beyond use."

"Well, he can rest assured," Booth said. "I plan on making my introduction when Mr. Lincoln's train reaches Albany."

"Not if you continue to make your opinions known so publicly." Molly feigned disdain.

"Yes, yes." He tried to dismiss her, but he turned in his chair again. She would have to reel him back in.

"Very well then," she said. "I will pass on your estimation. Mr. Sanders will no doubt be awaiting your news."

"Is that all you came for?" Booth asked. He turned back in his chair, trying once more to warm up to Molly. His voice found a certain playfulness. Though he slurred his words, muddying the beginning of each with the end of the last.

"Well, no," Molly said. "Mr. Sanders wanted to know if you secured some manner of funding."

"That is all?"

"And I hoped to catch a play, to see one of the finest actors this country has produced."

She quoted from the paper. A smile found its way across his face and he squared himself in his chair. He reached across the table to take Molly's hand.

"I should be able to resume tomorrow night, or the night thereafter. If you stay, you may yet see the nation's finest actor."

Molly pulled her hand away. Meaning to lead him on, her fingers lingered for a moment as she pulled her hand into her lap.

"I do not know that my affairs will lend me enough time," she said. "I must return to Baltimore. And you have not answered my question."

"What question was that?" Booth asked.

"Did you secure Mr. Sanders' funding?"

Booth took his hand off the table and sat upright in his chair. He crossed his legs and leaned back, attempting to relax. But he caught himself as he nearly tottered over.

"I meant to before this dreaded injury. I fear the theater manager will require me back upon the stage this weekend, and I will not have time to travel for it."

"Where do you have to fetch it?"

Her question leapt out before she thought to pose it in a manner that did not pry. Booth didn't seem to notice.

"I must meet a man in Montreal."

"In Quebec?" Molly asked. *The conspiracy crossed the border?*

"Indeed," Booth remarked. "You see my dilemma. It would take the better part of the day upon the train to arrive there, and then another on the trip home."

He leaned forward and indicated that Molly should do the same. Leary of his charms, she hesitated until he waved her closer with his free hand.

"And those men by the bar have kept a close watch upon me."

Molly turned slowly, hoping her observations would not draw their attention. Two men drank at the bar. Each dressed in a dark suit and bow tie. Nothing about them drew her to alarm. They spoke quietly amongst themselves.

"How long have they been here?" Molly asked.

"Each night," Booth said. "Since I criticized Mr. Lincoln and said I would take care of the man myself."

"That is why you should not make a spectacle of yourself," Molly scolded. "Who are they?"

Booth shrugged as he sat back once more. "I could not say who sent them. They follow me from the theater, to my hotel, and even watch when I am about town with my merrymaking. Even if I meant to make my way to Montreal, I fear I would lead them right into the hands of our dear friends."

Booth looked to the two men for a moment, then leaned into the table. From his expression, an idea grabbed his attention.

"You could go for me," he said.

His voice was earnest—excited. The bourbon poured off his breath.

"I don't know," Molly hesitated.

She had no desire to ever go back to Montreal. Instead, she longed to find Mrs. Warne before Mr. Lincoln's train made its way to Philadelphia. She hoped they still needed her. She worried she would be too late. *After this whole affair was over, with Mr. Lincoln in the White House, would they still have need of her?*

"It would be easy," Booth forced the issue. "I could write you a letter as a means to make your introduction."

An uneasiness overtook her. She fought it, but her face betrayed her. At the same time, this was another opportunity laid at her feet. The men behind the entire plot could be those in Montreal. If the Confederacy had agents in Quebec, then it might signal something far more sinister.

"I would have need to send a message and attend to other business before I could consent to such a task," Molly said. Her voice came out weak. She hated how it sounded. Her confidence had drained and lay in a puddle at her feet.

"Then it is decided. You make your arrangements and I will provide you a letter first thing in the morning."

"How am I to find you?" Molly asked.

"I am staying at the hotel across from the theater." He paused. "Of course, you are welcome to join me."

Molly stood from the table, longing for a few short hours of sleep.

"Mr. Booth," she began, "I would hardly wish to take you from your adoring public." Her hand swept out toward the bar where a few of his earlier companions remained.

"It would be nothing, Miss Lawton. You are infinitely better company."

Molly gathered her shawl around her shoulders. "Please know that I do appreciate the offer. However, I am afraid if I were to accept that, I would be forced to do all the work, while you would do all the storytelling. That would be enjoyable for neither of us."

Booth stood, unsteady upon his feet. His face contorted, no doubt trying to puzzle together the manner of her insult.

"Perhaps next time if you are less influenced by the whiskey," Molly offered, "I may consider such a proposal. I will find you in the morning."

Before Booth could say anything, Molly held out her hand for him to take. With a short curtsy she took her leave and headed for the door. As she crossed the room, the two men at the bar seemed not to notice. Pulling the door open to step into the night, the reflection of the room passed in the glass panel. Booth still stood where she left him, watching her every movement. She hesitated for a moment, bracing for the cold. Then she stepped into the night.

As darkness enveloped her, the sounds of the conversations felt so very far away. The cold penetrated deep through her dress. She watched for a moment, through the window. A dim light escaped, but it held her frozen in a manner worse than the cold.

Only one of the two men remained seated at the bar.

CHAPTER TWELVE

MOLLY FLED DOWN the street. The dampness had faded, and now the cold made her heel falls echo off nearby buildings. Her pace made it difficult to steady her vision to see what followed—*perhaps nothing but her own fear.*

Albany was a quieter city than New York. There were few people upon the streets, especially with the cold. Occasionally a wagon passed, loaded with lumber or other goods. Molly tried catching the eye of each wagon master. Most were too bundled to look her direction. She rounded a corner and pressed her body into a deep façade of worn sandstone that lined the building. It gave her solace to hide amongst the shadows. She forced her breathing to slow. With each exhale the mist from her breath extended into the dim moonlight. She waited.

Her ears strained against the dark. She imagined noises—footsteps echoing like hers had done. She held her breath searching for any sign that someone closed in upon her. But there was nothing. She wished Mrs. Warne allowed her a weapon, and the training to use it. Times like these haunted her dreams—*exposed and vulnerable.* She eased the clutch upon her handbag, and breathed deeper as her body relaxed. She had imagined it. *Why would they follow a woman, when Booth was the threat? But who were they?* Peering from her hiding spot, she saw nothing. She stepped into the moonlight and made her way back to the corner.

The street to the south was empty, except for a wagon. It was laden with stacks of lumber. But as she scanned the opposite direction, she saw him. He stood at the far side of the street, in the middle of the sidewalk. His back faced her. He hadn't heard her approach as the wagon had masked her footfalls. Its wheels turned with sharp squeaks at every rotation. The old machine sounded tired and worn. She took a step back, trying to once more ease into the shadows.

It came too late. He swung around to face her. His eyes were set deep in his face, with a dark mustache covering his upper lip. The rest of his face hid in shadow under the brim of his hat. They stood, staring at one another.

Molly froze. There was nothing to do. Her shoes would slip against the hard cobblestones if she ran. This man would be more than a match against her. If she was barefoot, and unburdened by this dress or the cold, she might have a chance. Instead, she forced her fear aside and stepped into the path of the oncoming wagon. Without taking her eyes from the man, she waved desperately at the driver.

"Help! Help!"

Her voice made it barely above the sound from the wheels. The wagon master pulled hard on his reins, bringing his horses to a stop. They were massive Clydesdales, with tufts of white hair hanging over their large feet. Molly stepped around the beasts, still watching the man on the far sidewalk. Finding the footholds, she pulled herself up.

"What are you doing?" the wagon master asked.

He appeared confused. Then he looked to the man on the sidewalk. The man watched, but made no move to intercept Molly.

"Drive, please," Molly pleaded. "That man means me harm."

The wagon master looked at the man, still confused.

"I will pay," Molly added. She held out a five-dollar bill she pulled from her handbag.

The wagon master stared at the bill—a large sum. He glanced at the man, and then whipped the reins as he yelled at the horses. With a start the wagon creaked and then rolled down the cobblestones. Behind them, the stranger stood in the same place, watching the wagon pull away around the corner.

Molly didn't care where she went. She had rented a room at a boardinghouse but felt little like returning immediately. Likely, it was not compromised. These men had not picked up her trail until she met with Booth. But still, the incident unnerved her. As they rode, she searched over her shoulder—*nothing*. The man could have almost kept pace with the wagon had he chosen to run alongside, though it was cold, and he appeared to not want the attention or trouble. He was not official like the New York detectives she encountered in Baltimore. Detectives would have no care if confronted, even outside their home city. These men were different.

The weight of the conspiracy pressed down upon her. She was more mired in it than ever. Forces she didn't understand shadowed her. She longed for Mrs. Warne and the safety of something solid under her feet—a place she understood.

The wagon master dropped her at the end of his line. He offered to drive her to her boardinghouse, but she refused—the fewer people who knew where she stayed the better. She darted down several streets, checking over her shoulder at each turn. When she came in view of the place, she remained outside until the cold seeped through her gloves. Her fingers went numb. She steeled herself from view. The wind cut through her shawl. When she was convinced no one awaited her return, she made her way inside. The warmth came as welcome relief.

Sleep did not find her—at least not easily. When she held her hands steady, they shook. She closed them into a fist and sat in a chair in the corner of her room facing the window. Daring not to light a candle and give away her room from the street, she waited. When she closed her eyes, she saw the face of the man from the bar. He had stared at her, not concerned in the least that she made her escape. A terrible thought filled her mind—*he could find her when he wanted, when he needed. They already knew her.*

She kept a vigil until a gray light lifted the veil of darkness. When the sun crested over the buildings, it cast enough light into the room. She changed into a new dress, hoping it might mask her appearance and make her less recognizable. This was her last dress from Mrs. Warne, and she carefully placed most of her money in a small pocket concealed at the top of the skirt. Mrs. Warne had insisted on these subtle modifications—a means to conceal messages or other items. She had to send a message to Mrs. Warne about Montreal. *Should she head north, or return to Baltimore? Let it be south.*

The telegraph office stood near the boardinghouse. Molly crafted her message. She tried to obscure the meaning from prying eyes without confusing Mrs. Warne. She waited until the operator sent the telegram, tapping out the little dashes and dots on his stylus. It would take hours to get a response—enough time to find Booth and recover his letter of introduction. At least she would return with his letter as proof of the conspiracy. That alone should be enough to prove her continued worth to both Mrs. Warne and Mr. Pinkerton.

Booth's hotel was a quick walk from the telegraph office. Molly checked over her shoulder with every few steps. She must have looked peculiar to any who witnessed. A nagging feeling haunted her.

At the hotel, her mood soured. Booth was gone. The desk clerk refused to provide a room number. Perhaps he assumed Molly was yet another adoring fan who hoped for a private interlude. When she went to leave a message using her assumed last name, the clerk recognized it.

"There is a letter for you," he said, handing an envelope across the desk.

Molly tore open the paper and read the contents. Booth had remembered. He provided an address, as well as a name—*William Norris*. But there was more. He had included a small silver locket. On the front was the Palmetto symbol of his secret society. On the back his name stamped into the silver, with a small tintype image of himself inside. Maybe he meant the locket as a gift. Or perhaps he intended it as a further means of introduction. With Booth, either made sense—another way to gain her affection. She read the letter again, all the while watched by the desk clerk. When she realized he regarded her so close, she stuffed the letter back in the envelope. Placing it into her baggage, she rushed from the hotel.

The telegraph office was her next stop. She needed to know what Mrs. Warne intended her to do—head north or south. She feared the answer. But she had discovered a name—William Norris. Perhaps that might suffice, and there would be no need to head to Montreal.

Inside the telegraph office she had to wait. Only one operator manned the lines, the same man from before. He finished with another client and then stood to greet her.

"There is nothing yet, miss. Maybe soon."

He looked out the door behind Molly, and then scanned the windows. It made her turn to look—nothing. His voice lowered as he leaned in on the counter and motioned for her to come closer.

"A man came in after you left, inquiring about you."

"About me?" Molly asked. "Are you certain?"

The words barely came out. Suddenly she wished to run to the train station and book passage to New York and then Baltimore.

The operator nodded. "Yes. He wanted to know what message you sent, and to whom. I refused, of course."

The operator looked away when he said this last part, not wishing to make eye contact. *He lied.* In fact, the concern in his voice was not about her. Some people were easy to read. He had taken money to give up her message. Now he assuaged his guilt with a warning.

"Who was he?" she pressed.

She could use this to her advantage—understand more about who stalked her.

"A British man. But plain in every other way."

"British?" She held her breath for a moment, her mind racing.

The operator nodded. "A bow tie and a round hat. That's all I remember of him."

"And how much did he pay you?" The question came without thinking.

The operator turned away, with a feigned expression of hurt. "Nothing."

She had her answer. This telegraph office wasn't safe. She would have to find another in the city. Turning from the counter, she pushed through the door and back to the street. She walked down the cobblestones, her luggage swinging at her side as she pressed her pace. The wind sent a biting blast, and she pulled her shawl over the lower portions of her face and tucked her chin. It blocked her vision.

At first she didn't notice the carriage approach. Not until the sunlight glared off the polished wood. Matching black horses pulled to a complete stop. The silver accents on the rigging sparkled in the light. The door on the near side of the carriage opened, and a man leapt from the opening. The man from the night before. Before she had let go of her shawl to unleash a punch, or grab at his face, he gripped her arms. Then he pulled her toward the carriage. Another man joined him. He grabbed her other side. Together they dragged her through the open door. One of the men pounded on the side of the carriage. The driver lashed the horses, and the carriage lurched forward.

Even if she had wanted to fight, there was no point. One man faced her. The other sat at her side. He held her down in the seat.

"Who are you?" Her voice came out as a hiss. Anger rose through her.

The man sitting across from her spoke first—his accent resoundingly British. He didn't even attempt to hide it.

"We'll ask the questions. Who are you sending messages to in Chicago?"

Molly struggled for a moment, but the other man held her fast. Her arm was in danger of going numb from his grip.

"It is none of your concern!" She struggled against the man to her side. As he clamped down upon her upper arm, the pain felt good. It stoked her anger.

The man across from her pulled his arm back and struck her across the face with a full fist. For a moment her world spun. She heard the strike before the pain reached her. Then she tasted the blood. She lunged forward, but the second man pulled her down hard. Both men laughed.

The man across from her enjoyed this. His eyes narrowed, bunching up the skin atop his close-set nose. He reminded her of one of the ruffians, or field hands, her father had hired. Not a man with much intelligence.

"I'll ask again. Who did you telegraph?"

She had checked on her message, but sent nothing—they couldn't know that part. They must have watched her, lying in wait at the end of the street. She summoned the spit in her mouth then hurled it across the carriage. The man reeled. He wiped his face. She enjoyed the moment, smiling to mock him. It only lasted that moment. His full fist crashed upon her face once more. Her head slammed into the seat behind her, and her body went limp. The man at her side let go as she slumped against the side of the carriage, but she didn't pass out.

"Bitch," the first man mumbled. He wiped his face again. "I'll search her bag. You talk to the telegraph operator again. If she sent another message, we'll need to tell Lord Lyons."

Molly waited, feigning the extent of her incapacitation. Her head rang, and blood flowed from her nose. The warmth of it crested her lip and dribbled onto her teeth. She longed for a pistol or some other manner of weapon to make this man pay. She wanted to hurt him—to stand above him as he lay on the ground bloodied and battered. The anger rose again.

The carriage came to a stop, and the man at her side rose and opened the carriage door. He left it partially opened. The man across from her paid no attention. He opened her baggage and searched through it. It contained nothing of importance, except the letter from Booth.

Molly waited—to ensure the other man had entered the telegraph office. Then she pulled herself up and lunged at the remaining man. He still rifled through her bag. Her knee hit him square across the head. She wished she had struck harder, but her dress constrained her swing in the tight carriage. He grunted and fell back, though his grip upon her bag did not diminish. She grabbed at the bag.

He held fast and pulled it toward himself. She tugged until her fingers slipped, but it did not free from his grip. The man glared, both hands firmly fixed upon her bag. She had only moments.

When the other man returned, she would be helplessly trapped, unable to fight off both of them. With all her strength, she heaved at the bag one last time. The man did not budge. She would have to sacrifice it for her freedom. She let go.

He had resisted her grip with such force that he fell hard against the back of the carriage. It was her only chance. She dove out the carriage door, falling hard upon the street. At first she was unable to get her feet underneath her. Her head throbbed from how hard he struck her. Scrambling to stand, she ran behind the carriage. Her shoes slipped against the cobblestones. She fought to stay upright. A man's voice called out behind her, but she didn't dare look behind.

She ran until she hit the first intersection, and then she turned sharply down the street. A horsecar approached, heading back in the direction she just came. She flung herself to the side of it, and then pushed through the rear door. It resembled a large railway car, pulled by a team of horses. Passengers filled the space. They gasped as she crawled inside. She lifted her head enough to see the team of black horses dash down the street—opposite the horsecar.

She stayed out of sight, then dared sneak another look. The man who had entered the telegraph office ran past, never looking in her direction. They hadn't seen her mount the horsecar.

"Miss . . ."

A man's voice startled her. He stood over her in the center of the aisle as she struggled to stand.

"Let me help you," he said, starting again. He wore a uniform, like a conductor. His face was the epitome of concern, and he eased her to a seat. Kneeling, he offered a handkerchief. It was white and clean. She pressed the cloth against her lip and nose. When she pulled it away, it had stained with blood.

"They attacked me," Molly said. "Took my baggage, and . . ." She didn't know what else to say.

"You are safe now," the man replied. "The police station is near the end of our route. We will drop you there."

"I am late for a train," Molly replied. "They took nothing important."

The man looked at her, uncertain. She wished only to leave—to put as much distance between herself and this city. She would find Mrs. Warne and Mr. Pinkerton. She had lost the letter from Booth, but she remembered both the name and the address from the letter. And she still had his locket, upon the chain at her neck where she kept the other medallion and the key from the brothel. That alone should prove something. They would welcome her back.

"All right then," the man said. "The train station is near the police precinct. I'll show you when we get there. Sit and rest."

The other passengers regarded her in an odd manner. One older woman gave her another handkerchief. As she sat, the blood dried upon her face. It made tracks, her skin tight underneath. She would need a washroom.

The horsecar lumbered upon its route for another hour. True to his word, the conductor let her off near the railway and gave her brief directions. Her head throbbed, and her heart beat in her nose—likely broken. She dared not touch it.

Molly entered the rail station after watching from outside for several minutes. She hurried through the waiting area and to the ticket counter.

"When is the next train south?" she asked.

"Do you mean to New York, miss?" The man behind the counter did not look up.

"Yes," Molly said. There were trains to Baltimore from New York. She would send another telegram once she left Albany.

"Not until this afternoon. There should be a one-fifteen heading to New York City."

The man looked up for the first time. He saw Molly's face and did not hide his shock. The blood had dried, but her nose swelled. At least one eye was turning black.

"I fell," Molly lied. "There is nothing sooner? What train is upon the track?"

She had heard the conductors yell out the five-minute warning. She wished to leave immediately, even if it meant heading in the wrong direction at first—anything to get away.

"That's the Rouses Point line." He said it cautiously, still studying her face.

"Rouses Point?"

"To the Canadian border. The opposite direction you desire."

The luck of it. She had no idea what Mrs. Warne would want her to do. She had lost Booth's letter, but Mrs. Warne would believe her, even without much proof.

"Miss, one ticket to New York then?"

Molly didn't answer. Her eyes welled, but she fought it.

"Miss, I have other customers in line. You can board a train and pay the conductor as well."

Several men waited in line behind her, looking impatient.

"Are there any sleeper berths to New York?" she asked.

"Of course. They are expensive. Do you wish one?"

Could she wait that long? It would be several hours.

"Miss?" He became impatient.

"Yes," Molly said, turning back. "One ticket to New York."

"And a sleeper berth?"

Molly nodded.

She fetched several bills from her handbag and handed them through the cutout in the bars of the window. He handed her a ticket. *What would Mrs. Warne say? That she quit?* But her strength had worn thin, and she required sleep. Her body ached—her face burned with a dull pain. She wandered away from the counter. A place to lie down would be heaven, but it might lull her to sleep and make her miss the train. She needed a breath of cold air to revive her.

She pushed through the doors to the station and stood atop the stone steps. The world around her slowed. People walked past. She caught snippets of their conversation. None of it made sense—as if everyone spoke a foreign language. Her head throbbed, and her vision blurred. She focused on things far away, like the statue across the street, or the carriage parked along the road. Forcing her eyes, she pulled the daylight into focus. The carriage gleamed with hints of the sun. The team of horses glistened. Silver buckles and black leather harness complemented their black coats. They had run recently, and hard. Her eyes grew heavy and closed. The man from the night before appeared as a mirage in front of her. He did nothing to move toward her. She startled awake—the carriage. It was still parked down the street.

Frantic, she spun in all directions. The men were not in sight. Turning, she rushed back inside the station. She searched every face she passed. Many looked back at her, likely appalled by the damage to her face. She pushed past them, searching for a corner to hide in. The conductor announced last call for the train. His voice drew her like a beacon. She made her way to where he called out and stepped onto the platform where the last of the passengers boarded their cars. At the front of the train, the engine stirred.

Bags piled upon the marble floor where other passengers waited. People sat upon wooden benches. Nothing. No men with bowler hats—no one about to catch her. *But they would find her.* The cars jostled together, as the northbound train started.

There was no choice.

She had a name, and an address. If she waited here, there was no telling she would escape this city alive. The train picked up speed. *North.* She stepped toward the iron beast. Then she broke into a run toward the nearest car, catching the handle from one of the doors in her hand. She pulled herself up, and stepped inside.

CHAPTER THIRTEEN

MOLLY PRESSED HER pace. Not even the biting northern cold could slow her mission. The city looked the same. The sound of French made the adventure exotic. She didn't dread the place, as she feared. In fairness, she pushed the old memories from her mind. Instead, she focused on what needed her attention—finding William Norris.

The trip to the border had taken longer than expected—a whole day longer. But that offered unique relief from her dilemma. She slept most of the way to Rouses Point. Once she woke, she found that deep snow delayed the trains to the north. They needed a special engine with a plow to clear the path. A particularly harsh blizzard had dumped feet of the frozen powder along the iron rails. She used the time well, first sending another telegraph to Mrs. Warne. Then she went in search of winter clothes. Mrs. Warne had left her with considerable money, and for the first time, she actually counted the amount. She had more than enough to find a heavy dress and coat and make it back south with plenty to spare.

Still, she worried. *Had she made the right decision?* Her face ached, and one eye had almost swollen shut. If she did not touch it, the throbbing subsided until she forgot and disturbed the bruising again. Perhaps she should have returned to Baltimore and sought out Mrs. Warne. But her answer came in the form of a telegraph, though it created more questions than it answered. It felt like a positive sign. They trusted her.

Use discretion. Make haste to Philadelphia after finished.
Find E.J. Allen at Continental Hotel.

She didn't know an E.J. Allen, and she hadn't been through Philadelphia for many years. But the relief the telegraph brought highlighted her worst fear—finding herself abandoned. She held the paper in her hands, rereading the words. They wanted her—she was not alone. She should have torn the message to bits. But she convinced herself there was no harm in holding it until she reached Montreal.

The men from Albany were her second greatest fear. They had her letter from Booth. He had foolishly written it in plain language. His friend, Mr. Sanders, understood the value in writing an innocuous letter. Anyone who found it would miss the true intent—an introduction between Confederate agents. Booth was either too stupid or too arrogant to mask his involvement. Molly assumed it was the latter—always the ultimate showman.

The railway finished plowing the rails to Montreal in the early hours of the morning. She had not woken in time to board the first train of the day. But once they started, they made good time upon the cleared track. The train deposited her at the southern end of the city. The timing left her with dying daylight in which to find the address Booth had left so unguarded in his note.

As she hurried upon the near barren streets, she ignored her anger at Booth. Her gloved hand felt the telegram in the pocket at the front of her outer skirt. Holding it, touching the paper, eased her mood. *Keep walking—keep walking.*

She kept her pace as fast as she dared. Though patches of ice formed where the snow packed firm upon the cobblestones, the

citizens here were particular about their cleared streets and sidewalks. They beat the snow back, pushing it into white mounds that
resembled mountains. Molly walked in the direction of Mount
Royal, the mountain that stood as the backdrop for the city. Her
feet led her north through the business district, toward the univer-
sity. She had a vague idea where she headed. It was not in the same
area of the city where her father had taken her—small virtues.

She found Pine Avenue without trouble. Her dress beat back the
cold, even when the wind tried its best to press through the thick
wool. Heading east, the numbers on the sides of a few buildings
moved in the right direction. They were one- or two-story brick
houses, with smoke exiting soot-stained chimneys. The smell of
burned coal lingered amongst the bite of the air.

Even this late into winter, Montreal was a city in motion. It had
become the epicenter of British North America. Though pockets of
French existed in the conversations of the people Molly passed, the
city had turned Anglophile with the British takeover of Quebec. But
there were those who kept their French heritage. Molly liked the
sound of it.

As she approached the address Booth provided, the neighbor-
hood felt empty. Smoke rose from the chimneys, but no one walked
upon the street. She walked past the address—on purpose. The lack
of pedestrians wore at her nerves. She dared not look at the building
but hurried her pace. From the side of her vision, all appeared
normal—or at least quiet. Curtains were drawn, and the chimney
told of a well-stoked fire. Someone was inside.

She turned the corner past the building, hoping to circle around
the block. If questioned, she could pretend she lost her way. From
the corner, an alley disappeared behind the building. It likely led
across the block. *A way to cut through?* Behind her, a large wagon
passed. A team of four horses pulled it along the rough street. In the

back of the wagon, two ordered rows of soldiers sat upon the side benches. They wore scarlet jackets with dark pants, each holding a musket. The last man, a boy really, stared at her. He looked so young, not old enough to be away from home. He might have said the same about her. Their eyes locked. The wagon rolled out of sight and turned at the next intersection.

Buildings loomed on either side of the alley, blocking the wind. It came as a welcome relief. The alley itself was narrow, likely too small for a wagon or carriage to make its way through. It jogged in the middle, where the buildings on one side jutted into the space. It left no way to see if the path reached the opposite street. *Surely it must.* Perhaps the building she sought had a back door. *That would work better—out of sight.* But the quiet, and the soldiers in the wagon, felt wrong. She steadied her breathing and glanced down the alley. There was no turning back. She had come too far and too much hinged on what she might discover.

After several steps, she stopped. A small pile of bricks and broken bits of masonry lay piled at the base of one of the buildings. She knelt and selected one that fit into her handbag. If Mrs. Warne would not let her have a pistol, she would find another means to stay safe.

Only a small amount of sun filtered between the buildings. It passed the narrow point between the roofs making the last of the daylight appear bleak. Pressing further into the alley she shifted her weight to keep her heel falls from echoing. As she approached the jog in the alley, she pressed her body against the brick wall to peer around the corner. A man stood at a back door—exactly the door she hoped to find. She cursed her luck. He paced back and forth, shaking his hands while he smoked. Easing back along the alley, she slid her back along the wall to keep herself out of sight. She hoped he had not noticed. He could be a lookout, or worse. She would use the front door and take her chances—a better option than a strange man in an alley.

But as she turned to leave, her grip on her handbag slipped. Her new gloves were not yet worn, and they made holding onto the handle a tricky affair. The weight of the brick only made it worse. The bag hit the ground. She froze, holding her breath.

The moments passed like an eternity. She forced herself off the wall and stooped to recover her bag. As she stood, someone grabbed her arm—the man from Albany. When he breathed, the smell of smoke fell heavy about her face.

"I rather thought you would use the front door," he said.

He grabbed her face. She winced and fought hard to not lose her grip upon her handbag. He pinned her arm to her body, so there was little room to swing it. Struggling, she tried to create the space she needed.

"Stop fighting!"

He gripped her face harder and then shoved her head back into the wall.

"Did you think we wouldn't find the letter? That we wouldn't follow? You took your time getting here—the train arrived almost an hour ago. But I appreciate the time. I have a squad of Royal Marines set around the corner."

Molly said nothing. The man held her head against the building. She stood upon her toes. He dragged her off the wall and down the alley, toward the back door.

"We were waiting for you to show," he continued, "to arrest you all at once. You can watch me give the signal, and your friends dragged into the street. I'll make certain you have a cold cell."

He pulled back his coat and produced a pistol. Cocking the hammer, he raised the weapon, intending to fire into the air. But with it, he gave her the space she needed. She swung with all her strength. As the bag hit his head, Molly slipped and fell backwards. The man crumpled, dropping his pistol, which skidded across the stone of the alley. Molly rushed to recover the weapon.

She gripped the pistol awkwardly. But the man lay upon the alley—facedown. A pool of blood collected near his head. She sat a moment, then scrambled to her feet. No one came down the alley—in either direction. With nowhere to turn, she rushed to the door.

She pounded with her fists against the wood, but dared not scream unless she alert the soldiers. They must have been the ones in the wagon and couldn't be far away. She drove her fists into the door. It echoed beyond. Then there were voices, muffled through the thick door. A moment later the latch caught, and the door pushed open, nearly knocking Molly over. A man stood and stared at her.

"Please," she said. "Please help me. I need to see Mr. Norris. The soldiers are coming."

The man stared at her, dumbfounded. Then he looked to her hand. She still gripped the pistol. He took a step back.

"No, no . . ." Molly said. "It's his. He attacked me. He was going to call the soldiers."

The man peered around the corner. His fear of Molly turned to shock. He saw the blood pooling in the alley.

"Get in," he said.

His accent was Southern. Despite the shock and the cold, it brought her comfort. As he reached to give Molly a hand, he took the pistol from her. He called inside for help, and another man met them down a long hallway.

"There's a man in the alley; we need to get him inside before someone sees. And get her to the study. She's here for Colonel Norris."

The two men rushed outside and picked up the injured man. They dragged his limp body inside and deposited him upon the hall floor. Then, after checking outside, the man closed the door.

"Follow me," he told Molly.

She didn't have a choice. He grabbed the top portion of her arm and thrust her down the hall. He walked her into a sitting room where a man sat by the fireplace. He rose as they entered.

"What's this about?" the man asked.

He was impeccably dressed with a full head of dark hair. His mustache lay upon his beard like an ornate roof. And his accent came from the Deep South.

"Sorry to disturb you, Colonel, but she came to the back door, and . . ." the man began speaking, but the colonel held up his hand.

"Who are you?" he asked Molly.

"My name is Hattie Lawton. Mr. John Wilkes Booth sent me," Molly answered.

The colonel nodded. "Mr. Booth sent a telegram. We've been expecting you."

"You don't have much time," Molly said. Her voice strained as she fought the panic rising like the tide within her. "Soldiers are coming to arrest us all."

"What soldiers?" the colonel asked. He looked to the man with Molly.

"We found her with this, sir." He handed the colonel the pistol Molly had recovered from her fight in the alley. "And there was a man out back clubbed about the head."

"He followed me," Molly explained, "from Albany. He beat me and took the letter of introduction from Mr. Booth. Mr. Booth wrote the letter plain, and it had your name and address upon it. The man out back said he staged soldiers nearby to take us all into custody. He went to signal them with the pistol. That's when I struck him."

The colonel shook his head, annoyed. "Where is this injured man?" he asked Molly's escort.

"We dragged him inside."

"And he's the one who did this to you?" the colonel asked.

He stepped forward and reached for Molly's face with one hand. His thumb streaked down her cheek. When he pulled it back, it had stained red. Instinctively, Molly reached for her face. Blood had splattered across it.

"Go search him," the colonel ordered his guard, nodding toward the hall.

The guard left Molly alone with the colonel. Blood covered her hand—not her blood.

"I am William Norris," he said. "Mr. Booth said he gave you something, something you could show me."

Molly nodded, still staring at her hand. Slowly she reached around her neck to pull out her chain. Her hand shook. She held up the locket without taking it from around her neck.

"Very well," the colonel said. "Tell me about these soldiers. British soldiers?"

Before Molly could answer, the guard came back. He held papers in his hand.

"Colonel Norris, I found these on the man from out back. He's dead."

Dead? Molly felt sick.

The colonel took them and read. He skimmed the first, and handed the letter to Molly. It was Booth's letter. Then he read the second paper.

"These are diplomatic papers, signed by Lord Lyons—the British emissary in Washington. How do you know this man?"

"He's dead?" Molly asked. Her world dimmed. The room became fuzzy at the edges of her vision. "I didn't . . ."

The colonel caught her arms, propping her up. He shook her and forced her to look into his eyes.

"What soldiers?"

It took Molly a moment. Numbness overtook her. Her breathing was shallow, and she feared she might be sick.

"What soldiers?" the colonel asked again. He strengthened the grip upon her arms, and his voice became more pressing.

Molly snapped back. "They're coming. I saw them in a wagon on my way here. They had red coats and rifles."

The colonel eased his grip. He turned to his guards.

"Get my coat and burn the papers. I'll take Miss Lawton to the apartment. Hurry."

The colonel walked Molly out the back, toward the alley. They stepped over the man she had clubbed, who lay faceup in the hall. Her knees became weak when she saw his lifeless face. The colonel lifted and pushed her along at the same time.

"Stay with me," he said. "We're going outside. The cold will do you good."

They pushed into the cold air. Night descended upon them, making their flight harder to detect. The colonel wrapped an arm around Molly and kept her moving forward. Molly played the sound of her handbag hitting the dead man in the head over in her mind. As they reached the jog in the alley, she doubled over and vomited. The colonel paused only for a moment. He pulled her upright and wiped her mouth with a handkerchief.

He led them across the street, back where Molly had seen the soldiers. They headed down a different alley, through a maze of alleyways, arriving at a door. The light faded fast, especially in the narrow places between the buildings. The colonel took a key from his pocket and let them both in. He secured the door behind them.

Once inside, he led down a small hallway and into a large sitting room. He eased Molly onto a couch, standing and stretching his back after she let her weight down.

"We have a guest staying with us," the colonel said. "But for now we can use this place. It will be safe. The Crown does not know we rent this apartment. But I will have to leave immediately to see the governor about this. He guaranteed our protection."

The flooring creaked behind them—another man appeared in the doorway. Her head spun. She held a hand over her mouth, trying to hold her stomach together.

This couldn't be happening.

He was older than when Molly last saw him. Gray filled his beard, and his hair had thinned. He looked at her as if he might recognize her. Her vision filled with the sight of Salvation Acres on fire—her mother screaming, and her father dragged off with the noose around his neck. And Isabelle.

Mason Cheeney stood in the doorway.

CHAPTER FOURTEEN

MOLLY AWOKE ON the couch. She had no idea how much time had passed. Her head spun with the light. Mr. Cheeney and Colonel Norris were deep in discussion about next moves.

"I must go to the governor's office," Colonel Norris said. "A Confederate courier has killed a British agent, who meant to arrest us. The Crown guaranteed our safety—the governor himself!"

"If they mean to arrest us, then there is no need to test their loyalty to the South," Mr. Cheeney countered. "We have their answer. We must head to the French envoy's residence. We can explain it to him and ask for council."

Molly dared open her eyes again. Anger replaced the fear. It even overtook the sick feeling in her stomach over the dead man. Without moving, she studied the room. They had taken the pistol. *She needed a weapon.* The object of her most intense hatred stood before her. And here she lay, completely unprepared. *How could this have happened—finding Cheeney in Montreal?* She had figured him for thousands of miles south, in New Orleans. In her mind's image, when next they met, she held a revolver while he pled for his life.

Cheeney glanced in her direction. His eyes met hers.

"She stirs. Let's see what else she can tell us."

There was no point in feigning any longer. She tried to sit, but Colonel Norris made his way to the couch and sat beside her. He laid his hand upon her arm and encouraged her to lie back. From the side table near her head, he retrieved a damp cloth and placed it upon her forehead. It seemed he had already wiped down her head or sat with her when she first felt ill.

"He beat you hard, didn't he?" Norris asked. His voice was kind, almost fatherly.

Molly said nothing, looking between the colonel and Mr. Cheeney.

"Was he the first man you've killed?" Cheeney asked.

Molly nodded and clenched her jaw. She imagined Cheeney a demon, sent straight from hell. His eyes stayed fixed upon her face. But he didn't seem to recognize her. She had only met him a few times, mostly with her family at social events upon his estate. When his son began courting her, Jonathon made his visits to Salvation Acres. She never went to the Cheeney estate. And the brothel had aged her in ways she wouldn't think upon. Her face had changed. She kept herself different now. Of course, the beating distorted her true identity further. She did not look herself. With no name to match the face, Mr. Cheeney appeared not to know her. She had time. But if he figured her true identity, she would have to act. *Could she take on both men at once? Could she kill again?*

Her stomach answered—an image of the pool of blood in the alley crossed her mind. She coughed, the prelude to a further emptying of her stomach. Colonel Norris reached for a wastebasket in time. She gratefully pushed her head deep into the receptacle. When she finished, the colonel handed her the washcloth.

"I am sorry you were put in that position," Mr. Cheeney said. "We are both grateful for the duty you performed for our cause. You did us a great favor this day."

Her stomach pitched once more. *She had done them a great service?* This man might have been arrested if not for her—she would have seen him in irons, though not for the reason she desired. But that might have placed him outside her reach. *This might be better.*

"A squad of Royal Marines raided my office right after we left," the colonel said. "We saw them take my men from the place and carry out the body of their colleague."

"He was a British agent then?" Molly asked.

She stalled for time as her eyes darted around the room. A pair of heavy brass candlesticks stood on a desk nearby—a perfect club.

"As you suspected. He had Mr. Booth's letter, and you were quite right, Booth was careless in his manner. The letter led them right to us."

"If the British governor knows about you, then why would they try to arrest you?" Molly asked—it didn't fit.

She hated asking direct questions. But she found little point of dancing around the facts before she killed Cheeney. She might never get a chance to report back to Pinkerton and Mrs. Warne, anyhow.

The colonel looked to Mr. Cheeney, who had not moved from where he stood—a foot or so inside the study. He still considered Molly. Her stomach turned with fear. Any moment his memory might place her.

"Our cause is in a precarious place, Miss Lawton," Colonel Norris began. "We need Europe. They are the hope to win our independence. War is coming, and both England and France have indicated they may back the South. But they hesitate."

Molly studied the colonel. He seemed a man much maligned with worry. The weight of his position held him hostage. The wrinkles in his face were new formed, and the dark rings under his eyes showed he either worked too hard or had trouble finding sleep.

"That's why you are here?" Molly asked. "To convince the British?"

"That's why I am here," the colonel answered.

"They want to back the winning horse," Cheeney added. "That is why, William, we should go to the French. They are already supporting my—" he hesitated, looking at Molly. *He had said too much.* "—my project. That will convince Europe to support us, especially when their markets are full of cotton. England will follow suit if the French back us. They hate one another and will compete for our affections."

The colonel stood, irritated. "Not here, not now." He glanced back at Molly. Cheeney had said something he wasn't supposed to reveal.

"Very well, but we must pick sides, too. Or our Confederacy will wilt upon the vine."

The colonel paced the room for a moment and then stopped in front of the bookshelf. He took three glasses from a silver tray and filled them with dark liquor from a clear glass bottle. Walking back, he handed one glass to Cheeney and then the other to Molly. Cheeney sat in a nearby seat. Molly refused the drink.

"Take it," Cheeney said. "You just killed your first man. A stiff drink will do you some good. That is a memory you will not soon forget."

Molly fought her hatred, not letting it bait her to action. With another drink, the candlestick would be a real option. But she needed help to pull it off—something to numb her fears. She took the glass.

"He won't be the last," Molly muttered, downing the brandy in a single pull.

Mr. Cheeney let out an enormous bout of laughter. It filled the room, catching Colonel Norris by surprise. He looked to the other man.

"By God, I would not want to cross her! This very evening, she killed a man and is already planning more. If the women of the Confederacy can fight like this, imagine the men!"

Cheeney raised his glass and then downed the drink. The colonel followed suit.

"Another round, Colonel. The young lady puts us to shame with her patriotism. Miss Lawton was it?"

Molly nodded, unable to answer.

"Where are you from, Miss Lawton?" Cheeney asked.

The colonel became interested in the question as well. She held her breath for a moment and then summoned her best acting skill.

"My mother was from Atlanta, though we had relatives in Richmond. I spent time in both cities."

She told the truth, though conveniently left out any mention of New Orleans. Mrs. Warne had told her to keep her backstory close to the truth—her lies to a minimum. It made it all easier to remember under stress.

"And now?" Mr. Cheeney pressed.

"Baltimore. I have spent a great deal of time in that city helping with a current operation. I was asked to transport a message to Mr. Booth in New York City, but I arrived too late. Mr. Sanders provided help in locating Mr. Booth. And as you know, he sent me here."

She hoped discussing names these men already knew would further cover her identity. It might make Cheeney forget her face or obscure it with twists in the truth. He had sold her to a brothel, killed her parents and Isabelle. She would carry the ruse, to see where it led. They might allow her even deeper knowledge of what they planned. Perhaps even the project Mr. Cheeney alluded to earlier.

"If you had them so convinced, William, why would the British wish to stop our plans with Booth?" Mr. Cheeney asked the colonel.

The manner in which he asked revealed more. From the tone in his voice he had an answer and wanted Colonel Norris to arrive at the same conclusion.

"I don't know, Mason. The governor gave me assurances."

"But the British governor in Quebec does not control Lord Lyons in Washington. This is about slavery. There *is* no other answer."

The colonel shook his head. He retrieved the glasses from Mr. Cheeney and Molly, before walking back to the liquor bottle. He refilled them.

"William, you have the ear of Jefferson Davis," Cheeney continued. "He will be sworn in as the Confederate President any day. Tell him of my solution. It will work. Europe will come on board."

Colonel Norris crossed the room and handed Cheeney a second glass.

"This goes beyond the question of slavery. Do you think that the newly sworn president of the Confederacy would free our slaves to bring England and France to our aid? Even you cannot believe that, Mason."

"But I have seen it, William. There was a plantation in New Orleans where it worked! It could be our salvation. Tell me you'll mention it to President Davis. Your voice carries weight."

It took all Molly's strength to keep her mouth closed. Cheeney talked about Salvation Acres. There could be no other plantation run in a similar manner. He had destroyed all her father built. *And now he advocated using her father's plantation as a model for the South?* The candlestick was close. It taunted her.

As she rose, Colonel Norris offered the second drink.

"No need to get up, Miss Lawton."

She eased back in the couch, accepting the glass. Taking on both men was foolhardy. Maybe they would have a third drink. She could hold onto this one, and not finish the glass while they consumed enough to be slow of reflex and mind.

"What was your message from Mr. Booth?" Mr. Cheeney asked. Once again he tested her with a loaded question.

"It was for Colonel Norris," Molly said, trying to deflect.

"You may speak openly," the colonel responded. "Mr. Cheeney knows of our plans."

Cheeney nodded, mirroring the colonel.

"Very well," Molly said. "He sent me to retrieve some manner of funding for the venture."

The colonel nodded. "I was afraid of that. The money is now in my office, likely confiscated by the Crown." Turning to Cheeney, he continued, "You have government funds here, do you not, Mason?"

"You can't be serious, William. I need those for my project. Every dollar is precious. If you want to ensure that Europe receives all the goods she needs to pledge her loyalty, then I need my money!" Cheeney's voice strained.

"We may not need Europe if the Baltimore plot prevails. Think of it. With Lincoln dead in Baltimore, Maryland will secede. Once Maryland goes, Washington will be cut off. We will have won the war with a single shot."

Mason Cheeney was quiet for a moment, staring into his glass as he swirled the liquid. The colonel looked to Molly and smiled—he held the power. Molly would get the money.

"How much do they need?" Cheeney asked.

"Five thousand."

"For what?" Mr. Cheeney protested.

"The conspirators must escape. They'll book passage on a schooner and get out of Baltimore. The effect is more pronounced if the federals capture no one from the plot."

"Do they need to move an army?"

The sarcasm came thick. Cheeney was disgruntled, but from his deflated tone he had no choice.

"I will take your plan to President Davis," Colonel Norris said. He offered it as a half-measure to gain Cheeney's compliance.

Cheeney looked at the colonel. He swirled his glass some more while studying the other man. Then he upended the glass, finishing the liquor. He placed the glass on a side table with a sharp report as it struck the wood.

"Very well. I will get you the money. I have a meeting with the French this evening to show them my drawings. I should not be late, but now I have another five thousand dollars I must raise!"

He started for the exit. Molly's heart rushed. She had to do it now. The colonel celebrated his victory over Cheeney by downing his glass. Molly went to stand, but her knees failed. She pushed up from the cushions but stopped. Cheency had turned and backtracked. He walked into the room and stood in front of Molly. Holding out his hand, he bowed slightly. She hesitated. *How could she take hold of it?*

She needed more time, or another chance. There was no way to attack here. Not in her current state. She breathed deep. Mrs. Warne always said that a good spy is an amazing actress. For this act, any stage in the world would put her on the marquee. She took his hand.

"A pleasure to meet a fine Southern woman," Cheeney said. "I wish you success, and I do hope our paths cross again. I am soon to relocate to Richmond. If you find yourself among your relatives, I do pray you will come pay me a visit."

"I will make certain of it."

As Mr. Cheeney headed out of the study, the colonel collected her unfinished glass.

"Are you done, Miss Lawton?"

Molly nodded, watching Cheeney leave. Her chance had slipped through her hands.

"Do not worry," the colonel said. "He is quite focused upon his project. I will get you the funding. Baltimore must not fail. You will stay the night, and at first light, I will escort you to the rail station. Mr. Booth may be a fool, but he seems to have been wise in sending you. A woman raises fewer suspicions. I will see the governor in the morning and clear up the misunderstanding."

Molly's mind was elsewhere.

"May I ask what Mr. Cheeney meant when he spoke of his plan for slavery?"

The colonel placed the glasses upon the silver tray with a small clink of glass against metal.

"There was some plantation in New Orleans. The owner freed his slaves and paid them as employees. A brilliant idea in some manner." He laughed, more to himself, as he shook his head. "The slaves never left. How could they? Their master paid them almost nothing—they could never be truly free. But they thought they were. And they worked like it—from bondage to servitude. Mason wants to use that as a model to show the Confederacy has abolished slavery. That issue keeps Europe from declaring their intentions. They have outlawed the practice and are quite against it."

Molly clenched her fists, then eased her grip. Cheeney used the very thing her father had built as a means to further the Southern cause. Her head spun, the anger arriving in waves.

"What happened to the plantation?" Molly asked.

The colonel turned. "If I remember correctly, Mr. Cheeney won the property in a game of cards. The owner became burdened with debt and gambled often. When Cheeney went to claim the place, there was a fight and it burned. A sad story, really."

Molly doubled over, as if punched to the gut. *Gambling? It wasn't true.*

"Miss Lawton, are you alright? You have had a rough day, let me show you to a room."

"Thank you," Molly said. "I was thinking of the plantation."

"I'm sure if you asked Mr. Cheeney, he would be happy to provide the details. He does like to talk about it."

Molly stood. "Thank you, Colonel. When I see him again, I will be certain to get the story out of him."

CHAPTER FIFTEEN

COLONEL NORRIS KEPT his word. Before the sun rose above the tops of the buildings, he knocked upon her door. She dressed quickly. A carriage took her to the rail station. She boarded the train he suggested—through Vermont and then to New York. It took longer but guaranteed to be less watched in case the British were on her trail. She saw nothing.

Her trip did suffer a familiar delay from deep snow in Vermont. Then she encountered another delay in New York before she dragged herself into Philadelphia—hardly the quick journey Mrs. Warne had urged in her last telegram. The newspapers published Mr. Lincoln's itinerary, making it a simple matter to track his whereabouts. He would arrive later in the day. That left them with less than a week to avert disaster before his train arrived in Baltimore.

Molly followed the instructions in the telegram. She found herself in the Continental Hotel exhausted—every corner of her being ached. Part could be accounted for in the days of travel. But a portion fell to disappointment. *Could she have reached the candlestick?* She had beat one man to death. *Could she do it again when she meant it?*

Before, she had thought it to be easy. Her hands went numb, and she balled them into fists to bring them back. Her courage had drained at the moment of opportunity. The combination bore down upon her. She had failed her father, her mother, and, most of all, Isabelle. She had faltered in their revenge. And now she stumbled into Philadelphia days late. She failed both the living and the dead.

Her face had turned black, with blue and yellow highlights where the bruising pooled. It matched her mood. Some studied it as she passed, perhaps trying to take stock of what had happened to her. She kept her mouth set tight and forced herself to the Continental Hotel's front desk. The man behind it tried not to stare, but he wanted to ask. His eyes lingered on her bruises.

"I'm looking for Mr. E .J. Allen."

"I am sorry, miss. We do not give out guest information at the Continental. Would you like to leave a message?"

"He asked me to meet him here. How am I supposed to do that?"

She willed herself to stay together, resisting the temptation to shatter into a million pieces. Her voice echoed her feelings. It took the man by surprise.

"Then perhaps he left you a message? Can I have a name?"

"Hattie Lawton."

The man studied her for a second, then looked through some papers behind the counter.

"I recall that name. I don't see a message from Mr. Allen, but I do see you have a room reserved. Mr. Allen paid for your accommodations. Would you like your key?"

Molly stood for a moment, uncertain. She expected to find a Pinkerton operative, and had hoped it would be Mr. Davies—the man who had found her in the brothel. He had been sharp-witted and interesting. But the thought of a bed and fresh sheets with a place to clean up overwhelmed her.

"Yes. Yes, please."

The hotel clerk pulled a key off a pegboard behind his desk. He handed it to her. With sparse directions, Molly found her room. It was elegant, with a thick carpet under her feet. She took her shoes off and stood upon it. She planned to wash up and at least hang up her dress. But the lure of the clean bed with fresh linen was too great. She laid down. A deep sleep claimed her.

Well after the sunset, Molly woke to a loud knocking upon her door. She had not bothered to pull the shades in the room, and the change in daylight disoriented her. She bolted upright, searching through the darkness, and opened the door. Mrs. Warne stood outside.

"Always check first, Molly."

The older woman walked past her. Molly closed the door and the darkness swallowed them. Mrs. Warne went to the nearest oil lamp, struck a match, and lit the wick. A soft light bathed the room.

"Where have you—" Mrs. Warne started to speak as she turned from the lamp. She stopped, staring at Molly's face. "Dear God, what happened?"

Mrs. Warne dragged Molly into the light.

"It's nothing," Molly replied.

"Have you seen yourself? I would hardly call that nothing."

She moved Molly in the direction of a mirror that hung above a small vanity. Mrs. Warne stood behind her, studying her face, gently probing her injuries.

"It looks worse than it feels."

"I should hope so. For it looks awful. What happened?"

"A British agent followed me after I met with Booth in Albany."

"British?" Mrs. Warne asked.

Molly nodded. "I don't understand it. Colonel Norris tried explaining the politics of it all. It was confusing."

"I am so sorry, Molly." Her hand found Molly's face, holding it lightly while she inspected the younger girl. "I had no idea this might happen. I would never have sent you alone if I thought there would be this much danger. You are not ready for it."

Molly pulled away—the image of a dead man lying facedown in an alley imposed itself on her thoughts.

"Come," Mrs. Warne said. "We need to see Mr. Pinkerton. I assume you received the telegram and that's how you received the room here."

Molly nodded. "Who is Mr. Allen? Is he the man who found me in the brothel?"

"No, that was Mr. Webster. You knew him as Mr. Davies, his cover in Baltimore. He is down South on other business. E.J. Allen is the name Mr. Pinkerton uses when he travels. The Pinkerton name is building quite the reputation. Remember when I told you to always blend in, to never be flashy or stand out?"

Molly nodded.

"It goes for names, too," Mrs. Warne said. "Let us find Mr. Pinkerton, and you can tell us the whole of the story. He will be most interested in anything you have discovered. It appears you found names as well, like this Colonel Norris. I will not make you bear it out twice—let us all talk at once."

Mrs. Warne led them down the hall and to another room. She knocked in a repetitive pattern. Molly tried to commit it to memory, but found she was too groggy to remember.

Several oil lamps filled the room with the same soft warm light. They were brighter than Molly's room, or the hallway outside. She squinted as her eyes adjusted, shaking off the fog of sleep.

"Miss Ferguson, whatever has happened?"

Mr. Pinkerton stood from a small table where he had been busy writing. Papers lay strewn about the table, and an inkbottle had recently spilled over some of them. They dried along the floor.

"A British agent followed her," Mrs. Warne told him.

"British? Are you sure?" he asked.

"Yes," Molly said. "He had diplomatic papers on him, signed by Lord Lyons—the British emissary in Washington."

"I know who he is," Pinkerton replied. "One of his men did this to you?"

"Yes," Molly said. "In Albany. They grabbed me off the street, thinking I was a Confederate agent. They found me again in Montreal."

"But you escaped him?" Pinkerton asked.

"He's dead."

Nausea overpowered her. Mrs. Warne steadied her and then eased her onto the bed. Then she pulled up a chair and sat opposite Molly. Tears streamed down Molly's face. They burned hot. The numbness broke like a dam, but she managed to keep her stomach down. So much went through her mind—the pool of blood, the burning plantation, her father dragged off by the horse. She heard Pinkerton ask questions. She heard herself answer—while the visions filled her mind. The story came out in exquisite detail. She pulled out the locket and showed them. By the end she poured out everything, like a pitcher of water fully emptied—a shell with nothing left.

Mrs. Warne sat next to her on the bed and pulled her close. Her free hand stroked Molly's hair. She let Molly cry, the tears building upon her cheeks until they broke free and fell upon her lap. The moments blurred into minutes. The chime of the clock on the wall heralded a new hour. Mrs. Warne held her as she spoke with Pinkerton.

"We should never have sent her alone."

"Nonsense," Pinkerton said. "Look at all she has done! We know the names of those involved at the highest levels of the Confederacy. We know the British are not yet decided on a course of action and that Lord Lyons may yet be an ally. And our agents down South gave us reports of William Norris, but we had no idea of his role. Now Miss Ferguson has met with him! She is deeper into the Confederacy than any of us could ever have hoped."

"Allan—" Mrs. Warne's tone of voice came out scolding.

"Do not take that tone with me," Pinkerton interrupted. "She has been through the ringer. I can see that as clear as you can. But she is strong. Look at her!"

He lifted Molly's face. Molly cleared her mind. She pushed the awful visions into the dark place where they would not surface— she hoped.

"You have done more than we could ever have asked, Miss Ferguson. Your nation will be grateful. I am grateful."

"Allan, I should take her back to her room. I'll clean her up and put her to bed."

Pinkerton pulled out his pocket watch, which hung from a gold chain and fitted into a pocket on his vest. He opened the face of the watch.

"Soon. I will need you before this night is done."

"What is it?" Mrs. Warne asked. "The girl needs rest."

"We all need rest. We can have that luxury when we see Mr. Lincoln safely through Washington. For now I need you on hand to tell this story once more."

"At this hour? To whom?"

As if their conversation had been overheard outside, a soft knock came about the door. He ignored Mrs. Warne's question, and knelt in front of Molly.

"Your timing could not be better, Miss Ferguson. I know this is hard, and you have been through much. But I need you to tell your story once more—what happened in Montreal, and New York, and even Albany. He needs to hear this."

"Allan, who needs to hear this?" Mrs. Warne sounded annoyed. He had not answered her.

Pinkerton strode to the door. He opened it without checking and stepped aside to let the stranger in. Stooping to get through the doorway, the man stood upright once in the room. Molly had seen him on so many photographs in newspapers—heralded as savior and villain alike.

"Mr. Pinkerton, I received your note. I remember you well from our time working for the Illinois railroad."

"That is good to hear, sir. Please allow me to introduce my two agents. This is Mrs. Warne and Miss Ferguson. Ladies, please meet Mr. Lincoln."

CHAPTER SIXTEEN

HER MOTHER WOULD chastise her, but Molly couldn't help but stare. All this time searching for the conspiracy against Mr. Lincoln, the man had remained an abstraction—as an image upon a newspaper, or a curse muttered under someone's breath. In person, his presence was overwhelming. She worked to save this man's life.

The wrinkles in his face were more rugged than the papers gave him credit for. Deep furrows lined his face around his cheeks. Little or no sleep plagued his eyes with puffy bags underneath. In the last newspaper tintype she had seen, his ears were not so large. Funny the things that came to mind as she faced the man himself.

"Mrs. Warne, Miss Ferguson. It is a pleasure to meet you both."

He nodded in their direction. Then he regarded Pinkerton who gave up his chair and motioned the president-elect to sit. Mrs. Warne pulled at Molly's arm to get her to stand.

"Please, there is no need," Mr. Lincoln said as he motioned to Mrs. Warne.

She continued anyway, only easing her grip once Molly stood. Mr. Lincoln studied her but said nothing. She preferred to stare at her feet than meet his eyes. Her face was puffy and distorted. Pinkerton produced another chair from the table where his papers were strewn about.

"Please forgive my state," Mr. Lincoln began. "It has been a long week of travel since Springfield, and I am afraid all the speeches and stops have worn on me."

"I will be succinct," Pinkerton answered. "Sleep is precious, and I myself have had far too little of it as well."

Pinkerton looked more worn and discarded than when Molly had last seen him. He set his chair across from Mr. Lincoln and handed him a letter. The positioning of the two men felt awkward. Mr. Lincoln leaned forward and rested his elbows upon his knees. He read the letter without reaction.

"As you can see," Pinkerton began, "this is from Mr. Samuel Felton—the executive of the Philadelphia, Wilmington, and Baltimore Railroad. He retained my services several weeks ago, fearing the election may lead to violence and the destruction of his rail lines. In particular, he worried about sabotage before your inauguration. He is most afraid the wooden bridge over the Gunpowder River or the ferry near Havre de Grace will be destroyed—preventing your arrival in Washington."

Mr. Lincoln nodded, seeming to read the letter again. Molly strained to see the paper, but he handed it back to Pinkerton.

"And I am assuming since you asked me here at this hour, you did indeed find something?"

"Quite," Pinkerton said. "With the time constraints, my more regular methods were ineffective—too slow. So I dispatched agents to Baltimore and other points in the south. They were to uncover the leading spirits of this plot and determine the actual danger."

"So they intend to burn the bridges and prevent my arrival in Washington?"

"I'm afraid it's worse," Pinkerton replied. "They mean for there to be no inauguration."

Mr. Lincoln nodded—he emitted a small noise that sounded like he might be amused.

"Will they take Washington by force before I arrive?"

"They don't intend you to ever arrive in Washington. They will set upon you when you arrive in Baltimore."

"Assassination?"

Pinkerton nodded, but said nothing. Maybe it was the lack of sleep, or something larger. But Mr. Lincoln showed no reaction—almost like he expected it. He breathed deep.

"Are you certain?"

Pinkerton carefully revealed all they had learned. He told Mr. Lincoln of the very details Mr. Webster had uncovered—the conspiracy with Otis Hillard, Mr. Luckett, and Cipriano Ferrandini. Mr. Lincoln's hand played with his beard, as if deep in thought. A melancholy overtook him. He sat up, then ran his hands through his hair.

"And you are sure of this?" Mr. Lincoln asked.

"One of my operatives infiltrated a secessionist movement—the Palmetto Guard in Baltimore. They drew secret ballots to choose the assassin. We know the ringleaders. I am quite certain this is real and you are within an hour of peril."

The moments stretched in front of them. Mr. Lincoln stroked his beard again, considering the news.

"Why not Albany or New York then?" Mr. Lincoln countered. "I was mobbed in Albany. If they meant to kill me, they could have done it then."

The itinerary for the special train carrying the president-elect was well publicized. Crowds met him at every stop. They waited to hear his words, hoping for a tone that healed the country and did not further drive it apart. Molly looked to Mrs. Warne. No one answered Mr. Lincoln. *But she knew.*

"Because they wish Maryland to secede," Molly spoke.

Pinkerton turned, irritated. Mrs. Warne reached out and took Molly's arm, as if she would escort her from the room.

"Not now—" Pinkerton began.

Mr. Lincoln interrupted him.

"Let her finish. What did you say, Miss Ferguson?"

Mrs. Warne slowly let go of her arm. She nodded, encouraging Molly to speak. Pinkerton maintained his fierce glare.

"They wish it to be Baltimore. It will be a smear upon the reputation of the city. These men think it will force a vote for secession. Once Maryland falls, Washington is cut off from the North. The war will end before it begins."

"Baltimore is the backdoor to the capitol," Mr. Lincoln murmured. "Who told you this?"

Pinkerton's expression softened. Molly looked to him. He nodded his approval.

"In Montreal I met with the man funding the operation—William Norris."

"We think he was appointed the head of the Confederate Secret Service," Pinkerton added.

"What is there to fund?" Mr. Lincoln asked. "A mob attacks an old man as he steps off a train."

"They want to escape unmolested," Molly answered. "If there is no one to punish, then it seems more organized. Baltimore will have no scapegoat. It makes a vote to secede more likely."

Mr. Lincoln took a deep breath, then exhaled. It filled the space in the room. Mrs. Warne's face remained stoic.

"But we have no proof of any of this," Mr. Lincoln said.

Molly no longer had the letter from Booth, or even the one from Sanders. She had lost both when her luggage was stolen. But she had the money. She hadn't shown it to Pinkerton or Mrs. Warne. She opened her handbag and withdrew a large roll of bills. She held it out over Pinkerton's shoulder. He looked back as Molly's hand crossed his sight.

"What is this?" he asked.

"The money I am to deposit in Baltimore for the escape. Colonel Norris gave it to me."

Pinkerton took it from her.

"That's—" he tried to estimate the amount.

"Five thousand dollars."

Pinkerton held it out to Mr. Lincoln. "This is real, sir. Very real."

Lincoln hesitated, then took the wad of cash.

"It's not often a man holds the very money paid to his assassins." He laughed. "What would you have me do, Mr. Pinkerton? I assume you have some manner of plan to avert this pending disaster?"

"Leave tonight, sir. We put you on a train and you are in Washington ahead of schedule. You must pass through Baltimore before they think you will arrive. Surprise is the essence."

"So you ask me to pick up and skulk to Washington this very night?" Mr. Lincoln asked. Pinkerton started to answer, but Lincoln held up his hand. "It is wise council."

Silence filled the room. Mr. Lincoln looked at Molly.

"Did they do that to your face?"

"It is nothing," Molly said. "An accident." She wished not to tell the tale again.

"An accident? You need to take more care or you will wind up with a face like mine."

Molly smiled but looked to her shoes. Her face ached.

"But please tell me, Miss Ferguson. Were you so hurt on my account? Looking out for my safety?"

"It was mistaken identity, sir. A British agent thought I worked for the South. He tried to stop me. I have had worse."

"British?" Mr. Lincoln asked. His voice changed.

"Yes," Pinkerton answered. "One of Lord Lyon's men."

"So the British are on our side?"

"Not entirely," Pinkerton offered. "I have a man in Charleston, who meets with the British emissary there. The Crown wishes to see you inaugurated because they hope for disunion."

"They want a war," Lincoln said.

"Yes. They can sell arms to the South, and the country will remain divided. United we are a strong rival. If we fall into disarray, then the British have less to compete against. And their cotton will remain cheap."

"And you are certain the men who attacked you were British?"

Molly nodded. The alley, the pool of blood—she pushed these images from her mind. She swallowed hard. This was not the time for tears.

"If the British believe the plot is real," Mr. Lincoln began, "it lends great weight to your work. I thank you, Mr. Pinkerton. I do have one question."

"Anything at all, sir," Pinkerton answered.

"Are you working with the superintendent of police in New York? Mr. Kennedy?"

"No," Pinkerton answered. He looked to Mrs. Warne. "My detectives met with him. His officers even arrested Miss Ferguson in the city, but we are not in league with one another. Why do you ask?"

"Just before I came here, I received another message from Washington. It seems New York detectives uncovered a similar plot to the one you mentioned. I wanted to ensure the information came from different sources. We could easily fool ourselves that there are wolves among the flock, when all we have are sheep. But I am more convinced than ever. I thank you all for your service, especially you,

Miss Ferguson. You seem to have borne a brunt of it in my defense. It is a sad day when our Southern brothers consider my death necessary for the furtherance of their cause."

"Then you will heed our council and make straight for Washington?" Pinkerton asked.

Lincoln shook his head.

"I cannot go tonight. I have promised to raise the flag over Independence Hall tomorrow morning and to visit the legislature at Harrisburg in the afternoon—beyond that I have no engagements. Any plan that may be adopted that will enable me to fulfill these promises I will accede to, and you can inform me what is concluded upon tomorrow."

He stood and offered his hand to Pinkerton. The detective rose to meet him. He nodded toward both Mrs. Warne and Molly, then headed toward the door. Pinkerton's shoulders slouched as the door shut. The weeks of frantic work weighed upon him, as if he had taken the beating Molly received.

He faced both Molly and Mrs. Warne.

"We have much work to do."

CHAPTER SEVENTEEN

OVERNIGHT, PINKERTON DEVISED the best plan under the circumstances. The official itinerary showed Mr. Lincoln staying overnight in Harrisburg before traveling to Baltimore by train. But Pinkerton arranged an earlier departure from Harrisburg. After dinner with the Pennsylvania governor, the president-elect would backtrack to Philadelphia. From there, another train would take him to Baltimore, where they could switch stations and continue on to Washington. There was no getting around Baltimore. All the rail lines converged through that city. But they could change the timing. With luck, Mr. Lincoln would arrive hours ahead of schedule. The conspirators would mob the wrong train while Lincoln would be safely in the capitol.

Pinkerton dispatched Molly and Mrs. Warne to follow Mr. Lincoln that morning. They watched him raise the flag at Independence Hall. He gave a speech in the hall and then stepped outside. A large entourage followed to a makeshift wooden platform. Two lines of soldiers stood at attention below the platform. The crowd expressed its boisterous approval as the president-elect made his appearance. He pulled off his overcoat, and then, hand-over-hand, raised an oversized American flag. The cheers drowned out the moment. The soldiers fired a salute. Molly jumped at the report of the guns. Even children perched in the few small trees around yelled with joy. As he finished, Mr. Lincoln stepped back and looked at the flag. Then he faced the crowd. His words were mostly lost to the wind and the distance, though he caught sight of Molly and locked eyes.

"I would rather be assassinated on this spot than surrender it."

He bowed to the crowd and took his leave.

Relief filled Molly as Mr. Lincoln's train left Philadelphia, bound for Harrisburg—a four-hour trip to the west. She hoped for sleep, but too much work remained. She followed Pinkerton and Mrs. Warne everywhere for the rest of the day, ensuring every last detail fell in place.

As dark descended over Philadelphia, her body begged for sleep. Even with the late hour, she let the cold find her. It kept her from falling asleep on her feet. She forced herself awake, for no other reason than she might die from exposure if she collapsed upon the stone rail platform. She had no rest the night prior, and her fortunes were looking rather bleak for what remained of the night ahead.

Mrs. Warne stood beside her. The last train headed toward Baltimore idled on the track. The timing would be close. Pinkerton had left an hour earlier with a carriage to meet Mr. Lincoln on the special train from Harrisburg. It arrived at a different station on opposite ends of the city—different railways. Molly was glad he had left. His mood had been foul, plagued by worry and lack of sleep.

As they waited for Pinkerton's return, Molly and Mrs. Warne guarded the last car on the train, a sleeper car with several open berths. Passengers filtered into the front cars as the train stood stubbornly upon the rails. Steam rose from the engine. The engineer stoked the fires to ensure they were ready for departure. A water pipe extended to the idling engine, keeping the tanks filled. It ensured they would have enough steam. The minutes passed slowly. Mrs. Warne checked her watch and searched in the direction where she expected Pinkerton to appear.

They had twenty minutes. Mrs. Warne sent Molly to check on the sleeper car once more. To avoid scrutiny, Mrs. Warne had not requested a private sleeper car. She feared it would draw too much attention. Instead, she relied upon the late hour departure with the hope it would leave the train sparsely attended.

At the head of the train, several men milled about the platform. At least one had some manner of lapel pin. Molly strained to see if it were a white cockade or a palmetto. Her furtive glances could not produce an answer. It should be neither—not in Philadelphia. The men smoked and paid Molly no notice. She entered the train at the head of the last sleeper car. Passengers filled some of the front benches, but it appeared to be a light run to Baltimore. The back half of the car contained four pairs of sleeping berths, still empty. It gave Molly an idea, and she headed down the aisle.

"Excuse me, sir." Molly pulled gently at the arm of the conductor. She found him two cars up, checking on passengers.

"May I help you, miss?"

"The back car, sir. My invalid brother is set to arrive at any moment with family. Could I ask your help in securing those last berths?"

She grasped hold of his hand, pressing a large bill into his palm. He looked down, then pocketed the money.

"Why certainly, miss. Your brother, you said?"

"Yes, sir."

Molly followed him down the aisle.

"I hope he is not too unwell?" the conductor probed.

"Well enough to travel, but his coughing might make quite the disturbance. I would hate to inconvenience the other passengers. Especially if his malady proves contagious."

The conductor glanced up from the tickets. He lost track of his count and placed them in a pocket.

"Well, let us secure that rear car and hope the trip passes quietly."

He led Molly down the aisle, stepping through the doors separating each car. The conductor brushed his way past the few passengers in the front half of the sleeper car. Then he looked into the
sleeper berths at the rear. They remained empty. He placed a rope
across the back half, securing it from the other passengers. He even
pulled a curtain across the narrow hallway that led to the berths.

"If anyone tries to pass, I will gladly remove them."

"Would you be able to unlock the back door?" Molly asked.

The conductor studied the bruising upon her face. She pressed
another bill into his hand.

"That might be best for the other passengers," he said.

"I thought so as well."

Molly accepted the key he handed her.

"I trust you will lock the door before the train departs?"

"Certainly," Molly replied.

He nodded, and then headed toward the front of the car. Molly
rushed to the back and opened the rear door. Waving, she attracted
Mrs. Warne's attention. The older woman joined her at the back of
the train.

"I must get out of this wind," Mrs. Warne said. She pushed past
Molly and entered the car.

"I talked the conductor into giving us the sleeping berths. There
is only a curtain separating the passengers in the seats up front. If
you wish, I can head outside and wait for Mr. Pinkerton while you
wait by the curtain."

Mrs. Warned nodded. She shivered, adjusting her shawl.

"Thank you, Molly."

Molly stepped outside. The men along the platform walked toward the front of the train in an ambling manner, away from her.
There were three of them, each wearing a bowler-style hat. They
talked to one another, gesturing with their hands. Molly found a
place out of the wind by a stone pillar to await Pinkerton.

She had no watch to check the time. But if she strained her eyes, the hour on the station clock came into focus—a quarter till the hour. She watched the men as they strolled along the platform near the engine. A few moments later, one of the engineers stepped from the engine. He tugged the water pipe away from the train. The engine hissed louder, as if someone stoked the fire to build steam. The conductor walked down the platform.

"All aboard! Last call for Baltimore!"

Molly strained her vision. A team of horses pulled a carriage down the cobblestone street, though the train drowned any noise from the carriage. She turned to see the conductor walking her way. She held up a hand to the man. He looked into the dark and saw the carriage as it pulled to a stop near Molly.

Mr. Pinkerton stepped out of the nearest door, followed by a tall figure. Molly stepped forward to grab hold of Mr. Lincoln's other side. As she held his arm, she pulled him ever so slightly. The conductor watched. Another tall man followed. His manner of dress appeared polished. His frame filled the carriage door as he pulled himself through the small opening.

"I told them we were expecting my invalid brother," Molly explained.

The conductor turned toward the engine and yelled, holding the train. It caught the attention of the three men who stopped their conversation.

Mr. Lincoln understood and stooped. He even feigned a limp, letting Molly and Pinkerton guide him toward the back of the train. Mrs. Warne stood at the door.

"Why, Miss Ferguson, it is good to see you," Mr. Lincoln began. "I am honored to have so charming and accomplished a female relation."

Molly had not the time nor breath to answer. The cold stung her lungs. She walked them to the door of the sleeper car, stepping aside as Pinkerton guided the president-elect up the stairs. Her attention focused on the men at the front of the train. They watched, their conversation interrupted.

The third man from the carriage started up the stairs behind Mr. Lincoln. He tipped his hat to Molly, smiling in a suggestive manner while examining her from her feet to her hat. She avoided his eyes. He mounted the first stair but then stopped to introduce himself—unaware or unconcerned with the hurried nature of their mission. It bespoke a certain arrogance.

"Mr. Lamon. And you are?"

"Miss Lawton," she answered. There was comfort in the assumed name, a barrier between herself and men like this. "It is time we left, sir."

He looked up the stairs and lingered a moment. Inside, Pinkerton looked out. He fumed. The man smiled, then mounted the stairs. He delayed for Pinkerton's benefit. She imagined the two men disliked one another. Looking down the line of train cars toward the engine, only one of the trio of men still stood upon the platform. The others had disappeared into the dark of the Philadelphia night. Or worse, they had entered the train. She mounted the stairs then pulled the door closed, then locked it.

As the party settled into the berths, Molly made her way to the curtain. Mrs. Warne stood nearby.

"We may have company. Those men boarded the train."

Molly had barely finished her sentence when the curtain pushed back. Only the rope separated one of the men from the two women. Behind them, Mr. Lincoln, Mr. Lamon, and even Mr. Pinkerton had already settled into their berths. They were out of sight.

"May I help you?" Molly demanded. She held her voice stern.

The man tried to see past her, but Molly forced him to look right at her face. He caught sight of her bruises.

"I'm looking for someone," he said.

Molly's eyes fell to the palmetto pin on his lapel—a bold statement in a Northern city like Philadelphia.

"There is no one here save my brother and some family. He is quite ill."

"All the same . . ." the man said, starting to lift the rope.

Molly pressed her hand against his chest. He looked to her hand, and then met her stare. With her free hand she pulled out her locket from Booth. It had the palmetto symbol on the front.

"I am already upon a mission for the guard," she said.

She let him study it until his expression mirrored his confusion.

"I am guiding a party of our supporters to Baltimore. Please, we need no commotion now. Not in this city."

The man hesitated, perhaps thinking through his options. Finally, he nodded.

"I am looking for someone," he said.

"I understand," Molly answered. "*He* is not here." She stressed the word *"He,"* as if they shared some common knowledge. She imagined whom he meant but couldn't know for certain. "All those with me are supporters of *our* Cause."

His face softened, and he turned. "Be safe."

"And you," Molly replied.

He walked down the aisle then stepped down the stairs at the front of the car. The engine started. Out the side window the three men stood along the platform.

"Excellent work, Miss Ferguson."

Pinkerton had listened from his berth. He eased himself out of it to stand behind Molly and Mrs. Warne. His hand gripped a pistol. Mr. Lamon pulled back the curtain from his berth. He lay on his back and also held a pistol. This was the kind of situation she meant—where she needed a gun. She couldn't catch Mrs. Warne's eye.

"We have cut the telegraph lines from Philadelphia to Baltimore," Pinkerton said. "Even the lines from Harrisburg to Baltimore. If those men suspect anything, there will be no time to warn anyone in Baltimore. I am surprised at how bold they are, especially here in Philadelphia."

Mrs. Warne steadied herself on Molly's shoulder as the train lurched. Ahead, the engine howled. Molly fixed the curtain back in place and pulled the rope as tight as it would go—at least it was something. The train built speed, and soon they had pulled out of Philadelphia, steaming south.

Molly slept in fits during the first hour of the ride. On a normal night, the route would take four hours. She lay in the berth below Mr. Lincoln. He spilled out of the small enclosure. Despite exhaustion, Molly's nerves held sleep at bay. And she startled each time Mr. Pinkerton opened the rear door to the train.

Part of Pinkerton's preparations included posting guards at each bridge. The men held a lantern aloft to signal the bridge was safe, and all was well. It eased Pinkerton's mind to see each flash of white light as the train made its way south. They still had the ferry crossing at Havre de Grace, and the Gunpowder River Bridge, both locations that Pinkerton had worried about leading up to the election.

The engine slowed as they approached the Susquehanna River. Molly stood, giving up on slumber. Pinkerton would interrupt her sleep once again as he opened the door to let in the cold night air. Mr. Lincoln opened his curtain. His berth stood at Molly's shoulder height. No sleep plagued his eyes.

"We are at Havre de Grace," he said. "We are getting along very well. I think we are on time."

His composure could have been made from granite. Only her lack of sleep competed with her fraying nerves. He had to worry about his life. A mob waited for him in Baltimore—if they knew he arrived early, they might be particularly vicious.

"You cannot sleep?" he asked.

Molly shook her head.

"Then talk to me awhile, for I am similarly afflicted." He paused. "Have you always done this work, Miss Ferguson?"

"No," Molly said. "I have only just met Mr. Pinkerton and Mrs. Warne. They found me in Baltimore."

"Found you?"

The carpet in the sleeper train was worn where she stood. She remembered the smell of the brothel—a mix of sweat and fresh linen. Mr. Lincoln must have sensed her hesitation. He changed his line of questioning.

"Where do you call home?"

"I guess New Orleans, at first. I lived there until my parents passed. Then Baltimore."

"And you like this detective work?"

"I don't know," Molly said. She hadn't thought about it. It had been a means to an end—to escape the brothel, to find the men she wished, though when she found the first of them, she failed. "I have nothing else."

"How did your parents die?" Mr. Lincoln asked.

She tried to hold back, but the memories overwhelmed her. Tears welled in her eyes until the first rolled down her face.

"I did not mean—" he began. Molly cut him off.

"They were killed. Men came in the night and burned our plantation. They hauled away my father with a noose, dragged by a horse. My mother they left upon the steps of the house after they defiled her. Then they took me to Baltimore."

Mr. Lincoln sat up—to the extent he could in the berth. He found her hand and clutched it.

"They found me in Baltimore . . ." Molly hesitated, then met his eyes ". . . in a brothel."

"Why? Why would men do such a thing?" Mr. Lincoln asked.

Her eyes traced the patterns in the carpet once more. She wasn't certain, not after what Colonel Norris told her—a gambling debt.

"We had no slaves. They were all free folk—freed when they came to the plantation. Someone talked. Someone told them the place was not a plantation. So men came and burned it."

Mr. Lincoln gripped her hand. She didn't know if he understood. She didn't anymore.

"There will be a war," he said. "I fear none among us can stop it. One way or the other, things will change."

The train jostled as the car slowed. Outside, rail workers readied to uncouple the cars and shunt them onto a ferry to cross the river.

"That doesn't mean things will be better," Molly said.

"I suppose you are right. We need to fight to make them so."

"Mr. Pinkerton says the coming war is like a fog. None of us can see through it."

"Then we must work together," Mr. Lincoln said. "There is nothing worse than traveling through a deep fog by oneself." He paused, looking out the window. Molly was about to slip away, to dry her face out of sight. "You seem to have a talent for this business, and Mr. Pinkerton seems to have a need."

Molly shook her head.

"I am no detective," she said. "I'm a whore they found in Baltimore."

Molly pulled away from Mr. Lincoln's grasp and walked toward the rear of the car. Pinkerton had the door open. The cold air felt good. She stayed a few minutes and was relieved to find Mr. Lincoln's curtain pulled back over his berth when she returned. She took one last look toward the rear of the car, then crawled into the lower berth. She pressed her face into her pillow to keep anyone from hearing her sobs. She hadn't expected to talk about the plantation, and she wished never to think of the brothel. But it all came back in flashes—flashes that overwhelmed her with anger, and shame, and sadness, and guilt at the same time. And something else edged upon her thoughts. Once they arrived in Washington, all would be done. Mrs. Warne would have no more need of her. She kept her face pressed into the pillow and allowed sleep to find her.

As the train slowed, Molly roused from her slumber. Baltimore grew around them. They had made it over the ferry crossing and across the Gunpowder Bridge. If the conspirators had planned an attack on either location, they did not anticipate an early arrival. But Baltimore presented the biggest challenge. Certainly, men watched each train as it arrived. This city was the most dangerous location.

Mrs. Warne manned the back of the car. Dark still wore at the windows. She held a pistol like the men. At best, the coming day lay several hours away. The train slowed to a stop, jolting as the cars settled upon the rails. A conductor called out for Baltimore. Some of the passengers in the front of the car stirred—the ones who wouldn't travel on to Washington. The car shifted ever so slight as they dismounted the stairs at the side of the car. Mrs. Warne still wore a determined yet concerned look.

Pinkerton had pulled most of the curtains closed in the back half of the car, yet he incessantly moved about and pushed open a corner to peer outside. Molly slipped out of her sleeper berth and stepped to where the curtain covered the aisle leading to the front of the car. A few passengers remained, and those who did were stretched in all manner across the hard wood benches. A hand fell upon her shoulder, and she startled. Mrs. Warne stood behind her.

"We'll get off here, Molly," the older woman said.

"We won't go to Washington?"

Mrs. Warne shook her head. "Mr. Pinkerton is worried. His plan will likely cause Mr. Lincoln a fair heap of criticism in the newspapers. We do not want them to discover that he traveled with women who were not his relations. That would not play well in the Southern press—or in the North, for that matter."

Molly followed her toward the back of the train. As they walked past, Mr. Lincoln pushed aside his curtain.

"Miss Ferguson," he called out.

She returned to the side of his berth.

"Thank you for all you have done for me."

"Of course, sir." She didn't meet his eyes.

"We both fear what lies ahead. But, you are an angel in disguise."

She thought of the brothel and shook her head. Mr. Lincoln reached out and lifted her face by the chin.

"Do not think of yourself in any other manner."

His words filled her with shame. She had not chosen this path, and even after Mrs. Warne found her, she had been consumed with personal motives. But this operation was larger than any of them. Getting Mr. Lincoln through Baltimore meant something larger for the nation. She met his eyes, then raced down the aisle to find Mrs. Warne. She feared the sadness and guilt would overwhelm her again.

Pinkerton still lunged from window to window. He stopped long enough to look out the back door.

"It appears to be clear," he said. "They will shortly uncouple us from the train and use horses to pull the car to the Camden Street station. But the real danger is here. This is where they will attack." He stepped aside to check out the window again.

"We will stay for a time," Mrs. Warne offered. "Observe from the station and give you a warning if there is a need."

"That would be splendid. And, Miss Ferguson, I'll need you to deposit the money from Colonel Norris. With it safe in the bank, the conspirators may not realize how their operation was compromised—your reputation as a Southern agent will remain intact. We may even capture some of the Palmetto Guard if they go to claim it. Colonel Norris gave you instructions, did he not?"

"Yes," Molly said. "I know what to do."

"Good. Then delay not and wish us Godspeed to Washington!"

Molly longed for a bed with fresh linen and a week of rest. She caught Mrs. Warne's eye. The older woman looked as weary. Mrs. Warne grabbed Molly's hand and pressed her through the back door. The two women descended the stairs, then found a place out of the wind to watch the train. Molly leaned against a stone pillar.

The railway workers uncoupled the sleeper car first—the last of the train. They shunted it to a side track, then hooked up teams of horses to pull the car away. Trains couldn't run through the city, but the horses provided the means to transfer across Baltimore and continue to Washington. Molly searched around them. Despite the early hour and lack of daylight, the station felt busy. A nervous energy permeated the area, like a heavy winter morning awaiting a storm. Mrs. Warne's voice rose above the noise of the railway workers.

"We are in a rare club, Molly. You and I. Where else could women do this work?"

The horses pulled at their harnesses, straining the leather. The sleeper car inched forward. Then it built speed, the rhythmic clacks of the hooves filling the night air. The women watched as the sleeper car rolled out of sight. There was something nostalgic in Mrs. Warne's expression.

"My husband would be proud of this," Mrs. Warne said. "He certainly would laugh knowing I was part of it. I miss him terribly, but

I also love this new life I have found. It is funny the turns one's destiny can take, is it not?"

Molly didn't know where the older woman led the conversation. Suddenly she worried. This was the end. They had no more use for her. She found herself short of breath, staring to her feet trying to gather strength. *What would she do?*

"Are you all right, Molly?"

Molly stood at a cliff. *Of course, this was the end. What use would she be now?*

"Is this it, then?" she managed. She would rather it be over fast.

Her eyes teared. *Where would she go?* Her mother had that friend in Richmond. But heading south felt like the wrong direction with the drums of war starting their call.

"Is what it?" Mrs. Warne asked.

"You no longer need me."

Mrs. Warne grabbed hold of Molly's shoulder and managed to angle the younger girl toward her. Molly braced herself for a blow that never came.

"We need you more than ever. Much work remains."

A tear broke free, but she grabbed it with her gloved hand before it could stream down her cheek.

"I feared you might not need me—or want me."

"I need you, Molly," Mrs. Warne confirmed, then drew Molly close. "You have talent for this work."

Relief flooded through Molly. She had a place. It felt good to fit somewhere.

"Will they make it to Washington?" Molly asked.

"Yes," Mrs. Warne answered. "They will make it. This station was the danger point, and now it has passed." She looked in the direction of the sleeper car a moment longer. It was nearly out of sight. "I have seen all I need. It is enough to know we played our role."

Mrs. Warne turned and walked toward the exit of the station. Molly stood for a moment, straining to see the car disappear into the heart of Baltimore. Mrs. Warne returned and grabbed Molly's hand, pulling her close.

"Come, Molly. Our enemies do not rest, so neither shall we. It is time to begin your real training."

CHAPTER EIGHTEEN

Molly stood where the wind bit hard. It didn't bother her, at least not yet. A line of bottles sat less than ten paces away, precariously balanced on a fallen log. She pulled a revolver from her handbag, and then set the bag on the ground. She had been training for almost a year with Mrs. Warne, and still they had not taught her to shoot. Standing in a small valley, she hoped the trees and the enormity of the park would swallow the noise. She cocked the hammer and took aim.

Her first shot went wide. Dirt kicked up on the ground behind the bottles. Her next shot did no better. It struck a rock. Bits of fractured sandstone flew into the hillside.

Her ears rang. She de-cocked the weapon and searched her bag. She had forgotten the cotton balls. She found them and then wadded them to fit in her ears. Then she faced the bottles once more, pulled the hammer back, and took a deep breath.

The bullet struck the ground behind the log.

"Damn," she muttered.

Again, no broken glass. She raised the weapon, but one of the bottles teetered. Then it slipped off the log, battered by the wind. It shattered as it struck the ground.

"Seems you broke one."

Molly spun. The voice came from out of nowhere. Mrs. Warne stood behind her. The older woman caught the barrel of the gun as Molly startled.

"How did you—"

"I guess it is safe to be a bottle when you have a gun?" Mrs. Warne asked.

From her tone she meant to mock Molly. Mrs. Warne took the weapon as Molly let go.

"I wanted to practice."

"And what have we talked about before?"

Molly glanced at the hillside.

"Guns are not tools for the female detective," Mrs. Warne said.

"But what if we have cause to use one? What if that's all I have?"

"Then you have failed. Let the men practice their crude methods. You and I have devices much more refined."

"But you used a pistol when we escorted Mr. Lincoln into Baltimore."

"Those were extreme measures," Mrs. Warne answered.

"That's what I am talking about!" Molly cried.

They had had this very argument before.

"When you master those skill, then perhaps we shall teach you to shoot."

"You'll never teach me." Molly said it under her breath.

Mrs. Warne didn't answer, but she certainly heard.

"Mr. Pinkerton wishes to see us."

"Fine." Molly crossed her arms and stared at the bottles.

Mrs. Warne started to walk away; her footsteps broke through the dead leaves and the light layer of snow. Molly didn't move. The defeat stung. She should have hit at least one bottle. She needed more time, but it was near impossible by how close Mrs. Warne watched all she did.

"She can't do it." Molly spoke to the bottles.

The crunching of the snow grew louder. Molly turned. Mrs. Warne made her way back to where Molly stood. A determined look set upon her face. When she drew even with Molly, Mrs. Warne cocked the hammer on the pistol. Raising the weapon, she fired the remaining three rounds in rapid succession. She shot so fast Molly scarcely turned in time to see the bottles shatter. Only two remained upon the log. She handed the empty pistol to Molly. The older woman turned once more and began to walk away. This time Molly followed.

Molly was sullen in the carriage ride. They rode through the streets of Washington. It had changed, become a different place from a year ago. War twisted the very fabric of a country, distorted everything—even small things. It became hard to find fresh produce, and the price of cotton soared. The people changed, too. It felt like a never-ending winter had descended—a blanket that smothered everything.

It had been almost a year since they watched Mr. Lincoln's train head to Washington. Molly hadn't seen him since. She did nothing except train and do menial tasks Pinkerton assigned. Mrs. Warne taught her things that felt far from detective work. She longed to head outside and follow a spy or saboteur. There were plenty set upon the city. Certainly, that would have been more use than reading books, or dining with the highclass of Washington. Molly found most of her excitement in leaving the city to deliver messages. But she always went to dull locations in Pennsylvania. Once, she traveled to Chicago, returning with an urgent message for Pinkerton. He wouldn't tell her what the message contained.

"Does he have another letter for me?" Molly said.

Mrs. Warne glanced at her, then turned her attention out the window. Molly did the same. Soldiers marched upon the streets.

Some stood on the corners near the gas lamps. Come nightfall, they would patrol. They searched out Southerners who sneaked into the city to retrieve messages before heading south again. Tents littered the city outskirts. Earthen breastworks fortified the approaches. War reached everyone and everything.

The war had dragged on longer than any expected. The fast victory the Union promised didn't come to pass. And with the stalemate, Pinkerton delivered himself to General McClellan to lead the new Secret Service. With each defeat or dispatch from the front, the hope of an early end to the conflict faded. Even the British across the ocean debated the merits of which side to back. And if the rumors held any truth, the French Foreign Minister supported rescuing Richmond and the Confederacy. Some claimed Europe would break the stalemate on her own, if the North couldn't trample the insurrection.

The carriage stopped in front of Pinkerton's new headquarters. Mrs. Warne stepped out first, with Molly following like a schoolgirl off to see the headmaster. That image matched her mood. Mrs. Warne knocked once upon Pinkerton's office door and then entered, as was her custom. He sat behind his desk, seemingly as tired as ever. A small fire smoldered in the fireplace. The man never ceased his efforts.

"I found her," Mrs. Warne said.

"We searched for you this morning. There are important things afoot, Molly. When I ask you to remain close, it means I may have need of your services." He looked at Mrs. Warne. "Where'd you find her?"

Mrs. Warne didn't answer, not at first. She turned to look at Molly. Something in her manner softened.

"I forgot that I set her upon one last training task."

"So it is you I should be cross with, then?" Pinkerton asked.

"Yes, quite."

"And she is ready?" he pressed.

They spoke of her as if she didn't stand just feet away.

Mrs. Warne nodded.

"Very well. Miss Ferguson, we have need of your talents."

Molly's breath drew in. She had desired the chance to shake off the boredom of the Washington political circuit. This certainly sounded different than delivering notes to Northern supporters.

"Yes, sir. Anything."

Pinkerton looked to Mrs. Warne. "You told her nothing?"

"I thought that best left to your devices."

Pinkerton stood.

"Please, Miss Ferguson, have a seat."

Molly walked deeper into the room until she stood before the great oak desk. She sat opposite Pinkerton, waiting for him to seat himself. Mrs. Warne had coached her through all manner of classes in etiquette. She hated them. It reminded her of the lessons from her mother.

"I understand you have been to Richmond before," Pinkerton said.

Molly nodded. "Yes, I spent summers there many years ago. It would get too hot in New Orleans, so my mother brought me to my grandmother's house."

"Do you still have family there?" From his face, he was concerned.

"No," Molly answered. "I have no family now . . . that I know. My mother had a close friend in the city. But I have not seen her in many years. Am I going to Richmond?"

Pinkerton paused then began to explain. "We have had an operative in Richmond for some time. But we are in need of deepening his cover amongst the Confederate elite. Mrs. Warne believes that softening his image will help in this regard?"

Pinkerton paused. He glanced to Mrs. Warne, then back to Molly.

"What do you need of me?" Molly asked. She followed his stare to Mrs. Warne who stood to the side, near the fireplace. The fire burned low.

Pinkerton cleared his throat. "Our man needs a wife."

The words didn't sink in, not at first.

"I am to find him a suitable match?" Molly asked.

Pinkerton shot a pleading look in Mrs. Warne's direction.

"You are to be his wife."

"Only playing a role, Molly," Mrs. Warne added.

A devilish delight danced in her voice. Mrs. Warne found humor in Pinkerton's discomfort.

"Who am I to marry?" Molly asked.

She wanted nothing to do with men. Her memory still held the smell of sweat as they pressed their fat bodies against hers. Even now, it took all her concentration to dine with the fat powerful men of the political establishment without gagging—made worse when Pinkerton and Mrs. Warne encouraged her to tease them along to extract their secrets and expose disloyalties. It was easy, but thoroughly distasteful.

"You will marry no one," Pinkerton said. "But we require someone who can think on her feet, to help Mr. Webster in Richmond. Do you feel up to it?"

He had regained his composure, leaning back and letting his hands smooth over the wrinkles in his vest.

"Mr. Webster is the one who found me in Baltimore, the man you called *Davies* for a time?"

The words leapt from her mouth before she had time to think. It meant a break in the routine. Mrs. Warne studied her. She had answered too quickly. Molly tried to suppress her smile.

"The same man. She is ready?" Pinkerton asked Mrs. Warne again.

"She is," Mrs. Warne answered without looking to Pinkerton.

"When do I leave?" Molly asked.

She had another chance—at Cheeney.

Pinkerton opened a desk drawer and pulled out a small steel box. Removing a key from around his neck, he opened the box.

"You should have left this morning," he answered, distracted as he counted through a stack of bills. He handed a large pile across the desk to Molly. "This should suffice, but do not spend foolishly. We get this money from the government now. It is meant to last several months."

Molly held the paper in her hands. It felt flimsy. Some of the corners were worn.

"When do I leave?" she asked again.

"You are already packed," Mrs. Warne said.

"I did not pack anything."

"We bought you all new clothes. We want you to take nothing that might give you away or be associated with Washington. Your bags are on the carriage."

Molly stood and faced Mrs. Warne. "Thank you."

Pinkerton held out his hand. She took it, letting him place his other hand on top. He held firm.

"Listen to Mr. Webster. He is an experienced agent. He knows Richmond well and has established himself upon the place. He is even a personal acquaintance of the Confederate Secretary of War! But Mrs. Warne convinced me we are missing valuable intelligence—the gossip amongst the womenfolk."

"Are you that anxious to be rid of us?" Mrs. Warne asked.

"It's not that I want to leave," Molly said. "I just want to be useful."

"An excellent sentiment." Pinkerton let go of her hand. "And Mr. Webster's wife will be happy to know we have paired him with someone who can watch over him. He will not be gallivanting in the saloons to the same degree."

"He is already married?" Molly asked.

"He is. But his wife could not do this task," Mrs. Warne said. "She is not trained as you have been."

"Mr. Webster has cultivated a new persona in Richmond," Pinkerton added. "I do feel I must warn you that he is not convinced in the necessity of this addition. He likes to operate by himself."

"I shall win him over then. Mrs. Warne has been teaching me."

Mrs. Warne stepped forward and took Molly's arm in hers. "There is little teaching I can do in that regard. You are a natural, when you wish it." She pulled Molly away from the desk and toward the hall. "I will escort you downstairs."

"Good luck and Godspeed, Miss Ferguson," Pinkerton called out as he sat behind his desk once more. "Above all, be careful. We will have a hard time if you need rescuing in Richmond."

"Yes, sir."

Mrs. Warne pulled the door closed behind them. She faced Molly.

"I would have liked even more time with you, but you are ready. Trust what I have taught you. Trust Mr. Webster. And trust no one else."

Molly nodded.

"Put your money in your handbag."

Molly opened her handbag and placed the bills on top. She struggled to close the latch. Mrs. Warne held out her hand.

"The pistol," Mrs. Warne said.

Reluctantly, Molly unclasped the bag. She removed the bills, and then pulled out the small revolver. She held it a moment, looking at the dull metal. It had cost her two weeks' earnings. It should have been less, but she liked the ornate engravings. She handed it over.

"What have I taught you?" Mrs. Warne asked, taking hold of the pistol.

Molly nodded, looking to the floor.

"Say it, so I know you remember."

"Women have better tools than guns."

Mrs. Warne smiled, lifting Molly's face.

"Trust in yourself—you will do just fine."

CHAPTER NINETEEN

THE SMALL BOAT pitched and rocked upon the water. The air hung heavy, pressing in on Molly as if it were a blanket. Small ice crystals formed with every breath. It hurt when she breathed deep. The Potomac River ran swift here, and the boat caught the current as soon as they put out. Only in the small waves could she find the water. It flowed with an inky blackness under an equally dark sky as the wind cut through her coat and her dress.

She sat by herself in the back of the boat. Webster helped the boatman pull at a pair of giant oars in the middle of the small craft. With two men at the oars, they hoped to beat the coming storm, which already battered the canvas of the small sail. Two children huddled against an older woman at the front. She was the wife of a Confederate officer who needed a guide into Richmond. It seemed a small miracle that the children—one boy and one girl—tolerated the cold without complaint.

Webster looked different somehow, though it was hard to place. A sadness possessed him. At once she had recognized him, but his cold manner made her feel small—not how he met her before, in the brothel. Mrs. Warne must have felt it, too. As she saw them off, she wished Molly luck, with a tone that conveyed she understood the challenge. Mrs. Warne had pried her way into the

Pinkerton agency and tirelessly built her reputation. Molly had to do the same.

In some manner that was lucky—exactly the reason Mrs. Warne wanted Molly in Richmond. Men talked around women, because they felt confident women could not be spies. They had not the intelligence, or the forethought, or the care of the business of men. So went the logic. Yet women heard everything and were privy to the deepest secrets. Around the sewing circles and sitting rooms they traded these secrets. They exchanged nuggets of information as they did patches of material. The key to some of the greatest men in the Confederacy came through their wives.

Webster strained at the oars. The travel weighed upon him. Molly had thought of him often over the past year. Even though Mrs. Warne had been the one to take her from the brothel, she still held in him the image of liberator. She hoped his energy waned because the war drew on—not that her presence was so distasteful to his sense of purpose. He had built his reputation as a trustworthy Confederate courier—a man who could smuggle messages north. The messages made it to their intended readers. But not before Pinkerton steamed open, read, and then resealed each one.

She yearned for more conversation with him, as their first meeting had been so curious. He remained the only man she had met who could hold a topic and make it worthy of discussion. But there would be no talking upon the boat. They kept quiet, hoping the Union patrols huddled somewhere warm and would not hear them from the shoreline. If discovered, the soldiers would fire upon them. Anyone crossing the Potomac was either a spy, or smuggled contraband. Both were capital offenses, dealt with in the field by troops who longed to break winter boredom with any action. As the wind picked up, their fear of being overheard faded. The weather had decidedly turned.

"Storm's a coming!" the boatman shouted. "Get low and cover up!"

Rain started the assault. It showed no mercy, blinding with small particles of ice embedded in each drop. Molly leaned forward and huddled into her shawl. She hoped the boat held—she hated swimming. The men weathered the wind without shelter, afraid to let go of the oars. To do so would leave them at the mercy of the wind, free to blow them however it desired.

Molly willed the minutes to pass. Each breath came as agony. She lost feeling in her hands and it took all her strength to hold her shawl against the wind. As she counted her breaths, grateful that each one came in the open air and not struggling upon the water, the wind shifted. It tugged the boat faster toward the opposite shore. It also pulled them along the river. The men fought at the oars, desperate to push back against the wind. It did no good. With a grinding, the boat came to a stop—grounded along shallow water as they approached the far shore. They were still hundreds of feet from land.

Webster leapt up with astounding dexterity in the face of the wind and cold.

"Lower the sail!" he commanded.

He waded to the front of the boat and grabbed hold of a lead rope. The water was only knee deep, but the keel of the boat had become wedged upon rocks. He used all his strength upon the rope to no avail.

Surveying the far side, he called into the boat. "We must wade ashore. Gather all that is necessary!"

Molly could barely gain her balance in the wind. She stepped over the side and plunged deep to her waist. The water was ice. She fought to breathe. Webster held out a hand and pulled her toward the front of the boat.

"I'll take Mrs. Horvath. You grab the little girl."

Molly helped Mrs. Horvath over the side of the boat. As the woman made it into the water, a small bundle slipped from her dress and landed back inside the boat. Molly managed to reach it with her fingertips, before she scooped up the little girl. The wind howled too loud to get Mrs. Horvath's attention. So Molly gripped the girl tight and placed the packet into her handbag.

The boatman was also upon the water and had reached into the vessel to take hold of the boy. As a group, they waded through the current. At times Molly fell waist deep. The girl clutched upon her neck, holding ever tighter the closer they came to shore. With her legs ready to give out, and no feeling in her arms, Molly stepped onto the far bank. She let the girl down, prying her free before setting her on the bank. Then Molly climbed up. She slipped twice, muddying her dress and tearing the hem.

Webster and the boatman arrived behind her. The boatman handed off his charge, then headed back out. As they sat upon the shore they saw him free the boat, jump into the vessel, and raise the sail. It disappeared downriver.

"My bag was in the boat," Molly said.

"We'll buy you new clothes," Webster responded. He sounded upset, like this had happened on her account. "I know of a smugglers cabin upriver along Monroe's Creek—near where we should have landed. Should have wood stacked and dry cots."

They headed in the direction Webster pointed. The land was soggy and the going slow. Molly's shoes dug deep with each step, forcing her to pull straight up. It sapped her strength. She still carried the girl. The boy walked beside Webster, holding his hand, while Mrs. Horvath followed behind. After a time, Webster slowed. He gave directions from behind the group, but he struggled to keep up. Molly hung back to talk with him.

"Are you unwell?" she asked.

He shook his head, but coughed—his voice raspy. "It's my rheumatism. The cold makes it all the worse. I need to get to the cabin."

With her free hand she grabbed his. Even through her gloves, the ice of his fingers made her shiver. She held fast and pulled him along, ensuring he stayed with the others and led them in the correct direction. Molly tired between holding the girl and pulling Webster. When they finally caught sight of the little cabin, hidden in the woods back from the riverbank, she gave a prayer of relief under her breath.

Molly rammed the door open with her shoulder. Inside, the air stood stale. No one had been there for some time. She deposited Webster by the hearth, placing a heavy blanket over him. His body shook uncontrollably. The cabin contained a second room, with another fireplace. She helped Mrs. Horvath light a fire, and then the woman went about stripping and warming her children. Molly pulled the door closed behind her as she stepped out of the room. She managed to start a fire in the first fireplace and pulled a chair near Webster. He rocked upon the floor. There was little to do other than stoke the fire.

When the other room fell silent, Molly dared removed the package Mrs. Horvath had dropped in the boat. A red ribbon bound the package in oilcloth. Inside, she found a stack of correspondence to Mr. Benjamin—the Confederate Secretary of War. It appeared Mrs. Horvath had the same courier job as Webster.

Before she violated the seal upon the first envelope, she crept to the door leading to the next room. Nothing other than a deep snore emanated from the room beyond. Only the snapping of a roaring fire punctuated the night. She made her way back to Webster and sat down. His shaking had eased and his breathing deepened. Sleep had found him.

She turned the first envelope over in her hand, and then ran her small finger under the flap. It popped open. Taking the letter out, she paused. Still nothing from the other door. She unfolded the paper and read.

One by one Molly passed the hours with the other letters. By the end she cared not how she tore the envelopes. These would never go back to Mrs. Horvath. The author remained anonymous—but the penmanship bespoke of one man. He documented the defenses of Washington, down to the last sentry. There were maps in one letter, illustrating the location of the heavy guns and artillery. Others gave near exact counts of troop strength. Some even contained General McClellan's personal assessments. The letters contained a blueprint on how to attack Washington. Only a few people could have known these details.

The flames danced while she enjoyed the irony. A woman had tried to deliver these damning messages. The information they contained could end the Union with one well-planned assault. And another woman had found them—foiled their delivery. This transcended the war. It wasn't about north and south. It was about her place in the world, and Mrs. Warne's place—even Mrs. Horvath's place.

Women were in the great game, and Molly would stake her claim to it.

CHAPTER TWENTY

THE CHILDREN FAIRED substantially better than Webster by the time they reached Fredericksburg. In fairness, the mighty Potomac had not soaked them as they waded ashore. They were happy to talk and run, after so much time traveling in hushed voices. Once in the city, Mrs. Horvath bid Molly and Webster goodbye. She secured a stagecoach to the Confederate capital, hoping to find her husband. Before leaving, she invited Molly to pay a visit once she and Webster arrived in Richmond.

But Webster's condition eroded, halting their trip. Molly had never heard of rheumatism. She suspected Webster contracted pneumonia. But he refused any attempts to fetch a doctor. Molly rented them a hotel room and set about nursing him to health. Molly desired to make the capital and figure out a means to get the letters north. She tried to show him the letters, the ones Mrs. Horvath dropped. He looked at the stack of papers, refusing to even take hold of them.

"Women don't courier messages of importance."

"If you would just read—" Molly started. He cut her off.

"Not now! Once my business is concluded with Secretary Benjamin, I will look at your *discovery*." He said the final word with a twinge of cruelty.

His words stung. Molly had hoped for a partner. But he rolled over in bed and pulled the covers tight. She kept close hold on the letters, knowing they were her issue now. She would have to find a way herself.

It took almost a week before Webster's condition improved and they made Richmond. Once there, Molly contented herself with learning the city and setting into the work Mrs. Warne had assigned. She had no way to get the letters north without Webster's help. He knew the city and had the contacts. So she hid them in the space behind the painting over the mantle.

She passed her time calling on Mrs. Horvath, who acquainted Molly with the women's auxiliary. They met every day, sewing or baking—all for the soldiers. Molly was instantly ingratiated to the group through the introduction. She had braved the Potomac crossing. While frightening, Mrs. Horvath exaggerated the ordeal. It cemented Molly's place as a fine secessionist without question.

"Has your husband recovered?" Mrs. Horvath inquired.

Molly swore under her breath as she pricked another finger. She sucked the blood from the tiny hole the needle made, then smiled.

"Not yet. He is still taken with rheumatism."

Several women nodded, as if they understood. They meant to be nice, but Molly hated them for it—worthless creatures sitting in pretty dresses amusing themselves with gossip. She feared Webster had been right. These women knew nothing of use.

"Is there a way to get a letter north?" Molly asked. "I hadn't counted on the telegraph lines being cut to Baltimore or Washington."

Mrs. Horvath looked up, seemingly startled.

"Why, whatever for?" she asked. Her eyes narrowed as she studied Molly. "There is nothing worthwhile in the North, especially in Washington!"

"There won't be for long!" one of the other younger girls added.

She was Molly's age, with dark red hair. They would have matched, except Molly had kept hers dyed coal black. This girl had a boy she fancied in one of the local regiments. He had bought a commission as a lieutenant, though the girl worried it wasn't enough rank to get her invited to the formal balls that would follow once the South won.

"There is nothing in Washington but that ape," another chimed in. "Can you imagine a man like that thinking he would be President?"

Molly suppressed a laugh, forcing her eyes into her lap. None of them could imagine that she had smuggled Mr. Lincoln through Baltimore. Molly sucked at her finger once more.

"Why, Hattie? Why did you ask such a question, dear?" Mrs. Horvath asked.

She feigned disinterest, though it came out disingenuous. The older woman played distracted while she fixed a seam.

"I need to get word to my uncle. He is in Washington and feared leaving with us. I told him he should have left when we did, that we would find ourselves among friends in our dear South. I wish to tell him we are safe and he might make the journey."

"I see. Shouldn't he have come south already and enlisted?"

"Oh no," Molly countered. "He is well beyond the years of leading men in the field. He is no longer strong and full of youth like Mr. Horvath. But he is quite wealthy and could help far beyond sewing shirts or marching to battle."

She meant it as a dig at the women around the circle. None of them acknowledged it, though they certainly heard the part about his money.

"Wealthy? What type of business does he engage upon?" the red-headed girl asked.

"He made his money as a slaver," Molly said. "It was quite lucra-tive. Do you know of a way to get a message to him?"

Horvath smiled politely. She answered without looking up from her sewing.

"Well, dear, Mr. Horvath told me your husband is renowned as one of the most reliable couriers, although I hadn't entertained that as a respectable job—nor particularly lucrative. I guess that is why you are living in a hotel. You should have your uncle purchase suit-able accommodations."

She stressed the lucrative part, mimicking Molly. She meant it as insult, exposing Molly's social status. Especially when she referred to the Spotswood Hotel, where Molly stayed with Mr. Webster. It came as a constant game these women played—vying for position through their husband's status or wealth. Mr. Webster, as dashing and handsome as some might consider him, did nothing more than deliver the mail. Mrs. Horvath was married to a colonel, as she liked to remind everyone.

Molly smiled curtly. "I haven't bothered him with it on account of the rheumatism. I will have to ask him this evening." She paused, but her mischievous side could not resist taking a swipe in kind at Mrs. Horvath. "The Spotswood is not so poorly off, after all. They have done wonders with the place. It is quite . . ." She paused while searching the room, letting her eyes fall on the curtains, then the sofas. "It is quite modern. As for Mr. Webster, you are correct. His current vocation is not lucrative, but it is physically taxing. It keeps him well in shape. Which, I confess I rather like."

Several of the women giggled. Molly seeded her comment with the right amount of implication. She had met Colonel Horvath. While he could get his portly frame onto a horse, he was in no danger of marching with his troops. He held a staff position, drafting letters and attending dinner parties.

"Maybe you could try the *Richmond Underground*!" The red-haired girl injected herself into the conversation. Laughter filled the room.

"Am I missing a joke?" Molly asked.

"No, dear," Mrs. Horvath said. "There is an old spinster up on Church Hill. We believe she is partial to the Union—she and her mother visit the federal prisoners. They have often refused our invitations to come and sew for the soldiers—*our* soldiers."

"Ridiculous," Molly answered. "You should have the colonel arrest her."

"Oh, Miss Van Lew is quite harmless."

"Elizabeth Van Lew?" Molly asked. It escaped her lips in a moment of surprise.

"Do you know her?" Mrs. Horvath's suspicion had returned.

"No," Molly lied. *Miss Lizzie—her mother's friend.* For a whole summer Molly practically lived at the Van Lew estate. She scrambled to think of an explanation. "My husband mentioned her name once, I believe. He wanted me to mind myself if I happened upon her here. It's such an unusual name."

"Lizzie Van Lew here?" Mrs. Horvath coughed the words out as she laughed. The others joined her.

"She would not dignify us with her presence—her or her mother. They are a pair. Unionists should all be rounded up and sent to the land they so love. Her brother fled to Philadelphia, they say, to avoid enlisting. Shame of it."

Molly put her finger in her mouth again, even though the pinprick had long since healed. It masked her face.

"You can tell your husband not to worry," Mrs. Horvath said. "There is little fear Lizzie would make her presence known among the respectable women of Richmond. Stick with us, and you will be fine."

"Hard to believe that a woman would be permitted to run . . ." Molly paused. "What did you call it, the *Richmond Underground*?"

"Those are just rumors, dear. I don't think Miss Van Lew is that smart. She may have provided messages to her brother, but what could she really know?"

Mrs. Horvath appeared bored of the conversation, reaching the limit of her attention span. It sounded in her voice, revealing her mood, like when she had been suspicious of Molly's questions. *Had it passed? Did she play it well?*

This job was harder than she imagined—not the glamor that came to her daydreams. Mrs. Warne had trained her well. Molly drew confidence from that. But even though the older woman was strict, Molly thought on her often. *Would she approve?*

When the daylight drew long, Molly left as the others filtered from the group. The red-haired girl gave Molly a ride in her carriage to the hotel. The girl talked on and on about her lieutenant. She wanted Molly's advice, as they were closest in age. Relief filled Molly when they arrived at the Spotswood. She flung herself from the carriage, scarcely saying her thanks before slamming the door in the cold.

As Molly entered their small hotel room, she found Webster seated. He leafed through her letters. Mrs. Warne would have chastised her—she needed a better hiding place. Webster's hair plastered to his forehead, except in the flat spot on the back, which had ground into his pillow. His shirt was half-unbuttoned, revealing a broad chest. She hadn't lied to Mrs. Horvath—he was fit, and once bathed, passably handsome. She liked the deep gray in his eyes.

"Do you believe me now?" she asked, nodding toward the letters.

"Where have you been?"

"Out listening. I was at a sewing circle."

"Aiding the enemy?"

He mocked her. It caught her off-guard, piquing her anger.

"Well, one of us had better settle into work. You have done nothing but lie in bed."

Her words bit hard. He glanced up from the letters.

"It is my—"

"—your rheumatism, I know." She cut him off. "I waded through the same water, and I am able to function. I am beginning to think men are made from weaker stock. At least *you* are made from weaker stock!"

He laughed. It drew more anger. She hurled her shawl his direction. He batted it from the air.

"And what did you find out in your sewing circle?" he taunted. "What useless gossip did the Richmond elite have to offer?"

His tone lashed out as much as his words. He clearly held Molly in no esteem. It burned. She had thought so highly of him, never realizing his playful taunts when they first met were not meant in jest. He looked down upon her, as he did then.

"The Richmond Underground."

"The Richmond Underground?" he asked. "Another sewing circle? Or maybe this time you will quilt."

"It is a courier service—sending messages north."

She didn't know what it was, if it was anything at all. But he had pushed her anger until she allowed it to mix the rumors and spew them back as fact. With the Van Lews there was a chance something substantiated the rumors.

"And who runs it?"

"Elizabeth Van Lew."

He scoffed, laughing as he shook the letters in his hands.

"A woman is running a courier service?"

Molly started to say something more, to expand upon the rumor to spite him. But she stopped. If there was nothing to it, he would laugh at her. This wasn't the way to earn his respect.

He lowered his voice.

"I courier messages—important ones, from important people. That is why we are here—for my work. You are here to help me blend in, nothing more. You play the wife. That is your role. You make it seem I could not be what I truly am. You are part of the deception, part of the icing. Go to your sewing circles and your baking parties. But do not try to do my job."

Her fists clenched—her knuckles white. The room stank, like perspiration and stale air.

"If you think so little of me, then why did you save me?" she asked. Her eyes welled. They were hot, filled with rage and sadness. He was not the man she wished.

"I hoped you would be a distraction."

He didn't even look up from the letters.

"A distraction?"

"For Mrs. Warne. I have worked with Mr. Pinkerton for a long time, long before Mrs. Warne arrived. She has too much influence upon him."

"And I was to distract her?"

He looked up from the letters—placing them upon his lap in obvious annoyance. He didn't mean these words to hurt, instead, he told her the truth. A tear rolled down her cheek. She wiped it away, unconcerned if he saw it.

"Yes. I thought you might be a good project for her. Something she could work on. She needs more women to sleep with powerful men— the real use for your sex. You were already a whore with no prospects, so it seemed an interesting turn to get her interested in you. It would give those of us serious about this business a chance to get back to it."

"So, women have no place in your world?"

"I didn't say that." He sat up and his voice softened. "To get important secrets, you have to meet with important people. As a man I can find any number of means to meet those most important to our cause. When they trust me, they tell me their secrets and give me messages to deliver. How is a woman to meet these people? What excuse would you use? Do you think these men will sit and sew with you?"

"Obviously by seducing them and then lying on my back as they have their way with me." Molly's sarcasm forced her words to a clip.

"That is the best way I can think. You will not find state secrets in a sewing circle."

"Then you would have me whore my way through Richmond?" she responded. Her eyes welled again. She remembered the chain at her ankle, and the fat bodies that lifted her undergarments and spread her legs.

"Not as my wife."

"So I am here only to entertain you?"

She let the implication stand in her choice of words.

"No. I am already married—to a respectable woman."

Another tear ran down her face. She was nothing to this man. He was like the others only he didn't touch her. She let the tear roll off her face, hitting somewhere on her dress or the floor. He watched it, and took a deep breath.

"And that is why you can do little here. I told Mrs. Warne as much, but she didn't listen. I don't need a partner, but if I am to have one, then you are to secure my cover story and make me less suspicious—nothing more. Play the role of my wife. It should be easy."

"I found the letters," Molly snapped. "I did that, not you."

"You picked them up from the bottom of the boat. That was luck, not skill."

He studied her face. She wiped her cheeks and looked away.

"I am grateful for that luck, Molly. But it was still luck—like finding you in Baltimore. *Luck*."

Her anger faded, as if he had pulled the drain at the bottom of a washbasin. Sadness flowed in. It filled her until it felt heavy—overpowering. She had worked so hard to push down her feelings, to feel like a real woman. But he would never see her like that. *Maybe no one would.* Even Mrs. Warne, who had preached her value, saw her as an opportunity. *She was a whore who had gotten lucky.* If she was anything more, she would have proven it when she saw Cheeney in Montreal. She should have reached for the candlestick and beat his head until he stopped breathing.

Webster turned back to the letters, oblivious of the impact in his words. Or he knew and didn't care. Without looking up, he spoke again.

"I leave in the morning, to Chattanooga for a few days. I'll help an acquaintance negotiate a leather contract for the Army. It will make me more of those *important* friends and get me closer to Secretary Benjamin. I expect you to have figured your place when I return."

Molly said nothing. Her tears dried, leaving a streak she didn't bother to remove. She picked her shawl up from the floor and made her way to the door. In the doorway she paused to look back. Webster remained focused upon the letters.

She closed the door behind her without a sound.

CHAPTER TWENTY-ONE

MOLLY PASSED THE night by the fire in the hotel parlor. At some point one of the hotel concierges brought her a blanket and asked to escort her upstairs. She used Webster's sickness as an excuse—she could not sleep and needed fresh air. The man left her alone after bringing a pot of tea.

In the morning, with the sun streaming through the windows, she startled awake. She found herself surrounded by strangers. They drank their morning coffee and engaged in conversation. She pushed the blanket off. Folding it, she left it at her seat. The fire had long since died. As of yet, no one had rekindled the flames for the new day.

She opened her room door, turning the knob and easing her shoulder into it to make no sound. She worried she might wake Webster. The bed was empty. He had left, evidently early. His bag was gone, as were most of his clothes. Relieved, she opened the window and let the room air out. The cold heralded a refreshing start—a new day. She took a deep breath and held it. In the distance the James River snaked its way through the city. If not for the circumstances, she would have liked exploring Richmond.

The wind picked up and filled the room. She closed her eyes. Breathing deep, she let the cold sink into her body. Her back ached

from the high-back chair, and she longed to lie upon the bed—
though it needed fresh linens. As she went to close the window, a
gust of air pushed past her. It swirled about the room, kicking up
the curtains and scattering a stack of papers—*the letters.*

She slammed the window shut and scurried to find the loose papers. Most of them remained haphazardly stacked at the floor near
the bed. As Molly clutched them, her anger built.

"How could he be so stupid?" she yelled to the room.

Webster had left the letters lying about, as if they mattered
little. She clenched her jaw, and she threw the stack of papers at
the bed. Whoever wrote these letters intended them to find
Secretary Benjamin's hands. They mapped out Washington's
strengths and weaknesses. Even worse, they proved a spy hid
amongst the loyal Unionists in Washington. He would send more.
The traitor had to be rooted out. It went beyond these letters. It
went beyond Molly, or even Timothy Webster. If Webster wouldn't
act, she would.

She grabbed her coat and then shoved the letters into her
handbag. She wrapped her shawl over her coat and headed for the
door, slamming it behind her. The sound of the heavy door
crashing into the doorframe soothed her. It blunted her anger.
Her feet fell heavy upon the stairs as she rushed for the entrance
to the hotel.

"Mrs. Webster," the concierge called out as she crossed the lobby.

She stopped long enough to stare at him, projecting her frustration. He shrunk, sensing the mood with no further explanation.

"Mr. Webster seemed in much better spirits this morning. He
did not wish to wake you. Can I get you a carriage?"

"No." Molly let the word out in a clipped fashion. "I wish to
walk."

She turned to leave, but then thought better of it.

"Can you provide me directions to Church Hill?"

"Certainly, madam. I will write them down for you."

Molly waited as the concierge walked back to the front desk. Around her, the bustle of the day had commenced. Men in fine suits strolled with one another. Most wore the white cockade upon their lapels—no longer the hidden symbol of secession. They flaunted it. She caught whispers of their conversations. Some spoke of troops and supplies. They plotted who would get the next contracts. They talked of the Union and when General McClellan would invade. But most of all, they talked of profit. These were the men Webster meant—the important people.

"Mrs. Webster?"

Molly startled and turned. The concierge held a piece of paper. She took it and glanced over it.

"Is there a particular place you need to find? It is quite cold. I can get you a carriage."

"No, thank you. I simply need to visit a friend. I have what I need."

She smiled and turned from the man, surveying the lobby. The business of the Confederacy played out in front of her. Taking a room at the Spotswood was no accident. Webster chose it for the men who stayed there and the meetings they held. The secrets and gossip floated on the air waiting for anyone to pluck them out and commit them to memory—as easy as taking apples from the branch. But he was also right. She would never be able to walk up and talk to these men. Not in the open. Not in the manner he could. Women didn't conduct this business. They sat in sewing circles and gossiped. But she had a role beyond playing the doting wife—*she would get the letters north.*

Outside, the air offered a welcome respite. She quickened her pace, walking fast along the sidewalks and the cobbled street crossings. The city churned. Not so much as New York, but it came close to Washington. Factories grew from older buildings. Looms worked the cotton crop, turning raw fiber into uniforms for the summer fighting. Other places made the soles of shoes. War was lucrative—to the important men in the Spotswood.

At each crossing she glanced over her shoulder—a habit Mrs. Warne enforced. She sought out the faces, looking for anyone who might be following along with her. But the mix of people was too great. She gave up and focused on her route, looking to the paper and counting the intersections.

It took her the better part of an hour to make her way through the jumble of the city. She slowed to match those around her, not wishing to seem eager. She had heard that General Winder—the Provost Marshal in Richmond—employed a following of detectives. The general sounded much like Pinkerton. Winder rooted out dissent among the population—hidden Unionists in their midst.

The area surrounding the Van Lew estate contained other upscale houses. The rich and elite lived here. The factories were far below, and the quiet that fell upon her ears was as welcome as the cold air in her lungs. The serenity of her walk beat back the melancholy of the night before. She pushed the thought of Webster from her mind. Instead, she focused on the task at hand. It gave her purpose.

Arriving on Grace Street, she found the Van Lew estate. The house encompassed a whole city block. A generation earlier, Miss Van Lew's father built the estate on the back of a prosperous merchant empire. Twin sweeping staircases led to the front porch and vestibule. A low white fence traced the property line for the entire block—quite stately in its manner.

What if Miss Van Lew wasn't whom she thought?

Building her courage, she clutched her handbag and stepped forward. If she revealed herself, her true self, then this might go horribly wrong. Mrs. Warne taught her to never leave her role—to never be anyone other than Hattie Lawton—Hattie Webster. But that wouldn't work. Hattie Webster had no business with Elizabeth Van Lew. But Molly Ferguson did. She stepped forward and opened the front gate.

With each step of the curved staircase, her breath grew short and her heart pounded. Facing the door, she realized she should have thought of another story in case she needed the escape. All her hope rested with one plan.

She had barely knocked when the door opened. A servant stood before her. The woman was older than Molly, with skin as dark as the night sky. Molly had a vague recollection of her, but couldn't place the name—something simple, something close to hers. The woman wore a freshly pressed apron over a neat dress. Her hair was pulled back under a bonnet and she smiled broadly upon Molly. At once she put Molly at ease.

"May I help you, miss?"

"I . . ." Molly stopped. "I was looking for Miss Van Lew."

"I gathered as much, but there's two of 'em. Do you mean Miss Lizzie or her mother?"

The woman stepped to the side to let Molly into the entranceway. Molly stepped inside, looking about the place. It was as grand inside as it looked from the outside—as she remembered.

"Miss Lizzie," Molly answered.

It felt wrong to call Miss Van Lew by her first name, especially since Molly hadn't seen her in years. Even then, Molly had only been a young child.

"Can I tell her who is calling?"

"Yes," Molly said. Then she paused. She played it safe. "Hattie Webster."

The woman smiled and showed Molly to the sitting room.

"I'll let her know she has company. It might be a few minutes. She didn't tell no one here she was expecting visitors this morning."

The woman pulled the doors closed behind Molly, as if sealing her from the rest of the house. Tall bookshelves lined the room from floor to ceiling. This had been Miss Van Lew's father's office. When she was little, Molly had stared through the threshold and looked at the books in wonder. When she stepped into the room, her mother caught her and pulled her out. Miss Van Lew had turned it into a sitting room.

The door cracked open. Molly spun to catch sight of an older woman in the doorway. She spoke to someone down the corridor.

"Mary Jane, can you help me with the fire? I think I will sit and read a spell after our guest leaves."

Of course—Mary Jane!

Miss Van Lew opened the door wider. Mary Jane followed her into the room and went about fixing kindling in the fireplace.

"Mrs. Webster, to whatever do we owe this visit?" Miss Van Lew asked.

Nothing on her face showed she recognized Molly.

"I am so sorry to intrude unannounced, Miss Van Lew. I am newly arrived in Richmond, and I had reason to believe you might be able to help me with a sensitive matter."

Molly had no idea how she might broach the topic of her true self. *It might be better to hold back.* Perhaps she might secure a route north for the letters without endangering herself or Webster.

"A sensitive matter?" Miss Van Lew inquired.

The older woman wore a dark dress, buttoned to her neck. It gave her a stiff appearance, which did not soften with her body posture—upright and rigid. Her chiseled features were fine, with an almost birdlike delicacy. She clamped her hands together and studied Molly. It made Molly uneasy.

"Yes, you see, I am trying to get a letter to my uncle in Washington."

"Ahh . . . I see. Did I hear correctly, Mrs. Webster? You came across the Potomac River at night and in a storm with Mrs. Horvath?"

"Indeed," Molly answered.

She longed to sit in one of the chairs, the ones set near the fire. It felt awkward standing, as if Miss Van Lew did not want her to stay. Mary Jane had gotten a small flame started. She used a billow to stoke the little orange tongues until they caught the kindling.

"Well, that must have been harrowing for you. But I must confess I am at a loss as to why anyone would point you in my direction for such a request?"

As Miss Van Lew spoke, ringlets of hair bobbed at the side of her head. They distracted Molly.

"The other women thought you might have a means to deliver messages to your brother in Philadelphia. Perhaps you have a way to get my letter to Washington?"

"Well, Mrs. Webster, I do not have such means. And quite frankly, you can tell Mrs. Horvath that I am offended she sends her friends here with such requests."

Her tone was cold and stern. Molly was a schoolgirl once more, standing in front of the headmistress.

"I am sorry, Miss Van Lew, I did not mean any offense. Mrs. Horvath did not send me. I came of my own accord. I am truly desperate for help."

"I am certain you are," the older woman replied. She turned to watch Mary Jane put a fire screen in front of the now crackling flames. "Thank you, Mary Jane. That looks fine." Then turning to Molly she continued. "If it is intrigue you seek, please go elsewhere."

"Intrigue?" Molly asked.

Mary Jane watched the conversation. She studied Molly closely.

"Please excuse my bluntness. But you and Mrs. Horvath must think me daft to come here to elicit a confession like this. I am not a damned Unionist to be found and drummed out of the city. Because I choose not to spend my time with petty gossip while sewing and cooking in your little group does not make me a traitor. As good Christians, my mother and I attend the federal prisoners at Libby Prison so they are well treated. It is the same we would expect for our good Southern boys in their custody. I am tired of the insinuations of your friends. I think it is time you left."

Molly shrank under the tirade. She hadn't expected any of this. Her hope was a pleasant conversation, easing into the topic of getting mail north. But it was all ruined. Even Mary Jane stood behind Miss Van Lew and stared with fierce determination.

"I think you misunderstand, I—"

"I understand you perfectly. I am a Southern woman and loyal to my country."

Miss Van Lew walked to the window facing the front of the house and looked out. She beckoned Molly to join her. When Molly stood alongside the older woman, Miss Van Lew pointed to a man on the corner. He wore a dark suit, with a wide-brimmed hat. Long dark hair flowed from under his hat, and his mustache was well waxed in an impeccable curve above his lip. He watched the house.

"One of your friends?" Miss Van Lew asked.

"I've never seen him before."

The man hadn't been there when Molly entered the house. Mrs. Warne had trained her well, and she would have spotted this man.

"One of General Winder's pug-uglies, I suspect."

She must have seen the blank look on Molly's face.

"His detectives," Miss Van Lew clarified. "They hound us at times, ever since we started visiting the prison. Your ploy is too transparent, Mrs. Webster. In fact, it is offensive."

Molly shook her head. "I meant no disrespect."

"And I will take none," Miss Van Lew answered as she left the window and settled herself in front of the fire in one of the chairs. "We can pretend this conversation never happened. I trust you can find the door and let yourself out. And tell your friend and General Winder that we are simply old ladies doing Christian charity work—nothing more."

Molly nodded slowly. Miss Van Lew did not acknowledge her. Instead, the older woman stared toward the fire. Molly took a step toward the parlor door, then two. She stopped. She took a deep breath and turned. *This could be a mistake.*

"You don't remember me, do you?" Molly asked both women—looking at Mary Jane, then to the back of Miss Van Lew's head. "The last time I was here, I was much younger."

Miss Van Lew spun in the chair. She studied Molly's face. She still held no recognition.

"Of course, I dyed my hair to hide my true self. And I changed my name. I am not Hattie Lawton or Hattie Webster. You knew me as Molly Ferguson."

It was the first time she had said her name out loud in months. Her voice choked on her last name.

"My mother was—"

"Annabelle's girl?"

Miss Van Lew cut her off. This time she rose from her chair to look at Molly.

Molly nodded. She fought but could not hold back her tears. Her mother's name had not fallen upon her ears in so long. Miss Van Lew stepped forward. She searched Molly's face. Her expression eased from the resolute composure of earlier. She knew Molly.

"Dear child, how is this possible?"

She reached for Molly's hands and then placed a hand on Molly's cheek.

"I don't know how I didn't see your mother in you. Why did you not say so when you first arrived?"

"I couldn't," Molly answered. "I work for people—no one must know I am here. They cannot know me by any other name than Hattie Lawton or Mrs. Webster."

"I don't understand," Miss Van Lew answered. "What has happened to your parents? I have not heard from your mother in some time."

Molly buried her face in her hands and sobbed. It came back in horrifying flashes. The scent of the fire made it worse. Her legs gave out from under her, and Miss Van Lew and Mary Jane grabbed hold. They eased her into one of the chairs.

The story came out in bursts—all of it. Numbness overcame Molly, like she floated and looked down upon the scene. Her voice filled the room. She told every detail—the fire, her father pulled away by the horse, her mother clutching the medallion, the brothel, Baltimore, the trip to Albany, John Wilkes Booth, Mr. Cheeney, and even Colonel Norris. Molly pulled out the chain around her neck that still held Cheeney's medallion, Booth's locket, and the key. She showed the faint lines from the scars around her ankles. She told them of Mrs. Warne, and Pinkerton. Even Timothy Webster was not safe in the tale. The floodgates burst. She talked until her energy drained, leaning her head against the deep backrest of the chair.

Miss Van Lew sat across from her and listened. Even Mary Jane never left the room.

"I don't know where to start, Molly," Miss Van Lew said.

"Please," Molly answered. "No one can know who I am. I cannot put Mr. Webster in danger. My mother said . . ."

She didn't finish her thought. Her mother told her to trust Miss Van Lew. *Could she?* It was too late. She stood before them as nothing more than an empty shell.

"You can trust us." Miss Van Lew looked to Mary Jane, who nodded. "Earlier, I wasn't truthful with you either. We have been gathering secrets. Mary Jane does work in Jefferson Davis' house where she learns all manner of things. And we have many friends. The Negro community hears so much. No one suspects them. It is like how they treat us women. Men don't think we own the capacity or the physical endurance for this work. But we do!"

Molly opened her handbag. She brought forth the stack of letters.

"Someone in Washington is spying against the Union. Mrs. Horvath brought these with her when we crossed the river. Mrs. Warne needs to see these."

Miss Van Lew took the letters.

"We have a man leaving in a day or two. He is a servant, so no one suspects him. We have been sending messages north, but I had no good contact to ensure they find the right people."

"Mrs. Kate Warne," Molly said. "She stays at Willard's Hotel in Washington."

Molly pulled out the chain around her neck and unclipped Booth's locket. She handed it to Miss Van Lew.

"When your man gives the letters to Mrs. Warne, give her this as well. She will know the message comes from me."

Miss Van Lew took the locket. She placed it on top of the letters, then turned to Mary Jane.

"Let's prepare the guest room. Molly needs to stay the night. It will not do sending her out into the arms of General Winder's lap dog out there. Then we should call Robert. We must get him north with these letters at once!"

CHAPTER TWENTY-TWO

WEBSTER'S MOOD HAD much recovered upon his return from his business trip. The journey earned him an audience with Secretary Benjamin. Molly could not fathom the singular fascination with the one man. After Webster returned, they did not discuss the fight. And Molly did not offer any clue she had made contact with the Richmond Underground. It would only serve to anger him.

Molly was also in better spirits. In Miss Van Lew, she found a kindred spirit—a woman who had been overlooked and dismissed as a member of the fairer sex. And yet she had set incredible things in motion. The woman had a small informant network, though only occasional access to export messages. She had walked the city and sketched the defenses. She even visited the Union soldiers in the Libby Prison—mostly the officers. She tried to ferry their messages home to family. Many of their loved ones had no idea they were still alive.

Miss Lizzie, as Molly now called her with no discomfort, started her efforts as Christian charity. But at heart she was an adamant abolitionist. After her father died, she insisted on freeing the family servants. Most in Richmond used the term *servant* to whitewash the ugliness of slavery. But those in the Van Lew household served true to the word. Most remained with the Van Lews, accepting a small salary rather than flee north. As for Miss Lizzie, her resistance to the Confederacy cemented during her visits with the prisoners. Their conditions were appalling, she told Molly. She resolved to end the war and suffering as quickly as possible.

And the new friendship brought unexpected benefits. Miss Van Lew was good friends with Captain Atwater and his wife—a friendship cultivated behind closed doors. By all accounts, the Atwaters were good Confederate loyalists. Their inclinations toward secession, however, were another matter. They were a key part of Miss Lizzie's extended network. And that was how Mr. and Mrs. Webster found themselves invited to an elegant and important dinner party hosted by the captain and his wife.

The invitation arrived addressed to Mr. Webster at the Spotswood Hotel. When he announced to Molly they would attend the event, she feigned surprise. It was best to let him believe his efforts in cultivating high-level Confederate contacts had garnered the request. After all, her job consisted merely of posing as his wife.

Knowing the invitation would arrive, Molly had found an exquisite scarlet dress. Mrs. Warne would have disapproved. It held her in too much contrast with the other guests—they would remember her. But Molly needed it. When she emerged from behind the dressing screen in their hotel room, Webster looked away. But he stole glances when he thought she would not see. The dress was her celebration—her rebellion.

As they alighted from the carriage, Webster escorted her awkwardly. He held out a hand to hold her arm. When they entered the house, his hand lingered upon the small of her back longer than needed. She had power on him, after all. It gave her confidence, knowing she had leverage and needed nothing in return. But after checking their invitations at the door, Molly discovered she had not prepared herself for the guest list.

A long table filled the sitting room, covered with wineglasses and hors d'oeuvres. Though they had arrived late for the cocktail hour, a number of gentlemen were still engaged in quiet conversation. One matched what Molly had heard of Captain Atwater, standing tall in a Confederate naval uniform. He looked worn—torn between his native South and his convictions. Miss Van Lew was certain which way he would land if pushed. He spoke to another man, standing with his back toward Molly. At once she recognized him. It took her breath away—*Mason Cheeney*.

As he turned to see the late arrivals, his eyes were immediately drawn to her dress. Instantly, she regretted her choice. She wished to melt into the wallpaper. But it was too late. As his eyes rose from her breasts to her face, he recognized her. With an enormous smile he excused himself from Captain Atwater. He made his way toward Molly and Webster. Molly clutched an arm around Webster.

"Please do not let me fall," she whispered.

He didn't have time to respond. Cheeney was upon them. Instead, Webster placed an arm behind her and held tight.

"Why, Miss Lawton," Mr. Cheeney began, "I did not expect to see you in Richmond. I must chastise you for your lack of civility."

"It is good to see you once more, Mr. Cheeney. I'm afraid you have me at a loss over my manners. Did I commit some trespass?"

Molly forced her words. Without looking toward the table, she searched for the nearest candlestick—*an idle thought*.

"When last we met, I instructed you to see me immediately if you found yourself in Richmond. And here you turn up without having first stopped by my residence."

Molly forced a smile. "You are too kind. Please, let me introduce my husband, Mr. Timothy Webster."

Cheeney took Webster's hand, studying the younger man who stood a good inch or two taller.

"Mason Cheeney," he said to Webster. "I had the pleasure of meeting your wife in Montreal."

Cheeney stopped. His face grew pale, horrified. He checked around the room and lowered his voice.

"I do apologize," he said. "I am uncertain if I am supposed to say anything about our last meeting."

He meant when they last met in Montreal, and Molly had saved Colonel Norris from the British.

"It is quite all right, Mr. Cheeney," Molly replied. "Although, I appreciate your discretion. Mr. Webster well understands. He knows of my trip and the great importance of our work."

"Well then, sir, let me first congratulate you on a fine selection in a wife. And then let me offer my humblest thanks. Miss Lawton—pardon me, Mrs. Webster—provided our cause a most invaluable service."

"I am happy to hear it, Mr. Cheeney. She is indeed a most unusual companion."

Webster looked to Molly. He shouldn't know the Montreal story—she never told him. She was anxious to change the subject, and she pulled Webster closer.

"Unless I am mistaken, you were not married when I saw you last year."

"It is a recent development." Molly locked eyes with Webster, trying her best to play the happy newlywed. "We felt we should not wait as the war began. We need to enjoy the time we have."

"Well said, Mrs. Webster."

Behind them in the main dining room, a servant rang a small silver bell.

"That looks to be our call for dinner." Cheeney regarded the door. "I suppose I should gather my wife. She is among the women in the other parlor." He sounded less than happy at the mention of her.

"Please come and sit with me and Mrs. Cheeney. It will be a welcome distraction. I shall introduce you."

Molly gripped Webster tight, then let go. Cheeney started for the dining room. Molly had met Mrs. Cheeney, though it was a lifetime away—a lifetime passed in two years. Molly had only seen her at church or at a few select social events. Her son's courtship had not progressed to the point she had been invited to the Cheeney estate. Mostly it consisted of late-night walks, or trips to the swimming hole with friends. But women were more observant than men. Even with her dyed hair, her makeup, and years of age, Mrs. Cheeney might see through it.

"I don't know I can do this," Molly said. Her ears buzzed and her head swam. *How could she sit with this man? What if Mrs. Cheeney recognized her?*

"Yes, you can," Webster countered. His voice was firm, not cruel. "This is what we do. This is where I need you. Mr. Cheeney is one of the reasons we are here."

He looked down to her. His face was kind, not wicked like last time. She nodded. But Webster didn't know. *How could she tell him now?* They could both be in grave danger.

In the dining room, Cheeney maneuvered such that Molly sat immediately next to him. Mrs. Cheeney sat on the other side of the table with Webster—the worst placing possible. Mrs. Cheeney stared at the dress. She also studied Molly. When their eyes first met, Molly smiled politely. She drummed up a confidence she had no right to claim. Her palms turned clammy, and her stomach tugged. The older woman smiled back, nodding in Molly's direction as Mr. Cheeney made the introduction. Her eyes narrowed—enough that Molly caught it. Molly smiled again, and turned away. Webster distracted Mrs. Cheeney, touching her arm to gain her attention.

So much space separated Molly from Webster. Her confidence melted. Only scraps of the conversation across the table reached her. The seating came as an awkward manner of pairing the couples. A few hours ago she drew strength from not needing him, and now she longed for nothing more than to sit at his side.

Cheeney leaned close.

"Am I to understand that Mr. Webster undertakes the same business as you perform for our cause?"

His breath lingered, full with bourbon.

Molly smiled. "If he were, decorum would dictate that I would not tell you. And if he was not, I would leave you guessing."

Mr. Cheeney laughed, picking up his drink and downing another dram of whiskey. "Very well, I shall leave it to my imagination!"

Across the table, Webster had found his domain. He spoke to Mrs. Cheeney, though the woman appeared more suited to sit at home in front of the fire. She remained quiet and withdrawn. *Had she recognized Molly?* Molly's eyes drew her attention to the woman's makeup. She had applied it heavy upon her left side, her face darker in that spot. Occasionally, she reached up and touched her forehead near her eye. Molly had once heard her mother mention Mr. Cheeney's temper.

Mrs. Atwater sat on Webster's other arm. His manner darted between the women. He remained lighthearted—well versed at making small talk. He came at this vocation naturally. He figured people easily. Like how he changed his manner to match the two women. Even his body posture flowed. He moved with ease from the talkative Mrs. Atwater to the withdrawn Mrs. Cheeney.

Beside her, Mr. Cheeney reached for a goblet of wine and poured both their glasses full. Molly's stomach could not handle the liquor. If it mixed with the nerves, she would be a mess.

"In a way," he said, "you are partly responsible for the success that tomorrow will be."

"Tomorrow?" Molly asked.

"Yes. Do you remember my project?"

Molly tried something Mrs. Warne taught her—to elicit information without asking a question. She issued forth a slight insult to test his response.

"I remember you were going to the French for support. Of course, I thought it to be a most odd selection in allies."

"That is the beauty of it!" Cheeney said.

He took a swig of wine and reached for his fork.

"We cannot rely upon the British to save us. We must make new friends in Europe, backed by regular shipments of cotton."

Molly stole glances at Mrs. Cheeney across the table. Several times the other woman matched Molly's stare, always forcing Molly to glance away. It made her feel guilty. And with it her heart beat faster, as if she might be exposed. Webster remained blissfully unaware. His smile filled him with an approachable manner. Molly wished he treated her like this.

In a sense, her nerves held a certain relief. They focused her on the woman across the table, letting her forget the monster at her side. *Don't think of Salvation Acres—or the rope at his neck.* She focused on breathing.

"New friends in Europe would imply you have a means to deliver cotton?" Molly asked Cheeney. "Will you swim the cotton across, then? Or bribe the ship captains in the Union blockade?"

Mr. Cheeney nodded vigorously. He had taken a bite of roast quail. The servants had brought out dinner plates, and were passing them around one guest at a time. Cheeney didn't wait for anyone else. He started on his food, oblivious that not everyone had been served. For the first time Molly noticed the dark hands of the women serving them. They performed a dance, bringing food from the kitchen and placing it in front of each guest before fluttering away without notice—almost choreographed.

"Your project?" Molly inquired. "I was made to understand you were a most masterful naval architect. I suppose if anyone built a ship to outrun the blockade, you would be the man to design it." She had moved to flattery—another means of elicitation.

He coughed as he tried to finish his food.

"You will get not a word from me." Then he leaned close. "We will not need to outrun the blockade if there is no blockade!"

Molly turned in her chair to face him. She had never been this close to the man, not even back in New Orleans. His face flushed with the alcohol, and little beads of sweat built upon his brow. They did not yet break free and streak toward his cheeks.

"A warship then?" she pressed.

Cheeney would only smile, then took more food.

"Well, I wish you the utmost luck in the endeavor. I hear the city is soon to ration items like sugar or coffee. I should hate to think of a morning without coffee."

"We shall know more tomorrow!" Cheeney announced. "If our trials go well, then the blockade will never see our attack. They will be at the bottom of the ocean trying to figure out the manner of our deception."

He leaned close and lowered his voice.

"A warship no one has ever seen the likes of before."

"Ships never impressed me much," Molly countered. "If you've seen one, they all look alike."

"On this evening, madam, you can offer no insult that I may take as offense! That is how great our trials will be tomorrow. They will herald the end of the war! You will long remember the name Mason Cheeney!"

Molly had only poked her food to this point. But at the mention of his name, of his declaration, something washed over her. A nearby candle blew out. The whiffs of smoke floated toward her. One of the servants leaned over and re-lit the flame. It danced as the air around it fluttered past. She fingered the knife at the side of her plate. Holding it, she allowed her thumb to probe the edge—so sharp it tugged at the ridges of her thumbprint. Cheeney leaned over his plate, heaving food into his mouth. She could so easily plunge the blade into his chest. The little flame of the candle danced.

On the other side of the candle, Webster stared back. He must have caught her ominous look. She met his eyes. He glanced to her hand. Her knuckles were white upon the handle, and a little trickle of blood came from her thumb. He shook his head ever so slightly. *Did he know?*

Molly tore her eyes from the flame and let the knife hit the table. It chattered on the side of her fine china plate and struck the other silverware. A few guests looked up. Cheeney stopped eating and glanced at her.

"Are you all right?" he asked.

"I am fine, thank you," Molly answered.

She plunged her hand into the napkin at her lap, binding the cut at her thumb.

The rest of dinner passed in a blur. There was a second course, though Molly barely ate. Her nerves consumed her. Luckily, Mrs. Cheeney gave no further sign of recognition. The servants brought dessert—a fine pineapple custard. And then after all had finished, the men excused themselves to smoke cigars and enjoy brandy. The women waited in the front sitting room. The large table was clear of the hors d'oeuvres and wineglasses.

Molly scanned the room. Mrs. Cheeney stood near the door. Her arms crossed her chest, as if she were cold. Molly walked up to her. *Was she recognized? She had to know.*

"I am sorry we did not get more time to talk," Molly said. "It appeared that my husband kept you well entertained. I hope he did not impose himself too much."

Mrs. Cheeney looked at her, but her lips remained taught. She forced a smile. The effort strained her face. It looked pained.

"Are you all right?" Molly pressed.

"I am fine, thank you. It has been a long week with Mr. Cheeney working toward his big day tomorrow. I am feeling drained."

Her eyes narrowed, as she studied Molly.

"Have you ever been to New Orleans?" Mrs. Cheeney asked.

"No," Molly said. She cleared her throat. "I haven't had the pleasure. I split my time between Atlanta and Baltimore."

"You look . . ." Mrs. Cheeney paused. "I find you familiar."

Molly forced a smile as Mrs. Cheeney had done earlier. She was certain her face looked as pained as the older woman's had been.

"I am often told I appear to be someone I am not. When we first met, even Mr. Webster mistook me for someone different. Perhaps I need to style my hair in another manner."

Molly desperately wished to change the subject, to leave something else on the other woman's mind before she left for the night.

"Can I ask what happened?"

The place on Mrs. Cheeney's face still bothered the older woman, where the makeup covered her bruising. It appeared fresh.

"An accident. I foolishly ran down the kitchen stairs with my good shoes. They are not meant for the old wood flooring."

Mrs. Cheeney looked away and gathered her shawl about her shoulders. Molly did not press further. The question made her uncomfortable. The impression of a hand floated beneath the makeup, clear to see this late in the evening as the powder faded.

"I did not mean to pry." Molly's hand found the other woman's arm. "Mr. Webster—" She stopped herself without saying anything further. "I understand."

Mrs. Cheeney glanced toward her. Their eyes met. Molly sensed something, some common bond. The older woman longed for kinship. But she broke the stare and looked away.

"I think I will venture home by myself. Mr. Cheeney may be some time."

"Of course," Molly said. "I hope to see you again soon."

Mrs. Cheeney smiled, that same thin smile. She made her way for the door. A servant met her and escorted her down the hallway. Cold air squeezed into the room as the main door opened and shut. It had barely closed when a hand touched her shoulder, startling Molly. Mrs. Atwater stood close behind.

"I am glad you and your husband could make it this evening," Mrs. Atwater began. "I understand we have a common friend."

"Yes," Molly said. "She suggested we meet. So I was most thankful for the invitation."

"How long have you known Lizzie?"

"For as long as I can remember." Molly paused. Uncertain of how much she should reveal. "Miss Lizzie was engaged to my uncle. He passed before I was born."

"I am so sorry to hear that," Mrs. Atwater said.

"I never knew him. But Miss Lizzie and my mother remained friends. I visited once or twice when I was a girl."

Suddenly Molly realized what she had revealed could destroy her identity as Mrs. Webster. She had eaten little at dinner but downed at least two glasses of wine. They had set no water upon the table. At once Mrs. Atwater understood.

"You are among friends. I will tell no one. Miss Lizzie explained the sensitivity of your friendship."

Molly nodded. "Thank you."

"You will join us tomorrow?" Mrs. Atwater asked.

"Join you?" Molly had heard nothing of a further invitation.

"For the launch. My husband will allow a small group to attend. Please bring Mr. Webster. You will both be amazed in what you witness." She lowered her voice. "It is important."

"The warship?" Molly asked. She matched the whisper of Mrs. Atwater's voice.

"I would show you the plans, but the men are in the study. I think seeing it yourself would be better."

"Mr. Cheeney appeared confident in it."

Mrs. Atwater leaned forward and grabbed hold of Molly's arm. The woman's face dropped any pretense of disguise. Gone was the easy manner of the hostess. True concern plagued her.

"We must warn the Union. It will change the war."

CHAPTER TWENTY-THREE

THE BANKS OF the James River were chilly, especially so early in the morning. Molly sat with the Atwaters—Webster at her side. He had not managed to garner an invitation from the men of the previous night's party. His melancholy returned by the time they returned to the hotel. It plagued him so much that it became hard for Molly to convince him to attend. It wasn't until she said they were joining Captain Atwater and his wife that he perked up. At once he understood what it meant. They would see the first trials of the new warship.

They sat in a reviewing stand, facing the river. Up front, rows of naval officers and other Confederate officials sat upon hastily built wooden seats. Most brought their wives to see the spectacle. Mr. and Mrs. Cheeney sat near the front. The captain insisted on sitting at the back of the stands where they could barely hear a junior officer narrate the action—his uniform, pressed and starched. He looked so young.

The only thing in view upon the water was a single barge. It bobbed with the light current, anchored in place. The boat appeared old. Captain Atwater kept calling it the *"target."* Molly strained her view in all directions to see the new warship that Cheeney had designed.

Captain Atwater's leg bounced against the seat. Twice his wife leaned over and placed a hand upon his knee to silence his nerves. While the government commissioned Cheeney to design the boat, Captain Atwater managed the project. His career was on the line— maybe more so than Cheeney's reputation.

"From which direction will the boat come?" Molly asked.

She had leaned close to Mrs. Atwater, as much for shelter from the wind as to make the older woman hear her. Without taking his eyes from the water, Captain Atwater answered.

"It's already here."

Molly turned back to the river. Only the barge floated upon the water. Still tugging at the chains that held it fast.

"You mean the barge?" Molly asked.

Captain Atwater pointed to the water in front of the barge.

"Do you see the float?"

A green ring, big enough to hold two men inside, floated upon the water. Molly had noticed it earlier but paid it no mind.

"I do."

"The boat is below the float."

Webster looked to her. He didn't understand either.

"How do you mean?" Molly asked.

"The ship floats below the waves. The only portion you can see from the surface is the float."

"Under the water?" Webster was confused.

"Watch the float," the captain answered.

Molly focused upon the green ring. It moved, or at least it appeared to move. The waves made it hard to tell. Then it definitely closed in upon the barge, getting closer with each passing moment. Mrs. Atwater leaned close.

"I wouldn't believe it either, if I hadn't seen it. We toured the Tredegar Ironworks last week, and John showed me the ship. It looked like a giant bumblebee, with iron on the outside. The floatation collar, the green ring—it's attached to a hose. Two men work a handle and gear, which runs a propeller. Then a third man exits the ship with another hose. He swims to the barge, plants an explosive with a fuse, and then they sail away."

Captain Atwater handed a set of field glasses across the women to Webster. He focused them and watched.

"What's happening?" he asked.

"They're fixing the explosives."

"From the boat?"

"This is where the diver swims on alone," Atwater answered. "We won't see much for a few minutes. Watch for the flotation collar to move. That way we know they recovered the diver and are heading back."

A few minutes later the green float headed back toward the shore. It skimmed the surface, bouncing upon the waves as the river flowed between the barge and the shore. When it neared land, a mighty explosion tore through the barge. Molly startled. She had forgotten about the barge. Webster jumped, too. He gripped her hand so tight she worried he might break her fingers. She liked the feel of it. When they looked at one another, he leaned close. Then his grip eased, and he stood.

"My God," he muttered. "It's not a trick?" He turned to Captain Atwater.

"Indeed, not," the captain answered. "Come, they'll need help recovering the vessel. You can see it up close."

He let go of Molly's hand, but she grabbed his coat and pulled him near.

"The water will be cold—remember your rheumatism."

He smiled, caught up in the moment. His attention fixated upon the shore of the river. The first glimpse of the mysterious underwater boat was coming into view. It broke the surface of the water. He leaned down and placed a hand along Molly's cheek.

"I'll be fine."

Then he leaned close, as if to kiss her. As he whispered in her ear, his lips brushed against her cheek and his breath lingered. It gave her goose bumps.

"I need to see this up close. Don't fret."

He followed Captain Atwater toward the water's edge. They walked down the stands. Then they dashed toward the others who were knee deep in the water and wrestling with the rope lines. More of the vessel appeared upon the surface of the water.

"He seems a nice man," Mrs. Atwater offered.

"Yes, I suppose."

Molly still watched the men. Webster was in the water, helping to pull the vessel to the rickety dock. It had been fashioned near the shore for the test. Mrs. Atwater moved closer, ensuring no one overheard.

"But he is not your husband?"

Molly shook her head. She diverted her attention from the mysterious warship and glanced at Mrs. Atwater.

"He would rather I was not in Richmond," Molly said.

"I don't think that's true. I saw how he looked at you last night."

"That was the dress," Molly said.

"I think not," Mrs. Atwater answered. "Thomas used to look at me that way. Sometimes he still does, but I am older. We are both older, I suppose."

Mrs. Atwater glanced to the men, still struggling with the ship. She held a whimsical look, as if she dreamed of times gone past. Then she shook herself from those thoughts, and once again faced Molly.

"You will join us tonight?" she asked.

"Tonight?" Once more Molly had not heard of any plans.

"Of course, there will be a tremendous celebration at the Cheeney estate. You can meet the intrepid sailors who attacked that innocent barge." Mrs. Atwater's sarcasm filled the space between them.

"I don't know," Molly said. *Did Mrs. Cheeney recognize her?*

"You can come with us. And I shall point out Mr. Webster's inclinations. He is certain to show his true self, especially if you have a similar dress."

Molly forced the thought from her mind.

"Do you know what happened to her?" Molly asked. She nodded in the general direction of Mrs. Cheeney. "She masked a large bruise upon her face last night."

"We hear the rumors. Mr. Cheeney has a mean streak when under the influence of the liquor. She is not a bad woman. Rather timid, but nonetheless respectable."

"That is a pity."

"It is," Mrs. Atwater said. "I am lucky to have a gentle soul in my husband. And I like Mr. Webster." She let her voice trail off with a devilish intonation.

"It's not like that," Molly said.

Webster still worked on the ship. He helped the others lash it to the dock. Standing in waist deep water, he shook hands with everyone he could find. Then he helped hoist the sailors from the ship onto the shoulders of several men. Despite the cold, and the likely freezing water, spirits were high. Webster played into the scene. He pulled himself out of the water as he stuck his head inside the hatch of the ship.

"If you insist," Mrs. Atwater said. "But I am telling you, that man fancies you."

Maybe Mrs. Atwater saw something she didn't, or the older woman read some sign from Molly. He made her feel so small. Yet, she craved his acceptance.

Webster trudged up the short hill along the riverbank and joined the two women, clutching Molly as he stopped. His arm was firm around her waist, and he leaned on her. The cold from his wet clothes pushed through her dress.

"What do you think of our ship?" Mrs. Atwater asked.

"I wouldn't have believed it without seeing for myself," Webster said. "Whoever would believe a ship could sail beneath the water?"

"They plan on attacking the blockade soon." She lowered her voice and looked around before saying anything else. "If they do that, the South will get anything they want from Europe—even rifles for cotton. Do you think you can get word North?"

"We will find a way." Webster looked directly at Molly, a faint smile coming from his blue lips. "Even if we have to take word ourselves."

Molly's face flushed. His hand tightened around her waist.

"You cannot fail," Mrs. Atwater said. "This ship will change the war."

CHAPTER TWENTY-FOUR

THE CELEBRATION AT the Cheeney estate began early in the afternoon. Unlike the Atwater party from the previous night, this gathering needed no invitation. Of course, only those in the know were the wiser about the festivities. Even so, a small crowd packed into the elegant Cheeney estate. The house was the equal of Miss Lizzie's grand house, finely decorated with a mix of polished silver and well-oiled mahogany.

The Cheeney servants tried to keep pace with the food. They placed it upon the great dining room table. Those who were hungry took plates and ate anywhere they found a seat. The discarded dishes sat no more than a few moments before the household staff ushered them down the stairs and into the kitchen. They were soon cleaned and recycled. Molly might have been the only one who watched the servants. No one paid them any attention, other than to grab one as they passed and make demands for more food, or silverware.

Molly studied their faces. They were tired. But they spoke to one another in their own language—a language of furtive glances and veiled smiles that were quickly tucked away. They mocked the fat old men who became more intoxicated by the minute. They mimicked the pretentious women who vied for social status next to their husbands. The servants saw everything. Nothing that happened in the household escaped their grasp.

Webster was in his element once more. He danced around the room, always with a bottle in his hands. He proposed toasts and filled glasses. He engaged in raucous laughter and fierce debate. But never did the bottle in his hands touch his lips. He made certain everyone else held a full glass. Alcohol worked wonders in loosening secrets.

And it was the perfect crowd to work. The cream of Richmond society showed up to celebrate. It looked like every general in the Army had made his way to the party. The Confederate cabinet stood among them—even Secretary Benjamin. Webster worked from man to man, filling their glasses and plying his trade.

For her part, Molly found a corner. She had worried that, in attending, Mrs. Cheeney might start to put the pieces together. Her husband remained oblivious. Molly feared seeing him up close again. Twice she had failed. She could not kill on purpose. Not like she planned. But she buoyed herself in the thought of knowing the house and where he lived. It might be useful in the future.

She walked down the hall, getting air and space from the noise. Exquisite artwork hung upon the walls, clad in gold gilded frames. Gas lamps hissed, the most modern lighting Molly had witnessed outside of the hotel in New York. The Cheeneys spared no expense upon the decoration of their Richmond house. As she made her way deeper down the corridor, she paused at one of the paintings. Her hand clasped her mouth—a rendition of Salvation Acres. *She knew this painting.*

Her mother had known the artist and commissioned the work. Long rows of old-growth southern oaks formed a canopied path leading to the estate. Spanish moss decorated the branches, hanging from the limbs. The air around her felt thick and laden with moisture, as it would have back home. Her feet knew the path, running barefoot, chased by Isabelle. Her fists clenched. She would kill Cheeney here, in front of everyone. She needed a weapon—a knife, or a gun. *She needed a gun.* That would make the most noise and draw in witnesses to see what she had done. Then she would turn it on Secretary Benjamin, on the cabinet, on anyone in uniform. Her mind drifted to the fantasy, letting it play out as revenge. They stole this painting.

"Do you like it?"

Molly spun, startled and angry all at once. Her jaw clenched, and her fists formed tight. She dropped her handbag as she turned. Mrs. Cheeney stood behind her.

"It is our property in New Orleans. But sadly, the house burned."

The breath sucked out of Molly. *Her property?*

"I like the trees," Mrs. Cheeney continued. "The air is much cleaner there. I might soon leave Richmond and go back to New Orleans."

Mrs. Cheeney studied Molly. The woman was suspicious. Molly let her hands ease, her fists melting away. She leaned down and picked up her handbag.

"You startled me."

"I am so sorry." The apology rang hollow. "You said you have never been to New Orleans?"

Molly shook her head. Mrs. Cheeney stepped next to Molly, looping their arms together and spinning her to face the painting.

"It is lovely. We will re-build the house—the land is remarkable. I dread winters this far north."

"What happened to the house?" Molly asked.

She calmed her voice, to make the question passable. In truth, she forced it. The scent of smoke lingered—something she would never forget. The house in the painting caught fire. Grotesque flickering shadows cast on the old-growth oak trees with the Spanish moss. She clenched her free hand into a fist once more.

"It is a sad story," Mrs. Cheeney answered. "The man who owned it came upon hard times. He gambled away his fortunes. Mr.

Cheeney lent him a substantial sum, but he failed to pay. He even refused to sell his slaves to cover the debt. When Mason confronted him, the gentleman burned the estate. Mason tried to salvage the house, but to no avail. We will rebuild, and style it even grander than before. We plan to retire there, after the war, and when the property can sustain an income once more."

Molly tightened her jaw and breathed deep. Perhaps Mrs. Cheeney tested her—wanted Molly to break, to expose both her and Mr. Webster. Cheeney's men slashed Isabelle's throat as she watched. Her father had been dragged off by a horse. And she had found her mother the next morning. Molly forced the images from her thoughts. Patience was her better option.

"You intend to head south soon, then?" Molly asked.

"Perhaps," Mrs. Cheeney answered. "My son may be furloughed long enough to escort me to New Orleans. He leads a company of cavalry, but Mason is trying to have him assigned in Richmond. After today, I imagine Mr. Cheeney's prospects for such a request will be more readily received."

Again, Molly found herself gasping for breath. *Jonathon Cheeney would arrive soon?* He would recognize her, even if his parents did not. Molly had to leave. Her presence endangered Webster. It would ruin the whole operation. Her stomach heaved, though she remained upon her feet.

"I hope for your sake he is successful," Molly said. Then she turned to Mrs. Cheeney and smiled, forcing it with all her strength. "I see your cheek is healing."

"Yes." Mrs. Cheeney touched her face, then her mouth. For the first time, Molly noticed the split along her lower lip. She had met the end of Mr. Cheeney's temper once again.

"Perhaps the weather in New Orleans will help with those prospects."

"I get so dizzy here," Mrs. Cheeney confessed. Her confidence faded. She covered the lie, but her voice deceived her. So quickly she transformed from antagonist to victim—her weakness.

"I am certain a break from Richmond would help," Molly said. "Mr. Cheeney seems much stressed with his work."

"As he has a right to," Mrs. Cheeney answered. Her words formed clipped and sharp. She averted Molly's gaze.

"It is important work," Molly confirmed. "All the same, such stress should not affect the family. I am certain some time away to recuperate will help you both. I find I am often refreshed after some time without my husband. Men such as ours, who hold faith with a singular purpose, come with a high-price. We are meant to bear that price, I suppose."

Mrs. Cheeney dropped Molly's arm and faced the younger woman. Her face changed. Gone was the scheming look that earlier held it hostage. The lines around her eyes softened. Her eyes dropped to the floor.

"No one else ever mentions it. I know they see. I know they talk about me. But you're the only one who says anything. He was never like this when we first met. So much has changed."

Molly took her hand. The woman looked up. Her eyes welled, but they did not break. She forced a thin smile. It faded.

"Thank you," she said.

Then she dropped Molly's hand. Stepping around her, she walked down the corridor away from the party. Mrs. Cheeney disappeared past the gas lamps. Her footsteps echoed as she found some back staircase. The painting once more filled Molly's heart. It ached. She couldn't bear to look at it any longer.

Back in the sitting room, the party had thinned. Only the dedicated remained. Webster stood with Mr. Cheeney and Secretary Benjamin. They were engaged in a heated discussion. Molly hoped to convince Webster to leave. As she approached, he glanced toward her. Her mood must have cast upon her face.

"Not much longer, my love," he said. "This is Secretary Benjamin, and of course you know the hero of the hour, Mr. Cheeney."

He played to Cheeney's ego, especially in front of the secretary. The older man nodded, but Cheeney could not help himself.

"Mrs. Webster is in the employ of our mutual friend, Colonel William Norris," Cheeney announced. "She provided an invaluable service to our cause just this past year. I will be forever indebted."

Molly did not wish to correct his mistaken impression. Of course, he had first met her with Colonel Norris, so he assumed they worked together. It blurred her past while further strengthening her credibility.

"I shall have to hear the story," the secretary replied.

He studied Molly, perhaps skeptical on what role she might have played. Molly reached out and placed an arm around Webster, as if to steady herself. He understood.

"I don't want to cut-off Mr. Cheeney's earlier topic," Webster said. "I believe he was about to enlighten us on how to win the war."

"Indeed," the secretary replied. "Please continue Mason, that is, if it can be told in mixed company."

"Yes, yes," Mr. Cheeney said. The odor of bourbon floated across the space to Molly. The man could scarcely stand, and his words slurred at their edges.

"I was telling them how we win Europe," Cheeney explained looking at Molly.

"With your blockade-breaking ship," Molly answered. Flattery would further hook him.

"That's only the beginning. We will soon get our cotton to Europe, but we still require their backing. We need France to recognize the Confederate government. It will line up credit for our cause, gain us recognition, and force an end to the war if we need intervention."

"I hope you're not implying we need French or British troops to win this war," Secretary Benjamin responded. "Need I remind you the year we have had upon the battlefield? The Southern soldier is unmatched!"

The secretary believed his own propaganda—fitting for a man who relied upon it.

Cheeney shook his head. "I'm being realistic. I am the most ardent supporter of our troops. But I see the losses. We win battles, but we have fewer men to lose. That is simple math."

"I take your point," the secretary conceded. "What would you do next?"

Cheeney looked around, seeing who else might be in earshot. Then he lowered his voice.

"We end slavery."

Webster's body tensed under Molly's arm. The secretary, to his credit, showed no outward sign of his thoughts.

"Are we not engaged in this conflict to preserve the institution of slavery? You would kill the very thing we fight for?" the secretary asked.

"We fight to save the South—to no longer be at the whims of the Union. I would rather win the war and end slavery than lose the war and have its end imposed upon us."

Molly's face flushed. She brushed her hair back from her forehead, her focus trained on Cheeney.

"So, it is inevitable?" Secretary Benjamin asked. He entertained the notion, perhaps for no other reason than amusement.

"Yes. The North will reach the same conclusion. And they will free any captured slaves and outlaw the practice. Then Europe will back them instead of us. Our fight becomes futile in such a case.

However, if we beat Lincoln to the act, then we win Europe and isolate the Union. Again, Mr. Secretary, it is simple math."

Secretary Benjamin nodded. His face formed an amused look, processing such an unusual proposition.

"And what then would we do with the throngs of liberated Negroes? How would we stop them from burning and pillaging? They would be so grateful for their freedom? And how would we get our cotton crops to market? It seems a serious flaw to win your European friends, Mason."

Cheeney smiled. "That's the best part. We pay them."

Molly clutched at Webster. He looked down to her, reacting to the change in her posture.

"You're too much, Mason," Webster blurted out, interrupting the conversation.

"I've seen it work," Cheeney countered. "It is possible."

"There was a plantation in New Orleans. The estate master there freed his stock of slaves. He didn't need them all, but those he kept, he paid a wage. They stayed, and they out produced any plantation for several counties."

The look upon Secretary Benjamin's face changed—no longer idle speculation. The man was drawn in.

"And what happened to this plantation?" the secretary asked.

"Well, that is another matter," Cheeney said. "The man was a fool. He became soft for the darker flesh—even took one as a mistress, I am told. Once his mind was affected, he went upon a splurge and bought all the slaves he could, never mindful of the profits. He gambled in hopes to win it back, and came to me for a large sum of money. Mind you, I didn't know this was happening until I took control of the property to cover his loans. He would still owe me money today, if he had not hung himself. Patrick Ferguson—ever the fool."

Molly's knees buckled. Her grip remained tight on Webster, and he caught her in time. Both Cheeney and Secretary Benjamin broke their discussion. They watched as Webster guided Molly to a nearby chair. Webster leaned close.

"I know, I know," he whispered to her. "We'll leave. Let me get our coats."

Webster turned to the two men who watched the commotion.

"I'm afraid you made the punch too strong, Mason!" Webster tried to cover for Molly.

He hurried from the room, likely searching for their winter garments. He needn't have worried. Cheeney nodded, forgetting all about Molly, and went back to his impassioned conversation. Molly strained to hear.

"The Union will end slavery as we have done, Mr. Secretary. It will appear they do it to mimic our motives. And with the extra Negroes, we send them North. Once there, they will fight for jobs with the Catholics, and whoever else has immigrated to the Union. They will collapse the economy for us."

The secretary stood quiet. He raised his hand to his chin.

"It is a most crazy, yet interesting idea, Mason."

Webster walked back into the room, holding their coats. He stopped by the two men, and bid his goodbye, once more congratulating Webster for the great success of the day. Then he held out a hand to Molly.

"I am fine," she said. "I need some air."

"As do I. We shall walk home."

"Really?" Molly questioned. "But you were soaked today, and I wish not to nurse you to health once more."

"I'll be fine," he insisted. "And I wish some time with you. There are things I need to say."

His face revealed none of what he meant. The butterflies in her stomach appeared again. He helped her put her coat on and wrap the shawl around her shoulders. Then with an arm around her shoulder, he escorted her to the door.

As they entered the foyer, a young girl—a servant—held the front door. Molly almost passed her without notice. But something about how the girl stared caught Molly's attention. Molly turned. There was no mistaking it. The girl recognized her, too. Their eyes met, shocked to see one another. Webster's firm arm at Molly's back kept her moving. They stepped through the door, and down the stairs to the sidewalk. The girl stood in the doorway.

Jeanine—Isabelle's sister.

CHAPTER TWENTY-FIVE

WEBSTER SET THE pace—purposeful yet unhurried. Molly walked at his side, a quarter step behind. His body sheltered what wind blew down the boulevard.

"Are you all right?" he asked.

Molly's thoughts fixated upon the girl at the Cheeney estate. It rattled her. The Cheeneys' had stolen more than the painting. *How many others had been forced back into slavery?* Likely every last one of the plantation workers. She hadn't thought much on their plight. They had their papers, but those were easily fixed with a match or fireplace. Her stomach pitched.

"I am fine," she lied. Her thoughts lingered upon Jeanine. The name was the last thing Isabelle had said before the knife drew across her neck and tore at her flesh. Molly shuddered.

"Did something upset you?"

She hadn't told him about the Cheeneys, and in truth she had no desire to broach the topic. In all regards, he had a right to know. It affected him, or it might. If her cover unraveled then they were both in danger. She didn't know where to start, and she didn't have the energy to attempt the endeavor.

"It was a long day," she lied. "I am tired."

They walked in silence. Molly's thoughts tossed between Jeanine, the painting, the Cheeneys, and Miss Lizzie. She had forgotten Webster's words before they left. He finally broke the quiet.

"I wish to apologize."

His confession pulled her from the swirling memories. The moon held high, casting a pale glow upon his face.

"I understand you are responsible for setting all this in motion," he said.

"All of what?" Molly asked.

He looked at her briefly, then slowed his pace. His hands met behind his back as he leaned forward. His shoes clicked upon the pavement with each step.

"The invitation to the Atwaters' dinner party, then the demonstration this morning. You made that happen for us. It was not of my doing. Captain Atwater explained that his wife met you through a friend. She garnered our invitation."

Molly nodded. "I should have said something—I didn't want to upset you further."

"Before I left for that trip south, I was harsh in my words. I should not have taken them out on you in that manner. My conflict with Mrs. Warne is my own. And then I was still sick and upset my rheumatism had claimed me at such an important time."

"It is no bother," Molly replied. Secretly, she loved the apology. She pondered if she had need to tell him of Miss Lizzie and her network.

"It was not fair. You have been a true companion. Mrs. Warne said you were ready for this assignment, though I fought against it. I wanted no company. But I take great comfort from you."

Guilt washed over her. He did not know of her tie to the Cheeneys. She had to tell him. Her fingers played upon the chain about her neck. It still contained Cheeney's medallion and her key.

"And my outburst that day was fueled by a letter I received. Another courier brought it through the lines. It came from my wife."

"The respectable woman?"

Molly regretted her words as soon as they left her mouth. At the time he uttered them, they had stung—holding her in direct contrast. If she was honest, there was more to it. She played his wife, but another woman had his true affection.

"Yes. I am sorry for those words as well. I was angry at her letter—at her. I used it to lash out upon you. You see, it was the first time I had heard from her in over a year."

"You've been gone a year?"

Webster nodded. "Longer. I haven't seen her in more than two years. And before that there were long absences. I left the job for a time."

"But you came back?" Molly asked.

"We had a daughter. I saw her a handful of times before she died, but I was absent most of her life. My wife never forgave me. I should have been home, but I was not. I tried to stay after she passed, but I was not welcome. I should have tried harder. And for that shortcoming, I do not have a marriage—though I will not leave her destitute without an income."

His voice choked. He persisted in looking forward and not to Molly. She took his arm, prying it free from behind his back. He finally looked down and smiled. He had been crying, though Molly had not seen the tears. They caught in his beard.

"I have a son who is likely your age. He looks after home in a way I could not. I hear from him from time to time. He doesn't understand, and I cannot explain why I am always gone. In his last letter he said he might join the Army. I urged him to reconsider. I would hate for him to follow in this path."

Molly didn't know what to say. She walked on, holding tight upon his arm. It blocked the wind, but it felt good to have someone. She had hoped for a partner in Richmond, not a conflict.

"Be mindful, Molly, what you choose in this life. This job will take everything you have at some point. I wish I had known that earlier. No matter what good we do, there is always a price. Sometimes those we love most pay it for us."

They walked on for a time in silence. She should tell him about the Richmond Underground, but it could wait. She didn't want to shatter the peace that descended upon them. She wanted this moment to last as long as possible, savoring every second. She matched his stride as their footfalls fell in step—the only sound to penetrate the dark. He finally spoke.

"Did you know the girl back there? The one who held the door? She looked at you in an odd fashion."

The peace she had enjoyed disappeared. Lying would not help.

"Yes." Molly drew in a deep breath. "She lived on my father's estate."

"The one that Cheeney destroyed?"

Molly's pace slowed. She let go of his arm.

"You know?"

"Pinkerton told me. I argued with him that it made you a liability. I was afraid you would be recognized. But they insisted."

"Why?" Molly asked.

"Mrs. Warne has great respect for you. They told me about Montreal. That could not have been easy. But it was your efforts that brought us to Mason Cheeney. He is the target of this operation."

"Mr. Cheeney?" Molly asked. She didn't understand. "Mr. Pinkerton and Mrs. Warne said nothing."

"I know. They didn't want you to become fixated on Cheeney. After what you discovered in Montreal, Pinkerton had concerns. It seems his fears were well founded. He sent us to uncover Cheeney's special project and find some way to stop it."

"We can send word of the ship, can't we? Once they know, they can look for the floatation collar. It seems a flaw in his grand design."

Webster drew her close, hooking her arm and holding her tight. He lowered his voice. No one else walked nearby, but it made good sense to keep the conversation low. Molly enjoyed the warmth.

"We will. I plan to leave as soon as possible, perhaps tomorrow. We can tell them what we witnessed."

He paused, looking to her before continuing.

"I am more concerned in the second part of his plan. It would be a dangerous course if the South freed their slaves—with or without shipments of cotton to Europe."

"Dangerous to who?" Molly asked.

"To the Union."

Molly stopped. Webster took another step before he realized she was no longer beside him.

"You wouldn't want slavery to end?" she asked.

"I fight to keep the Union whole. No matter what."

"That's not an answer. You would save the Union even if it meant the South kept their slaves?"

"I think it little matters, Molly. The Union will win. We will see to it."

"And will the Union free everyone? Will President Lincoln set them all free?"

"I don't know," Webster admitted. "The President said he would keep slavery if it meant an end to the war. These things are hard to know."

The Union might keep slavery?

"If the South moved first," she asked, "if they liberated everyone, what would we care? Let them do it."

"Because it complicates matters," Webster replied. "That sounds cruel, but that is the truth of it. The Union first—then the slaves."

Molly shook her head. The turn of fate was awful. The man she most wanted dead held the best hope to liberate millions. While the man she saved might yet be the one to maintain their bondage. *Everything was backwards.*

"Does Cheeney's plan have a chance?" she asked.

"Not immediately," Webster said. "But when they become desperate—when the resources of the North press down upon them—they might consider it. But that could be years."

Molly started walking again. Webster matched her steps beside her.

"How do we hasten it?" Molly asked.

"Cheeney's warship. It might force Mr. Lincoln's hand. Pinkerton said the President considers emancipation. But he worries that would drive Maryland and Kentucky into the hands of the Confederacy. It's a tightrope. If Cheeney's idea spreads, Europe may back the South. So we could force Mr. Lincoln's options. He will have to declare it first."

"Would the President believe us? Would he believe that one man could convince Jefferson Davis to free the slaves?" Molly asked.

"Cheeney's more than a single man. We looked at him hard this past year, after you highlighted his importance. Pinkerton intercepted messages from the French ambassador. Cheeney works for the French. If Cheeney can break the blockade, then he has the contacts to convince the French to join the fight."

They walked on in silence. The weather had turned, and with each breath the mist in front of their faces grew dense. Webster coughed and leaned on Molly.

"We should have taken a carriage," Molly said.

"I needed the walk. And I wanted to talk to you in peace."

Molly was still thinking of the dilemma with Cheeney.

"I could kill him."

Webster laughed, but it turned into a coughing fit. Molly took his initial laughter to mock her.

"You don't think I could?"

"Oh no, I have no doubt in you. I laughed because it is exactly what Pinkerton feared—you might kill Cheeney."

"It would solve our problem."

Webster coughed again, and then cleared his throat.

"It would create new ones. It would be better to discredit him, to push him from the French so they distance themselves from the affair. There are fates worse than death."

"You sound like Mrs. Warne."

"Do I?"

He pulled Molly close.

"We should get you out of the cold," she said.

"Yes. I need a fire. And we need to get back to Washington. We can tell Pinkerton of the ship, and then of Cheeney's plan."

"I thought we are to stop him."

He leaned upon her with more weight.

"We will, but for now we should leave Richmond. Tomorrow—first thing. Mrs. Atwater is right. We have to warn Pinkerton."

"When will we come back?" Molly asked.

She thought of the painting and of the bruises on Mrs. Cheeney's face—the burning mansion, the rope around her father's neck, and the medallion she wore. She wanted her painting back. *Cheeney had to pay.*

"We might not. It becomes too dangerous in Richmond for us. That girl worries me."

"It was several years ago. I look much different."

Her words rang hollow. There could be no doubt. Jeanine recognized her. *Would she tell the Cheeneys? Why?*

"No," Webster said. "She most certainly recognized you. I'm afraid our time in Richmond has come to an end."

CHAPTER TWENTY-SIX

THEY DIDN'T LEAVE Richmond the next day—or the day after that. The rheumatism returned, and Webster could hardly roll over in bed, let alone walk. His excitement over the warship spelled the beginning of this round in his affliction. Wading into the water to better inspect the vessel was a mistake. And he ensured its effects to be particularly strong with the walk home from the Cheeney party. Molly didn't leave his side, ferrying him soup and hot tea from the kitchen. She slept in the chair next to the bed and kept an ever-watchful vigil. At times, he murmured in his sleep. Molly clutched his hand and comforted him.

In truth, she liked this role. While he fretted about getting north, part of her longed for the time to stretch. She wanted him healthy, but the shared solitude came as a comfort. Perhaps a deluded comfort, but comfort nonetheless. She hated the intrusions of the outside world, trampling upon their long conversations. His manner toward her had eased entirely. When not running errands, she sat close, barely any space between them.

When Webster recovered enough to sit, he worried their enemies would close around them before they could leave. And then he grew concerned that, while he recuperated they wasted time to get valuable intelligence into Pinkerton's hands.

"You should go without me," he pleaded. "Take my pass to travel and get the information to Pinkerton."

Molly didn't dignify the request. He gave up trying to convince her. But she had other reasons to resist the temptation to leave. She longed to find Jeanine. The girl would never give them up. Molly convinced herself, though it worried her. They had never been close. Jeanine was younger, two or three years in arrears of Molly. And Jeanine felt neglected. Isabelle said so. As was the custom in the South, Isabelle tended to Molly throughout the day. Jeanine stayed with other servants or worked the mending pile once old enough.

Isabelle and Jeanine's mother had left the plantation. She planned to send for them when she found a better life. But she never did. While they waited, Molly occupied the better portion of Isabelle's time. Jeanine received the leftovers, when Isabelle returned to her cabin on the plantation tired from a day of chasing Molly.

Jeanine won't say anything.

Molly muttered those words to herself. They sounded hollow, no matter how she said them. She pictured how Jeanine used to look at her. Not the shocked expression from the party, but an intense gaze. Isabelle told Molly not to fret about it. Molly didn't. She looked down upon the girl who mended the clothes and kept house with the other staff. Thinking on it, she treated Jeanine something awful. They competed for Isabelle's attention. Molly always won. But Molly was jealous of the bond the girl had with Isabelle—real sisters. Molly would have done anything for a sibling.

Mrs. Warne was the closest thing to Isabelle that Molly had found since. She closed her eyes and remembered Baltimore—their training sessions. She longed to see the older woman, even Pinkerton. Mrs. Warne would never leave anyone behind, and neither would she. When Webster was better, they would leave together.

Webster lay in bed next to her as she sat upon the old wood chair. He read the newspaper that Molly found downstairs. The news was stale, but he did not care. She liked watching him read— the way he sighed at certain articles or threw the paper aside in disgust. Her eyes followed the curve of his jaw, or the outline of his shoulders under his loose undershirt. Her face flushed when- ever he caught her. She kept her glimpses short, like sips from a cold glass.

A knock roused Molly from her thoughts. They both looked to the door. A few days ago a knock like this would have panicked them both. But Webster had begun receiving a steady stream of visitors. All were acquaintances who had heard of his affliction. Molly rose to answer the door as Webster propped himself higher in the bed.

"Captain McCubbin, it is good to see you again. Two days in a row. To what do we owe the pleasure?"

The young man stood in the door. He appeared Molly's age, though he wore no uniform to distinguish his rank. His compo- sure marked his fine upbringing. His hair and mustache were well groomed and fitting of the most current Southern style. He worked as the chief detective for the military provost. Webster had cultivated him as a friend—mostly for better travel passes from General Winder.

"I thought I would see how Webster fared. He mentioned yes- terday you might need some air, so I suggested I would return today and take over for a spell."

"Really?"

Webster nodded.

"You've watched me around the clock for days. I figured you could use a walk."

She had already grabbed her overcoat and her shawl. Making good as the dutiful wife, she danced back over next to him as the captain settled into her chair. She pressed her lips against his forehead. She let them linger for a moment.

"Thank you," she whispered.

Outside, the air bit harder than she imagined it for the time of year. A cold snap had landed upon them. But it felt good as she drew it into her chest. The twinge woke her body and eased her stiff limbs. She walked with a purpose—toward the Cheeney estate. She had no plan. She wanted to see Jeanine, to steal a moment alone with the girl.

When she arrived on the street where the Cheeneys' lived, Molly stopped at a street corner. She leaned against an old light pole. The gas lamp above her had long been turned off with the arrival of dawn. But she studied it as a manner to distract herself. Terror gripped her. Not the sudden fright at being startled. Rather, it was a growing fear of climbing the stairs and knocking upon the door. *What if Jeanine answered? What would she say?*

Molly stayed fixed to the street corner. Wagons passed, and servants flowed from the various estates. They carried baskets and hurried in the cold, making their way to market. The embargo of Richmond had begun to play out upon the rich. There became fierce competition to make it to the stores early to get what fresh goods could be had. Even then, the prices trended ever upwards.

Amongst the flurry of activity, Molly stood like a statue. No one paid her any mind, especially not the servants who wouldn't meet her eyes. *The servant entrance.* She would claim she lost a scarf at the party and had come to find it without bothering the lady of the house. That might be plausible, without breaking decorum. It might also draw attention if Mrs. Cheeney heard. But she had to try something.

Breaking free of the lamppost, she started down the street. The wind bit, and she pulled her shawl over her face. Crossing the street between wagons, she hurried along the sidewalk. Up ahead a man walked toward her. She tucked her chin low and kept her shawl pulled over her shoulders. As he passed their eyes met. She breathed sharply with the shock of it—*Jonathon Cheeney.*

He stopped walking.

"Molly?"

She had no answer. She took a step backward and shook her head—the movement barely noticeable.

"Molly, is it you?"

He stepped forward and reached for her upper arm. She backed away. He stopped and held his hands out.

"No, no...I won't hurt you. What are you doing here? How did you . . ." His words trailed off.

Her heart led a furious pace below her dress. He was older, more worn. Wrinkles had formed in his forehead from time in the elements, under the sun. But he held himself taller, and more filled out. His eyes—a deep blue.

"Why are you here? What happened to you?" he asked.

She studied his face. *How could he not know?* His expression contained no deceit.

"You don't know?" she asked. It came out as a whisper, barely above the wind. She wasn't certain he had heard, but then he shook his head.

"No."

"But your father. He was there."

Molly's heart beat faster. Anger ate into her shock. She drew strength from it, feeling it grow.

"I had nothing to do with it. I swear it."

"Nothing? You told me to go to the swimming hole that night—to be out of the house. That's when they came."

"I know, Molly. I swear, I didn't know," he said.

His voice pleaded. He took another step forward. She retreated. Her anger rose. The unsteadiness in her legs faded, like fog melting in the sun.

"I watched them die, Jonathon! All of them. They killed Isabelle in front of me. She stared at me as . . ." A bitter taste built in her throat. Tears gathered in her eyes. They were hot tears, filled with anger. They burned.

"I know, I didn't think—"

She stepped forward and slapped him across the face. The violence of it startled her. But it felt good. She hit him again. And again. He backed up, absorbing the blows without defense. She sobbed as she struck him. He grabbed hold of her, pulling her close. She struggled, but it was no use. He was stronger. He clutched her, not hard—just enough to stop her thrashing. He placed his lips against the top of her head and pulled her in. His breath was hot upon the top of her head. She held on to him, trying to vanquish the images of the burning plantation. Isabelle stared at her, the life draining from her eyes.

"I didn't know what my father planned. I had no idea."

Her breathing slowed.

"Forgive me," he said. "Please."

She pulled back from him. He tried to pull her close again, but she shook free. She took a step back. He didn't try to stop her.

"I never thought I would see you again," he said. "My father said you ran away. I didn't know how to find you. But you're here, and—"

"He told you that? He told you I ran away?"

"Yes," he said. "Where did you go?"

Her thoughts filled with the brothel—of sweat smeared into fresh linens.

"It doesn't matter," she answered.

The street was clear. *She had to get away.* She was supposed to find Jeanine—to see if the girl had talked. It was a futile point now.

"How do I find you again?" he asked.

He stepped toward her. She mirrored him, pulling away.

"You can't say anything," she said. "You can't say anything to anyone."

"Why, Molly? Are you—"

"Promise me!" she yelled, cutting him short.

"I promise."

She stepped forward and shoved him, pushing hard against his chest. He stumbled.

"Mean it this time!"

He looked shocked at the ferocity of the act.

"I loved you, Molly. I truly did. I still—"

"Tell me you mean it. Tell me you won't say anything."

He nodded. "I mean it."

He would talk. How could he not? Maybe she had time—the one thing she needed.

She took a step back.

"How do I find you?" he called out.

"You don't."

She locked eyes with him. He had grown—tall and strong. She remembered how each time she saw him she had to look away. She remembered the first time he grabbed hold of her hand, how her knees buckled. *What would her life have been? Maybe he had nothing to do with any of it.*

"I need to see you again," he said.

"I'll find you."

She took one last look at him, lost for a moment in those eyes. She had loved him—or the idea of him. She shook her head, dislodging the thought. Then she ran.

She needed to get to Webster.

CHAPTER TWENTY-SEVEN

MOLLY BURST THROUGH the door of the hotel room without thinking. Captain McCubbin was still there, sitting in a chair beside Webster. The two precariously perched a chessboard between them. They both turned and stared.

"What happened?" Webster inquired.

Molly froze, glancing between the men. She closed the door, trying not to look at either man.

"Nothing," she lied. "It is so cold out. I just need the fire."

She stepped to the fireplace with her hands outstretched to the flames. Captain McCubbin examined her, even as she stood with her back toward him. There was no trusting this man. Webster dismissed her concerns. But he was a serpent in their midst—friendly but able to turn with the slightest provocation. She kept her conversation to a minimum near him. She feared he would catch any slip, even the smallest mistake.

As the men played, she caught a glimpse of Webster over her shoulder. She gained his attention. But there was no chance to talk, not with McCubbin close by. The wait would be agonizing. Molly turned to the fire, hoping to compose herself before dreaming up some excuse to get Webster alone.

A knock upon the door drew her attention. She took a sharp breath. *Had Jonathon followed her?* She had checked, watched behind at every intersection, even took a tortured path to the hotel.

"Are you expecting anyone?" she asked.

"Our regular guest is already here," Webster said, not looking up from the chessboard.

Molly made her way to the door. McCubbin's eyes remained upon her. She paused, drew in a deep breath, and then opened it. Two men stood outside. Neither were Jonathon Cheeney. She exhaled in relief. Their manner of dress did not match Richmond, as if they tried too hard—out of step with the style.

"Good day, ma'am. We're looking for Mr. Timothy Webster. I understand he may be here."

Molly nodded. But she did not open the door wider.

"May we call upon him?" one of the men asked. "We have a message for him from Baltimore."

"Who is it?" Webster called out.

"I don't know."

It was a partial lie. Molly didn't know their names, but she had seen them before—with Pinkerton. She opened the door wide so Webster could see. McCubbin studied both men. His eyes lingered upon their clothing. Even their accents were wrong. They tried too hard. The man who spoke heralded from England, more recent than Webster. America had blunted his accent but hadn't erased it. Molly let them into the room.

"I apologize for dropping by unannounced," the first man said. "I'm Mr. Lewis, and this is Mr. Scully. We promised a mutual friend we would deliver a letter. The manager at the *Richmond Enquirer* told us we might find you here."

"Very good," Webster said.

His voice tremored. He shifted nervously on the bed. Webster often ran messages for the *Enquirer* to their Northern contacts. Sometimes he brought back delicacies through the lines. The story sounded plausible. But Webster's color had drained. He recognized them, too. The first man came forward and handed Webster a letter. Webster studied the envelope but did not open it.

"Well, what does it say, Webster?" McCubbin prodded him.

Molly didn't like the tone. From his body language, Webster didn't want to open the letter. But with McCubbin watching, he had little choice. He tore at the seal and then removed the paper. As he read it, his color returned. He relaxed.

"My route to Washington is compromised. General McClellan has posted units upon the path I normally take. My dear friend Mr. Scott has sent warning."

"I hope it is news of use," Mr. Scully said. "We had a devil of a time making it to Richmond. Those damned federals seem to be everywhere." He looked to Molly. "Pardon my language, ma'am."

Molly nodded. The room went cold—rigid. Every motion fell under intense scrutiny from McCubbin. It all felt wrong.

"Indeed," McCubbin said. "Did you just come across the Potomac then?"

"Yes, sir. We barely made it through the pickets."

"And, of course, you stopped at General Winder's office when you arrived?" McCubbin pressed.

"General Winder?" Scully asked. "We haven't heard of him."

"He is the provost marshal of Richmond. It is necessary for all those who newly arrive to have an interview with the general or myself. You, of course, understand the necessity of such precautions."

"I'm afraid," Mr. Scully began, "we do not know who you are, sir."

"Quite easily remedied. I am the chief of detectives for the general—Captain McCubbin."

"Well then, Captain, we submit to your inspection," Lewis said.

He kept his tone light, trying to deflect suspicion—the more natural spy between the two men.

"You are then in good fortune," Captain McCubbin said. "For I am about to defeat Webster here at this very game of chess, and I can then escort you to the provost marshal's office. I am certain the general would like a word of introduction."

"The hell you are," Webster grumbled.

He focused upon the game in front of him, sitting straighter and studying the chessboard. He wanted to distract McCubbin, but his voice betrayed his concern.

"Well, here you go, Webster—check, and I believe, mate."

McCubbin moved a piece upon the board and captured one of Webster's bishops. Webster stared at the game.

"Take your time, and I will stop back later," McCubbin said. "I expect you will concede defeat and have the board re-set for your second drumming."

Then he stood from his chair.

"Gentlemen, if you would be so good as to follow me, I will be most happy to make the necessary introductions."

McCubbin grabbed his coat. Looking back upon the room, he bowed toward Molly.

"It is always a pleasure to see you, Mrs. Webster."

Mr. Lewis followed his lead, also taking a slight bow.

"We are off to our doom!" Mr. Lewis declared, using the same lighthearted voice. "It was a pleasure to meet you, Mr. Webster, and also you, ma'am."

Then both men disappeared through the door with McCubbin. Molly and Webster listened as their footsteps echoed down the hall.

"You have to leave!" Webster held his voice low, and it came out as a hiss.

The sound startled Molly. He threw the covers off and tried to swing his legs free. But he wound up coughing, then doubled over in pain.

"I need to tell you what happened," she said.

He held up one hand as his coughing fit died.

"Yes," he said. "You looked terrible when you came in. Are you alright?"

She knelt. He reached out and took her hands. She enjoyed the warmth as it spread through her fingers. She took a deep breath, then let it out.

"I ran into Jonathon Cheeney."

"Who's that?" Webster asked. "Related to Mason Cheeney?"

"His son."

Webster clutched her hands, squeezing lightly. "He knows you?"

Molly nodded.

"And he recognized you?"

"Yes."

She avoided his stare. Webster studied her, then reached out with one hand to lift her chin.

"He was someone important?"

Moly tried to look away, but he lifted her head again.

"No. I mean . . . it doesn't matter."

"It is alright, Molly. We have all loved." He paused. "And lost."

Molly nodded and looked down again. He let his hand brush against her cheek. She grabbed hold of it and pressed it to her face.

"What do we do?" she asked.

"Does he know your name?"

"Of course," Molly said, confused.

"I mean, does he know you by Hattie Lawton? By Hattie *Webster*?"

He stressed the Webster part when he said it. She tried to hold back the smile at the sound of it, but it crept across her face.

"No," she said.

"Then we have some time. He won't know how to find you.

"But if he says something to his father?" Molly pressed.

"We have to assume he will. But Mason Cheeney may not understand he means you. Mason knows you as my wife, as Hattie Lawton. It gives us time, but not much. I'm more concerned with the men who just came. Do you know them?" Webster asked.

Molly shook her head. "I've seen them before, at Pinkerton's office in Washington. But I never met them."

"It's Lewis and Scully. Why would Pinkerton send them?"

"What did the letter say?"

"It said nothing," Webster answered. "At least nothing important. But it's in Pinkerton's hand. He meant it as a signal."

"When were we supposed to return to Washington?"

Webster sat at the edge of the bed. A coughing fit took over, only easing after a few moments. Molly poured a glass of water from a pitcher and handed it to him. He drank it, in small sips at first, before draining the entire glass.

"We should have left a few weeks ago, but I wanted to finish the mission with Cheeney. I was to find and disrupt his plans."

"I still don't understand how you meant to do that," Molly answered. "You never told me. And when was the last time you sent word north to Pinkerton?"

"I haven't," Webster confessed. He looked up to catch Molly's eyes—his face grim. "Pinkerton's courier was supposed to meet me on the business trip in Chattanooga. He never showed." Webster ignored the first part of her inquiry.

Molly sighed. He had been so harsh with her at first, not wanting her to do anything other than play the doting wife.

"So he has no word from us," Molly said. "Of course, he sent men looking. He was worried. I would be, too."

She pulled his hand from her face and held it in hers.

"I have a means to get messages north," she said. "Elizabeth Van Lew has a network—the Richmond Underground. We could have sent Pinkerton word that we were safe."

Webster looked to the ground and shook his head.

"A fine time to tell me now!"

Molly dropped his hands and stood. Anger flushed through her.

"Well, you wanted the doting wife, not a partner. So I did my part on my own. And a lot of help you've been, wallowing in bed." She surprised herself at the anger—how quick she snapped at him.

She walked away, toward the fire. The dancing flames held her attention. It reminded her of the painting at the Cheeneys' estate— Salvation Acres on fire.

"Molly . . ." His voice trailed off into a coughing fit.

She let him finish this time, without bothering to hand him the glass with fresh water.

"Molly. Come here . . . please."

She turned, but did not move.

"I am sorry. I should have trusted you earlier. I told you that before. I meant it then, and even more so now. I need you. *Please.*"

She broke his stare. Then she moved toward him. He reached for her hands.

"You have to leave," he said. "I don't want you to go, but I need you to do something for me."

"What?"

She kept her voice level, further revealing her anger. Webster pointed to the painting above the mantel.

"There is a stack of letters behind the painting. In the same place you hid the other letters. I brought them with us to use against

Cheeney. They need to get back North. We are surely detected. Pinkerton will send someone else to finish what we did not accomplish."

"We?" Molly asked.

"What I did not finish," Webster conceded.

He clutched both her hands, then pressed them to his lips.

"Please, Molly. This is my folly. Help me make it right before they come for me."

"They might not, have you thought of that?"

Webster shook his head. "Scully is weak. He will break if they take him. I am certain McCubbin suspects them both. You saw it. I know you did."

"I don't want to leave you."

She meant it. Her anger subsided. He needed her, and she liked it—she needed it. With his sickness, she was an equal partner, nursing him to health. She wasn't ready for it to end.

"I don't want you to leave." He pressed her hands against his face. "But you must."

"What do the letters say?"

"I am not supposed to tell you."

"I thought we were past that," Molly said. Her anger simmered. Her cheeks flushed.

Webster nodded. He pulled her to the sit in the chair, then released her hands.

"They are a correspondence between Cheeney and a Union general. Cheeney tried to sell the plans for his warship to the North. They will need those plans now. No one would believe it to be a ship that sailed under the waves."

"He was selling them? Why?"

"I don't know. I was to negotiate their sale, and bring the plans home. Pinkerton would send the funds through the courier, the one

I was supposed to meet in Tennessee. He didn't want us traveling with that much money in case we were caught."

"Mason Cheeney is betraying the Confederacy?"

"I think he's a pragmatist. He knows they'll lose the war eventually. They're outnumbered. You heard him—*it's all in the math*. And there's only a slim margin he could get his other plans through the Confederate government—freeing the slaves and making a deal with Europe. If he sells out, he wins either way. He's betting on both sides."

"What were you to do with the letters?" Molly asked.

"If he didn't sell the plans, I was to blackmail him with them. Pinkerton didn't want you to know."

"Why?" she asked.

"We want to turn Cheeney, to flip him against the South. That's why we couldn't just kill him. Do you see now?"

"Pinkerton worried I would try," Molly muttered, working it out for herself. "I could still do it. I could get the plans from him."

"You'd have to confront Cheeney. Could you do that alone?"

She had failed every time with Cheeney. She had wanted to kill him—but failed. Every time she saw him she was the little girl, barefoot in the New Orleans mud watching her house burn. Her eyes fell to her lap. She shook her head. A tear rolled down her cheek. Webster reached out and lifted her face by the chin.

"Don't. You are stronger than you know. I've seen it. Take the letters and go North. Tell them what you saw with the ship. And convince them, Molly. They need to know what's coming. You have to make Pinkerton believe."

She nodded.

A knock fell upon the door behind them.

"They've come. Get the letters!" Webster said.

He whispered to Molly; his face was so close his breath fell upon her neck. Molly stood and rushed to the mantel. She found the packet behind the painting. The knock at the door fell louder.

"Put them out on the window ledge," Webster instructed. "If they search the room, they won't look there. You can retrieve them later."

Molly rushed to the window. She was about to open it when she saw the man below, staring up at their room. He was the same man she had seen outside the Van Lew estate—the detective from General Winder's office. She turned from the window. The knocking grew louder.

"Webster! Are you in there?"

It was McCubbin.

Molly pushed the letters into the pocket on the front of her apron, then rushed to the door. She opened it.

"I'm sorry, Captain McCubbin. He was caught in a fit."

Webster began coughing, as if on cue. McCubbin studied them both, then stepped into the room. Molly took some comfort that he was alone. She shut the door behind him.

"Have you at least admitted defeat, Webster?"

Webster stopped coughing. Molly froze. They looked to one another, then Webster turned to McCubbin.

"At the chess game," he clarified, pointing to the board. It remained perched upon the chair.

Webster shook his head, relief claiming his face. "Yes, I admit you have me."

"Good," McCubbin declared. "Though I am sorry to say that I won't be able to deliver you another defeat just yet. Those men from earlier, have you met them before?"

"Never," said Webster. "I know the man who wrote the letter—W.H. Scott. He is a true champion of our cause. I am grateful he gave me warning. I was to travel back to Washington soon and carry dispatches for General Winder."

McCubbin nodded, still studying Webster's face.

"Would you mind if I see the letter?" McCubbin asked.

"Not at all."

Webster picked it up and handed it to the younger man. McCubbin opened the envelope and read the contents.

"May I take this to General Winder?" McCubbin asked.

"Certainly. Keep it. I have what value I may extract from the message. The general is welcome to it, especially if it helps him know the enemy's intent."

"Thank you, Webster. I am most grateful."

Captain McCubbin turned to leave.

"Is there something wrong with them?" Webster called out.

McCubbin stopped and turned. He studied Webster before answering.

"I'm not certain. Good day."

And with that he turned and left, seeing himself out. Webster reached for the side table next to his bed. He yanked open the drawer and pulled out his pistol. He pulled Molly close and pressed the weapon into her hands.

"There can be no question, Molly. You need to go now!"

CHAPTER TWENTY-EIGHT

MOLLY KNOCKED UPON the back door of the Van Lew estate. She used the servants' entrance to remain unseen. No one had tailed her from the hotel. Not that she saw. She had taken the offer from the concierge for a carriage. She let the driver drop her off several blocks away, and then pretended to visit a different estate. Once he drove off, she doubled back and made her way to Miss Lizzie.

Mary Jane answered the door. She dragged Molly through the threshold the moment she saw who stood outside. Mary Jane looked both directions around the house before closing the door.

"Molly, what are you doing at the back door, child?"

Mary Jane scolded while she pulled Molly into a light embrace. She worried. Her body language betrayed her feelings.

"I need to see Miss Lizzie."

"Of course, of course. Whatever has happened? You wouldn't be here two days in a row if it weren't important."

She gripped Molly's hand and started her upstairs.

"Mr. Webster thinks we are discovered, and that he is soon to be arrested. I need to get more messages North."

Mary Jane ushered her upstairs and then toward the same sitting room where she always met with Miss Lizzie.

"I'll be getting Miss Lizzie and then will make up some tea. You look frozen."

Molly sat near the fire. "Thank you, Mary Jane."

Mary Jane had scarcely left the room when Elizabeth Van Lew flew through the doorway. She must have heard the commotion.

"Molly!"

Miss Lizzie rushed the length of the carpet, and clutched Molly. Concern wore at her face.

"Is everything all right?"

"No," Molly said. "Mr. Webster believes we are caught. I was careful, though. No one followed me here."

Miss Lizzie nodded. The curls of her hair bounced with her head. It always drew Molly's attention.

"How does he know?"

"He doesn't, but I trust his instincts. Mr. Pinkerton sent two men to find us. We were supposed to make a trip back to Washington by now. They must have grown worried. And then those men came at the worst time. Captain McCubbin was there."

"General Winder's chief detective?"

Molly nodded.

"I do not like that man," Miss Lizzie continued. "He is always suspicious. He came here once, to talk about the prisons. But I gathered he meant to snoop and see what mischief an old woman might be up to."

"Well, he took the men to General Winder's office and then came back for the letter they brought. He suspects them for certain. And Mr. Webster says one of the men is weak and will talk."

Miss Van Lew pulled back from Molly, deep in thought.

"Well then, as much as I have enjoyed your visits, it seems we must smuggle you out of Richmond."

Molly shook her head. "No. I need you to get more letters to Mrs. Warne. I need to stay and get Mr. Webster."

"You must not. They will come for you next!"

"You said it yourself," Molly pleaded. "Men do not think women could be engaged in this work. I will be safe. If I leave, they will know for certain that Webster is a detective from the North. I will not condemn him to save myself."

"I have not met your gentleman, but from what you have told me of him, he would rather see you safe than both of you captured. We must get you out of the city now."

Molly shook her head—more forceful this time. She clenched her jaw.

"I cannot. I will not leave him."

Miss Lizzie's face softened. She took Molly's hands.

"Molly, he knows his role, and the risks. I know you care for him, but I cannot let you put yourself in more danger. I would rather see you safe. You are Annabelle's child. How will I meet her in the afterlife and explain that I did not courier you to safety when I could have done so? Listen to me. I will work on Mr. Webster's behalf. I will get him out—perhaps before they come for him."

At the mention of her mother's name, she came undone. She turned from Miss Lizzie, covering her face. She fought the sobs, but they came forth. This house had been one of safety for her. But it reminded her of something else—a deep-harbored guilt.

"It's not just Mr. Webster. I need to get Jeanine out."

She had told Miss Van Lew about the girl.

"I don't know how we get her out, Molly. But we can try."

"I have to. It's my fault."

Her voice came out weak between the sobs. Miss Lizzie tried to comfort her, placing an arm around her shoulder.

"I came here to kill Mason Cheeney—for my father. But I couldn't, even when he was right in front of me. I was too scared. And Pinkerton needs him for other purposes. But I found Jeanine. I can get her safe. I have to do that for Isabelle. I have to."

Miss Lizzie put an arm around her.

"I don't know, Molly. Let's get you safe first, and then Mr. Webster."

"I have to do this."

"No, Molly. You don't. You need to get safe. For me . . . for your mother."

"I don't deserve it. It's all my fault!" Molly screamed.

She tore away from Miss Lizzie's clutch. Her sobs deepened. Her mind filled with images of the burning plantation—of hiding with Isabelle in the woods. The men came, galloping on horses into the underbrush, calling for them. Molly and Isabelle ran. Molly was always faster in the thickets and small trails. Isabelle screamed behind her—caught.

"None of this is your fault, Molly."

Miss Lizzie tried to comfort her. Molly sank to her knees and rocked. She pulled at her hair on the sides of her head, vanquishing the images from her thoughts. They persisted—stubborn ghosts.

"No, it's my fault. I told him." Molly's voice came out barely above a whisper. "I told him. It all happened because of me. It's my fault."

"Who, Molly? What did you tell him?"

"Jonathon. Jonathon Cheeney. I told him about the plantation. I told him they were all free. He said he loved me. He said he would ask my father to marry me. And so I told him about everything. They're all dead because of me."

Molly's sobs turned into a wail. She clutched at the carpet in front of her as she rocked upon her knees. Miss Lizzie held her. Mary Jane stood at the door, watching the scene.

"It doesn't matter what you said, Molly. It's not your fault."

Molly tried to break free, but Miss Lizzie held tighter.

"They'd be alive if it wasn't for me. They'd all be alive." Molly continued to rock. Her hands were numb. Resting her forehead against the floor was the only thing that fought against her spinning vision.

"We'll rescue them both. We'll do it together."

Miss Lizzie looked over her shoulder. Mary Jane still stood at the door.

"Get the carriage ready."

Mary Jane didn't reply. She rushed from the room. Miss Lizzie clutched Molly until Molly let go of her hair and pushed her forehead into the carpet. Miss Lizzie whispered into Molly's ear. Her cheek fell upon Molly's neck—warm and comforting.

"You'll have to help me, Molly. But we'll get them both out."

CHAPTER TWENTY-NINE

THE CARRIAGE ROCKED as they descended from Church Hill. One of Miss Lizzie's servants, a broad-shouldered man named Robert, drove the vehicle. They could hear his booming voice outside, coaxing the horses.

"How will we do this?" Molly asked.

She had settled but felt drained.

"I haven't told you everything we have engaged in, Molly. The Underground has helped prisoners escape. They make their way to my estate, where I have a hiding place. Then we smuggle them to a farm outside the city. They wait until we can cross the lines. If it works for soldiers, it can work for you and Mr. Webster. He can recover at the farmhouse. And then I can work on Jeanine."

Molly nodded.

"Mrs. Atwater came to call yesterday after you left," Miss Lizzie said.

From the tone of her voice, she wanted to tell Molly but maybe felt uncertain to add more stress. Molly gazed out the window, relieved that someone else now told her what to do. It felt comforting, like when she was younger—happier.

"She asked if you had all you needed about the ship," Miss Lizzie explained.

Molly shook her head. "Mr. Webster thinks we need the plans. But I would rather have him than the plans. Together we can convince Pinkerton."

Miss Lizzie laughed.

"What?" Molly demanded.

She was in no mood to be trifled with. Though immediately after she snapped, a pang of guilt fell across her. Miss Lizzie had done so much for her.

"She offered the drawings."

"She did?"

Miss Lizzie nodded. "Captain Atwater is trying to slow the work at the Tredegar Ironworks. But he may need to flee at some point. The Atwaters want to head north, though he is frightened over his prospects. He is a Confederate officer and might be jailed. But if I get you the plans . . ."

Her voice trailed off.

"He won't be imprisoned," Molly said.

It wasn't her promise to make, though she could argue the case to Pinkerton. Captain Atwater might know more about other projects at the ironworks. He would be a valuable ally.

"I will get the drawings. And you and Mr. Webster can courier them north when you leave."

"That would be wonderful."

Her voice was flat, her mind consumed with other matters. Her gloved hands sat in her lap. She dreamed of a warm bed, a bath. The nightmare would end. It had to end.

"Molly . . ." Miss Lizzie's voice was soft, soothing.

Her face was free from judgment.

"It doesn't matter what you told Jonathon Cheeney. You were young—you still are. What happened is not your fault."

Molly shook her head.

"It does matter," she said. "My father told me that no one could know. I thought Jonathon would say nothing—that he could keep it a secret. I told him that afternoon. That very day."

She went quiet, letting the motion of the carriage carry her thoughts. That night came back so easily when she stopped fighting the memories.

"Isabelle and I weren't home. We had gone to the swimming hole."

Miss Lizzie clutched her hands. Molly had no more tears to give. Her face felt flushed—hot.

"Jonathon said he would come that evening—to ask my father to marry me. He didn't want me there in case my father rebuffed him. I trusted him. And so Isabelle and I went swimming. It's all we talked about. I was so nervous. I kept asking Isabelle about where I would live—what it would be like. I was so stupid. I should have been there."

Miss Lizzie squeezed her hands.

"If you were, you might have wound up like your father or mother."

"That would have been better."

"Never say that, Molly."

"They put me in a brothel!" Molly clenched her jaw, grinding her teeth. "Those men . . . they were awful."

"You survived. And you will survive this, too."

She stared out the window. Shades of gray fell over Richmond. It had to be the winter weather, but the place felt heavy. The chill in the air came laden with moisture, and the sluggish wind tugged upon the carriage. Outside, soldiers milled on the corners. Some were younger than her—their faces smooth and never touched by a razor. The homespun uniforms gave them away, the ones she helped sew. They hung crookedly over shoulders or were too long in the sleeves. But the boys were proud. Their faces displayed undying optimism.

"I don't see where I go from here. I can't see what's next."

Miss Lizzie slid closer in the carriage. Her hand reached out and grasped Molly's arm. She squeezed.

"We get you home. That's first—you and Mr. Webster. And you let me fret about Jeanine. That way I know I have done some small service in honor of your mother."

Molly breathed deep and held it. Then she let the breath out. It formed a small cloud of mist, even inside the carriage. With it, she let go. Her forehead rested against the window, and she let her eyes close. The jolts from the carriage kept her from thinking—her mind a blank piece of paper.

The carriage ride lasted only another ten minutes, maybe a stretch longer. Molly had no memory of it. She might have slept. She only remembered the pressure as Miss Lizzie gripped her arm.

"Molly . . . wake up, dear."

The older woman's voice strained. It shook Molly from her peace, forcing her back to the world.

"Molly, is that Mr. Webster?"

They had reached the hotel, or at least approached it from the main thoroughfare. Outside, two men dragged another between them. They stood on the street in front of the hotel. The man in the middle had a blanket thrown over his shoulders, and he walked unevenly. A third man led them toward a waiting carriage—Captain McCubbin. Molly didn't need to see the ailing man's face. She recognized his body, his movements.

"Dear God . . ."

It came out as a whisper. Miss Lizzie pounded on the side of the carriage.

"Robert, back to the estate and fast. Do not stop!"

Then she caught hold of Molly, dragging her down in the seat by the shoulders.

"Get down, Molly!"

Molly slid, but not fast enough. Webster looked into the window as they passed. For a fraction of a moment no one else existed—just Molly and Webster. Then it was gone. He turned his head. Miss Lizzie managed to push Molly below the line of sight of the window.

But she saw him. She saw the terror upon his face. And at his waist his wrists were bound in irons.

CHAPTER THIRTY

THE DETAILS OF the ride back to the Van Lew estate escaped Molly's memory. She sat in a fog. Robert and Miss Lizzie managed to drag her inside. At some point, Mary Jane drew a warm bath. Molly remembered sitting in the water until it became tepid, and then changing into a nightgown. Mary Jane showed her to a spare room, turned down the bed, and left Molly alone.

She may have slept, but she didn't know. She didn't care. She wanted to scream, and cry, and fight, and rip her clothes and her hair—all at once. The conflict raged within her. Nothing came out. Instead, the numbness gave way to something serene. The ceiling above her was a blank canvas.

Outside her door, Miss Lizzie and Mary Jane spoke in hushed tones. They were scared. Molly couldn't blame them. If Captain McCubbin came to the estate, Molly would be a liability. Or *when* Captain McCubbin came to the estate. Molly focused on the words between the two women. They planned to get her out of Richmond the next day, maybe even at daybreak. Robert would bundle her up and take her to the farm. Her mind went back to the irons at Webster's wrists. If she left, he would be doomed. So many people had died on her account. She had hurt so many.

And with that thought calmness descended like a warm blanket, enveloping her and vanquishing the fear and doubt. *The answer was so clear.*

She waited until the house quieted. The last chime from the hall clock felt like ages ago. She had not bothered to keep the count in her head. She figured it to be well past midnight. Outside, the wind raged, as if the conflict inside her had been excised past the pane of glass. She lifted the blanket and swung her feet until they reached the floor.

At the bottom of her bed she found her dress. She put it on, careful not to make any noise. Miss Lizzie believed every room should be well stocked with pen and paper. Molly sat at the small desk and rummaged for what she needed. She had no way to light the oil lamp, but she needn't have worried. Enough moonlight fell through the window.

She opened the inkbottle by feel, careful not to spill. Then she applied enough to the pen before she scratched her note upon the paper. It was fine stationary, and her hand flowed over the words.

Miss Lizzie—

Please accept my sincerest regards for all you have done on my behalf. I am grateful that fate put me upon your path. I fear I may have caused you more trouble than I intended. I will be forever indebted to you for your kindness. If there is one favor you might still do for me, please look out for Jeanine as we discussed. I hope someday that I will see you again. Please send my apologies to Mary Jane for not bidding her goodbye in person.

I think my mother would be happy that we met again.

—M. Ferguson

She closed the inkbottle, and then laid the note upon the desk to dry. Without wasting time, she reached into her handbag and produced the letters. She left them next to the note. Finally, she removed Webster's pistol. It felt so heavy and awkward. A crude weapon—the tools of men, Mrs. Warne would say. Manipulating the weapon, she eased the hammer back until it locked in the cocked position. Then she eased it forward, pulling the trigger to release the mechanism. *She could work this gun.*

There was no need for the handbag. She had no need for anything else. She found her shawl and pulled it around her shoulders. Then she grabbed her boots but did not put them on. The floor would creak and wake Mary Jane or Miss Lizzie. She made her way down the stairs, only stopping once she reached the basement and the servants' entrance. She pulled her boots on, tied the laces, and then unlocked the door.

The same pale moonlight bathed everything. It soothed her. The calmness persisted. She crept along the side of the house. Not even the cold or the wind could penetrate her peace of mind.

Richmond lay before her. She had a twenty-minute walk. Even though it was well past curfew, the patrols of soldiers rarely came through this part of Richmond. Most of the patrols scoured the city below Church Hill, in the underbelly of Richmond. She pressed into the shadows and hurried her pace.

She found the estate without trouble, stopping to observe it from afar. She stepped out of the shadows of the nearest gas lamp, casting its pale light past the sidewalk and onto the cobblestone street. Staring at the building, a rustling at the top of the lamp drew her attention. She spun to face a large black crow perched upon the light. It looked right into her eyes. They stared at one another for a few moments. The bird stretched its large wings, and with a sudden jump lofted into the night sky. It soared past Molly and toward the house, disappearing into the dark.

She watched the bird fade into the night, then stared at the estate. Despite the hour, a light shone in the front parlor. The rest of the house lay dark. She stepped past the gas lamp and made her way to the front gate. The staircase consisted only of a few steps. She did not have to do more than stand upon her tiptoes to see into the great window. The glow of the gas lamp reflected in his spectacles. She mounted the few stairs, and without hesitation, knocked softly at the door.

It took a moment. Her thumb rode the hammer of the pistol, pulling it back until it locked in place. Then her finger pressed into the trigger, taking all slack out of the mechanism. She would not hesitate.

A sliver of light fell upon the stairs as the door opened. The man holding the light peered out. When he saw the familiar face, he swung the door wide open.

"Why, Mrs. Webster. Whatever are you doing out this late?"

Jonathon hadn't said anything.

"I've come with an urgent matter to discuss," Molly answered. "One which cannot wait until tomorrow. I do hope you have a few moments for me, Mr. Cheeney."

Then she lifted the pistol until the weapon gleamed in the lamplight. The barrel pointed directly at Mason Cheeney's chest.

He staggered backward. She stepped toward him, crossing through the doorway.

"What's this about?"

His voice held panic. He fought to suppress it, but it leaked in. His eyes never left the gun.

"There are so many things this could be about. But tonight I am happy to limit the discussion to one. I need your help with my husband."

Molly took another step inside. Mason Cheeney stepped back, focused upon the pistol. Molly closed the front door behind her.

"Why don't we move to your parlor? But slow."

Cheeney nodded. "Yes, yes."

He backed away, leading them into the parlor.

"Sit in the chair in front of the desk," Molly ordered. "And it would be most convenient if you placed the lamp upon the desk and left your hands in your lap."

Cheeney obeyed. He placed the lamp in a position where the soft light filled the room.

"I heard General Winder had your husband arrested."

"And that is where you will help me."

"Help you?" he asked.

His eyes moved between the barrel of the pistol and Molly's face, then back again. Her focus turned to his body language—for any sign he might try to get up.

"Cross your feet," Molly said.

"What now?"

"Cross your feet," Molly ordered.

If he was off-balance, it would buy her time to pull the trigger—if she had the need. He followed her instruction, though he did it slowly, conveying his reluctance.

"What do you think I can do for your husband?"

"You will go to General Winder and vouch for him. Your reputation has grown considerably with your successes. You will see him set free."

"And if I do not?" Cheeney asked.

He had recovered slightly. A bit of bravado crept into his voice.

"Then I will expose your letters."

"My letters? What letters?"

"The ones you wrote offering to sell your ship to the Union," Molly answered.

Mr. Cheeney stared. A smile broke out across his face. He began to laugh.

"Are you mad? Sell my plans to the Union?"

"I have the letters, Mr. Cheeney. They are safe. You get my husband free, and I'll return your correspondence."

"I never wrote anything of the sort! Never would I betray the South!"

Molly studied his face. She hadn't expected this. He should have crumbled, understanding her leverage.

"So it's true. Webster is with the Union?" he asked. "Who are you?"

At first Molly said nothing. Then she took a step closer, raising the gun until the front sight covered his forehead. With such little pressure the trigger would break—the bullet would split his head open.

"You don't remember me?"

He shook his head.

"I remember you. I remember how you torched my house. I remember how you put the rope around my father's neck, then let the horse drag him. I remember how your men slashed Isabelle's throat. I remember the blood mixed with the mud. I remember the flames, how you killed Big John. I remember it all."

He stared. Fear returned to him. As he leaned forward, Molly raised the gun again. He eased back in the chair.

"Ferguson?"

His voice came as a whisper.

Molly nodded. "Molly Ferguson. And I remember the brothel in Baltimore. You will get Mr. Webster out, or I will send those letters to General Winder. You'll have the cell next to my husband."

"How?"

He stared at her.

"How is it you?"

"I dyed my hair. I changed my clothes. I covered the freckles upon my face. And I'm older. I was raped night after night. That'll change anyone."

"I don't understand—"

"You don't have to understand. For now, we want you alive. First thing in the morning, you go to General Winder. If you do not, I will tear your life down starting with those letters."

Molly thrust the pistol toward him. It gleamed in the light. She kept the pressure upon the trigger. If not for Webster, she would kill this man where he sat. She no longer doubted that she could do it. He shook his head and raised his hands.

"I never wrote such letters."

"Lying comes easy to men like you. Like how you won my father's estate in a game of poker."

"I was ordered to do that. It wasn't personal."

"Ordered?" she asked. "Ordered to burn my house and kill my family?"

"Yes!" His voice rose, filled with excitement. "Your father was a British agent. He worked for Lord Lyons. I work for the French."

Her calmness began to fade. None of this had turned out how she expected.

"You're lying."

"No, I'm not," Cheeney pleaded. "Did you never wonder how an Irish immigrant found the money to purchase a large Louisiana plantation? Did you ever ask?"

Molly shook her head—nothing she had ever thought upon. Her father came from Ireland, her mother from Richmond. She never knew more, and she never asked. Studying Cheeney, truth and fiction were impossible to separate. His face appeared sincere, and his voice did not waiver.

"We had to stop him," Cheeney argued. "I was told to stop him."

"Why?"

Her confidence drained. But it mattered little. She needed this man to go to General Winder. The rest was history that would not save Webster.

"Your father found a way to make the plantation work—without slaves. Slavery was always the objection of the Crown. They would buy more Southern cotton if it were not harvested by slaves."

"Why do you care?"

"I am *against* anything England does."

Molly studied his face. None of this made sense.

"Why? Why do you care so much about Europe?"

"I don't," Cheeney answered. His tone turned cold. "I don't care about Europe. I hate the British. They killed my father in the Battle of New Orleans. I was a boy when he died."

"So you killed my parents and burnt Salvation Acres because your father died?"

"No!" he yelled. "I did it to save the South. If your father's plan had worked, then there would be no Confederate States. *We* would be *slaves* to Northern industrialists."

He argued in circles. Her anger rose until her finger tensed upon the trigger.

"But you promote the same plan now. I heard you!"

"Because it is the only way to win this war. Think about it. We use your father's plan but do it right! He didn't free anyone. He fooled them. That's all he did. Put the gun down and you can help. I am not a secessionist. I am a revolutionary!"

"No!" Molly yelled back. "He gave them papers. I saw! They could leave whenever they wanted."

"Could they? He paid them so little they could never leave. They weren't free. They only thought they were. And your father was no saint. He kept a Negro mistress!"

"Liar!"

The door to the parlor opened behind Molly. She spun to see who joined them. Even through the dark, as he stood in the door partially bathed in the light, she recognized him.

"Molly?" Jonathon called out.

She had no answer. Then out of the corner of her eye she saw the movement. Mason Cheeney lunged forward. Her finger pulled down upon the trigger. The flash from the barrel bathed the room in an instant of light.

"Father, no!" Jonathon yelled.

He gave no sign the bullet had struck him. Her thumb fought for the hammer again, but it came too late. The older man ripped the pistol from her hand. Cheeney threw her to the ground and pressed his fat body upon her. She stiffened. It was the brothel all over again. She fought, pushing him off. But he was too strong—too heavy. She struggled to breathe, but the air in the gap next to his chest grew stale with perspiration. She gasped at it as her world grew dim.

CHAPTER THIRTY-ONE

MOLLY STIRRED. HER head throbbed if she moved fast. Her ribs hurt near as much as the side of her head above her ear. A large lump had formed there, and her hair plastered to the side of her scalp. Flakes of dried blood came loose upon her fingers. They were barely visible in the dim light.

She found herself upon a rough-hewn wood floor. The gaps between the planks showed little care was taken in aesthetics. This was a functional place. Her hands pressed up against the wood, forcing her body to sit. She had trouble staying upright, using one hand to balance upon the floor. A voice came from the front of the room. It reached her muffled and distant. She didn't know this man.

"She's awake. Get the captain—he wanted to know when she stirred."

A chair scraped along the floor, and then footsteps trailed into the distance. Another person watched—his eyes were heavy upon her. She tried to find him, to see through the fog. But bars blocked her sight. They rose from the floor and made their way to the ceiling as if they were a row in a pine forest without branches. The footsteps returned. There were more this time—and a dog. His nails scratched the wood.

Two figures stood alongside the bars. They blocked the dim light. One stood smaller, though maybe he was farther away. The other wore all black. A large dog sat at his feet. The man banged the bars.

"Stand when I speak to you!"

Molly lifted her head but did not move from the floor. Her world spun—she might retch.

"Wake her up," the man ordered.

The other figure turned, stooping to recover an object from the floor. He hurled it against the bars. Molly raised a hand to cover her face, but the object hit the bars and bounced off. A wave of water crashed onto her. It dripped down her face and left her gasping. She spit upon the floor. The men outside laughed.

"Welcome to Castle Godwin."

His voice was deep and commanding.

"I am Captain Alexander, the warden. While you are here, you will not eat without my permission. You will not sleep without my permission. And you will not speak to anyone but me. Is that understood?"

Molly didn't understand.

"Where is Castle Godwin?"

She pushed up upon her hands, but her strength waivered. The man picked up the wooden bucket from the floor and slammed it against the bars. They rang a dull metallic song. It echoed in her head. She cringed, holding her ear—the one with the large lump.

"This is where we put traitors and whores. I understand you are both." The man held out his hand, pointing across the room. "Get dressed. There are clothes on the bed. You will wear them and place your soiled dress upon the floor outside the bars."

A small cot took up the far wall at the other end of the cell. On the thin bed lay a homespun dress.

"I will return in a few minutes. If you are not changed, then I'll have the men here do it for you. And they can take what they want as they dress you."

Placing one hand in front of the other, she made her way toward the cot. Outside the cell, the man walked away. He left two others. Their eyes weighed heavy upon her. The dog remained. He stared through the bars, towering above Molly on hands and knees. She was grateful for the bars.

"Come, Nero!" Captain Alexander called.

The dog hesitated. It took one long look at Molly, as if it memorized her face, then it turned and sauntered after the man. It disappeared past the edge of her cell, its nails scratching the floor. Molly continued to crawl. She reached the cot and pulled herself to her knees. Then she dragged the dress to her lap. It was a coarse fabric—rough and ill-made.

As she worked the clasps of her dress, the men outside the cell began to make comments. They prodded her with insults. They asked to see her breasts, to have her take it all off and bare her skin for them. She stood, balancing upon the cot. Slowly she pulled off her dress, letting it fall upon the floor. She would not take off her undergarments. She pulled one arm through the dress when one of the men slammed the bucket into the bars. It startled Molly and she almost fell.

"Take it all off, or we come in to help. Everything."

A fierce joy flooded his small features. She clutched the homespun dress to her chest as if it were a shield.

"Maybe I should go in and search her myself, anyway." He laughed and jingled a set of keys. "What do you boys say?"

Several men hollered with glee. He slammed the bars again. Molly jumped.

"Drop the dress and take it off!"

Molly hesitated a moment. The man took the keys out again, this time finding the right one to put in the lock. At the sound, she dropped the dress, and pulled at her undergarments. The keys stopped jingling.

Slowly she pulled off her undergarments. She turned so her back faced him as they fell to the floor.

"Turn around!" the guard ordered. "We need to see you have nothing on you."

He jingled the keys as a threat. Molly turned, her arms wrapped around her chest. When she faced the men, one stuck out his tongue in a lewd manner, as if he lapped milk from a saucer.

"Lift your arms," the guard said. His voice fell softer, oozing with lust.

Molly let go of herself, letting her arms fall to her side—her chest bare to the men gathered in front of the cell. They let out crude gasps, enjoying the eyeful. A tear rolled down her cheek, but she caught it. She forced her eyes to dry. They would not get that pleasure, too.

"Get dressed," the guard ordered.

Molly turned and picked up the dress. Despite the coarse nature, she coveted it. The rough material blocked her from these men. She pulled it on to cover her body, then she sat upon the far end of the cot—hidden amongst the shadows.

The days passed in slow anguish. Molly lost all sense of time. The guards banged upon the bars, as they liked to see her jump. The noise preyed upon her nerves until it wore her thin—like an old cloth washed too many times. They tortured her at all hours. She had no window to judge the days. At first, she kept track of her meals—if one could call them meals. However, the guards did not keep a regular schedule. At times her stomach tugged with hunger. Other times they brought her food before the last meal had eased upon her stomach.

Captain Alexander and the dog came every so often. He placed a chair at the bars to the cell and asked questions. Molly answered none of them. She sat in the shadows with her knees pulled to her chest. They gave her no shoes or socks. The patched blanket upon the cot was her only means of warmth. But the candlelight at the guard table reminded her of what fire felt like—soft and dancing. It teased her with the memory of warmth. Closing her eyes, she hoped that alone would stave off the cold.

Her mind wandered to that time with Webster at the cabin. He shivered until he rested peacefully. His back turned toward her—broad and muscular. She had watched over him all that long night. She longed to see him. Or to see Mrs. Warne. The older woman would be so disappointed. Captain Alexander asked about Webster often. Molly gathered a trial had formed to determine his fate. But she would give up nothing they might use against him.

Time passed without meaning. And with it, she lost hope. The more she held on, the more she slipped through her own fingers. But she didn't care. She had stopped eating. The food offered nothing in the way of incentive—either stale or rotten. She lost the will to do anything other than lie upon the cot with the blanket pulled to her chin.

That was how she found herself, startled awake. One of the guards slammed the bars with a metal food tray. He had come for her dinner, removing it and placing the tray upon the desk. After he closed the door, hushed voices overtook the hallway outside. They reached Molly, but the words remained jumbled. It mattered little. But then the guard took the metal tray and slammed it against the bars.

"Get up!" he ordered.

Molly didn't move. The man worked the keys in the lock and then pulled the door open. Stepping into the room, he made his way to where she lay. He pulled the blanket from her then took a step back, repulsed.

"You need a bath."

Molly didn't respond. He grabbed her by the arm, dragging her to her feet. She floated as he walked her through the cell. Her legs were weak. She hadn't used them in days, maybe weeks. She didn't know. The guard escorted her, still holding up most of her weight. He looped one hand around her back as her feet lagged.

"Walk," he ordered.

Molly tried. They made their way down a hall. She hadn't left the cell since she arrived. Light shone through a window. Dust swirled in the strands of the day, the little sun that made it past the bars. He ushered her farther into the prison, stopping outside a wood door. Then he opened the door and shoved Molly inside. She stumbled and fell, catching herself as she landed on her hands and knees. The man pointed.

"Clean up. There's a fresh dress."

His voice had eased, no longer so calloused as he looked down upon her. She sensed pity. He turned and shut the door behind him. A window on the far side of the room let in light, revealing a tin bathtub in the middle of the floor. It passed far from luxury, but a gentle steam rose from the surface of the water. A small table stood next to the tub, with a similar homespun dress. Molly pulled herself to her feet.

Her head swam. It came from hunger. When she stood over the washtub, the face that peered back in the reflection looked foreign. Her cheeks had sunk. She held her hands to her face. Even her wrists were more slender. As she slipped off her dress, she realized how thin and worn she had become.

Easing into the water spelled a certain relief. The warmth penetrated through her in an instant. She had been so cold. Though now her stomach tugged. The heat awakened hunger from the hopeless slumber that bound everything about her. As she soaked in the water, she came alive, like her very soul rose to the surface. She dipped her head under.

A bar of soap and a towel sat near her dress. She used the soap, as awful as it smelled, to work out the dirt that layered her body. It came off like a snake shedding its skin. She worked as quickly as her malnourished state allowed. But the water cooled fast with the metal tub. Her muscles slowed as the temperature dropped. As she finished, a knock fell upon the door. She stood and grabbed the towel, placing it over her chest. The door cracked open and the guard stood in the doorway.

"One minute more—Captain Alexander has a surprise for you."

His voice revealed nothing about what he meant—nothing sinister nor anything to excite her passions. She pulled the new dress on, trying to keep his eyes from her body. He looked away. She had lost much of her figure. As she washed, she had been amazed how her ribs were so defined under her skin, which seemed paper thin.

Freedom was not the surprise. They wouldn't release her with these clothes—Captain Alexander had some other notion. The guards had rumored she was the only female prisoner.

She shuffled toward the door. The guard pushed it open, revealing the full extent of the hallway. Captain Alexander and the dog stood outside. His smile concealed something.

"You look better. I understand you are not eating."

Molly said nothing.

"Still not talking? Well, General Winder is concerned with your condition. He has ordered a different approach. Come."

"Where are we going?" Molly asked.

Her voice came out raspy and distant.

"You will enjoy it—though not for long," he said. Turning to the guard: "I will escort her."

He took hold of her upper arm and pulled her through the door. Remaining a half step behind, he walked her down the hall. Her heart beat faster. Men like this took what they wanted. She resolved to fight. He would kill her before she surrendered. He pushed her farther down the hall, winding through other corridors. Finally, he stopped before another wood door. Removing a key ring from his pocket, he let go of her arm long enough to search the keys. The dog issued a low growl.

"Do not think it," Captain Alexander said.

He may have been speaking to the dog. He selected a key and unlocked the door.

"You have tonight. I will come for you in the morning."

Then without further ceremony he pushed her through the door. The lock issued a metallic clang as it sealed the room once more. A dim light filled the space, flickering from a candle at the far end set upon a table. In the middle of the room was a bed with a thin mattress.

"Molly?"

She made out the form of a man. He sat upon the bed. But she already knew the voice—*Webster.*

She rushed into the room. He stood and caught her as she ran toward him. She buried her face in his chest. He gripped tight, holding her and pressing his face into her neck.

"I am so sorry," Molly said. "I'm so sorry . . ."

Sobs overcame her. He held tight until she eased.

"This is not your fault. None of this is your fault," he said.

He pulled back to see her, wiping her cheek with one hand.

"Scully folded—then Lewis," he said. "General Winder provided a sham trial and sentenced both to hang. Scully confessed everything. Lewis even escaped for a time but was recaptured. Pinkerton should never have sent them."

"What's going to happen?" Molly asked. "Does Pinkerton know we are discovered?"

"I don't know," Webster offered.

"But Captain Alexander said we had only tonight? What does he mean?"

Molly pulled back far enough to see his eyes, but she did not let go. She reached up until her free hand held his face.

"Tell me what he means," she pleaded.

"They are taking you to Libby Prison tomorrow. They keep the officers there, so it should hold better conditions. I asked to see you before you left."

He looked to the door, then lowered his voice to a whisper.

"I told them nothing about you. They know you only as *Hattie Lawton*. I said I tricked you into helping me courier messages, and that you are a good and loyal servant to the Confederacy."

She placed her head against his chest and held him tight.

"I don't want to leave you. Pinkerton will get us out. He must."

Webster ran his hands down her hair.

"They'll release you. No one rightly believes you were involved."

Molly shook her head. She didn't want to look at him.

"No," she said. "I tried to free you. I went to Cheeney and threatened him with the letters."

"What? Molly, why?"

His hands gripped her upper arms and pushed back enough to see her face.

"So Cheeney knows?" he asked.

Molly nodded.

"That's how they caught you?"

"Yes," she said.

"What about the letters, Molly? What happened with them?"

"I gave them to Miss Lizzie. I told her to get them North. She was going to get me out of Richmond, but I couldn't leave without you."

"Why, Molly? I wanted you out safe."

His voice contained a mixture of desperation and sadness.

"I couldn't lose you," she answered. "I failed everyone. I wanted to kill Cheeney, but I couldn't. I wanted to do something for Isabelle, to get her sister out. But Miss Lizzie didn't know if it were possible. I couldn't leave without you. I had to try something—anything."

He brought her close. She pushed back against him and reached for his face. For a moment they locked eyes.

"Is the rheumatism gone?"

He nodded. "Mostly."

"How long have we been here?"

"Three weeks—maybe more. You look like you haven't eaten. I can feel your ribs."

His hands held her sides. She reached for one of his hands, clasping it. They stayed like that for a minute. He leaned forward. She rushed to meet him. Her lips found his. He lifted her up, and she reached around his neck holding fast. She breathed deep when he exhaled. Stepping backwards, they fell upon the cot. It crashed to the floor, the legs of the crude bed giving out at both ends.

"Are you okay?" he asked, still clutching her.

She nodded. He began to laugh, but she didn't let him finish. She pushed him onto his back and lay on top of him. She pressed into his lips, feeling their warmth. After a moment they stopped. His hands held her face, brushing some of her hair behind her ear.

"Molly, you don't have—"

She cut him off, placing her hand over his mouth. His breath worked its way between her fingers.

"I want to. I never . . ." she trailed off.

She didn't know how to say what she meant—she had never given herself to a man willingly. He sensed her reluctance and grasped her hand. Their fingers interwove. Then she leaned forward upon him and found his lips again.

She reached between them and tugged his pants off. Then she pulled up her dress. She pulled him close, easing onto him. She grabbed both of his hands, weaving their fingers until they locked together. She leaned forward and placed her forehead upon his and stared into his eyes. He pulled tight, easing her back and forth. Then he drew her close, pulling her lips to his.

They stayed like that for hours. After they finished, she lay next to him. They talked as they held each other. He wanted to know about Salvation Acres—the good times. She told him about Isabelle and the trails. She remembered the water in the swimming hole and the feel of the dirt under her feet. It came easy. Not the fire, or the terrible night—but everything before that. She even told how the air smelled in the spring before the first rains. The candle at the table went out—neither of them cared. For the first time in as long as her memory held, she was safe. Her stomach tugged, then rumbled.

"Promise me you'll eat," he said. "You cannot waste away."

She nodded. "If you'll promise we'll get out of here."

"I do. I promise. We'll both get out of here."

She held him tight until her mind wandered. They talked, but slowly sleep pulled him under. His body shook once as slumber took over. She wanted to wake him, to keep talking until they came for her. But instead she wedged her face into his neck. He rolled toward her and clutched her body. She fell asleep in his arms—happier than she had been since she ran barefoot upon the trails at the plantation.

The morning came with a jolt. The door rattled. Webster kissed her upon the forehead. He had been awake. Then he sat and pulled his pants on. Captain Alexander opened the door.

"Not yet," she said.

He rolled back and kissed her upon the forehead, pressing his lips against her skin and holding it there. She closed her eyes and breathed deep, holding the smell of him, committing it to memory.

"Are you ready, Webster?"

Molly reached out and put a hand upon his shoulder. She pulled herself up to sit.

"What is he talking about?"

Captain Alexander laughed. "He is to hang within the hour."

The words struck Molly in the gut, sucking out all the wind. Webster turned to her. She clutched him around the neck. He whispered in her ear.

"I die a happy man."

"No—you promised," she said. "You promised we would leave together."

She stood at the edge of the clearing once more, watching her world burn. Webster pushed her back far enough to see her face. He looked into her eyes.

"I promised we would both leave. And we both will. Get yourself free."

"They can't do this. They—"

Webster cut her off. He placed a hand upon her mouth, then leaned close by her ear so no one else could hear.

"I confessed, Molly."

She wanted to scream. Instead, she clutched at his neck and pressed her head into his. *This can't be happening.*

"Why?" she whispered.

"So you would go free. Make this matter—make it all matter."

His words made no sense. He kissed her and stood. Captain Alexander grabbed his arm as he stumbled near the door. Molly collapsed in disbelief. The feeling of safety from the night before shattered. Her world fell to shambles and she found herself clutching the bed like those first days in the brothel. Nothing made sense.

Captain Alexander dragged Webster to the door. But he paused, standing framed in the open doorway. Before the door closed, Molly caught a final glimpse. For a moment the rest of the world fell away—only the two of them existed. In her mind she reached for his hand. He took it, letting their fingers intertwine. They walked upon a dirt path, barefoot and happy—headed to the swimming hole to make love upon the rocks in the afternoon sun.

Then the door slammed shut. He was gone.

CHAPTER THIRTY-TWO

NUMBNESS CRASHED UPON Molly like a wave. It drowned her until nothing mattered. Once more she floated, looking down upon the happenings around her. In it all, she retained a memory of Captain Alexander. He warned her that the clerk of Libby Prison would not match his generosity. And with that, they placed her in a carriage and delivered her across Richmond to a new jail.

By all measures, Libby Prison held luxury compared to her old cell. She had her own room, this time with a door—not merely bars. Even with the small window inset in the door, it afforded a modicum of privacy. The best part came from the window. She counted the rising and the falling of the sun. She scratched them upon the wall with the spoon they left her for meals. It mattered little to her. She ate, from a promise to Webster. He had died—confessed—so she would go free.

Spring came upon Richmond, throwing off the shackles of the gray winter. She stood for hours on the small stool in her cell, facing out the window. She danced among the clouds, imagining their touch as she jumped from one to the next. But when the sun fell, it returned the dark to her room and with it, captivity.

The prison held captured officers. She had heard Miss Lizzie talk about this place. Miss Lizzie made it out to be a wretched existence, though she had likely not visited Castle Godwin. The commandant of the prison cared little for the prisoners, or at least took no interest in the daily operations. But Captain Alexander was right about Mr. Ross—the clerk. He had a reputation for beating the men. He walked through the halls with a riding crop in one hand. He beat anyone within an arm's length. At times he stopped by Molly's door and peered through the small window. He stared without uttering a sound. It made Molly's stomach turn, and she always said a prayer as he walked away.

When she had been at the prison for nearly two weeks, she received her first visitor. Up to that point no one paid her any mind, except for taking her bedpan or bringing food. They let her walk in the yard a few times each week, but it came in fleeting spurts— nothing regular. So when the key worked her lock and the door opened, she stared at the familiar face—*Miss Lizzie.*

She started to call out in surprise, but noticed the finger held over the older woman's lips. She wanted Molly to remain quiet. The guard watched for a moment. Miss Lizzie remained characteristically stiff and formal.

"Mrs. Webster. I am Elizabeth Van Lew. I look after some of the prisoners here at Libby Prison. After I was made aware of your detention, I made a request to see you."

Molly nodded. This was an act for the sake of the guards. She stepped down from her stool, and pulled it toward her bed.

"It is good to meet you, ma'am. I am afraid I have little to offer in terms of comfort. If you'd like to sit." Molly motioned to the stool.

"Thank you."

Miss Van Lew sat. Molly smiled at the guard. Seemingly convinced, he pulled the door shut. His footsteps faded down the hall.

"I just heard you were here," Miss Lizzie lowered her voice.

"They brought me from Castle Godwin."

"I heard. It is an awful business about Mr. Webster."

"Is it . . ." Her words failed her.

"It is done. I am most sorry for your companion."

Molly held back the tears. It came hard, but they remained at bay.

"If I had thought you would have run off that night, I would have posted Mary Jane at your door," Miss Lizzie said.

"I had to try and save him," Molly offered.

"I understand. Foolish as it was—I understand. I called in many favors to get you here, but I managed."

"Why?" Molly asked. "I did not want you to put yourself at risk. That's the last thing I would wish."

"I know. But it is what we do. And we have lost several couriers. It is becoming harder. When we get you out, I need to make contact with General McClellan. I still have no trusted route to the true government with the information we collect. And I have your letters. Mrs. Atwater is working on the plans for Mr. Cheeney's infernal ship. She had a copy of them, but Captain Atwater feared he would be implicated. He may be cooling to our plan. Mrs. Atwater remains steadfast. She will provide them when her husband leaves with Mr. Cheeney this afternoon."

"I did not kill him then?"

Miss Lizzie shook her head. "No. But I do hear that he has nasty powder burns upon his face. You must have come close."

"And he's leaving Richmond?"

"Yes—to New Orleans. They will start building these ships at a second ironworks."

"But how will you come for me . . . and when?" Molly asked.

Footsteps came from the hall again. The guard returned. Miss Lizzie looked to the door.

"They only granted me a few minutes. I cannot tell you when. But you need to be ready always."

Molly held up her hands. "I'll pack."

Miss Lizzie cocked her head. The humor was lost upon the older woman. Before she could respond, the door behind them opened. Mr. Ross stood with a guard.

"I trust you had a good visit?" he asked Miss Lizzie. "And you can see that we treat our female guests with as much respect as the officers."

"She is a prisoner, not a guest. If she was merely a guest you would have permitted her to stay at my house as I requested."

A thin smile formed across Mr. Ross' lips. He seemed a nervous man—skinny and not quite composed.

"I will leave such decisions to General Winder. In the meantime, I have come to escort you out, Miss Van Lew."

He motioned to the door. Miss Lizzie stood.

"I enjoyed our talk, Mrs. Webster. I will be sure to bring you the things you requested when I have the chance. Perhaps in a few days."

And with that, Miss Lizzie turned and walked to the door. She disappeared through the doorway. Mr. Ross held the door open for a moment. He looked Molly up and down. Instinctively, she curled in her shoulders and tried to make herself small. She had seen this look before—on men at the brothel. Mr. Ross closed the door and Miss Lizzie's shoes punctuated their walk with a staccato rhythm.

The days blurred together after that. But Molly ate more voraciously. Before, she would finish half her food. The meeting with Miss Van Lew inspired her. She polished her plate every night—no matter how awful. She would need the strength. Even though spring had found them, crossing the Potomac could still be a dangerous affair. And if they headed over land, then it would be even harder.

A week after Miss Lizzie visited, one of the guards left her with a small basket. It contained homemade biscuits with a small jar of honey. Molly recognized Mary Jane's cooking. She searched the basket, but there came no word on how or when she might depart. She spent her days at the window. But Mr. Ross visited more often. He peeked through the door without making any sound. She turned one day, with the uneasy feeling of being watched. She found him on the other side of her door. He left immediately. *Miss Lizzie, hurry. Please.*

That evening, as the sun dropped below the horizon, it filled her cell with a dying gloom. She had taken to small naps so she could stay awake at night. The best time for any escape would come after dark, with a light guard force. It would be a harder prospect to walk out of the place during the day. And night harbored a certain dread. She did not feel safe sleeping during the quiet hours.

As she sat upon her cot, a dim light built in hallway outside. It started weak, like when the guards walked the halls with lanterns to check on the prisoners. They never paid her much attention. They housed her on her own end of the building. But this light continued to build. She tucked into a ball on the cot.

No footsteps accompanied the light—not until the light came closer. Then someone held a lantern to peer into the room. Keys rattled and the door opened. Mr. Ross stood in the doorway. A grin plagued his face.

"You're awake."

Molly said nothing. Her heart beat fast. With her foot, she brought the stool closer. It would make a club.

"Come with me."

"Why?" Molly asked. She kept her voice meek. She wished to find some answer to his intentions without angering him.

"Now!" he ordered.

He looked out the door. He didn't want others to see. Her discomfort grew, but she stood. For a moment she lingered by the stool. *A foolish thought.* She could survive this. She had survived so many others—*what would one more matter?* When she approached the door, he grabbed her by the arm.

"Where are we going?" she asked.

"My quarters."

Molly breathed deep. It steadied her nerves. She didn't like the smell of him—tobacco. With a firm grip, he guided her through the hall. Behind them, he left her door open. She wanted to ask but thought better of it. Maybe he would let his guard down and give her the chance to slip from the prison on her own. She would hide in the shadows until she reached Miss Lizzie's house. And this man would not raise an alarm—not after he had roused her for his own desires.

He walked her down several corridors, stopping in a doorway to wait for a guard to pass at the far side of the complex. Then he guided her across a short courtyard. He ushered her inside an office, closing the door behind them. A bedroom branched off the side of the room. The opposite end contained a small stove with a kettle. There was even a back door, which faced toward the street—*freedom*. Taking off his coat, he pointed to the room.

"In there and get dressed."

As he turned his back, she searched the room. A pistol lay upon a desk a few feet away. He did not see her pounce, but he must have heard her sudden movement. She grabbed the weapon and cocked the hammer. When he faced her, she pressed away, creating enough distance. She did not want the weapon taken as Mr. Cheeney had done. He stared at her.

"You'll find a change of clothes in the other room," he said. Then he turned from her again and sat on a chair near the desk. He started pulling off his boots.

"I'll kill you." She meant it.

"That would be stupid."

"You would be dead."

"And you would be caught," he countered. "The moment you fire that weapon, every guard in the prison will descend upon this office. Now . . . go in the other room and change."

His confidence was confusing—so cavalier with his life upon the line in this manner. She feared the pistol might be unloaded. So she pulled the weapon back to check the front of the cylinder. All the chambers contained a bullet.

Mr. Ross proceeded to pull off his second boot. Then he placed both feet upon the ground.

"This is useless, Mrs. Webster. You waste time. If you change, then you'll have a better chance to escape."

"Escape?"

"Yes. Why else are you here?"

Molly shook her head. She didn't understand. His brow furled. He must have realized.

"No, no. I'm not like that," he said. "I work with Miss Van Lew. I thought you knew."

Molly shook her head.

"There is a Confederate uniform in the other room. It is big, but it will help get you out of the city this evening. You must hurry. Miss Van Lew's colored man is waiting to escort you."

"Robert?" she asked.

"I think that is his name."

Molly peered into the bedroom without lowering the pistol. A gray uniform lay upon the bed. Her mind processed this twist. Mr. Ross opened the door to his desk and took out a chain—her chain. It still held her medallion and the key.

"I thought you might want this back. They took it from you at Castle Godwin."

Molly lowered the weapon. It wasn't a trick. She stepped forward, tentatively at first. Then she took the chain.

"You'll need to leave the gun," he said. "I won't be able to explain how you have it. But as for the rest, I'll claim they left your cell open and you fled. When you leave, I'll burn your dress."

"You're the one who helps Miss Lizzie get prisoners out?"

"Yes."

"But you're so . . ." She paused.

"Cruel?" he asked.

She nodded.

"I don't enjoy it, but it makes me the last one they'd ever suspect. I've helped dozens escape. I believe it justifies my methods."

"And when you came to my cell?" Molly asked. "All those nights?"

"It's a different part of the jail. The superintendent has changed the rotations. I was working out the best night and time to get you. But you must hurry."

She had been wrong about him. She handed him the pistol, holding it by the barrel. He took the weapon and de-cocked it, letting the hammer down easy. He pointed to the room.

Molly closed the door and changed. He had even thought of cheesecloth wrapping, to bind her breasts tight. She had lost so much weight it seemed to matter little, but it might still help passing her off as male. The uniform was loose, and well worn. Both facts helped to disguise her body even more. She pulled on the boots. It had been weeks since her feet had either socks or shoes upon them.

When she stepped from the room, he nodded in consent.

"I chose well. It was the smallest I could find. If you come here, I'll cut your hair."

"Cut it?"

"Do you wish to get out of Richmond?" he asked.

She didn't answer. Instead, she stood in front of him and turned so he had her back. He picked up a pair of shears from his desk. Her hair fell in large chunks.

"I'm afraid I've never done this before," he said. "It won't be pretty."

He worked fast. She hadn't seen a mirror in some time. It surprised her how much of the black dye had faded or washed out. Much of the hair at her feet revealed its deep auburn color.

"Thank you," she said as he finished.

"You are passable—from a distance. One more thing . . ."

He stepped toward the small stove in the corner of the office. His hands picked up some of the ash and charcoal. He rubbed them together, shaking off the excess. Then he stood before Molly. He wiped her cheeks down.

"It makes you more soldierly."

"Full of soot?" Molly asked.

"Soldiers are soldiers everywhere—they sleep by the fires, they camp in the mud. It is a dirty profession. It's why I prefer the prison."

He pointed toward the back door.

"Cross the street," he said. "You'll find Miss Van Lew's man. They'll find you missing at roll call. I'll have to make a report to General Winder before breakfast, and they'll be sure to search for you. They wanted to exchange a female Confederate spy captured in Washington. With you gone, they lose that leverage."

Molly went to the door and turned the knob. Then she stopped.

"Thank you," she said. "I'm sorry I thought ill of you."

"Don't be sorry," he replied. "When this war ends, I may need friends. The Union will imprison me for my . . ." he paused ". . . for my cruelty."

"The truth has a way through the fog," Molly said.

"I hope you are right. Good luck, and Godspeed, Mrs. Webster."

CHAPTER THIRTY-THREE

MORNING CAME WITH little rest. Miss Lizzie pushed the set of drawers away from the wall and then opened the small door. Molly crawled through. The hidden room was almost worse than her cell. The walls closed upon her. Every time she closed her eyes she saw Jeanine. One more way she had failed. Miss Lizzie brought her downstairs and they huddled near the fire in the kitchen.

"Robert is getting the wagon ready," Miss Lizzie said. "As soon as the sun rises and the curfew lifts, you will start out."

"I can't thank you enough," Molly said. She clutched a cup of tea, warming her hands.

"Mrs. Atwater was here last night. Her husband left with Mr. Cheeney. She provided two copies of Cheeney's plans. Mary Jane is sewing them into your dress. We hope it will make the papers less obvious. I do not think anyone will search your clothes. Robert will drive you out of the city and then to the farmhouse."

"Do we have passes to get through the pickets?" Molly asked.

"No," Miss Lizzie admitted. "We have had trouble in that area for some time."

"When I get to Washington, I will ask Mr. Pinkerton to help," Molly said. "He'll have someone come through Richmond and pick up dispatches."

"That would be splendid." Miss Lizzie took a deep breath. "I fear I will cry if I take too long in this goodbye. I am so sorry, child—about your mother, your parents."

"I know."

"You must get yourself safe, for me and your mother. And you must not come back—not until the rightful flag flies over the city. Then we will have a grand time visiting all the sights in Richmond."

She clutched Molly, the rings of her hair bouncing upon Molly's face.

"It is time."

Miss Lizzie escorted Molly toward the servants' exit. Mary Jane helped Molly change. She showed Molly how the plans were sewn into panels on her dress. The papers felt like waxed parchment—with luck they would last until she arrived in Washington. There could be no wading across the Potomac on this trip. Molly hugged both women, and then met Robert at the door.

"Do not forget these," Miss Lizzie said as she handed Molly the packet of letters from Webster—the ones between Cheeney and the Union general.

"They were too thick to sew into your dress," Mary Jane added. "You will have to carry them."

Molly clutched both women. Miss Lizzie held on an extra moment, then let go. Her eyes moistened but did not break. Her strength and courage were boundless. Molly summoned her own brave front. She would rest easy once outside Richmond.

Robert drove them on a wagon once dawn broke over the city. Molly had a couple hours before the prison realized she had escaped. They roused the prisoners and gathered them for a headcount each morning. Then she would discover how much they wished to recapture her.

Her hands shuffled through the stack of envelopes in her hands as they descended from Church Street. All her plans, the things she would do to exact her own revenge—she had failed. Jeanine's face haunted her. Molly placed a hand upon Robert's arm.

"What is it, Miss Molly?"

He brought the wagon to a stop. Standing still made him nervous.

"I need to go somewhere first, before we leave," Molly said.

"But Miss Lizzie said to get you straight out of town. That's what I intend."

"I know," Molly said. "But I have to find someone. She has to come with us."

Robert tilted his head, then looked over his shoulder. They were still the only ones upon the street.

"It isn't a good idea, Miss Molly. I'll take a message once we see you clear of the city."

He went to start up the carriage again, but Molly tugged at his arm once more—this time with more force.

"What did it mean to you, when Miss Lizzie set you free?"

He let the reins fall, his curiosity piqued.

"What did it mean?"

"Yes," Molly said. "Do you remember what it felt like?"

"Of course, Miss Molly. That's something I guess you white folk will never understand. I have my papers. They show me to be a free man."

"What if your papers went away?" Molly asked.

He turned in his seat. His look filled with suspicion.

"No, no..." Molly said. "Can you imagine if someone took your papers? Can you imagine how that would feel, to be free then made a slave again?"

He nodded, uncertain what she meant.

"There's a girl here in Richmond," Molly explained. "That happened to her. She lived with me when she was young. She was born free, but now she's not."

"She's a slave?" he asked.

"She wasn't, but when my plantation burned, Mr. Cheeney took our servants and made them slaves. They all had papers like yours. He took them from her."

"That's not right."

"I know. I need to get her. Will you help me? We have time."

He shook his head. The nervousness returned. He looked around—still empty.

"They killed her sister in front of me," Molly said.

"They'll come a looking soon, and if they catch us, they'll take *my* papers."

"I know," Molly said. "And you know how that would feel. She's not far, back down the road a bit."

"Can you be fast? She knows you're coming?"

"She doesn't know. But if it were you, would it take you any time to get ready?"

He looked at her for a moment longer, then picked up the reins.

"Lead the way, Miss Molly, lead the way. But if I done get caught up in this, you have to promise to get the two of us out!"

Molly directed him to the Cheeney residence, stopping well down the street. She sat for a moment gathering her courage. Mr. Cheeney had left, and if he went to New Orleans, only Mrs. Cheeney would be in the house. Jonathon Cheeney had likely gone with his father. It was a risk, but she had to do this for Isabelle. She had lost Webster, and her chance at Mr. Cheeney. This was all she had left.

She stepped from the carriage and made her way to the servants' entrance with fleet feet. Looking back, Robert shifted in a nervous manner. She had to hurry. Her fist rapped upon the door. Inside, the servants were stirring—likely getting breakfast ready for Mrs. Cheeney. The door opened.

The girl stared at her. Molly hadn't anticipated seeing Jeanine right away.

"Miss Molly? It's really you?"

"Yes," Molly said. "It's me." She paused. "I'm glad to see you."

Molly's tone didn't confirm her words, and she heard it as soon as they left her mouth. Her guilt overwhelmed her. The girl looked so much like Isabelle, though her skin was lighter. Molly looked into the room beyond. The kitchen was empty. She stepped inside and pulled the door shut behind her.

"Why are you here?" Jeanine asked. "I thought you were gone up North."

"Gone?"

"Mr. Jonathon said that after the fire they took you North to relatives. That you were gone."

"No," Molly said. She fought a moment of anger. *Jonathon said that? Gone to relatives?* "They took me away, but not to any relatives."

Noises came from upstairs.

"I'm sorry, Jeanine. I really am."

"For what, Miss Molly?"

"For everything." Molly stopped to collect her thoughts. "I loved Isabelle. I wanted a sister. I wanted *her* to be my sister. But you were her real sister, and I...," Molly paused. "I wasn't. I was jealous."

The girl set her lips firm.

"Did they tell you what happened?" Molly asked. "What happened to Isabelle?"

"A little."

"I'm so sorry, Jeanine. I couldn't do anything. They held me down, and . . ." She pushed the image from her mind. "I came for you. I'm leaving Richmond."

There was no way to apologize for all this girl had been through. For what Molly had done in their youth. They both lost Isabelle. She didn't want to relive that night. In truth, if it weren't for the painting, all she would remember of Salvation Acres would be flames exploding through the windows.

"I can't leave, Miss Molly. They'll find me."

"Is Mr. Cheeney here?" Molly asked, hoping to press the issue.

"Mr. Cheeney is a cruel master, Miss Molly. He beats on Mrs. Cheeney something awful. You don't want him knowing who you are. He'll kill you like he did Big John. Like . . ."

"Like Isabelle?" Molly asked.

Jeanine didn't answer.

"Is Mr. Cheeney here?" Molly asked again. "Is Jonathon here?"

"They both left the other day. I think heading to New Orleans." Her voice trailed off. "I lost all I had, Miss Molly. No more Izzy, no mother. And I'm here stuck with a beaten woman and a cruel man. I don't ever know when that man will show up in the basement at night all drunk. After he's had his fill of Mrs. Cheeney, he comes and finds me. Do you want to hear the things he does?"

Molly shook her head. It wasn't fair—she caused none of those things. And she needed no imagination to know what Mr. Cheeney did to her at night. Man after man had lain atop her at the brothel and done the same. Molly shook her head. This wasn't the time or place to argue.

"I'm leaving Richmond," Molly offered.

"What's that to me?"

"Come with me. I'll take you North."

Jeanine studied her. Molly matched her look, staring straight into her eyes.

"You mean it?"

"That's why I'm here," Molly said.

Jeanine didn't answer. Instead, her hardened look eased, maybe in puzzlement.

"Where would I go?" the girl asked.

"Anywhere you want. I'll find you money to go anywhere."

The girl nodded, though the movement was slight.

"Is Mrs. Cheeney here?" Molly asked.

"She stayed behind," Jeanine confirmed. "You must go now. If they find you, I don't know what they'll do to you—or to me."

"I know what they'll do to me," Molly said. "They'll hang me."

"Like your husband?"

Molly thought a moment. "Yes, like my husband. Show me to Mrs. Cheeney and then gather your belongings. We leave right away."

"Why?" asked Jeanine.

"Because I promised. And I'm here now. You can stay if you want, but this is the last time I'll be in Richmond. If you wish to leave, you have to go with me now."

Jeanine studied Molly. Her hard look remained, but Molly sensed something. The girl looked away.

"I'll come."

"Good," Molly said. "Get warm clothes. Where is Mrs. Cheeney?"

"She's in the front sitting room, waiting on her breakfast. Are you going to ask her?" Jeanine asked.

"No. I have something for her."

Molly made her way up the stairs. She walked down the hall, pausing only a moment to look at the painting of Salvation Acres. Then she walked into the front sitting room. Mrs. Cheeney sat in front of the fire. She spoke without looking up.

"Place my breakfast on the small table, Jeanine. I hope you remembered my tea."

Molly said nothing. Her heart beat fast in her chest—so much so that each heartbeat made her vision jump. Her mouth dried.

"Jeanine . . ." Mrs. Cheeney's voice faded as she turned to see Molly. "What are you doing here?"

"I came to see you."

"I know who you are. The last time you came to kill my husband!"

"I did," Molly said.

"Thank God for my son."

"Are you trying to tell me you wouldn't be better off without him?" Molly asked.

She hadn't thought this plan through, but there was no turning back.

"How dare you—"

Molly cut her off.

"I've seen your face. When I lived in New Orleans, I heard the rumors. Everyone talked about it. Everyone here talks about it. I know he beats you. And . . ." Molly paused, stepping closer to take a better look at the older woman . . . "it looks as though he has been at it again."

Mrs. Cheeney stared into the fire. A bruise covered the right side of her face. The skin under her eye had turned yellow in the healing process.

"I will scream for help," Mrs. Cheeney said.

"I am your help," Molly answered.

Mrs. Cheeney looked to her. "What do you mean?"

"Do you wish to continue to live this way? Or do you wish to be free of him?"

"I am serious," Mrs. Cheeney said. "I will scream, and you will go back to jail."

"Then do it," Molly said. "Or shut up and listen."

Mrs. Cheeney made to stand, but then she eased back into her chair. She stared at Molly a moment, but then looked to the fire.

"I see it upon your face," Molly said. "Do not feel bad about hating him—about wanting him gone. He is an evil man."

"No," Mrs. Cheeney countered. "I love my husband. He is not evil."

"He killed my father and burned Salvation Acres. There was no gambling debt. Then he raped and killed my mother."

Mrs. Cheeney stood. Her fists clenched at her side.

"Liar! You have lied since the moment I met you. You told me you had never been to New Orleans. My husband had nothing to do with your plantation burning. Your father betrayed his people. He betrayed the South. It was God's vengeance!"

They stood like that for a moment, both fierce in their determination. But the older woman didn't believe her own words. It played upon her face. Molly reached around her neck and pulled out her chain. It contained her key and Mason Cheeney's medallion. Undoing the clasp, she took the medallion off her chain. She turned it over in her hand, looking at the back one last time. Molly held it out to Mrs. Cheeney.

"What is this?" she asked.

The older woman studied the medallion. She recognized it.

"I did lie to you," Molly said. "But you knew who I was. I saw it in your face. And you know I'm telling you the truth now. This is your husband's medallion. I found it in my mother's hands. Her dress torn open—her body violated. He was there that night. He raped her. He killed her. He killed my father. He burned my home. You know it. You've always known."

Mrs. Cheeney took the medallion. She turned it over in her hands, studying the little metal object. Her eyes lingered upon the back, tracing the initials. Slowly she sunk to her chair, staring into her hands.

"He is evil," Molly said again—softer. "Maybe he wasn't always that way. But he is now. I came to kill him, but I couldn't do it."

Mrs. Cheeney was quiet for a few moments, then her hand clasped over the medallion. She stared into the fire.

"He rescued me, you know. My father . . ." Her words faded off. "Mason saved me from that man. And for a time, we were happy."

"But you aren't now." It came out as a statement—not a question.

Mrs. Cheeney shook her head. She looked to Molly.

"I tried once, too," Mrs. Cheeney said. "He slept in our bed, and I put his pistol to his head. But I could not. He is still my husband."

"You don't have to," Molly answered. "There's another way."

Molly reached into the pocket on her skirt. She pulled out the packet of letters.

"What are those?"

"Your husband wrote to a Union general, offering to sell the plans to his ship."

Mrs. Cheeney stared at the letters in Molly's hands.

"Why would he ever betray the South?"

"He plays both sides—to make money no matter which way the war breaks. He doesn't love the South like you do. He loves nothing but himself."

"What do I do with them?" Mrs. Cheeney asked.

"Take them to Colonel William Norris. I understand he recently moved to Richmond. He is in charge of the Confederate Secret Service. He will handle your husband."

"I know the colonel," Mrs. Cheeney said.

She reached for the letters. Molly pulled them back.

"There is one more thing," Molly said.

"What is it?"

"I want Jeanine."

"My Jeanine?" Mrs. Cheeney said.

"She belongs to no one," Molly answered. "She was born free— the letters for Jeanine. Your freedom for hers."

Mrs. Cheeney stared at the letters. She nodded. Molly handed her the stack of envelopes. The older woman stared at the medallion and papers in her hand.

Molly walked from the room. She made her way down the hall but stopped in front of the painting. Her eyes darted across the canvas—the canopy of trees that led to her home. She imagined the good times, running after Isabelle. The smell of the place flooded her memory, the feel of the dirt upon her feet—forever gone. She pulled the painting from the wall and headed downstairs to the kitchen.

Jeanine waited, a small bag in her hands. She wore her coat, ready to go.

"Are you taking that with us?" Jeanine asked.

Molly didn't answer. She took one last look at the painting. Then she walked to the fire and tossed it in. The little orange tongues devoured the canvas and lapped at the gilded frame. That was how she remembered Salvation Acres.

"It's time to go."

CHAPTER THIRTY-FOUR

MOLLY AND JEANINE slipped the bounds of Richmond with Robert at the carriage. He steered them to the farmhouse north of the city. It took them the better part of the day as the road had mired in mud from the onset of spring. The man who ran the farm, Mr. Rowley, took them in that evening. He fed them well. By then, the jailers had certainly discovered Molly's escape. If they needed her as leverage as Mr. Ross believed, then they likely scoured the city. It would not take long to realize she had fled. She fretted, wondering if they needed her enough to pursue outside Richmond.

Jeanine remained quiet. She spent her time braiding little figures out of the hay she found in the back of the wagon. She did not talk to Molly, although she spoke with Robert. They talked about New Orleans, and how she made it to Richmond. It seemed he tried to flesh out Molly's story. And he was not disappointed in Jeanine's tale. It balanced with all Molly had said.

But Jeanine's manner toward Molly remained steadfast and cold. At first it stung, but Molly figured it for normal with what the girl had been through. Molly reaped what she sowed. And this wasn't about Jeanine—it was about Isabelle. With that thought, a lightness filled her. She made good on *something* from Richmond. And she had the plans to the ship sewn into her dress. She told no one about those.

Early in the morning, farmer Rowley headed to the nearest town. He wanted to hear the news before he let them go, to better tell which direction to point their flight. He came back hurried, his horse worked into a lather from the hard pace he drove it.

"The cavalry's a coming. They've been searching the outskirts and towns 'round here. You got to get moving. Head west. They expect you to make for the Potomac."

Robert's face soured. He glanced to Molly. They had wasted time getting Jeanine.

"You can head back, Robert. Jeanine and I will go on alone."

At this suggestion, Jeanine became alarmed.

"And who will defend us? You?" she snapped—*a fair point.*

The land between the armies became more desperate—more dangerous. The newspapers carried stories of roving bands of thieves and plundering militia units. One or both armies would be on the move soon, likely to clash somewhere in the middle. So the region transformed into a lawless place, trapped in a calm before the fury.

"No, no, Miss Molly. I made a promise to Miss Lizzie to steer you safe. And I plan on keeping it."

Farmer Rowley nodded. "You need to make it to the Shenandoah Valley. Head to Harrisonburg, then toward Morgantown. That'll swing you 'round the Union positions. It's longer, but safer. This time of year the pickets are jumpy and liable to shoot at anything trying to cross the lines."

Robert loaded the wagon and got them under way. The further they put Richmond behind them, the less he fidgeted. Molly hoped Farmer Rowley steered them right. He provided several baskets of food, blankets, and even an old carriage gun with a few shells. He warned them to stay clear of other households. He couldn't vouch for the loyalties of those around. And traveling with Robert and

Jeanine might cause trouble. Either could be accused of being run-aways. Rewards were paid for less.

The trip went slow. They passed few wagons heading the opposite direction. On occasion, they overtook other travelers who looked upon their group in an odd manner. Molly placed a firm and determined expression upon her face, matching every eye that befell her. It worked. Still, the road behind them kept her attention. If the cavalry came, it would be from behind.

By nightfall on the second day they reached the outskirts of the Shenandoah Valley. The trees grew tight and full. It would be better to push through the night to Harrisonburg, but Robert did not fancy the idea. He worried about the dark in the forest. He claimed he feared falling into a ditch and ruining Miss Lizzie's wagon. Molly suspected he feared the spirits amongst the trees. He talked about them often. The moon was plenty bright overhead, and even the weather favored pushing forward. But Molly conceded.

They camped along a small creek off the main road, at the edge of the forest. Robert didn't want to be too deep in the woods, but they needed shelter from the road. It became hard to find a compromise where they both succeeded in their aims. Molly acquiesced to a place that provided some shelter from the road, or at least would once the fire died.

They ate a light dinner as Robert and Molly prepared beans and cornbread. Jeanine kept wandering off. She came back once Robert called in his booming voice. Molly shuddered each time he yelled—exposing their presence to whomever might be upon the road.

"Where did that girl wander off to again, Miss Molly? Does good to call out loud though. Scares all them spirits away."

"I'm more scared of what else may be out there, Robert."

He looked at her as if she were silly, then called into the dying light once more. Jeanine came in from along the road.

"I was seeing if we was followed," Jeanine explained.

The girl settled across from Robert by the fire. Her hands continued to work the little straw figures. She refused to look at either of them—even giving Robert the cold shoulder. He shrugged at Molly. Molly had no idea what she would do with the girl. Getting her out of Richmond was as far as her thinking on the subject extended.

As darkness surrounded their little clearing, they pulled blankets from the wagon. Molly spread hers on the ground next to the fire, watching the embers. Robert and Jeanine also crept close to the warmth, surrounding the small fire pit. In the distance a single wolf called out. Its voice rose and fell. Robert shuddered as it sang, pulling the carriage gun close.

Night came as a restless sleep. Molly woke repeatedly with the wind whipping through the branches. The trees groaned as they tugged in the early spring weather. Sleep finally claimed her as she stared into the dying embers, under an extra blanket. The ground remained hard, but anything was better than the miserable cot in Castle Godwin.

Deep in the night, Molly bolted upright and listened. She cast off one of the blankets. The other she pulled around her shoulders. Her heart raced. Robert heard as well. He sat up, holding the carriage gun. Through the wind and the trees came another noise—horses.

They were in the distance but neared. The uneven rhythm of the hoof falls told Molly there was more than one rider. *But how many more?* They were deep enough in the woods—no one would see them.

"Do you know how to use it?" Molly asked, nodding to the gun.

Robert nodded. She grabbed the long-cold pot of coffee and poured it over the embers, trying to kill any light. Instead, it threw steam into the night.

"Damn it!" she muttered.

"Where's Jeanine?" Robert asked.

His voice came out barely above a whisper. The horses were close. Molly peered over the fire, to where the girl had fallen asleep. She was gone.

The horses slowed. The dim moonlight cast confusing shadows. Then her eyes picked up the movement. They walked, slow. Then they stopped.

"Molly! Jeanine!"

The voice crashed over them—*Jonathon*. Molly froze. These weren't mere riders upon the road. They searched for her. And Jeanine.

Robert looked to her, panicked.

"How did they find us?" Molly asked. It came out as a hiss.

Robert shook his head. His hands trembled as he held the gun.

The shadows dismounted—two of them. Their footfalls broke sticks as they stepped upon the undergrowth. The cracks broke the night. Along the road, their horses whinnied. The animals pushed plumes of mist into the night air. Both figures stopped, then one pointed in their direction. Even with the dim light, the shape of the men came clear—both held weapons.

"Molly! It's Jonathon Cheeney. It's okay. You're safe! My father's not here. Come out, please."

"Where's Jeanine?" Molly asked as she pressed in toward Robert.

"The girl done run off. We need to make haste, Miss Molly."

He grabbed her by the arm. They fled a short distance through the woods. But it came as a hurried escape, making too much noise as they tripped through the branches. Behind them the figures rushed forward. Robert hurled Molly to the side. He raised the carriage gun and fired. One of the figures spun. A man screamed. Then the other man fired—several shots. Robert teetered. He fell forward, landing upon his knees. For a moment he fought it, but he crashed toward the earth. His eyes looked Molly's direction—lifeless. The gun lay at his side.

Molly dove for the weapon. She grabbed it, and as she brought it to her shoulder a shadow flew at her from her other side. She spun.

Jeanine stood above her with a large branch. Molly raised her hand to soften the blow, but it came too late. The impact echoed. Molly's grip upon the carriage gun slipped, and then she fell forward.

CHAPTER THIRTY-FIVE

MOLLY AWOKE BY a rekindled fire, her hands bound together in front of her. Her thoughts came slow. The blow to the head hurt, but there was something else—something familiar. She had a hard time placing it. Her body moved as if it were a thousand miles away. She willed it through the distance.

Jonathon and Jeanine dragged the body of the other rider away from the fire and toward the road, where the horses were tied. The girl made her way back toward the dancing flames. Molly struggled to sit.

"She's stirring!" Jeanine called to Jonathon. "I thought you gave her plenty of laudanum."

Laudanum. Of course, it felt familiar.

They drugged her with it at the brothel to dull her fight. Her wrists were bound tight. But nearby the flint and steel that Robert had used to make the fire remained in the dirt. One end of the flint was sharp. She grabbed it, clamping her palm around it before Jeanine made her way into the clearing.

As the girl neared, she circled the fire pit and stopped at Molly's feet. She glared down. A hateful look preyed upon her face. She kicked Molly's feet with the point of her boot.

"Why?" Molly asked. It came out as a whisper.

"Why?" Jeanine mocked. "Need you ask, bitch?"

"I got you out of Richmond."

"Why would I want to leave Richmond?"

"I thought you . . ." Molly stopped. She didn't understand.

"You thought I was the little girl who needed saving?"

Jonathon Cheeney walked through the woods behind them. He twirled one of Jeanine's little figures in his hand. Jeanine turned to him—her tone commanding, not the meek girl who acted as a servant.

"You didn't give her enough laudanum," Jeanine said.

"Easy." Jonathon's voice was deep and commanding—the slave master's son. "Remember your place."

Jeanine looked down. "Please. You hate her as much as I. Give me the laudanum."

"I gave her plenty. It'll kick in. We don't want to kill her. She goes back to Mr. Barbusca. He gave me assurances he could hold her this time."

Molly reeled. *Jonathon?* He had lied to her when they met on the street. He knew exactly what happened to her after the fire.

"She needs more. And I don't care if we kill her."

None of this made sense.

"She's confused. At least tell her," Jonathon said.

"She doesn't deserve to know. Give me the laudanum. I'll make her drink the whole bottle."

"Tell her first."

His expression contorted with pleasure. It took all her strength not to stand and rush him—to tear the look from his face. She tested the ropes. They remained fast. When she went to move, she found her feet bound as well.

"She must know," Jeanine said.

"She doesn't," Jonathon answered. "Why would she have come back for you if she knew?"

Jeanine looked to Molly, then knelt. Molly pushed away to make more space.

"Isabelle didn't tell you?" Jeanine asked.

"Tell me what?"

"The truth."

"What are you talking about?" Molly yelled.

Anger surged through her. She pulled at her wrists. The pain felt good. She wanted to strike Jeanine. *Why would she be with Jonathon? Why did she help him find them?*

"About my mother. And your father."

"What about them?"

"When my mother came to the plantation, it was just her and Isabelle. Your father bought her separate from her husband—on purpose. He didn't *buy* the family."

"He tried to keep families together. He went broke trying!" Molly yelled.

"Don't get me wrong, Miss Molly," Jeanine mocked. "I'm glad he didn't. I wouldn't be here if he kept them together. I came after. Your father bought my mother for other reasons."

"What reasons?"

"Because he wanted her."

The words didn't make sense. Molly struggled to make the pieces fit.

"My father was your father," Jeanine said.

"We're—"

"Sisters," Jeanine finished Molly's thought.

"You're lying."

"I'm not. That's why he moved Isabelle to the big house, so he could be alone with my mother and me. Your mother hated him. We were his *real* family."

Isabelle had moved into the plantation house—that much was true. She had the room alongside Molly's, to attend to Molly when she was younger. That's when they grew close. But Jeanine wasn't right. *She couldn't be.*

"You're lying. My father loved my mother."

Jeanine spit upon the ground. "Your mother was a whore!"

"Bitch!"

Molly kicked at Jeanine with both feet, bound as they were. Jeanine avoided them. Then she knelt and slapped Molly across the face. It stung. Jeanine grabbed Molly by the front of her dress, forcing Molly to look at her. Jonathon stood behind them and laughed.

"Your mother sold my mother. She made *our* father do it. He sold her back into slavery!"

"No!" Molly yelled. "My mother abhorred it. She was the reason he freed everyone."

"Everyone except my mother. He sold her!"

"No!" Molly screamed. "My mother gave her money to travel to Montreal. I remember."

Molly's voice betrayed her uncertainty. It happened years before the fire, when Molly was quite young.

"Liar! Your mother sold her. Isabelle told me."

Molly shook her head.

"No. Your mother left for Quebec. They have no slaves there."

It didn't make sense—why would Isabelle have said such a thing? Isabelle knew her mother hadn't been sold. A few years after her mother left, Isabelle said she would leave the plantation and follow her mother north. Molly had clung to the older girl and begged her to stay. Isabelle relented. She never left.

"Isabelle was going to take me to Mother," Jeanine continued. "But you sold her where we couldn't find her."

"We didn't. I saw her in Montreal when I went with my father. Maybe two years before the fire. Isabelle could have left any time."

❖

Jeanine grabbed Molly's face again, holding it harder.

"We weren't free to leave. Your father paid us nothing. He made it seem he was generous, a liberator. But he forced us to stay all the same. We were slaves. He fooled the men—the dumb field hands. They had their papers. Then he raped my mother. She didn't love him. She didn't want him. He sold her and kept me."

Could she have missed this?

"Isabelle stayed because she didn't want to leave!" Molly screamed. "She chose *me* over you!"

Molly meant it to hurt.

"Well, I'm free now," Jeanine said. "All I had to do was lead Jonathon to you, and I have my papers!" She fetched a bundle of parchment from her pocket and shook it. The paper crackled with each shake. "And I'm the reason our father is dead—and that whore you called a mother. I told Jonathon about your father. I told everyone what Planation Acres really was!"

"Why?" it came out as a whisper. *It made no sense.* Isabelle was free, Jeanine was free—their mother was free. *Why would Jeanine tear down everything? Unless... she hated Molly the way Molly had hated her.* Molly's head pounded. The rage built inside until it was unbearable. She lashed out but couldn't strike Jeanine with her hands bound so tight.

"And then you came to Richmond!" Jeanine said. "To rescue me? I wanted to tell them right away, as soon as I saw you. But I waited for Jonathon. And he was right. Hanging is too good a fate. We'll bring you back to Baltimore."

She held her hand out behind her, though her eyes never broke from Molly. They held nothing but hatred.

"Give me the laudanum."

Jonathon fished in his vest pocket and produced a vial. He handed it to Jeanine.

"Don't," Molly begged.

Jeanine grabbed Molly and squeezed her face harder. She uncorked the bottle and spit the cork aside. Then she dumped the bottle into Molly's mouth. Molly coughed, fighting the liquid. When the bottle emptied, Jeanine threw it aside. Then she pushed Molly's face into the dirt as she stood. Jonathon pulled at her.

"Come, we need sleep before dawn. Baltimore is a journey still."

They settled at the far end of the clearing, arranging the blankets upon the ground. Molly rocked. *Jonathon had sold her to the brothel?* Her stomach pitched. She had not swallowed most of the liquid. It remained in her cheek. A trick she learned at the brothel. As they walked away, she let it drain to the ground. Some made it through. She sobbed as the drug took hold. She hated the feeling, robbing her senses. Before she lost, she worked the rope. But her mind ran through her childhood. Isabelle could have left. She chose to stay. She chose it. The laudanum closed in, bringing numbness with it.

When next she stirred, cold had seeped into her body. She lay upon the hard ground with nothing to cover her, and no idea how much time passed. Across the fire Jeanine and Jonathon slept. Molly stressed at the rope binding her wrists—tight. She searched the ground until she found the flint. Working it, the rope frayed, then cut. With her wrists free, she slashed at the rope holding her ankles. It went faster.

The laudanum hung heavy about her balance. She headed away from the fire, tripping once and landing hard upon the ground. Next to her lay Robert, his eyes still open. She startled, then reached to his face. He was cold as the night around them. She tried to force his eyes shut, but they were frozen in place.

"I'm sorry, Robert."

Then as quick as her legs would hold, she ran through the woods.

CHAPTER THIRTY-SIX

MOLLY STOOD OUTSIDE the Barbusca brothel. She had made it to Baltimore—a miracle in its own right. She should have returned directly to Washington—to Mrs. Warne and Mr. Pinkerton. But she had unfinished business. This time, she would finish it all.

Jeanine was her sister?

When she arrived in Baltimore, she went straight to the bank—the one where she deposited the money meant to help President Lincoln's assassins escape the city. Her signature matched the card on file, and she closed the account. They had not touched a cent. She had more than enough money to make things right.

She stood down the street from the brothel, waiting for Jonathon to leave. He had entered the night prior. And she had been there then, watching. There was no sign of Jeanine. In fact, she had watched all week. Tracking his movements every day. She watched when he left. She watched when he returned. Jonathon emerged and walked down the street. When he was out of view, she crossed the worn cobblestones. She paused only a moment before pushing through the brothel door.

Inside, the place flooded back to her memory. This is where it all started. She looked different now—much different. She had bought several fine dresses, and wigs to disguise her short, rough-cut hair.

It transformed her. The mirror contained little resemblance to the ragged girl who Mrs. Warne had pulled from the brothel so long ago.

"May I help you, madam?"

One of the girls approached her. Molly said nothing.

"I think you may have the wrong establishment. This is a—"

Molly held up a hand.

"I know what this place is. I am here to see Mr. Barbusca."

"Is he expecting you?"

"No. But I have a business proposition. Tell him I am here."

The girl looked at Molly, then glanced up the stairs. She hesitated.

"He is likely asleep or drunk behind his desk," Molly said. "It is not yet noon. I can find my own way."

She brushed past the young girl. Her feet creaked upon the stairs. She avoided the one step that produced the loudest sound. She still remembered. As she made her way down the hall, she hesitated, stopping a moment outside one door. She wanted to push into the room, to see who it held now. But she resisted—nothing but bad memories lived inside. Instead, she continued to the end of the hall and opened the office door unannounced. Mr. Barbusca sat behind his desk, hung over. He had become older, and fatter. A pistol sat upon his desk, holding down scattered papers.

"Who the hell are you?" he demanded.

"It does not matter who I am, it matters what I want."

He studied her for a moment, then leaned back in his chair. He wore an old nightshirt with stains.

"What do you want?"

"I need help with a client of yours," Molly said.

"And what is in it for me?"

Molly smiled. It always came down to this with Mr. Barbusca.

"You get your money back," she answered.

He stared at her, narrowing his eyes. He didn't understand.

"I get my money back?" he repeated.

"Yes. I visited you last night and relived you of the contents in your safe."

Molly pointed to a painting of water nymphs. Behind it, a safe set into the wall—the same one she had once broken into in her attempt to escape. He looked to the wall, then began to laugh. It came deep from his belly.

"I don't have a safe," he declared. "I am afraid, madam, that you have me mixed up with someone else."

Molly smiled. She let him finish laughing. He studied her face, trying to place her. Something about her was familiar to him, though he did not yet see it.

"Of course, you do," Molly answered. "Ten thousand, two hundred and forty-seven dollars. I left the coins. You've done well this month."

The amusement faded from his face. There was only one way she could have known that sum. He looked to the gun in front of him and picked it up. Molly didn't move.

"I also took the liberty of emptying your weapon for this very reason," Molly said. "I figured you might not see reason."

Mr. Barbusca looked to the gun, then back to her. He pointed it at her head and pulled the trigger—a metallic click. His face went white. With his other hand he pulled at the weapon, opening the cylinder. The bullets and powder were gone.

"I also cleared the ones in your desk and the shotgun in the corner."

"Who are you?" he asked.

"I am the woman who holds all your money."

His eyes darted to the painting.

"I will kill you," he muttered, pushing up onto his hands.

"And then you would never see your money. I am counting on logic, Mr. Barbusca. I have no desire for your cash. I will, in fact, pay you for your efforts—another five thousand dollars. I took your money not to rob you, but so that you would listen."

He eased back into his chair, though anger still fixated upon his face.

"And what is it you want?"

"I have need to get a client of yours back to Richmond. You see, I work for the Confederate government."

His eyes narrowed. He had Southern sympathies, and she played upon those.

"I can help with that. Give me my money and I will be most glad to be at your service."

Molly smiled but shook her head. "You will get your money once the job is done. Do you still have contacts among the Baltimore secessionists? With the Knights of the Golden Circle?"

Mr. Barbusca leaned back in his chair. He refused to say anything, as if she might be tricking him into a confession.

"This is not the time, Mr. Barbusca, to hold anything from me. If you want your money, I need your cooperation."

He considered for another moment, then nodded. From around his neck he pulled out a chain. It held a medallion—the same as Cheeney's medallion.

"Excellent," Molly said. "Do you know Cipriano Ferrandini?"

He nodded again. "I do."

"This evening, I will require help in capturing and returning a man who has been staying here. If you will be so good as to help me get manpower from the secessionists, and have him delivered to Richmond. The Confederate government will pay both you and your friends handsomely. And you can rest assured that at the same

time you are doing a great service to our Southern cause. I understand you are a supporter?"

"Yes, I am. Which man are we speaking about? I have many customers who come through here to spend time with my girls."

"Jonathon Cheeney."

Shock crossed Mr. Barbusca's face. It was genuine. Molly counted
on his greed being more important than loyalty—with this man it
felt a certainty.

"Are you certain?" he asked.

"Quite. And I will have proof this evening. Which girl does he
visit?"

"He likes redheads."

Molly smiled—*of course.*

"This is what I require. You will provide me a room. When he
arrives this evening, you will send him to me. Tell him you have a
new redhead he would enjoy. And then round up several of your
contacts who can ferry him back to Richmond. Once delivered, you
get your reward."

"You know, he is the son of Mason Cheeney. I hope your proof is
substantial."

Molly made to stand.

"It is. He is a traitor. He sells secrets to the Union—secrets that
will crush our cause. Together, we must stop him. And you will be
both a hero, and rich."

Mr. Barbusca nodded. Greed reflected in his eyes. The trap had
sprung.

"Well, he tricked me this very week. So I suppose I already knew
he could not be trusted."

"Tricked you?"

"Sold me a Negro for the brothel. I thought I was getting a white
girl, someone he has long promised to return. Never you mind. This
will serve as sweet vengeance."

Molly made her way to the door and began to leave.

"Thank you, Mr. Barbusca," Molly said. "I will be sure to bring your money this evening, once Mr. Cheeney is in custody. I suppose you have a stock of laudanum?"

"I do."

"I will require several vials and a bottle of your best whiskey. Please place them in my room and have it cleaned and ready this evening. I will return in a few hours."

Mr. Barbusca began to make his way around the desk.

"You look most familiar," he said. "But I am unable to place it. Have we met before?"

Molly's heart beat fast until she was certain he could see it through her dress. Even if he did recognize her, he would play along. Greed served as this man's greatest weakness.

"I don't believe so, but I do work in very sordid circles. My name is Hattie Lawton."

CHAPTER THIRTY-SEVEN

MOLLY TOOK A deep breath and then finished her glass of whiskey. It calmed her nerves. Mr. Barbusca made good on his promise. Several members of the Palmetto Guard waited in the next room. He had also provided the master suite to Molly. She had seen this room once or twice, saved for high-class clients. Her room had been down the hall—the opposite end of the scale.

When she returned, she had changed dresses to make her appearance less recognizable. Mrs. Barbusca was not around. She took comfort in that. Women were better judges of faces, and she might see through Molly's veiled appearance.

She set the room to work in her advantage—a large changing screen separated the back half. Then she turned down the gas lamps until the light was held dim and poured a glass of whiskey she left on the nightstand. She placed a chair in the middle of the floor. When the door opened, she took a deep breath. Jonathon Cheeney called out from the other side of the screen.

"Is there anyone here?"

Molly concealed her voice, leading with her best Irish accent. *She could have acted upon any stage.*

"Have a seat, and I will be right with you. I poured a drink."

The chair scratched the floor as he sat, and then again as he moved to pick up the drink. She waited.

"Where are you from?" he asked.

"Dublin," she answered.

"I have never met anyone from Ireland."

"Well then, you are in for a treat. We do things different across the ocean," she answered. Her accent came out thick, disguising anything that might be familiar.

"How so?"

"It's not something I can explain. I'll have to show you. But I find men understand better with a few drinks. It loosens inhibitions."

"I can tell you I have none of those," he bragged.

Molly laughed. Then tossed a set of stockings upon the dressing screen.

"I come from an island of Catholics—perhaps they are too obsessed with sin and cannot relax," she explained. "Have a drink."

She heard him stand. Her mind raced; he couldn't see her—not yet.

"Sit back down," she said. "There is no rush."

"I downed the first glass. I was getting another drink," he answered. "Your orders."

He poured, slamming the glass bottle down upon the nightstand. The chair dug into the floor again as he sat back down.

"This whiskey is strong. Normally Barbusca waters it down."

"I told him, nothing but the best," Molly answered. "He said you were important. What is it you do?"

"I command a cavalry unit. But soon I will return to New Orleans and help my father build ships. Glorious ships. Have you been to New Orleans?" he asked.

"Yes," Molly said. "Do you have a girl back home?"

"I did. But not now."

His words slurred. Molly peered around the screen. Jonathon pulled the chair up to the nightstand, pouring a third glass. He downed it in one swallow.

"What happened to her?"

"Are you ever going to come out?" he asked. The glass slipped from his hand and crashed upon the floor.

"I am getting ready, and I like to know about you first. You were telling me about your girl."

"She was beautiful. But she is gone."

"How?" Molly pressed. Her heart raced. She wanted him talking.

"Her father. He would not let me marry her. I asked. I begged! But he was cruel and said I was not good enough for his daughter. He was nothing. *Nothing!* And now she is a whore. Who isn't good enough?"

She held two vials of laudanum. They were empty. She stepped from around the screen. He sat splayed out in the chair. In the dim light he could not recognize her.

"What's your name?" he asked. The words jumbled together.

"Molly."

"I knew a Molly."

She took a step closer and dropped her accent.

"I know."

He looked to her—confused. Then he saw it. He knew. He tried to stand up, but his arms didn't work right. Molly tossed him one of the vials of laudanum. It landed in his lap.

"Did you put the whole vial in there?"

He looked to the bottle of whiskey on the nightstand. Molly tossed him the other vial.

"I put in both."

"Oh God."

From his face, his mind raced. He reached for his side, pulling his pistol. She was faster. She grabbed the weapon by the barrel, taking it from his hand.

"What will you do? Kill me?" he asked.

"I'm not here to kill you," she answered. "There are fates worse than death."

"What?"

"Patience, Jonathon. Patience."

"Molly, please. I saved you."

"Saved me?" Molly asked. "Saved me from what?"

"From my father. He wanted to kill you that night. You should have seen his rage."

Slowly Molly circled the chair. Jonathon slouched, unable to follow her with his eyes.

"You should have let him kill me," Molly answered. "Now look where we are."

"I begged your father. I did! He told me I would never be right for you!"

He reached out and grabbed her arm. The pistol scattered across the floor. He fought the laudanum, pulling her toward him. She panicked, trying to yank back. He was still strong. He dragged her into his lap where he clutched her tight.

"I loved you. We were to marry, and I was to have the plantation. Your father owed us."

Molly struggled, but Jonathon proved strong. She needed to keep him talking, to give the laudanum more time.

"He owed you nothing. You lie like your father!"

"No. He owed us a vast sum. I told him my father would forgive the debt for you—for your hand. He told me I could never have his daughter."

"I don't believe you," Molly said.

She struggled, but he held fast. His eyes burned, and he pulled her close.

"I am sorry, Molly. But we can still do it. We can rebuild the plantation—together."

"Sorry for what?" she asked.

His hands gripped at her back.

"Sorry for what?!" she screamed.

He locked eyes with her.

"I'm sorry for everything."

"For taking me here in the first place?"

"Yes."

"For burning my home?"

"I didn't start the fire. Your father did. I ran home humiliated. And my father came back with me. I told him what the plantation was, and we came back with his men. He saw us and knew he could not win. So he threw an oil lamp upon the stairs. *He* burned it down. My father would have killed you. But I saved you. *I* did that!"

"Liar!" Molly hissed.

He shook his head.

"I loved you, Molly. I still love you."

He pulled her in, pressing his lips against hers. He held her face against his as she fought with all her strength. Then she bit down hard upon his lip. He screamed and pushed her off him. They both fell to the floor. She spit out the piece of lip.

"Bitch!" he swore. Blood gushed from his face. She had taken a gash from his flesh.

Slowly she stood. He tried crawling toward the gun, but she beat him to it. His reflexes had slowed. The laudanum took its toll.

"Molly. Help me from here."

She shook her head.

"Where is Jeanine?" she asked. "Mr. Barbusca said you sold him a girl. Was it Jeanine?"

His head bobbed. His words slurred further, making them almost indistinguishable.

"I don't want her. I want you."

"There are men next door," Molly said. She stepped closer and lowered her voice. "They will take you back to Richmond, with these."

She unfolded a set of the plans from the pocket in the front of her dress. He looked to them. Panic crossed his face. He tried to swat at the papers, but he had lost most of the use of his limbs. He knew what they were. His eyes rolled back in his head. It bobbed. Molly stepped forward and leaned down. She grabbed him by the hair and pulled his head upright. She had no idea if he could hear.

"Once I loved you. Or I thought I did. But *you* made me what I am today. After this I will think of you no more."

His hair slid through her fingers. His head struck the floor. She stepped over him and pounded upon the wall—the signal she arranged with Cipriano Ferrandini and his men. The door to the room opened.

"This is the man?" Ferrandini asked.

He stared at Molly. She wiped her mouth. Her fingers came back bloody. In the mirror beyond the bottle of whiskey her lower face was stained crimson. She wiped at it.

"This is the man," she said.

She handed Ferrandini the set of plans.

"Bring him and these plans to Colonel William Norris, in Richmond. When the colonel asks who sent you, tell him it was Hattie Lawton. He will pay your reward. Above all, guard those plans. They will make all the difference to our Southern cause."

"Upon my honor, Miss Lawton."

Molly grabbed his arm, holding it fast as he took the papers.

"The colonel knows who you are, by name and reputation," Molly said. "I know you were unable to aid us in our cause when Mr. Lincoln came through Baltimore. This is your chance at redemption, Mr. Ferrandini. Do not squander it. We get so few second chances in this world."

He stared at her, and then nodded as he looked away. She meant it as a means to shame him. He would not fail. Not on this assignment. Molly handed him several more vials of laudanum.

"When he wakes, give him more. It will keep him quiet all the way to Richmond."

Ferrandini accepted the vials, then snapped his fingers. Two of his men pulled Jonathon Cheeney to his feet. They hauled him from the room, dragging him down the stairs. His feet played upon each step. Molly followed to the top of the stairs, watching the foyer below. Mr. Ferrandini held the door to the brothel and then bowed to Molly. The door closed behind them. She stood for a moment. Outside, a carriage started upon the road. Jonathon Cheeney headed home.

Oddly, nothing reached her—no guilt, no sorrow, and no relief. Nothing.

"And now that I have done what you have asked of me, can we settle the other part of our bargain Miss Lawton?"

The voice came from behind her. Mr. Barbusca stood in the hallway.

"Yes. I have it in the master suite. Let us go to your office, and I shall count out your reward."

The fat man pressed his palms together then turned toward his office. Molly followed him, stopping only to gather her bags. Then she stepped into Mr. Barbusca's office. He had already opened his safe to accept his money. For a moment he stared at her face. She had clearly not wiped all the blood from it. Molly dropped one of the bags upon the desk. Eagerly his eyes darted to the bag, and he rushed to open it. His face bolted upright, turning red.

"What manner of joke is this? It's empty!"

"I apologize," Molly said. "Your reward is in here."

She reached into her other bag and produced Jonathon Cheeney's pistol. She pulled the hammer back.

"What is—"

"You don't recognize me?"

He looked at her, narrowing his eyes as if squinting brought back his memory. Molly pulled at the wig she wore. It dropped to his desk. Her short auburn hair felt the air in the room for the first time all day. Maybe it came from the color of her hair, but something brought the memory to his mind.

"Molly Ferguson."

His voice faded as he looked at the pistol. Then he smiled.

"You couldn't use the gun last time if I remember right."

Mr. Barbusca started laughing. It didn't bother her. She held the weapon steady, easing her finger onto the trigger. It would take almost no pressure to set the gun off.

"Where's my money!" he screamed.

"Do you remember what you took from me?" she asked.

He squinted again, his face growing flushed.

"You took something you can never give back. I remember it—before you gave me the laudanum. I still remember your fat body upon me."

"So you will steal from me and make Jonathon Cheeney out as a traitor? I'll tell everyone who you are. You'll never get away with it."

"I will," Molly answered.

The gun kicked in her hand. Blood splattered across her dress. The warm mist hit her face. She tasted the iron in it. It surprised him—he hadn't expected her to fire. Struggling, he started toward her. She pulled the hammer back on the pistol and fired again—then again, and again. More blood splattered. He slumped onto the desk then slid off as a snake might slither from a high object. She walked around the desk, aimed once more, and fired the weapon into his head. His body rocked. His fat carcass filled the floor.

This moment should have felt better. Mrs. Warne was right. The gun was not her path. It should have been more therapeutic. But she cared nothing for this man, or the fact she just killed him.

She picked up her wig. Before she left the room, she stopped at the entrance. Her reflection caught in the mirror upon the wall. She took a handkerchief from her pocket and wiped at the blood upon her face. It was impossible to get all the little spots. It didn't matter. She placed the wig back on, adjusting it as if nothing had happened. Then she started down the hall. She stopped at each door, opening it and leveling the weapon at the man inside.

"Get out!" she ordered.

She made them flee the room without clothes, heading into the streets of Baltimore naked. Then she ordered the girls out. None tried to stop her. They fled from their rooms, filing down the hall.

Finally, she stood in front of her door. She opened it. A girl sat upon the bed—Jeanine.

"It's time to go," Molly said.

Jeannie looked at her, then turned her head in defiance. Molly leveled the weapon in her direction. She had one more bullet by her count.

"Kill me," Jeanine said.

Molly fired, but it went wide—on purpose. The younger girl startled, shrinking back onto the bed. Tears filled her eyes.

"It's time to go," Molly said again.

Jeanine stared, then produced her leg. She tugged at it—chained to the bed as Molly had been. Molly nodded. She dropped the empty gun upon the floor and pulled the chain from around her neck. She tossed it to Jeanine. The chain held the key. Molly turned and started down the stairs.

At the bottom she waited. The other girls had gathered around the waiting room. They stared at Molly. None dared challenge her. When Jeanine emerged from the room, she hurried down the stairs. Molly pulled an oil lamp from the wall. *Was Jonathon right? Had her father started the fire?* It didn't matter. None of it mattered. She threw the lamp onto the carpeted steps.

At first nothing happened. Then the flame in the lamp jumped, spreading across the carpeted surface. It flared, giving off immense heat. The girls ran for the entrance, pushing their way out into the

Baltimore night. Molly waited a moment, watching the little orange flames cleanse the building. She turned and left.

She found a better vantage point across the street. The smoke rose into the dark of the night. She hated the smell. Jeanine stood by her side. Shadows from the fire danced upon the girls face.

"What do I do now, Molly?"

Jeanine's voice came out meek. She stood in her nightgown. Molly paid her no mind, preferring to feel the heat of the flames across her face.

"Where is Jonathon?" Jeanine asked.

This was not the ferocious woman who had attacked Molly in the woods. She held true concern for Jonathon Cheeney. It didn't seem possible.

"He is gone."

"Gone?" Jeanine asked.

Molly nodded and went back to watching the brothel burn.

"My papers were in there," Jeanine said.

"You never needed them. You were born free."

"But the Cheeneys, they . . ."

"They made you a slave," Molly finished her thought.

Maybe Molly had never seen it—the plantation workers weren't free as she had believed. Maybe they stayed because they had nowhere to go. They had their papers but they were bound to the plantation like any other slave in the South. And perhaps her father had loved Jeanine's mother. They had found her in Montreal on that trip north; Molly had seen them. That was why her mother had sent the woman away. Jeanine was wrong on that count. The woman didn't hate her father. Molly stared at the fire. Perhaps the truth lay somewhere in between. It didn't matter.

Slowly, she held out the other bag from the brothel.

"What's this?" Jeanine asked.

"Mr. Barbusca's money. I don't want it."

Jeanine opened the bag then closed it in a rush.

"But what do I do with it?" Jeanine asked.

"Your mother's in Montreal," Molly said. "I don't know how you go about finding her, but I know that much to be true. Other than that, I don't care." Molly paused, looking at Jeanine. "I hated that you were Isabelle's sister and I wasn't. I never treated you well. For that I am still sorry. But you're not *my* sister."

Then she walked away, leaving Jeanine in front of the burning brothel.

CHAPTER THIRTY-EIGHT

2 MAY 1862, WHITE HOUSE, WASHINGTON, D.C.

"I CAN'T TELL her the truth," Molly said.

Mrs. Warne shook her head.

"Of course not."

"Then why am I talking to her?" Molly asked.

"Because the woman needs closure. She needs to know her husband died for something. You will give her that much."

Mrs. Warne hesitated, stepping closer to put her hand on Molly's stomach.

"And if we wait much longer, you will start to show. Then we will deceive no one. She has given birth to children—she will know the timing. You may fool Pinkerton, but you do not fool me."

Molly held her stomach, protecting it with both hands.

"I'm not judging you," Mrs. Warne said, her voice soft. "I know things happen and that he was a good man. Tell her the good—leave out the rest."

Mrs. Warne walked to the door and opened it. Beyond the threshold sat a small yet comfortable sitting room. A woman stood from one of the seats. Molly took a deep breath and followed Mrs. Warne into the room.

"Mrs. Webster, I would like you to meet Miss Ferguson. She worked with your husband in Richmond."

The woman hid herself behind a thin smile as she studied Molly. Her eyes made Molly uncomfortable.

"It is nice to meet you, Miss Ferguson."

It was odd to hear her real name.

"I am most sorry for your loss, Mrs. Webster. Your husband was a good man."

It felt worse to bestow her adopted name back to its rightful owner— Mrs. Webster.

The woman said nothing. Molly's words rang hollow. They both knew it. The woman continued to study Molly. A bead of sweat dripped down Molly's back. She shifted her weight in an awkward fashion.

"What exactly was the nature of your relationship with my husband?"

"I helped him in Richmond," Molly said. "We worked together."

"Yes, yes," the woman said. "But what exactly did you do together?"

Seeing Molly struggle, Mrs. Warne stepped in. "The details of our work must remain secret, Mrs. Webster. I hope you understand. Miss Ferguson acted as part of Mr. Webster's cover. I sent her to listen to the women of Richmond and give us better perspective."

The thin smile returned. This woman did not believe what she heard, or they were not telling her what she wished to know.

"And did you . . ." Her voice trailed off. "You're very beautiful, Miss Ferguson—and young."

"Oh no," Molly lied. Her hand drifted to her belly. Mrs. Webster didn't notice—Mrs. Warne did. "I spent much time with your husband. When he became ill, I nursed him to health. That was how we passed our time."

"So you were close with my husband?"

Her voice implied something more. Molly chose to ignore it.

"Yes."

Mrs. Warne shot her a glance. It was the wrong answer—at least for what Mrs. Webster needed.

Molly continued. "I know what you want to know, Mrs. Webster. I understand. I may be young, but I have seen many things. I was close to your husband. He was a good man and he spoke of you often. He loved you."

"Which is why he went to Richmond with you instead of returning home?"

Mrs. Warne wore a stern look—*tread carefully*. Molly drew in a deep breath.

"There is no way I will be able to give you the certainty you desire," Molly said. "I won't even try. But he told me of you. And he told me of your daughter. He said he wished he had more time before she died—that he had been home more often. I think..."

The woman began to soften. Her eyes glistened, and her accusing expression dissolved.

"You think what?"

"I think he didn't know how to get back to you. I mean, he knew where you were, but he didn't know how to go home. It was not your fault. He held much guilt over your daughter. He loved you, but he was lost."

Mrs. Webster looked away. She dabbed at her eyes. Then she reached out and took Molly's hand.

"I am sorry for accusing you, Miss Ferguson. That was not very Christian of me." She smiled, her thin smile. "I'm glad someone was with him at the end. Someone who cared for him."

Molly felt cheap. Maybe Mrs. Webster believed her. Or maybe, Molly had said enough to give the older woman hope. But then Mrs. Webster reached forward and took Molly up in an embrace. The woman cried—her chest rose and fell erratically. Molly's eyes filled, but she caught sight of Mrs. Warne. The older woman shook her head ever so slightly. Molly fought the tears, walling them off behind a dam.

A knock fell upon the door behind them. Mrs. Warne stepped aside and opened it a crack. She spoke in hushed voices to a man who stood outside. Mrs. Warne turned to them.

"I'm sorry to interrupt," Mrs. Warne said, "but I have to escort Miss Ferguson to a meeting with the President. Mr. Lincoln would like a word, but we will return."

Mrs. Webster nodded, releasing Molly. Molly made space between them but did not fully let go of the other woman.

"He loved you. Please know that."

"I do."

Mrs. Warne caught Molly's arm, easing her away.

"I'll return in a few minutes, Mrs. Webster," Mrs. Warne said.

And with that, Mrs. Warne escorted Molly through the door. They followed the man down several hallways. He wore a dark suit. When he glanced over his shoulder, his eyes always met hers—deep brown eyes. There was something about his face. She didn't know him, but he felt familiar. His skin was darker, not quite white. It gave him a strong appearance—striking. That alone made her curious. But there was something else—in how he walked, or in how he held himself. Something about him reminded her of Webster.

Pinkerton greeted them at his office door. It was a small room, exactly what he wanted. His main office was back along I Street. So this place served to keep his prominence among those who contended for the President's attention.

"The President will be along shortly," he announced.

He ushered Molly to a chair near the fireplace. The fire burned low and bore little heat into the room. Spring came with its chills. It came in handy to have the fire started, ready to stoke in case the weather turned.

"I don't know if Mrs. Warne has had a chance to tell you, Molly. But the plans you delivered did much good this week. We forwarded a warning through the Navy, to be on the lookout for the floatation collar. One of our vessels discovered one. The sentries fired upon it, and no attack took place. We cannot ascertain if this was another Cheeney ship, but we are confident it might have been. The Navy has begun using nets in the water around their ships. It should prevent further aggressions of this type. If you and Mr. Webster had not uncovered Mason Cheeney's work, then who knows where we would be today."

Molly nodded, happy yet subdued. It seemed a small matter, so far removed from delivering the plans. She couldn't bear the thought of Webster in the jail. Her hands held her stomach. A strange life this had turned out to be.

"And speaking of Mason Cheeney—did Mrs. Warne show you the reports?"

He looked to Mrs. Warne who shook her head.

"What reports?" Molly asked.

"I told you to give me some time, Allan."

She did not want Molly to know. Mrs. Warne used his first name whenever he annoyed her in some manner.

"She has a right to know," he protested.

Pinkerton spread a newspaper upon his desk. He pointed to an article. General Winder hung Mason Cheeney for treason. The paper was recent. The trial had been quick. Her stomach rolled—she had caused it.

"So Colonel Norris received the letters."

"He believed the letters, which is more important," Pinkerton replied.

"Why wouldn't he believe them?" Molly asked. She turned her attention to Mrs. Warne, then to Pinkerton. There was something they weren't telling her.

"They were forged," Pinkerton said. "Not even Webster knew. He was supposed to use them as a last resort to pass to Secretary Benjamin. It would be a move of desperation to push the fog of war into the secretary's eyes. They wouldn't trust Mason Cheeney."

Forged? She had sent him to his death over faked letters. Mrs. Warne moved to her side and leaned close.

"He deserved his sentence."

"And his son?" Molly asked.

"He was set for a trial as well," Pinkerton answered. "But never made it to Richmond. He fled his captors in the woods. They gunned him down." Pinkerton studied Molly's face for a moment. "I understand he was a cruel man."

Molly nodded. She led both Cheeneys to their deaths. She had her revenge   done the things she had failed at so many times earlier. It wasn't a candlestick that killed Mason Cheeney, it was paper. But she felt no closure. Instead, there was empty space. Nothing would bring her parents back. Nothing would bring Isabelle back. She wondered where Jeanine found herself. Molly hoped the girl made it North. She had enough money to live comfortably the rest of her life.

"I am puzzled by another report from Baltimore," Pinkerton said. "The Barbusca brothel appears to have burned to the ground. Witnesses claimed a woman drove everyone from the establishment before setting it ablaze."

Mrs. Warne looked away. She shook her head ever so slightly. She had not told Pinkerton this part of Molly's adventure.

"The place was always a tipped oil lamp away from disaster," Molly answered.

"I see," Pinkerton said. He looked at Molly, waiting until she met his eyes. "The witnesses described an elegant woman, with long red hair. Of course, I worried you were involved. But when you arrived with quite a different hairstyle, I realized the folly in my assumption."

Molly smiled—the same thin smile Mrs. Webster had just used upon her.

"Well, before the President arrives, Mrs. Warne and I have something for you."

He turned to Mrs. Warne.

"She is ready?"

"She is. I told you last time she was ready, and you see how that turned out."

Pinkerton nodded. He opened his top desk drawer. He produced a small metal badge and laid it on the desk over the article about Mason Cheeney. A six-point star sat etched in the middle. Across the surface it read—*Pinkerton National Detective Agency.*

"Mrs. Warne says you will make an excellent detective."

"She already is," Mrs. Warne said.

Molly held her belly. It would take only a short time to become obvious. She wouldn't be able to work for some time. *What would she do after the baby came?* Mrs. Warne understood.

"Miss Ferguson will require some time—a few months. I can help her with those arrangements."

Pinkerton looked puzzled, but seemingly thought better of questioning further. Mrs. Warne wore a stern expression aimed at him.

"Of course. Whatever you require. You have well earned it, Molly."

Molly stood, looking at the badge upon the desk. Mrs. Warne nodded Molly forward. Pinkerton held it out for her. Molly accepted the badge from his outstretched hand.

A knock came from the door at the side of the office. It immediately opened. The man from earlier, the one who had escorted them to Pinkerton's office, opened the door. He stepped inside, and President Lincoln followed. The President took stock of all standing there. Pinkerton said nothing.

"Miss Ferguson, it is so very good to see you again," Mr. Lincoln said. "I understand we owe you a huge debt of thanks for your service in Richmond."

"Thank you, sir," Molly said. "However, I was not alone. I had much help."

"I know. Mr. Pinkerton has filled me in on the details. In fact, I am on my way to see Mrs. Webster. I understand you were with her husband when he was sentenced."

Molly nodded and looked to the ground.

"Please know that his contribution, and yours, is not forgotten. What you did to get the plans for the underwater vessel is extraordinary. What may prove more important is uncovering the meddling of both Britain and France upon our affairs. I will shortly have to make an important decision."

"Slavery?" Molly asked.

The word came out before she even formed it in her mind. Mr. Lincoln smiled.

"As long as this stays within these walls—I am considering how to emancipate all those in bondage. I find it ironic that the South could well win this war if they abolish the peculiar institution they so cherish. At the same time, they will likely perish because they fight so hard to hold onto it. We must beat Jefferson Davis in freeing the slaves. But those are treacherous political waters. And alas, that is my worry."

"Miss Ferguson will be with us for some time," Pinkerton added. "She has accepted our offer to stay."

"Excellent, Mr. Pinkerton. I would have it no other way." He turned to look at her. "I have a feeling I will rely upon you for a long time to come, Miss Ferguson."

"Thank you, sir," Molly managed.

He leaned close, so that no one else could hear.

"You are my *angel in the fog*."

She was at once elated and numb.

"If you can forgive me," Mr. Lincoln said. "I need to see to Mrs. Webster. I'm afraid I only have a few minutes before my other meeting, but I owe her my gratitude for her sacrifice."

With that he turned and left the way he came. Pinkerton walked him to the door, and then addressed Mrs. Warne and Molly.

"Stay here for a few moments longer. There is someone Molly needs to meet. I will return shortly."

He closed the door behind him.

"Are you all right, Molly?" Mrs. Warne asked.

Molly nodded. "I think so. It's just that I thought that Cheeney's plans were the most important thing from Richmond."

Mrs. Warne shook her head. "They were, until they weren't. You and I, or even Mr. Pinkerton, may never know what will be most valuable. So we never presume to know. We bring back all we can."

Molly nodded but looked to her belly. *How would she do it all?*

"You're not alone—I will help," Mrs. Warne offered.

"I know," Molly answered. "Thank you."

"I asked you once, if you looked for justice or revenge."

Molly nodded. She remembered.

"I won't ask which one you found. But I will ask this. Would you do it again?"

"What?" Molly asked.

"Everything."

She paused. "Different. I would do it different."

Mrs. Warne reached out and held Molly's arm.

"Good. You're learning."

"How do you do it?" Molly asked.

Mrs. Warne took a deep breath. "You find someone broken. As broken as you, and you hold on—through everything."

The door behind them opened. Pinkerton emerged with the man who had been with Mr. Lincoln—the man who escorted them earlier.

"Molly, I would like you to meet President Lincoln's bodyguard—Joseph Foster."

Molly smiled. He wore a large knife to his side, tucked high in his trousers. His hand clasped hers, then his other hand rested on top of hers. He did not let go.

"When you return from your rest we will partner you and Joseph to further protect the President," Pinkerton said. "You will spend quite some time with one another."

"I believe you will make an exceptional team," Mrs. Warne added.

Joseph still held her hand.

"And as I have long learned," Pinkerton said, "on matters such as these, Mrs. Warne is always right. You two will do magnificent things."

AUTHOR'S NOTE

Those of you who have followed Joseph and Molly's adventures in my earlier novels—*Lincoln's Bodyguard* and *Land of Wolves*—know that those stories are not only historical fiction but works of revisionist history. The timeline in those novels departed from the history we know when Joseph saved President Lincoln in Ford's theater—14 April 1865. *Angel in the Fog* starts before that historical bifurcation and is therefore the first book in the series that is a pure work of historical fiction. The challenge in this genre is to fit the story within the history we all know. I had the great luxury in my previous novels to explain away small historical inaccuracies as a result of the "new" timeline. That wouldn't be the case with *Angel in the Fog*.

At first, I worried that I would not be able to find a way to weave Molly's story into the fabric of our history at the dawn of the Civil War. However, as I started my research, her story emerged as if I were lifting it from a history textbook—though much more exhilarating. Almost all of the events as well as the backstory in the novel are true—or primarily based on truth. Many of the characters existed, and I used their role in history throughout *Angel in the Fog*. Let's start at the beginning.

Allan Pinkerton, one of America's most famous detectives at the time, was hired by Samuel Felton, the president of the Philadelphia, Wilmington, and Baltimore Railroad. Pinkerton's charge was to investigate whether separatist elements might burn railroad bridges to prevent Abraham Lincoln from arriving in Washington for his first inauguration. During the course of that investigation, Pinkerton learned of a plan far more sinister than burning bridges. A secretive group in Baltimore, led in part by Cipriano Ferrandini, planned to assassinate Lincoln when he transferred train stations in the city. Pinkerton and his operatives, including Mrs. Kate Warne, were able to thwart the attempt by sending Lincoln through Baltimore earlier than expected, just as presented in the novel. Some of the characters we meet, including Kate Warne and Timothy Webster, were instrumental in this operation—particularly Mrs. Warne.

Kate Warne is truly a fascinating character. The often quoted saying by Laurel Thatcher Ulrich applies: "Well behaved women seldom make history." Kate Warne made history. As a young widow, she marched into Allan Pinkerton's office and made a proposal to the famous detective—she wanted to be America's first female detective. Despite his initial hesitation, Pinkerton accepted her to his burgeoning detective agency. She soon proved her worth in a variety of cases, and by the time we meet her in *Angel in the Fog*, she is a seasoned operative. Kate Warne was a true pioneer, blazing a path for other women to follow at a time when acceptable careers were limited to teaching and nursing. She was therefore the perfect person to advocate for and train an apprentice—Molly.

Throughout the novel, Molly uses a cover name—Hattie Lawton. The historical records show Miss Lawton was a real person, though her identity has been lost to the ages. Some references refer to her as Carrie Lawton or have a different variant of her last name. What is clear is that her exact background before she came into the Pinkerton

organization is not known. The same is true about what happened
to her after her time with Pinkerton. She comes in and out of history like a breeze and leaves nothing more than anecdotes of her
accomplishments and stories of her bravery. She became the perfect
cover for Molly. I did take some liberties with her story, in particular in including her complicity with Mrs. Warne in thwarting the
Baltimore plot. It seems Hattie Lawton was involved during that
operation, but in a different city. She posed as Timothy Webster's
wife, and they lived among railway workers on the outskirts of
Baltimore who were suspected to be planning the bridge burnings
that Samuel Felton initially feared.

* * *

In the first half of the novel, Molly also travels to several Northern
cities. In New York she meets George Sanders. Mr. Sanders was a
Confederate official who conducted business in New York and
Montreal. He is credited with working in the background of the
Confederacy, traveling to Europe and supporting the Confederate
Secret Service in Montreal. Although I could find no record of him
meeting with John Wilkes Booth, as is portrayed in the novel, the
two men certainly traveled in similar circles and could have met and
worked together. While in New York City, Molly also meets
Superintendent Kennedy, the head of the New York Police
Department. He was also a historical figure, who helped guide
Lincoln through New York on his trip to Washington, D.C., despite the fact that the city mayor, Fernando Wood, did advocate for
New York City seceding from the Union. In Albany, Molly finds
John Wilkes Booth who needs no introduction. In the novel, he is
recovering from a self-inflicted wound endured during a theatrical
performance. Booth did, in fact, injure himself with a dagger during

a show in Albany, NY. Finally, Molly meets with Colonel William Norris in Montreal. Colonel Norris is also ripped from history, though I embellished his role in the Confederate Secret Service and his presence in Montreal.

* * *

During the second half of the novel, Molly accompanies another Pinkerton operative to the Confederate capitol—Richmond, VA. Timothy Webster was by all accounts a brave and talented man. He also has the misfortune of being the first American executed for espionage since Nathan Hale in the Revolutionary War. While I did expand Timothy Webster's role in uncovering the Baltimore plot, deliberately conflating his contribution with that of Mr. Harry W. Davies—another Pinkerton operative—Webster was nonetheless a real person. In addition, as portrayed in the book, Webster did work as a spy for the Union while in Richmond, where he was accompanied by none other than Hattie Lawton posing as his wife.

In Richmond, Molly's role was exactly the same as Hattie Lawton's in real life—to enhance Webster's cover as well as to "worm out secrets" from the wives of the Richmond elite. During the course of her time in Richmond, Molly and Webster discover that Mr. Cheeney is devising a devastating new type of ship to break the Union naval blockade. This is also based on real events. The display in the James River of this new naval technology—a submarine sinking a barge—occurred in the summer of 1861. This was the scene that Molly and Webster witness, along with Captain Atwater and his wife—also real people. The submarine was developed by a man named William Cheeney. I changed his name to Mason Cheeney as I also changed his backstory by making him part of Molly's past in New Orleans. However, I did maintain the Cheeney name as a tip of the hat to history.

During her time in Richmond, Molly also encounters another famous female operative—Miss Elizabeth Van Lew. Miss Van Lew grew to be one of the most important sources of intelligence for the Union throughout the war. She was so important that General Grant personally paid her a visit once he entered the fallen city. If anything, her role is downplayed in the novel. She formed and ran an extensive spy ring in Richmond. She figured out how to get messages out of the city; she tended to Union prisoners, even helping them escape from prison with the help of the clerk at Libby Prison—another aspect we see in the novel as Molly escapes. Miss Lizzie, as she was known, even planted a servant in the Confederate White House, offering Mary Jane Bowser's services to none other than Varina Davis—Confederate President Jefferson Davis' wife. We meet Mary Jane in the novel, though there is no mention of her incredible service of stealing secrets right under the nose of Jefferson Davis himself.

Molly's time in Richmond ends sadly when Timothy Webster is arrested and executed for espionage. The details of his capture in the novel are largely accurate. He did fall sick with rheumatism and was unable to send Pinkerton messages about his status. Fearing the worst, Pinkerton sent two operatives—Scully and Lewis—to find Webster. These men inadvertently cast suspicion upon Webster, and when they were arrested, they pled guilty to save their lives. That sealed Webster's fate. Hattie Lawton was there when Webster was hauled away to the gallows, as was Molly in my story. After Webster's execution, Miss Lizzie visited Hattie Lawton, just as she pays a visit to Molly in the novel.

Finally, I added a bit of international intrigue in the form of Europe's interest in the American Civil War. This is also based on fact. In turn, the intense interest from Europe shaped how we responded. For instance, England longed for cheap cotton to feed their textile mills. Their biggest dilemma in supporting the South to secure that commodity was the use of slave labor. Intense debate occurred within their society about whether they should back the Confederacy and turn the tide of the war. England had abolished slavery in 1833, nearly three decades before the U.S. Civil War, and the moral elements in their society were successful in maintaining a perceived sense of neutrality throughout the war. This did not prevent England from selling goods to the naval blockade runners, nor did it stop Confederate officials from lobbying England and France for assistance. England's teetering viewpoint on Confederate support may have been a significant factor in President Lincoln's Emancipation Proclamation, which threaded a fine line to keep border states in the Union while sending a signal to Europe. One of Lincoln's principal fears was that the South might emancipate the slaves—as seen in Cheeney's plan in the novel—in order to curry favor with Europe as a means to break the stalemate of the Civil War.

*   *   *

Hopefully these notes have helped show how intertwined Molly's story is with the real history of the time period. In fact, there are more real-life characters in the book than fictional ones. Throughout my research I was struck by one common theme—the incredible bravery of a small group of people who altered the course of history for our nation. This includes a cadre of women operatives—Kate Warne, Elizabeth Van Lew, Mary Jane Bowser, and, of course, Hattie Lawton. This list is by no means exhaustive and includes none of the Confederate women who engaged in similar activi- ties—Belle Boyd, Nancy Hart Douglas, and Rose Greenhow to name a few. These women, on both sides of the battle lines, chal- lenged the norms of the day. They participated in espionage and scouting the enemy lines at a time when men considered them to be too weak or lacking the intellect to carry out such activities. They not only proved these notions ridiculously false, they succeeded in a way that their male counterparts could not match, forever shaping our nation.

Although my ideas for the novel drew from many sources, I recommend the following references, both fiction and nonfiction, which outline this incredible time in our nation's history.

Liar, Temptress, Soldier, Spy: Four Women Undercover in the Civil War, by Karen Abbott

The Hour of Peril: The Secret Plot to Murder Lincoln before the Civil War, by Daniel Stashower

The Spymistress (a novel), by Jennifer Chiaverini